To Kathie + Scott, Here's to a slippery Rocket! (handwritten)

Night Terrors

Merry Christmas 2001 (handwritten)

A Novel By

Drew Williams

Drew Williams (signature)

Published By
Barclay Books, LLC

P.S. And tell Rita to tell Mina that Drew (the villain) says hello! (handwritten)

St. Petersburg Florida
www.barclaybooks.com
A Spectral Visions Imprint

PUBLISHED BY BARCLAY BOOKS, LLC
6161 51ST STREET SOUTH
ST. PETERSBURG, FLORIDA 33715
www.barclaybooks.com
A Spectral Visions Imprint

Copyright © 2001 by Drew Williams

This novel is a work of fiction. The characters, names, incidents, places, dialogue, and plot are the products of the author's imagination or are used fictitiously. Any resemblance to actual persons, living or dead, or events is purely coincidental.

Printed and bound in the United States of America
Cover design by Cathi Gerhard

ISBN: 1-931402-24-8

Acknowledgments

There's a lot of people I'd like to thank for their assistance and encouragement while I was writing Night Terrors. In no particular order I'd like to thank: Becki McNeel at Barclay Books for taking a chance on an unknown writer; Joe Nassise who pointed me toward Barclay Books; Ed and Katharine Whitelock who were the first to have Dust visit their dreams; my parents, Robert and Evelyn Williams, who got by the "dirty parts" and still liked the novel; Shelly and Carol Gerhard, who are waiting for the next one; Susan Bodendorfer at Wordbeams; and my wife Cathi who's been helping me in about a thousand different ways. Thanks also to Steve Alten, Douglas Clegg, and Jeff Strand, three great writers who were kind enough to answer my e-mails, and Mr. S. for treating me like a writer instead of a student. Twenty years later, I still remember. And I have to mention Ed Brady and his wife Maria because ten years ago I promised them that I would.

This novel is dedicated to my kids, Elizabeth and Robert, because it's their turn.

Prologue

In all my dreams, before my helpless sight
He plunges at me, guttering, choking, drowning
Wilfred Owen

Slaughter Saturday: June 3

Alllll Abbbooaarrrrrd !!!!!

Davie Cavanaugh rubbed his eyes with the backs of his ten-year-old hands. He couldn't believe it. In front of him atop a pair of shiny copper rails sat a life-sized Casey Jones Model-A train engine, complete with a cast-iron cowcatcher and a silver-plated stack that blew real smoke. Hitched to the engine was a long, red passenger car, the words SOUTHERN PACIFIC stenciled in bold, white letters on its side.

Davie blinked again. There was no doubt about it. It was the Toy Train.

"You gonna come aboard, Davie?" a familiar voice whispered in his ear. Davie spun around and was greeted by the smiling, round face of the conductor, Mr. Biggler. A plump, gnome of a man, Mr. Biggler wore his usual conductor's uniform—a pair of purple-spotted coveralls over a white shirt, and a bright yellow conductor's cap that fit snugly atop his round head. Completing the costume was a stick from a red lollipop that jutted from the side of his mouth like a thin, white cigar.

"Mr. Biggler. Is it really the Toy Train?"

The conductor laughed and clapped his thick hands together. "It sure is, Davie-boy," he said, lifting his cap and making a broad sweeping gesture toward the engine car. "The Toy Train, just as you remember it." Mr. Biggler handed Davie a red lollipop before dancing a quick jig to the boy's delighted laughter. "All the toys you can imagine are waiting inside for you. The bikes, the baseballs, the cars. And of course, the dollies are there too," he said with a wink.

"I never play with dolls," Davie shot back.

Mr. Biggler hooked his thumbs in the belt loops of his coveralls and looked down at the boy. "Is that so? I could have sworn you played with dollies. Perhaps you just don't remember that. Or maybe I have you confused with some other little boy."

Waving the lollipop in front of him like a wand, Davie politely told the conductor that, while other little boys might like to play with dolls, he most certainly did not.

"I do believe you are right. What ever could I have been thinking?" Mr. Biggler bent forward and placed his hands on Davie's shoulders. "Why don't we climb aboard and see what new surprises are on the Toy Train?"

Needing no further encouragement, Davie bounded up the steps of the passenger car. His eyes widened when he saw the stacks of toys that jammed every corner of the Toy Train. There were model airplanes, tennis rackets and just about every board game imaginable heaped about. Davie looked up. Above him thousands of footballs and basketballs hung from the ceiling, suspended like rawhide planets from thin strands of silver thread.

"Wow," he whispered. "I can't believe it, the Toy Train." Davie turned and ran to the conductor, wrapping his thin arms around the man's waist.

Mr. Biggler laughed and lifted the boy into the air. "Believe it," he said. "It's all for you." The conductor lowered Davie to his feet and gently ushered him deeper into the car. "And here's something new for you to play with."

8

"Wow," Davie gasped when he saw the hobbyhorse in the rear of the car separated from the other toys. It was an exquisitely carved mare, captured in midstride on its two runners. Davie shuffled over to the horse and ran his fingers against its polished wood surface that was black as midnight, allowing his hands to caress the smooth muscles that bulged from its flanks. Standing on his tiptoes to look into the deep black marbles that were its eyes, he saw his own reflection staring back at him. "She's beautiful."

"Yes she is," the conductor said, holding his arms out to Davie. "Do you want to ride her?"

"Oh yes," he answered, but before Mr. Biggler could place him on the horse, Davie heard a phone ringing. As if reacting to the sound, the train lurched forward sending Davie crashing to the floor. "What was that?" he asked, pulling himself off the floor. "Why did the train . . .?" Davie's question was swallowed back into his throat.

Mr. Biggler stood next to the horse, glaring at Davie through two narrow, gray slits that moments before had been green, oval eyes. The pleasant grin had also vanished. "Play time is over," Biggler said through a mouthful of broken, jagged teeth.

Davie gasped at the transformation, but he was too frightened to move or cry out. Even when Mr. Biggler started to make his way toward Davie, the boy remained paralyzed. "You wanted the Toy Train so badly. Nothing could make you happy but the Toy Train." Mr. Biggler removed the conductor's cap revealing a thick mat of greasy black hair. Beside him the mare kicked on its runners and screamed. "Well, you got your wish. Your precious train is back. And I'm on it." Mr. Biggler said something else but Davie wasn't paying attention. His eyes were fixed on two long fangs that were sprouting from the conductor's mouth.

"The better to gobble you up," Biggler laughed, running his pointed tongue across his lips.

Davie felt his heart about to explode within his chest. "No," he screamed. "You're not the real Mr. Biggler."

"Doesn't matter now, Davie-boy. This is my train. Mine." A long claw that barely resembled a hand slowly uncurled from the end of the conductor's left sleeve. Inside was a plastic toy phone.

"Answer it, Davie," the thing said. "It's for you."

"No." Davie jammed his ears with his palms. "I don't believe you."

The phone rang louder.

He opened his eyes just in time to see his wife return the cordless telephone to its spot on the nightstand next to their bed. "Linda," thirty-three-year-old David Cavanaugh said, his breath coming in hitches. "Christ, did I have a bad dream."

Linda ignored her husband's shaking body and laid her head back on her pillow. "We have to go home," she said softly. "My father died." Then closing her eyes, she drifted off to sleep.

***

Phillip Slaughter watched the thin sheet covering his wife's naked body rise and fall with the gentle rhythm of her breathing. Every time she inhaled, the sheet slipped a fraction of an inch down her chest toward the curve of her breasts. Phillip leaned across her body and kissed the exposed part of his wife's chest, savoring the salty taste of her perspiration. He carefully moved his head toward the small bump in the sheet that covered his wife's left nipple.

"And what do you think you're doing, young man?" Alicia Slaughter whispered.

"Nothing, go back to sleep."

"That's going to be kind of hard with you biting on my boob, don't you think?"

Grinning, Phillip snapped the sheet away from his wife and rolled on top of her.

"Oh, so that's what you have in mind," Alicia said, laughing.

They made love, quickly and playfully. It was too hot for any type of extended sex. When they finished, they were both coated in a thick layer of sweat.

"Ick," Alicia said as her husband rolled off of her. "You're all slimy, but I still like you." She reached out to grab his waist, but Phillip was already out of the bed and slipping on his robe. "Where are you going?"

"I have to go downstairs for a second."

"Sure, sure. If you want to leave a beautiful, naked woman all alone in your bed, you go right on ahead. I'll just have to jump in the shower."

"You do that, and I'll join you later." Phillip hurried out of the bedroom and headed downstairs to the kitchen. As he descended the stairs, Phillip heard his nine-year-old son, Sam, in the living room laughing at a Saturday morning cartoon. Phillip stuck his head into the doorway and peeked in on his son. With his dark brown hair and large, hazel eyes, the boy was a miniature image of his father. Wearing his favorite Batman pajamas, Sam sat on the floor staring at the television. Phillip tapped on the doorframe to get his son's attention. "Hey champ. Come here, I got something to show you."

Reluctantly, Sam followed his father into the kitchen holding a Pepsi in one hand, a half-eaten chocolate cupcake in the other. "Huh?" Sam asked, irritated that his father would interrupt The Real Ghostbusters.

Half chuckling, Phillip shook his head when he saw what his son was eating. "Is that your breakfast? Don't let your mother see you with that junk this early in the morning, or she'll skin us both alive." Sam nodded and took a large bite from the cupcake while his father reached into a cabinet above the sink and pulled out a plastic jug.

"What's up?" Sam asked, sending small, black crumbs spraying from his lips.

"Neat trick I learned." Uncapping the lid, Phillip winked once at his son then raised the jug to his lips. "Bottoms up."

Sam didn't start screaming until he saw the green Mr. Yuk sticker on the side of the bottle; but by that time, Phillip Slaughter had already swallowed a quart of drain cleaner and was far past the point of caring.

**

"Too fucking hot," Dick Oldfield cursed. "Too damn, fucking hot."

9

It was not an unusual complaint for the obese, school bus driver. When the temperature got above seventy degrees, Dick Oldfield's pores opened up like valves. It was a lifelong discomfort that did little to improve his normal shitty disposition.

As did the kids.

Dick knew all their nicknames for him like "Blubber Butt" and "Old Smelly." For the most part, Dick ignored their giggles; he had grown accustomed to taking shit off people because of his size. But yesterday, that little Mike Peters called him "Fatso" right to his face. Dick told him to sit his ass down, but what he really wanted to do was twist his skinny arm behind his back until it snapped. That would teach the little brat a lesson.

They were too brazen, thinking they could get away with that type of disrespect. It was all the parents' fault though. Dick knew that. If he had been caught mouthing off to an adult, his father would have opened up the side of his lip with the back of his hand. No doubt about it. Step out of line and whack, the knuckles on Ben Oldfield's hand would be meeting flesh.

But all the crap Dick had to put up with was during the week. The weekends were his, and besides, the little bastards would be out of school for the summer in a couple of days, and he wouldn't have to see their pimply faces until September. It was best not to think about them at all, especially on a Saturday morning.

Morning.

Dick glanced at the clock beside his bed. 12:28 p.m. "Shit," he said, not so much surprised at the time, but the Pirates were playing the Phillys at one o'clock, and he didn't want to miss the pre-game show on the radio. Dick hoisted himself out of bed and slipped a pair of ripped shorts over his boxers. Bypassing the shower, he went directly to his kitchen and started loading a Styrofoam cooler with a twelve pack of Iron City beer. After dumping two trays of ice onto the tops of the cans, he grabbed the transistor radio from the kitchen table and waddled through the screen door into his backyard. He made his way through the ankle-high grass to a lawn chair that he kept chained to a dead apple tree. Around him, scores of beer cans lay in various stages of decomposition.

Dick flipped the chair open and lowered his enormous ass into it. The chair bulged beneath Dick's three hundred-plus pounds, but somehow it held together. Comfortably nestled into his seat, Dick thrust his hand into the cooler and lifted out one of the cold brews. With the experience that comes from years of practice, he flipped the pop top open using only the thumb of his right hand then drained half of the can into his stomach. "Oh yeah," he said in mid-belch. "Breakfast of ex-champions." Dick placed the can in the grass and searched through the static on his radio until he found the ball game. He let the radio rest on his stomach, content to sit in the shade and listen to the Buccos whip the shit out of Philadelphia.

Sipping at his beer, Dick glanced up and watched a red pickup truck rumble up the cement incline less than twenty feet above the roof of his house. *What a place to build a house*, he thought. *Right under a goddamn overpass.* But then again, that was probably why he got the place so cheap. Who else but a bus driver wouldn't mind living beneath the on-ramp of a bridge?

Dick finished his beer as the starting lineups were being announced. "Now we'll get down to some serious ass kicking," he said as his hand fished into the cooler for another Iron City. He was just pulling one out when he heard the blaring of a car horn. Dick looked up in time to see a yellow Ford Fairmont crash through the overpass guardrail and explode above his roof. Hunks of concrete and steel rained down about his chair as the car flipped end over end and finally landed at the far end of the lawn. Dick remained motionless as the remains of the Fairmont burned about him.

When the fire truck arrived three minutes later, Dick still hadn't moved from his chair, but he had chugged four more beers and vomited, adding little to the colorful mess.

***

"Honey, are you okay?"
No answer.
"Larissa," Mrs. Montgomery called. "What was that noise?"

Silence.

"Larissa, answer me." Mrs. Montgomery stood at the base of the stairs waiting for her daughter to reply. There had been a thud, she was sure of that.

"Larissa," she called out sharply. "Now you answer me."

More silence.

Moving slowly, she made her way up the steps toward her daughter's room. The door was slightly ajar.

"Honey?" Mrs. Montgomery whispered pushing the door open. The first thing she caught sight of was the mirror. There was something written on it.

SECRETS

Mrs. Montgomery pushed the door open further and stepped into the room. One step was far enough for her to catch sight of her daughter's body slowly turning in circles as it hung from the ceiling fan.

Part One

Chapter One: June 5

Detective Gary Overton was not an excitable man. Whether discussing proposed cutbacks in police funding with a member of the city council or arresting a drug pusher in a back alley of one of McKeesport's three housing projects, his calm demeanor never changed. He possessed an easy-going style that hid the intense drive for which the twenty-nine-year-old Connecticut native did his job. Gary came to McKeesport four years earlier after a stint as a Connecticut State Trooper, and the quiet, young man had little trouble adjusting to his new job as detective in the small, western Pennsylvania town. And, at six-foot-four and two hundred muscular pounds, his intimidating physique was a definite asset in winning the approval of those on the force who thought he was too young to be a detective. But as far as Gary was concerned, most of the credit for the ease of his transition went to Steve Wyckoff, chief of McKeesport's detective force and Gary's most vocal supporter. He was the man who had convinced the mayor and city council that the young trooper was a perfect fit for the McKeesport police department. He was also the man who now sat in front of him grinding a Marlboro into a clay ashtray.

"Those things are going to kill you," Gary said. The senior detective looked up and slowly uncurled the middle finger of his

13

left hand. Gary laughed and plopped himself in the seat opposite Steve. "Oh, I see we're not in a good mood then."

Steve grunted and reached for a pack of cigarettes in the chest pocket of his drab, gray shirt. He was a short but powerful man whose thick muscles were deceptively hidden by a layer of fat. He had a round, uninteresting face with deep set brown eyes and a square jaw that in the past few years had begun to be swallowed by an extra chin. Blessed with an almost unerring natural intuition, Steve Wyckoff was generally considered to be one of the best police officers McKeesport ever had—smart, fair, and definitely someone who didn't take shit from anybody. He looked at the junior detective and snorted. "Every day you tell me smoking is bad, and every day I tell you to stick it. Don't you think I'm sending you a message?"

"Just keeping the status quo," Gary said. "What's up?"

Steve rose from his seat and walked to the lone window in his cramped office. Poking his head out, he took a deep breath. Immediately a wave of hot, stale air pressed against his face as the sound of a lawn mower roaring to life filtered into the room. Steve reached up and shut the window. "Too damn hot for this early in June," he said.

The younger man remained silent.

From his trouser pocket, Steve pulled out the silver Zippo lighter he was never without. With a quick snap, he flipped open the top and a small, orange flame shot out and lit the tip of the Marlboro tucked neatly between his thin lips. He let the smoke settle in his lungs and then slowly exhaled, all the while staring out the window. His eyes rested on the bronze statue of John F. Kennedy outside of McKeesport's city hall. The twelve-foot statue stood on a slab of granite in the middle of a small memorial garden named after the slain president. It stood on the same spot that Kennedy did when the president paid his only visit to the small steel town. Nine-year-old Steve Wyckoff had stood with ten thousand other McKeesport residents to hear the president speak on that sunny, October day in 1962. Three years later, Steve Wyckoff had been there again when the statue had been unveiled in a cold, February drizzle.

Steve turned and snatched a yellow file folder from his cluttered desk. He skimmed its contents then handed Gary a photograph of a burnt Ford Fairmont implanted in the backyard of the unfortunate Mr. Oldfield. "The car belongs to a guy named Merrill Toth," Steve began. "I went to high school with him."

Gary picked up the photograph and examined it. It was not unlike the hundreds of accident photos he'd seen in his career, a grainy black and white picture of a twisted hunk of what used to be an automobile. He handed the photo back to Steve who tossed it onto his desk. "He's the guy who drove off the Josslin Bridge the other day, right?"

Steve didn't answer the question. Instead, he handed Gary two other file folders. "Two people killed themselves Saturday morning. Phillip Slaughter," Steve said, pointing to the top folder in Gary's hand. "Up in the Grand View area. And a girl over on Willow Street."

Gary bypassed the first folder and opened the second file and looked through the report on Larissa Montgomery's death. "Jesus," he whispered. "Her mother found her."

"Uh huh," Steve half grunted. "How many suicides have their been in town this year?" Steve asked, not expecting a reply.

"None. At least none that we know of. And only one the whole of last year." Steve sucked sharply on his cigarette and frowned. "Slaughter here had a kid, a son. And Larissa Montgomery's father died two years ago. Christ, if this doesn't kill Mrs. Montgomery I don't know what will."

Gary glanced curiously at Steve. "You knew them too, didn't you? This Slaughter guy and the Montgomery girl?"

Steve nodded and pushed his chair away from the desk. "Yeah. Phil Slaughter worked at the Ford dealership in town, and Larissa's father used to be a sports writer for The Daily News. But hell, that's not surprising. It's not a big town. I've probably met or arrested just about everybody who lives here."

Gary had no trouble believing that. There was very little that happened in McKeesport that Detective Steve Wyckoff didn't know about.

"It is sad, Steve. And a shame, but I don't know what to make of it."

Steve jerked his head and pointed to Gary. "Now don't even say shit like this happens all the time," he said with a crooked smile.

The younger man returned the grin. "No, shit like this does not happen all the time, but it does happen. Look at that guy in California who killed all those people in McDonalds, or Charles Manson, or even the Challenger blowing up on national TV. Go try to figure out Dahmer. You have to face it, bad shit sometimes just happens."

"McKeesport isn't California or New York. People don't cannibalize each other here or whip out Uzi's and start shooting up the local citizenry."

"Right," Gary agreed. "So our bad stuff is on a smaller scale. Instead of Son of Sam, we get a few suicides on the same day. It sounds bad, but it really isn't major headline news."

Steve shook his head. Gary was right; bad shit just sometimes happened, and after two and a half decades as a cop, Steve had seen more than his share of it. Yet for some reason this was different. "I can't explain it to you," he said. "It's just too damn out of the ordinary for me."

"I'm not denying it's odd, but you have to look at this objectively. People do kill themselves all the time. Maybe not here, but perhaps we're due."

"Horse shit," Steve barked.

The edge in Steve's voice made Gary take notice. "Okay," he said. "Something's bugging you, and I have a feeling you're not going to relax until I end up with a stack of paperwork. So what's on your mind?"

A small grin played at the corners of Steve's mouth as he noticed his friend's sour expression. He was glad Gary was there. He was a good cop. "Think about it," Steve began. "Saturday, June 3. Three people die in one day. Not so strange in itself except that they all die in rather nasty fashions. And two of them were known suicides."

"And you think that Merrill Toth may have been a suicide too," Gary interjected.

Steve shrugged his shoulders and stuck his palms out. "Could be. I'm not saying it was or it wasn't, but driving your car through an overpass would definitely do the trick."

"But we're not sure."

"Right. We're not sure, but I'm not satisfied with what I'm seeing in here," he said, tapping the files on his desk. "Look at this." Picking up Larissa Montgomery's folder, he started to flip through the pages. "Cheerleader, honor student. Never in any trouble. Not fighting with her parents, no dope, no booze. Nothing."

"Doesn't sound like your typical suicide candidate."

"But that's not what's really bugging me. It's how she did it. Teenage girls are three times more likely to attempt suicide than boys, yet they only account for half as many deaths. Why? Because they're mainly looking for the attention when they do it. They try to overdose on pills, or they slice their wrists. Stuff that takes time. However," Steve said, flinging the folder onto the desk. "They don't hang themselves."

Gary took Larissa's file off the desk and skimmed through it. SECRETS written in red lipstick. No motive. No note. Unusually violent method. "You're right, it doesn't make sense. But," he added. "When does a kid killing herself ever make sense?"

"Never, but then there's this too." Steve handed Gary a second file. "Another not-so-typical candidate for suicide. Bio stuff is in there, but take a look at the method."

Once again, Gary scanned the report until he came to the line that read Cause of Death. "Self-inflicted ingestion of poisonous liquid—drain cleaner," he read aloud. "Christ, he did this in front of his son."

"In the kitchen. Talked to his kid for a minute and then whipped out a bottle of Drano and started gulping. He polished off the entire bottle, all two quarts of it."

"Two quarts." Gary looked back down at the report. "How could he drink two quarts of drain cleaner?"

"That's the same thing I wondered," Steve said. "So I called Dr. Mendez at the free clinic this morning and asked her how much drain cleaner someone would have to drink in order for it to be fatal. I told her about Slaughter but left out the amount he ingested. Anyway, Dr. Mendez told me that about a coffee cup full of grade-A cleaning solvent would do the trick. Two cups definitely, the body will go into shock, followed by heart failure. I asked her about anything over a pint, and she said it can't be done. Gag reflex would kick in and the throat would clamp up. Nothing goes down, not even air."

"Except for Phillip Slaughter and an extra quart and a half of Drano," Gary added.

The two detectives stood silent for a moment before Steve plopped himself back into his chair. "Merrill Toth driving his car through the overpass, I would call a terrible accident. A suicide on the same day, I would call a pretty shitty twenty-four hours. But Merrill Toth and two suicides, I say that's just too much to swallow. June 3 was not a normal day for these folks, and I want to know why."

"I know I'm going to be sorry for asking this, but what is it you want me to do?"

"I don't know," Steve said. "Poke around a bit. Ask a few questions. Try to find out if there was anything going on in the Montgomery girl's life that might drive her to suicide. Same thing for Slaughter."

Gary wasn't thrilled with the request, but agreed to take on the assignment. "Alright," he said as he got out of his chair with the two files in his hand. "I'll do some checking, but I don't know what you think I'm going to find."

"Hopefully nothing," Steve replied. "I really hope that you tell me everything's kosher. Then my funny feeling will go away."

Gary started for the door. "And if I tell you differently?"

Steve clapped his hands on the top of his head and sighed. "Then that would be a problem."

Gary nodded and left the office. Steve listened as his footsteps faded down the hall, then he rose and walked to the window. He pushed the sash back open and stuck his head out. The smell of fresh cut grass hung heavy in the air. Steve could feel the heat of the morning sun directly on his face, but for some reason, he felt cold.

***

June 5 continued

Nathan Espy stared at the sleeping figure of his father and wondered how it would feel to bash in his head with a baseball bat. A few good swings with a Louisville Slugger and Marcus Espy would be nothing more than a bad memory and a nasty red stain on the sofa. And the sofa could always be cleaned.

Nathan stroked his right cheek with the tips of his fingers. It was still slightly discolored and sore to the touch. Next time, he thought. The next time his father hit him, Nathan swore he would get his bat from the cellar and pound his father's face into a pulp. Next time. It was a promise he had been making to himself for nine years.

"Dad," Nathan whispered. "You asleep?"

Marcus rolled onto his side, one beefy arm dangling off the edge of the sofa. He was an enormous man, a two hundred and fifty pound slab of useless flesh. Unemployed for the last four years, Marcus was content to spend the rest of his life living off welfare and beating the crap out of his kid in between naps.

"Dad," Nathan said again, this time poking his father in the arm. When it twitched, the boy wisely stepped back.

"Hmmm," Marcus mumbled, opening his eyes to see the nervous figure of his son. "What do you want?"

"I got to go to work now. Your dinner is in the microwave. You just have to heat it up whenever you want."

"You woke me up to tell me that. What's wrong with you? I would've figured that out." Marcus glared at Nathan taking a perverse pleasure in knowing his son was scared shitless.

Nathan lowered his head and mumbled an apology. "I just thought I should tell you."

Marcus huffed and rolled over onto his stomach. "Don't think next time. Just get out of here and let me go back to sleep."

Nathan took the cue and headed for the door as his father buried his face back into the sofa. As he walked out of the house, Nathan could almost feel the comfortable weight of his Andy Van

Slyke autographed bat nestled in the palm of his hand. Just one good swing right above the bridge of the nose. One good shot and then you could kiss that son-of-a-bitch goodbye. Smiling, Nathan strolled out of the house and into the hot, June sun.

It was going to be another scorcher of a day and that meant business would be brisk at the Tasty Cone where Nathan worked four afternoons a week. The prospect of spending an afternoon busting his ass making frosties and milkshakes for a bunch of little leaguers and old farts who make a big production out of ordering a chocolate swirl was definitely not appealing. At least he'd be out of the heat he told himself.

After walking a little more than a block, Nathan stopped and pulled off the red polyester shirt that made up half of his uniform. He closed his eyes and turned his thin frame toward the sun and tried to remember if there had ever been a time in his sixteen years when life seemed better. Ever since his mother died when he was eight, Nathan had lived alone with his father. There wasn't much that Nathan could remember about Gloria Espy, except that she was a brunette and had a temperament like her husband. What he did remember were the fights. Usually late night screaming battles when both of his parents were drunk. He never really understood what they were fighting about, but there was always a lot of yelling and the occasional sound of breaking glass or furniture being knocked over. When the breaking glass started, Nathan would hide beneath his bed. Even at six years old, Nathan knew better than to ask his mother about the black eyes and bruised arms she always seemed to have. It was what grownup people did when they were married.

And then Nathan's mother died at the age of thirty-eight leaving Nathan to bear the weight of his father's drunken rages.

"Screw it," Nathan said and spat on the ground. There was no sense in crying about what you couldn't change. At least that's what that counselor at the youth center had told him. Accept reality. And the reality of Nathan's life was simple. His father was an asshole, his mother was dead, and if he didn't hurry up, he was going to be late for work. And if Nathan lost the eighty bucks a week he brought in from working at the Tasty Cone, Marcus would knock his teeth down his throat. That too was a reality.

His eyes still closed, Nathan slipped his shirt back over his neck and was pulling it over his shoulders when a strange sensation came over him. For a moment, he felt as if he was being watched. Not by just one person, but by a hundred pair of eyes gazing down at him from all directions. Nervous, Nathan glanced up and down the street. It was completely empty, no cars, no people. Even the sound of birds was missing. But still, he felt the eyes boring into his body.

It was the dead silence of the street that set off the slight tinge of fear in his stomach. Something wasn't right, his mind told him. That tinge ballooned into a full-fledged panic when he realized what that something was. The sun.

He could no longer feel it.

The day, which had been unmercifully hot a moment ago, was now bitterly cold. A blast of frigid air bit into Nathan's skin, freezing the thin film of sweat that covered his body. Nathan turned his attention to the tall trees that lined the far side of the street and watched astounded as they swayed against the force of some hidden wind. As the trees whipped back and forth, their dark green leaves began to turn brown and brittle and fall to the ground. Above the tree line, the sky turned a pale gray as winter storm clouds filled up what had been a second before, a field of pale blue. As Nathan stood wide-eyed watching a winter storm developing above his head, another sharp blast of wind blew down the street, catching the thousands of dried leaves that were falling from the trees. For a moment, Nathan was blinded by the leaves slapping into his face. Nathan turned away from the onslaught and clapped his hands over the deafening roar of the wind. He glanced upwards in time to see the leaves form a funnel cloud and zigzag down the street.

"Naaathaannn," a high-pitched voice called from above the din.

Nathan looked in the direction of the tornado as it made its way to the end of the block. It stopped, forming a wall of leaves in the street.

"Naaathaannn," the voice repeated. The leaves separated and a tall, bald man in a black suit stepped forward. In one hand he held a skull while the other gripped a baseball bat. "Batter up," the man yelled, tossing the skull in front of him. Nathan heard the sound of the bat connecting as the skull flew into the air. "Pop up, Nathan. Go get it."

Nathan screamed as the skull flew toward him.

Chapter Two: June 6

David Cavanaugh shifted uncomfortably on the metal chair, fighting back the urge to check his watch. When he looked at it five minutes earlier, Linda had fixed him with an icy stare that seemed to scream, "You're pissing me off, buster." David sighed and shifted again. No sense tempting fate.

It wasn't that David was trying to be rude, but after the testimonials and speeches about Dr. Smith had gone into their second hour, he thought that enough was enough. Everyone knew Linda's father was a pillar of the community and a great humanitarian, "One of the giants of goodwill and service," the beefy fire chief had called him half an hour earlier. But in God's name why did it need to be said by every politician and community leader in McKeesport that Henry Ellis Smith was one hell of a good guy?

At the moment, the head of the town's city council was praising Dr. Smith for his involvement with the Boys Club and the Youth Outreach Center. "Dr. Smith loved the young people of McKeesport. And they have lost their best friend." David stiffened. He was certain the Parks Commissioner had said the same thing three speakers ago.

The council president ended his remarks and quickly exited the podium, only to be replaced by yet another dignitary. David didn't hear who the short, round woman was. He was thinking about the

23

three days since his wife had received the news of her father's death.

They spoke little during the nine-hour drive from their home in Raleigh, NC to McKeesport. Several times David tried to start a conversation only to receive a curt, "Not now, David," from his wife. David gave up before the trip was halfway through, and the couple drove the last three hundred miles in silence. As they made their way up Interstate 95 through Virginia and on into Maryland, David thought of the different worlds he and his wife were from. Linda Smith Cavanaugh belonged to one of the wealthiest and most established families in her hometown; her father, a fifth generation doctor, and her mother, a wealthy socialite, Linda had grown up accustomed to every privilege wealth brought with it. Instead of McKeesport High School, Linda had attended an exclusive private school in Connecticut where she graduated first in her class. After that, four years at Columbia, followed by graduate work at Yale and in England, where she received her Ph.D. at the age of twenty-eight. After a year's travel in Europe, Linda accepted a faculty position at the University of North Carolina, teaching Native American History.

David's childhood was decidedly different. David's father had died when he was nine, and for the next two years, David and his mother were shunted between a succession of cousins and aunts until Mrs. Cavanaugh was lucky enough to find a decent job in a Laundromat. Not yet twelve, David and his mother lived alone in a two-bedroom apartment in Raleigh's lower east end. While his mother often worked double shifts to make ends meet, David did odd jobs after school for a local building contractor. The pay was usually the pocket money the building foreman had on him, but the experience taught David how to build and fix nearly anything. Between the Laundromat and David's odd jobs, the Cavanaugh's scraped by.

Never a stellar student, David attended community college and earned a degree in history. After graduating he applied for an assistant curator position at the museum of the Raleigh Historical Society. David didn't have high hopes of getting the job, but his experience with tools and construction made him an ideal candidate for the struggling historical society. As the assistant curator, David's duties were evenly split between organizing exhibitions and maintaining the building and grounds. After six years, the society's board of directors appointed David the museum's full-time curator.

When David and Linda met during an exhibition of colonial weapons, neither thought the other looked the part. With her striking good looks and athletic build, David thought Linda looked more like a fashion model than a history professor. For her part, Linda had concluded that the broad-shouldered man with thick, calloused hands would be more suited with a hammer than explaining the intricacies of Napoleonic battle tactics. After the tour, Linda surprised David by inviting him out for a drink. He accepted, and a little over a year later the two were married.

At the wedding, David sensed that he was definitely not the type of man the Smiths had envisioned for their daughter. Though they never openly voiced any displeasure, he felt a distinct coolness from Linda's parents, especially from her mother. Mrs. Smith had tried to mask her disappointment in her daughter's choice by taking complete control over the wedding preparations, presiding over the ceremony and reception with an authority that David recognized as natural for her. Linda's father chose a different tactic; he ignored David all together. Only her brother, Harris, was honest enough to tell David that he thought he was marrying Linda for her money.

The morning after the wedding, the trio flew from Raleigh back to McKeesport. It was the last contact David had with Linda's family.

Now as he sat in the sweltering heat listening to the drone of politicians, David sensed that little had changed. Mrs. Smith seemed particularly intent on ignoring her son-in-law, and at those times when she was forced to acknowledge him, she was quick to introduce him as Linda's husband, the historian. David imagined that historian sounded better in society than curator--or "glorified janitor" as he was first referred to by Mrs. Smith before the wedding. He didn't bother to correct her.

Harris, however, was a bit of a surprise. He seemed to be

making an effort to treat David with some civility. The day before the funeral, in what amounted to their first extended conversation, Harris took David to the Smith Rehabilitation Clinic.

"Come on," Harris said when they arrived at the four-story building. "We can't go inside now; they're getting things ready for the funeral, so I'll give you the abbreviated tour." He stepped out of his car and walked to the edge of the parking lot. David followed.

Architecturally, the Smith Rehabilitation Clinic was not impressive. Built in the early 1920's, it was a boxlike structure of brick and mortar, slightly taller than it was wide. Over the decades, its red brick surface had faded in spots, leaving a patchwork of dull, yellow discolorations across the front of the building. Though he wouldn't admit it to anyone in the Smith family, David was a bit disappointed in what he saw.

But any disappointment David felt about the structure was overshadowed by what he knew of the history of the Smith Clinic. Though Linda was never fully forthcoming about what she called "the family business," David knew that for several generations, the Smith family owned and operated one of the most successful private hospitals in the country.

Harris made a broad arc with his arm. "This land, the building, and all the property down to the river bank has been in our family for a over 150 years. The annex over there was the original hospital. Built around 1860 by my great, great, great grandfather." Harris paused, checking his fingers. "Yeah, that's right, three greats. During the Civil War the hospital was primarily for soldiers with massive injuries. Burn victims and amputees mainly. In fact, some of the earliest experiments with reconstructive surgery and prosthetics were done here."

"Impressive," David admitted. "What happened after the war?"

"After the Civil War came the Indian wars, then the Spanish-American War, a rather disappointing one for profits, so I've been told. Right after the First World War the new building was constructed, and the old hospital became the administrative wing. Then came WWII, Korea, and finally Viet Nam."

"I imagine that one was good for business," David said.

Harris didn't pick up on the sarcasm. "The opposite actually."

"How's that?"

"Well, it was because of Viet Nam that my father became mainly interested in treating substance abuse. You see, the hospital started filling up with kids, eighteen and nineteen, many of them strung out on dope, but the government wasn't paying any attention to that. So when Nam was over, my father severed his ties with the Veteran's Administration and the government, and took the place in a new direction. Over the years he did a lot of good for a lot of people, but there's no money on the curing side of addiction. In the end, it was a bad business move, and he had to shut down a few years ago."

The two men stood staring at the large, empty building. Tomorrow the grounds would be turned into a temporary monument to the man whose family name was chiseled into the granite slab above the front door.

"What happens to it now?" David asked.

Harris didn't hesitate to answer. "Sell it."

***

The speeches were finally over, and as the friends and well-wishers filed past Mrs. Smith, David couldn't help but be surprised by her calm demeanor. In the few days he'd been in McKeesport, he had seen no show of emotion from his mother-in-law. No tears, no anger, no sadness. It was oddly similar to his wife's behavior.

When the last of the mourners was gone, Linda motioned for David to follow her to where a line of limousines waited in the parking lot. David took Linda's arm and the two of them made their way to the third vehicle where they were joined by the president of the local chamber of commerce and her husband. Mrs. Smith and Harris rode in the first limo.

As the slow parade of cars started the four-mile trip to the Versailles Avenue Cemetery where the Smiths owned a private, family vault, Linda took David's hand. She squeezed it gently and laid her head against his shoulder. "Thanks for being here," she whispered.

27

He wanted to tell her that she was welcome, but he didn't. Linda closed her eyes, and David was thankful for the silence. While she rested, he looked out the window, not paying much attention to the town that passed in front of him.

June 6 continued

Standing in front of the open window in his office breathing in the humid, night air, Steve could hear the hum of the traffic on Fifth Avenue heading eastward toward the Josslin Bridge and out of McKeesport. He fixed his eyes on the well-trimmed lawn in front of him as the last rays of sunlight bathed the statue of John Kennedy in a pale, orange glow. Staring at the statue, Steve wondered what it was like to be dead.

A Roman Catholic, just like Kennedy, Steve had been raised to believe in heaven and hell, and God and the trinity, and all the other mysteries of the faith that the nuns at St. Pius elementary school drilled into his head. As a kid in the pre-Vatican II days, faith was easy. It was just a matter of memorizing a bunch of questions and answers from the Baltimore Catechism, and knowing the difference between a venal sin and a mortal sin. Religion was simple; go to church on Sundays and Holy Days of obligation, don't eat meat on Fridays, and don't piss off the nuns. Do that and God would take care of the rest.

But that was before he turned twelve and his brother Terry was killed in an accident at the mill. Eight years older than Steve, Terry never wanted to do anything besides work in the mill, making steel like his father and grandfather had done for nearly forty years. Two weeks after graduating high school, Terry got a job at the Imperial Tube works. Like most kids right out of school, Terry started on the bottom rung. Janitorial work mostly. But he was smart, and he put in his time, and within three years he had gotten a pretty good job as a flow regulator. Terry liked the work, and the paycheck was certainly welcome in the Wyckoff house. All that was left, Steve's mother would say, was for Terry to find some girl and start making grandbabies.

But Terry never found the girl. Four weeks before his twenty-first birthday, a steam valve exploded while Terry was taking a routine pressure reading. The steam struck Terry squarely on the chest and face, melting away most of his top layers of skin. He was rushed to McKeesport Hospital but there was nothing anyone could do for him; the burns were too severe. While the doctors worked furiously over his brother, Steve got a glimpse of Terry through the glass wall of the Intensive Care Unit, and for a moment, the brothers' eyes met. It was only for a second, but that was long enough for the sight to be burned into Steve's memory. Even at 12, Steve knew what terror looked like.

Then Steve and his parents had been ushered to a waiting room outside of the I.C. unit.

Three hours later Terry Wyckoff was dead.

Steve inhaled slowly and tucked Terry's memory back into a corner of his mind. The sun finally set, and the small row of lights in front of the Kennedy statue flipped on. Four incandescent bulbs bathed the entire thing in a soft, white glow. To Steve, it looked as if the statue was standing in the middle of a cloud.

Steve glanced at his watch. 8:00 p.m. Normally, he would have left the office over an hour ago, but tonight, he couldn't seem to take his eyes off the statue. It was a remarkably good likeness of the former president. Especially the face. It showed more than just Kennedy's handsome features; it captured the subtleties, the thin laugh lines around his mouth, the slight squint of his eyes which gave the impression of a deep sadness behind the permanently cast smile.

A hint of a breeze blew into the window; the first one Steve had felt the entire day. Steve turned his face toward it. Looking past the Kennedy memorial, up Fifth Avenue and Broadaire Street, he could see the remnants of the Imperial Tube Works where Terry had his accident. Like most of the mills in the Monongohelia Valley, it hadn't survived the strikes and cutbacks of the early 1980's. It closed in 1985. In 1987, after all of the salvageable equipment had been removed and sold piecemeal to Japanese companies, two of its three blast furnaces were razed, leaving behind a giant graveyard of twisted metal and brick.

Steve stepped away from the window. Glancing at the pile of

folders that cluttered his desk, he sighed knowing what was in store for him. Tomorrow he had to attend the Montgomery funeral, and he wasn't looking forward to it. The night before, when he stopped at the funeral home for Larissa's viewing, Mrs. Montgomery had seemed catatonic, oblivious to her surroundings. Two women Steve didn't recognize sat on either side of her, propping the grieving woman up by her elbows. The funeral director, Neville King, told Steve that Mrs. Montgomery had not spoken to anyone since finding her daughter's body. "She's gone away," Neville had said not unkindly. "And I don't think she's ever coming back."

Steve started for the door when he caught sight of a memo on his desk stamped with the mayor's seal. Steve gave it a quick once over. The mayor wanted details about the number of extra officers who would be working the combined dedication ceremony for McKeesport's new marina and Fourth of July celebration, both slated for July third. Following the example of Pittsburgh, McKeesport's Independence Day parade and fireworks were to be held July third, thus saving the city the expense of paying the police and fire departments double overtime for working on a holiday. It was not a popular decision among the rank and file of the police and fire departments, and while Steve, like the rest of his colleagues on the police force, complained about it, he recognized the logic behind the mayor's decision. The town needed to save money any way it could. The new marina and entertainment complex would go a long way toward revitalizing McKeesport's economy, but there was still quite a way to go, and if the mayor could save some revenue with a little creative scheduling, more power to her.

Steve tossed the memo back onto his desk and headed to the door. But still, he thought, flipping off the lights, celebrating Independence Day on July third didn't seem all that American.

Chapter Three: June 7

It was an unbelievably high pop-up, and for a moment, Nathan lost it in the sun. But then, as quickly as it disappeared, the ball was back, streaking down toward the earth. Nathan jumped, his legs swinging gracefully across the outfield. Eyes on the ball, his arms and legs pumping furiously, he felt his heart pounding in his throat. Behind him twenty thousand voices chanted: Nathan, Nathan.

Just a few more steps and . . .

He leapt, his body stretching horizontally in the air above the green Astroturf. For that moment he was free. Somewhere where his father couldn't touch him. He was Superman and Cal Ripken Jr. all rolled into one.

Smack.

Stinging his palm, the ball hit his glove as the boy landed hard. All around him the crowd was going crazy, chanting his name and tossing beer cups and nacho plates into the air.

Oh, it was soooo good to be the hero.

"Nice catch."

Nathan bounded to his feet. He was no longer in Three Rivers Stadium, and the cheering crowd was gone. Instead, he found himself in the alley behind his house.

He turned suspiciously to the tall, bald man who had launched a skull in his direction two days earlier, and asked him who he was.

Still dressed in the black suit, the man was now holding a baseball in his right hand. In his left hand was a catcher's mitt. "Me?" he replied, smiling. "I got lots of names. I've been called Sombus. Incubo. Dust. I've been called the 'bringer of wonder' and the 'dark despair.'" He tossed the ball to Nathan before crouching down into a catcher's stance. "But you can call me Coach, how's that?"

Nathan nodded. That was fine with him.

Pleased, Coach slapped his fist into the mitt. "C'mon boy, put it right here. Right down the pike. Let's see what you got."

Nathan eyed the catcher's mitt then looked up at Coach who was chanting, "Here we go, batter, batter." Gripping a two-fingered split fastball, Nathan went into his windup and whipped a perfect strike down the middle.

"Impressive," Coach grinned, tossing the ball back to Nathan.

It sure as hell was, Nathan thought. That pitch was faster and straighter than anything he had ever thrown before. Nathan was about to go into his windup again when Coach stood up.

"Plenty of time to deliver the heat later," he said. "How about a nice game of catch, Nathan? How does that sound? Just you and me tossing the old ball around, a real father and son kind of thing."

Why not? Nathan thought. It wasn't like his old man ever wanted to play catch. Nathan flipped the ball to Coach. A game of catch would be fine.

"That's absolutely right," Coach said, tossing the ball back to Nathan. "Your father doesn't seem to appreciate America's favorite pastime the way that you and I do. As a matter of fact, I don't believe that your father even appreciates you."

Nathan agreed.

"Such a shame." Coach paused. He shook his head sympathetically before tossing the ball back to Nathan. "What a waste of energy your father is. A complete misuse of flesh and bones. I simply don't understand how it is possible that a man could be so ambivalent about his own son, especially when he's a fine, athletic lad like you."

Damn right, Nathan thought. He fired the ball back to coach as hard as he could. He wanted to demonstrate his fine athleticism.

"Now, if you were my son, I certainly wouldn't treat you the way your father does. No siree bub. We'd do things together, me and you. Yes, we would do things, and go places together. Places like the ballpark." Coach eyed the baseball for a moment then tossed it underhand toward Nathan. The boy watched, amazed as the ball floated impossibly slow toward him. It inched its way across the space between Nathan and Coach, rolling lazily so that Nathan could see every thread stitched into its rawhide cover. Nearing the boy, it slowed until it came to a stop, hovering just a few inches in front of Nathan's outstretched glove. The ball turned on its axis as if held up by an invisible string, but it came no closer. Coach smiled. "If you'd like that, if you think that would be fun, just grab the ball. Just reach right out and take it."

Without hesitating, Nathan snatched the ball out of the air. That's when the crowd roared its approval.

Nathan beamed. He held the ball above his head to let the sold-out crowd at Three Rivers Stadium see that he had just made another game-saving catch.

"Bee-uu-ti-ful," Coach yelled from the dugout. He was wearing a Pittsburgh Pirates uniform and waving a ball cap in a circle above his head. "Absolutely-beautiful."

Heaven, Nathan thought. I'm in heaven.

Coach put the ball cap on his head, and Nathan immediately found himself back in the alley. Coach stood opposite him still dressed in his Pirates uniform. He was eating a hotdog. "These are fantastic," he said between bites.

Nathan told him he wanted to go back to the ballpark.

"Of course you do." Coach took a last bite of the hotdog then threw his napkin over his shoulder. He moved closer to Nathan, close enough that he could rest his outstretched arms on the boy's shoulders. "We'll go back, Nathan. We'll go back there, and other places too. Fenway, Candlestick, all the ballparks. We'll visit everyone, you and me. And you'll get to play in them with all the greats. And I promise, Nathan, you'll be the hero of every game."

Tears filled the grateful boy's eyes as Coach pulled Nathan close, wrapping him in a tight, but gentle hug. "Oh Nathan, you've lived with so much pain, so much. I can feel it all around you. I can smell it, taste it." Coach stopped. He pushed Nathan away from his body, but still maintained his grip on the boy's shoulders. "Now it's time for you to give a little of the pain back. It's time for you to be free."

Nathan nodded. The feeling of soaring through the air at the fly ball was still fresh in his mind.

"We'll be free together," Coach said. "I'll help you to be free, and you'll help me to be free. Okay?"

Of course it was okay. It was perfect. Nathan looked at the baseball in his hand. Stitched into it was the face of his father.

"Of course, first things are first. You have to work on throwing strikes."

Nathan's eyes were still locked on the image in the baseball. Throwing more strikes; that seemed reasonable. He asked Coach to teach him.

"Certainly," Coach whispered. "Right after you wake up."

June 7—night . . .

"Davieee-boy! Yoo-hoo, Davieee-boy," a familiar voice rang out. "Aren't ya comin' to play?"

David stood on the side of the railroad tracks staring at the open door of the Toy Train. Come on in, it seemed to whisper. You've been here before, hundreds of times, and it's always been fun. Standing on the platform in front of the doorway to the passenger car, Mr. Biggler still wore his conductor's uniform, only now dark crimson stains were splattered across his coveralls.

"Here you go, Davie," Mr. Biggler said, holding out an oversized red lollipop. "Take it. A nice treat and we'll be friends again." David didn't move. He stood staring at Mr. Biggler's empty white eyes.

"No?" the conductor replied. "Oh well." Mr. Biggler tossed the sucker over his shoulder into the Toy Train behind him. The lollipop disappeared, followed by a sudden, powerful crunching sound as the train jostled on its tracks.

Ba Boom

Ba Boom

"I'm not going in there," David said. "Ever again."

Mr. Biggler shook his head and sighed. "I figured as much. Especially now that we've gotten to know each other a little better." Mr. Biggler laughed and his face became transparent. For a split second, it flickered like a candle that was about to go out, then it began to liquefy and reshape itself. "I do like this look, Davie-boy. I'm so glad you came up with it." Mr. Biggler shook a bent finger at David's puzzled expression. "Don't forget the cardinal rule, Davie-boy; you're responsible for what goes on in your head. You dream of the Toy Train, you get the Toy Train. You want a conductor, you got a conductor. Me, I'm just the uninvited guest at this particular junction. But, that's neither here nor there, is it, Davie-boy? Neither here nor there. But oh my," Biggler said, slapping his knees with his clawed hands. "I am sorry. I really can't call you a boy anymore. Look at yourself. You've done gone and grown up."

"I don't need you," David said. "I'm not a kid anymore."

"Daviee, Daviee," Biggler began, his voice growing melodic. "I'm heart-broken. Don't you remember all the fun we had together? When there was no one to play with, there was always me. I was the one you went to, David, when your father died and your mother was too tired to pay you any attention. I was the one you turned to in your dreams. Me and the toys." Biggler stepped to the side of the door and waved his left arm like a model on a game show. As he did, the doorway became illuminated in yellow light, revealing the scores of toys waiting inside. "So don't be too quick to abandon us yet, David. Come on, let's go and play. If you do, you'll never be lonely again."

Biggler stepped to the side giving David a clear view of the Toy Train's interior. The entire car was coated with mud as if a river of filth had been diverted through it. Even worse, globs of thick brown shit had been smeared across the walls. The toys that once hung from the walls and ceiling had been smashed and were now scattered across the floor. Nailed in their place were the crucified limbs and torsos of a thousand dolls furtively wriggling their plastic arms and legs in an attempt to free themselves. In the middle of the Toy Train, untouched by the blanket of mold and shit that covered the other toys, the Black Mare pitched forward spewing white foam from its mouth. Biggler sighed and snatched one of the broken doll arms off the wall, leaving behind a dull, black stain. "Souvenirs," Biggler said. "Little mementos of others who dreamt of the Toy Train." Biggler examined the still wiggling arm, then flipped it into his mouth.

David shuddered. "It wasn't you I dreamt about. I don't know what you are, but you're not Mr. Biggler," David said, his voice rising. "And I'm not lonely. I don't need the Toy Train anymore."

Biggler laughed. "Oh David, you got it all wrong. You never needed me," he said, taking a step forward. As he did, his arms came thrusting out of the sleeves of his conductor's uniform and stretched across the platform. The claw ends of Biggler's hands clicked together as they halved the distance between himself and David.

"No," David screamed, throwing his hands out in front of his face.

Biggler stopped and grinned. "Certainly," he said, snapping his arms back to their normal size. "No playing now. But there is something you need to see." David's eyes followed Biggler's finger to a long cattle car that was hitched to the back of the passenger car. From inside erupted a chorus of high-pitched screams. "Inside that car is what is left of those who have tried to imprison me." Biggler chuckled. "There might even be one or two people you know."

David made a motion toward the cattle car when the train began to move backward. "What is it?" David shouted, but his voice was drowned out by the loud whine of the train whistle.

Mr. Biggler focused his blank, white eyes on David. Behind him the door to the passenger car was once again illuminated in yellow light. "You'll visit us yet, Davie-boy." Inside the train, the yellow light grew brighter allowing David a glimpse of a figure kneeling amidst the toys. As the train passed in front of him, David screamed.

"Now, now, none of that," Biggler chuckled, hopping back into the cabin of the Toy Train. He paused for just a moment, long

enough to let David get a last look at his wife before the door
slammed shut.

June 8

Stopping her car in the middle of a bridge was against the law,
but Gladys Decorta didn't think the police would mind her doing it
just this once. It was a nice June afternoon, and the police had
more important things to do than to bother about her Ford Escort
blocking an entire lane of the Josslin Bridge. After all, she had
some very important business to attend to.

Very important business, Gladys told herself, and if the police
department didn't like the fact that she parked her car in the middle
of the right hand lane of the bridge, well, they could just go and
fuck themselves.

The retired schoolteacher giggled at the brazenness of the
thought. It was very rare, if ever, that she cursed, but considering
the importance of her work, it was appropriate. If the police, or
anybody, tried to stop her, she would simply tell them to go and
fuck themselves.

Gladys's head snapped back, her eyes trained on her thin hands
clutching the steering wheel. *This wasn't right*, she thought. She
was supposed to be in her kitchen making a cup of tea. But now
she was in the car thinking terrible things about . . .

(. . . the enemy)
. . . the police.

Yes, that was it, the police. But how did she get here? She
remembered putting the water on the stove and sitting down on the
sofa. Then there was a knocking at the back door.

The back door. That was it. She had to answer the door and
that's when she realized she had to do something very important,
and very secretive. It all came back to her. She let her hands fall
away from the steering wheel and undid her safety belt. Everything
was clear now.

Gladys stepped out of the car and made her way to the hatch.
She paid no attention to the cars that sped by her. Instead, she
calmly reached into the back of the car and removed a grocery bag.

She took a quick peak inside, then satisfied with its contents, carried it to the edge of the bridge. From the bag, she pulled out a thirty-foot length of rope. With a quickness and dexterity that surprised her, she firmly secured one end of the rope to the bridge's metal handrail. With the other end she fashioned a hangman's noose and slipped it around her neck.

Gladys tightened the noose just enough so that she could feel a slight pinching about her throat. It was the first time she ever had a noose wrapped around her neck, and she wasn't exactly sure how much give it should have. Satisfied with the fit though, she leaned her body against the flat handrail and peered down at the river flowing sixty feet beneath her.

"Mrs. Decorta?"

Gladys turned to see a young woman standing beside a red pickup truck that was now parked behind her car. The woman looked nervous as she raised a shaking hand.

"Hello, Mrs. Decorta. It's me, Megan Tallbright. I graduated in '88. Remember?" the young woman said, her voice coming in quick gasps as she stared at the noose wrapped around the neck of her former science teacher. "What are you doing, Mrs. D.?"

Gladys raised a thin finger to her lips. "It's a secret," she whispered. Then offering Megan a warm smile, she leapt over the handrail.

Gladys fell for only a second, but it was long enough for her to notice how brown the water below her was. *Filthy*, she thought just before the rope went taut. Gladys heard a popping sound as her neck snapped back.

There was no pain, only a sudden sensation of weightlessness and a soft, reassuring hum in her brain. For a moment she was surprised to find herself looking up at the bridge. Her eyes traveled the length of the rope that hung limply from the guardrail toward the face of a young woman (Megan?) whose eyes bulged and mouth hung open in horror. Gladys smiled at the girl. She wanted her to know that everything was alright; this was important work she was attending to. There was nothing to be afraid of.

Then Gladys felt her head twist downward, once again giving her a clear view of the river. Far below she saw a decapitated body in a pink summer frock plunge into the dark water. At that moment, the reality of the situation hit her. This was not important work. This was her death. It was all a lie.

She tried to scream, but the only sound that came out of her was a shrill whistle from the air that sped into her mouth and out her open neck. As her head teetered on the coarse rope, the last bit of life mercifully left what remained of Gladys Decorta. She blinked once in darkness as her head fell toward the river.

Chapter Four: June 9

Nathan Espy was aware of two smells emanating from his body. The first was a sticky mixture of sweat and grease, a byproduct of his six-hour shift at the Tasty Cone. Normally, the first thing Nathan would do when he got home from work would be to shower the stink of French fries and choco-burger deluxes off his body. Though his shift had ended over three hours ago, Nathan still wore his red, polyester uniform top. Splatters of grease and ice cream mixed with a few drops of blood to create a strange quilt pattern on the shirt. Some of the grease stains were over three weeks old, but the blood, of course, was fresh. That had been dripping from his nose for the past two hours.

Nathan had no idea why his father hit him this time, not that Marcus Espy ever needed a reason to knock his son around. When Nathan came home, Marcus was in his usual spot, passed out on the couch. Nathan slipped past his sleeping father and went into the kitchen. He had just finished making a peanut butter and jelly sandwich when Marcus strolled in and, without a word, sucker-punched his son in the nose. As Nathan hit the floor, Marcus calmly turned around and went back to the couch.

Nathan wasn't aware that his nose was broken. True, it hurt, and if he took a look in the mirror, it would be impossible to miss the purple swelling and misshapen features of a busted nose. However, he could still smell and that meant the nose was working. And, of course, what he smelled was wonderful.

It was linseed oil. For the past hour Nathan had been working it into his baseball glove. It coated his hand and arm as he rubbed the oil firmly into the palm of the mitt. Slowly, always in a counterclockwise motion, Nathan's right palm massaged the soft leather of his Spalding Willy Mays autograph special-edition outfielder's glove. After a few rotations, Nathan would bring the mitt to his face and take a deep breath through his mangled nose, inhaling the wonderful sweet smell of oil and leather. It was intoxicating, better than the whippets he had done with some of the other guys at the Tasty Cone, better than the paint cans and magic markers. This was no phony high. This was the smell of . . . freedom.

Yeah, that's the word he was looking for. Freedom. Good old-fashioned American as apple pie freedom.

And baseball. He couldn't forget baseball.

Nathan brought his hand to his face and carefully licked the oil off his fingertips. There was no taste, only the aroma. Surprised, but not disappointed, Nathan made a fist and punched the center of his glove. It made the same popping sound as when his father had punched him in the mouth. Nathan giggled.

The similarity was rather striking. He struck the glove again. Pop. No mistaking it, the sound of a fist against flesh. He slapped the glove against his thigh like some of the big leaguers did before they caught a pop up. It made a softer thud, more like the sound of being slapped in the head. Nathan began to laugh out loud. Why had he never noticed it before? A fastball hitting the catcher's mitt; that made the same sound as his father kicking him in the back. A fly ball; that made a thud like getting punched in the stomach. A grounder; well, that skipped just like being thrown down the steps.

It was becoming so clear to him now. Everything had to do with baseball. Wasn't that what Coach told him? He *was* baseball. He *was* the game. Who gave a shit if it was a dream? It worked. Baseball was in every drop of blood that soaked through his work shirt. It was in every cut and bruise on his body. He was the infield, the outfield, the whole damned field. He *was* the game, and he would be played.

Nathan walked to the mirror and looked at his misshapen nose.
That's taking one for the team, eh kid?
Nathan nodded. He took one for the team all right. A fastball
to the old shnozz.
Then take your base
Of course. A free pass.
Softly, Nathan began humming John Fogerty's "Centerfield" as
he slipped off his work clothes. He would never make it to the big
leagues dressed like that. No, he needed the proper uniform and
equipment. "No problemo," he whispered to himself. All around
him was the smell of freedom.

***

Marcus Espy didn't hear his son's humming or the opening and
closing of dresser drawers. If he would have, Marcus would have
told Nathan that he better stop making noise if he knew what was
good for him. It wasn't often that a man could get a blowjob from
Marilyn Monroe, and Marcus was savoring every delicious
moment. Dream or not, this was a once-in-a-lifetime opportunity
and nobody, especially his crybaby shit of a son, was going to
mess this up.
"How's this?" dream Marilyn asked before wrapping her
perfect lips around Marcus's bulging cock.
"Perfect," Marcus moaned. "Just don't talk." He looked down
at the top of Marilyn's blond head. It was bobbing up and down in
agreement. "So fucking good," he sighed. Not like his wife. That
bitch would never go down on him without a little persuasion. She
thought she was too good for that, but Marcus wasn't fooled. He
knew that whore sucked off everybody in sight. But a couple of
wallops to the back of the neck usually changed her attitude. A few
good smacks, and she would suck him all right. Sure, she would
blubber and cry while she did it, but his dick was in her mouth and
that's all that mattered.
But now, oh God now, this was so perfect. Marilyn Monroe
had strolled into his living room wearing that white dress from The
Seven Year Itch and asked Marcus if he would mind if she

shwonked his gator. "Marcus, I would very much like to shwonk your gator," she huffed in that breathless, little-girl-voice of hers. And Marcus had smiled and said, "Sure Marilyn, here you go." Dream Marilyn grinned and sashayed over to the couch. There was no small talk, no bullshit. She just knelt down and started the serious business of shwonking.

"As it should be, eh Mr. Espy?"

Marcus looked over his left shoulder to see a man in a black suit standing next to the couch. Marilyn paid no attention to the newcomer as her mouth and hands worked furiously over Marcus's dick. Marcus didn't mind the intrusion either. Hell, he didn't give a shit if the Vienna Boys Choir popped in for the show.

"Marilyn Monroe is sucking me off," Marcus said matter-of-factly.

"I see that," the man replied. He walked around the couch for a better look. "She seems to be doing an excellent job. Stunning technique."

"Oh yes," Marcus purred. "Stunning." The first stirring of an orgasm was beginning to tingle in his balls. "Oh Christ yes," he groaned. Just a few more seconds; a few more . . .

Marilyn stopped.

Immediately, the buildup that was about to erupt ebbed away. "Hey, what's going on? Why did she stop?"

"Because, Mr. Espy," the man said, helping Marilyn to her feet. "She never really began, now did she? Marilyn Monroe has been a corpse for over thirty years. Even an idiot like you should know that. How can a corpse give you a blow job?"

Marcus was stunned. "You son-of-a-bitch," he shouted. "She was doing a fine job 'till you showed up."

"Of course she was, Mr. Espy. She was doing a most wonderful job of exciting a piece of excrement like you. Truthfully, I don't know how she does it. I mean, if you were a young, strong man, I guess it wouldn't be so bad to have your penis inside her mouth. Actually, I imagine she would enjoy it. But you are a grotesque bag of fat. A petty, abusive drunk. To have your shriveled lump of dick in her mouth must have been a revolting experience, even for a corpse. Wouldn't you agree, Mr.

Espy?"

Marcus couldn't believe what was happening. One second he was getting the blowjob of his life, and the next, some bald guy was calling him a piece of shit. "I'm going to break your fucking head open," Marcus said, reaching for his shorts. As he struggled to get them on, he heard a voice call out, "Batter up." Marilyn and the bald man cheered. Then Marcus heard the crack of the bat before being swallowed by blackness and a new, much darker, dream.

***

Marcus knew from the smell that he was in the cellar. Its unmistakable scent of mildew and decay was all around him. But how did he get there? The last thing he remembered was falling asleep on the couch. And then there was this crazy dream, something about Marilyn Monroe. But everything else was a blank.

"Dad?"

At the sound of his son's voice, Marcus's eyes flickered open. "Nath . . ." he started to say but stopped when he saw the absurdity in front of him.

"Hiya, Pop." Nathan was grinning, his wide chipped-tooth smile stained from the blood from his broken nose. Beneath his swollen eyes, dark yellow bruises were starting to form. However, that wasn't what struck Marcus as odd; Nathan was wearing the uniform of the McKeesport Bombers, the ten and under little league team Nathan had played for seven years earlier.

And the uniform did not fit. The gold and red shirt squeezed so tight at Nathan's neck, purple veins were visible beneath his pale skin. The sleeves weren't any better, stretched around his bony arms making him look like a scarecrow. The shirt barely covered his breastbone leaving his gaunt stomach bare. However, considering that the rest of Nathan's uniform consisted of a jock strap and cleats, the bare midriff seemed fitting.

Marcus also noticed that his son was wearing a new ball cap—one with a skull and crossbones on it. It took only a second for

Marcus's brain to absorb the sight in front of him. "You fucking little freak," he said, and then started to laugh. His head hurt like hell and he was still groggy, but the sight of his son looking like some transvestite baseball player at a faggot Halloween party was too much.

Nathan's smile didn't waver. "Fuck you too, father."

Marcus stopped laughing. It was the first time his son had ever spoken back to him, and by God it would be the last. Who the hell did this little freak think he was, parading about like some goddamn queer, and then having the nerve to say fuck you to his old man? Marcus would kill him; he would rip that jock strap off his little prick and jam it down his son's throat. He would . . .

Do nothing because he couldn't move.

"What the hell?" The grogginess in Marcus's head subsided enough for him to realize that his wrists were suspended above him. Marcus looked up to discover that his hands had been tied with clothesline to the water pipe. Confused, he looked down to see his feet poking out from a sea of silver. His legs wouldn't budge.

"Duct tape," Nathan said. "There are six rolls of duct tape wrapped around your legs. You were out for quite a while, Dad."

"Duct tape," Marcus repeated. He looked again. Hundreds of feet of the silver tape covered his lower body from his ankles to where his boxer shorts hung at mid-thigh. "What the fuck are you doing, boy? Get me out of this," he yelled. "Get me out of this right now!"

"Can't do that, dad," Nathan replied. "Don't want to do that."

Marcus screamed and tried to lunge at his son, but his body went nowhere, which only made him scream again. Content with his handiwork, Nathan sat his bare butt down Indian-style on the cold floor of the cellar. He watched his old man thrashing about, enjoying the sight of his father struggling against his bonds. Nathan could have told Marcus that there was no way he could escape, but then again, Marcus never did listen to anything Nathan had to say, so why bother now?

Especially today of all days.

So Nathan watched Marcus squirm and scream. After nearly

ten futile minutes, Marcus stopped. He swung there panting, his enormous fat body dripping with sweat. A trail of blood from where the ropes cut into his wrists had dripped onto his shoulder and was inching its way down his chest. Gasping for breath, Marcus glared at his son. "I'm going to break every bone in your body."

Nathan didn't answer. Instead, he lifted himself off the floor and strolled to the opposite end of the cellar. Marcus watched his son remove the plastic tarp that covered the snow tires in the corner of the basement. Only now, several white boxes sat atop the tires. Nathan carefully picked up two of the boxes and brought them over to where he had been sitting. He set them on the floor and went back for the tarp. As he did so, Marcus could see the word Spalding on the side of the boxes. They were full of baseballs.

Making a wide berth around his father, Nathan dragged the blue tarp across the floor and proceeded to hang it from two hooks that normally would have held the clothesline. Nathan spread the tarp out its full length and tied the ends to two mortar blocks he had brought into the cellar earlier in the day. When he was finished, Nathan again stepped around his father to admire his work.

Coach was right. The tarp made a perfect backstop.

"What are you doing?" Marcus asked.

Nathan looked directly at his father. There was no sign of malice in his expression, no anger in his tone. "I'm getting the field ready for the game. Gee dad, you really don't know much about baseball, do you? You can't play a baseball game without the proper equipment and preparations." Nathan spoke deliberately, as if instructing a slow-witted child. "All the big leaguers have the proper equipment, you know. They have customized uniforms and specially made bats. They even have gloves that are specially molded for their hands. Can you believe that? Baseball gloves that are made just for their hand."

Marcus didn't reply.

"Anyway," Nathan continued. "You would know all that if you liked baseball. But you never did like baseball, did you?"

"I like baseball," Marcus offered weakly.

Nathan chuckled and wagged a finger in his father's face. "Now don't start that. If you like baseball how come you never took me to a game? Huh? How come you never bought me a baseball glove, or a ball? Huh? How come we never played catch? Everybody else's fathers played catch with them. Everybody else's fathers took their kids to the Pirates games. But not you. You were too busy being an asshole, weren't you?"

Marcus began to cry.

"Tears," Nathan said, his voice mimicking his father's. "Quit your fucking crying, you little shit." It was a remarkably good imitation.

Nathan waited until his father's sobs trailed off before continuing. "I bought these today," Nathan said, holding one of the boxes of baseballs out to his father. "Four dozen official size and weight. Pretty nice, huh? Well, we're going to have a baseball game, just me and you. A regular father and son thing. Won't that be nice? I'll be the Pirates and you can be the Phillies. Okay? You're the visiting team, so you're up first."

"Nathan, please," Marcus blubbered. "Stop this. For Christ's sake, stop this."

But Nathan wasn't paying attention. He slipped his well-oiled mitt onto his hand and took one of the balls from the box. Taking five steps back, he stared at the obese wiggling figure hanging from the ceiling. Digging his fingers into the hide of the baseball, Nathan glanced at the backstop. Deep within its blue, he could see the catcher giving him the sign, two fingers against the left thigh. Nathan blinked and shook off the sign. The catcher smiled. A new sign.

Nathan approved. He brought the ball chest-level and checked off the runner at first base. No free passes today. No way. He turned back to the batter and went into his windup.

"Naaathannn, nooo!"

But all Nathan could hear were the cheers of the fans as he delivered the first pitch of the game; a fastball that smacked Marcus right above the upper-lip, knocking two of his front teeth down his throat and opening a deep gash above his chin. The ball caromed off Marcus's face, rolling to a stop in the far corner of the basement. Its pure white cover was now stained.

"Steeeerike one," the catcher/umpire in the backstop called. Nathan grinned and picked up another ball. He felt strong, like he could go a full nine innings.

***

With each moment his strength increased. Almost effortlessly, he was able to slip through the darkness of the neither-place and take shape in the young one's dream. The boy was so full of sadness, surrounded by so much delicious pain. It didn't take much to break down the walls that divided the boy's waking and sleeping worlds. Soon, he would be strong enough to push his will into the boy's mind; to see with his eyes, touch with his hands. But that would have to wait. There were others whose dreams had been left open to him, whose minds the old one had left unprotected. He would seek them out. Touch them and scar their sleep. But he needed to be careful. There were still those who knew of his presence, who were aware of his power. He would deal with them later. For now he would feed.

June 10: Morning

Peter Lichfield was showered and dressed before his alarm went off at 7:30 a.m. It was unusual for Peter to roll out of bed before noon on a Saturday, but this was certainly no ordinary Saturday. Oh no, it was THE Saturday he had waited for all year. In a little over two hours, the Elks Society Annual Bowling Tournament would be underway. And this was the year that Peter Lichfield, who had finished no higher than ninth-place the past six years, was going to win it.

Peter checked his appearance in the bathroom mirror. Two swipes of the comb and his few strands of hair covered the top of his head like five, outstretched fingers. Forgoing a shave, Peter smiled broadly and checked out his teeth. They were still crooked and yellow.

"Hot stuff," he said to his reflection.

Peter hummed as he strolled out of the bathroom. There was no doubt in his mind that this was going to be his year. He just knew it. For the past week he had been dreaming of the tournament. Not just winning it, but rolling a perfect game. Every frame, every shot, his mind's eye watched the pins falling. Strike after strike. Oh yeah. This was his year.

Peter smoothed his yellow bowling shirt over his protruding gut and slipped his Sports-A-Go Watch over his wrist. 7:45 a.m. Excellent. There was plenty of time for some breakfast at Carl's Diner. Registration didn't begin until 9:00 a.m., and the first-round matches wouldn't be underway until an hour later. Peter scooped his wallet and keys off the unmade bed and headed for the stairs.

As he rounded the corner of the first floor landing, a strange odor greeted his nostrils. *Christ*, Peter thought. It smells like something died in the living room. Maybe a mouse got trapped in the crawl space under the house and was only now stinking to high heaven. Or worse yet, a rat. Peter hoped that wasn't the case. He didn't relish the idea of crawling around under his house looking for decaying rodents.

As he came to the bottom of the stairs, Peter glanced about his living room. Almost immediately, he located the origin of the smell. It definitely wasn't a dead rodent under his house. Actually, the source of the smell was the coffee table in the middle of the living room. "Oh no," Peter whispered sickly as he gazed down at his bowling ball. It rested squarely in the middle of the table, exactly where someone had left it the previous night after covering it with shit.

Noon

Marnie Baxter was cold. Despite the eighty-eight degrees outside and the blankets that covered her, she still shivered. Eyes shut tight, Marnie hugged her pillow against her chest and waited for the shakes to end.

God, could she use a drink. Anything. A shot of rye, a glass of wine. She'd be happy with a bottle of warm beer. Anything.

Anything at all, just to make the shakes go away. One drink. One lousy drink was all she asked. And then she would stop again. She promised.

But Marnie knew that's not how it worked.

It was her twelfth day without a drink, and her third serious bout with the DT's. The first day sober hadn't been too much trouble for Marnie. She'd felt edgy and a bit sick to her stomach, but that had been nothing compared to the next two days on the wagon. That's when she started seeing the flying monkeys. Most people see pink elephants when going through the DT's; Marnie saw the flying monkeys from The Wizard of Oz. Tiny, thumb-size monkeys floating about her bed with their teeth chattering away. For two nights they visited her, and then, as quickly as they had come, they had gone.

After that, the next few days had been tolerable, but this last night had been rough. A seasoned, twelve-step veteran, Marnie knew what she was in for. The anxiety, the shakes, the nausea—all the little goodies associated with the DT's. She hoped that with a little luck she might be able to beat them before they really kicked in. If she could make it to the shower—soak her head in some cold water—that might ward them off. But even with all her might, she couldn't summon the strength to get out of bed. All she could do was roll over on her side and curl up in the fetal position. Several times during the last four hours she tried to get up, but each time she did, she was racked with a wave of nausea and double vision that sent her back to clutching her knees to her chest.

This was a bad one, perhaps the worst she'd ever felt. But Marnie knew, no matter how bad things got, they would get better. That was the one solace of going cold turkey. The DT's always went away. *Everything's gonna be okay*, she told herself. Marnie Baxter was not about to fall off the wagon.

But right now she would kill for a drink.

Marnie opened her eyes and waited for the double vision, but it didn't come. Relieved, she focused on her thin fingers clutching the blankets. *Take it slow*, she cautioned herself. She waited a minute and then carefully started to open and close her fist. Gently at first, and then with more force each time. No pain greeted her.

Marnie smiled even though she still felt like shit. Once again, she had proven that she was stronger than the damn booze. She carefully inhaled and then held her breath as she straightened her body. Once she stretched out the whole way, she exhaled. No pain, no blurriness. Confident that the worst was over, Marnie carefully rolled over onto her back.

That's when the flying monkey leapt from headboard of her bed and onto her chest. Only this one wasn't of the thumb-sized variety. It was full-grown, dressed in a snappy red vest and wearing a Shriner's hat. With one clawed hand, it pinned Marnie's head to the pillow while its other claw sliced through the covers and Marnie's nightgown. Marnie felt the bristles of coarse hair that lined the back of the monkey's paw scraping against her skin. It was trying to get at her heart.

Marnie screamed, but the sound was drowned out by the howling of the other flying monkeys. There were four of them hovering above the bed, all wearing the same stupid hats. A too-small fez, cocked slightly to the right. Marnie would have laughed if they weren't drooling as they stared down at her prone body.

But they couldn't see, Marnie realized. They had no eyes.

Marnie felt her head being yanked forward until it was about two inches from the face of the monkey on her chest. She gasped for air, but the weight on her chest made it impossible for her to breath. All around her, the insane squealing of the other monkeys increased. Marnie opened her eyes to see the monkey who had her pinned to the bed break out into a wide grin. Unlike the other monkeys who had fangs, this one had a nice set of human teeth.

Still unable to breathe, Marnie felt her consciousness slipping way. A breeze from the flapping wings of the circling monkeys hit her chest and face, but none of the air would go down her throat. *Well this is a stupid way to die*, she thought. *Killed by a fucking monkey in a vest.*

The monkey on top of her jerked her head forward, sending a sharp stab of pain through her neck and shoulders. Marnie's eyes flew open again, and she found herself staring into a pair of blank, colorless eyes.

"Empty," she said.

As blackness engulfed her, a familiar churning crept into the pit of her stomach. Seconds later, she could taste the bile making its way up her throat. Even in her stupor she realized that she was about to vomit all over the flying monkey.

She opened her mouth and wretched, but as she did, the weight that had been crushing her chest vanished. She sprung up in bed, her upper body whipping painfully forward as the contents of her stomach splattered over her covers.

The flying monkeys were gone.

"Oh Jesus," she whispered when she finished vomiting. "Oh my sweet, Lord Jesus."

Sobbing, she tossed off her ruined covers and fell out of bed. She looked down at her nightgown. There were no rips in it. Frantically, she snapped back the blankets, causing globs of her puke to smack her in the face and hair. She ignored them as she examined the blanket for evidence of the monkey's attack.

Of course, she knew, there was no evidence. There had been no winged simians fluttering about her bed. No monkey trying to rip out her heart. It was all the DT's.

Marnie began to laugh even though the tears still flowed freely down her cheeks. If this was the price of sobriety, visits from life-size flying monkeys, it wasn't fucking worth it.

Still shaking, Marnie slipped a pair of sweat pants and a sweatshirt over her nightgown. Wearing her bedroom slippers, she hurried out of her room, pausing only to grab her purse. With the taste of vomit still fresh in her mouth, she ran out of her house leaving the front door open. She didn't care.

The Blue Note Tavern was only two blocks away.

Evening

The knife fit very comfortable in Helen Bly's hand. It was a silver carving knife with a thick, wooden stock. A wedding present. *Now, isn't that fitting*, she giggled to herself.

For the past hour she stood in her kitchen sharpening the blade until it could slice through a page from the phonebook. She didn't know why she chose the phonebook to test the knife. Maybe something she had seen on television. But it really didn't matter. The blade sliced cleanly through a Yellow Pages listing for chiropractors.

Helen took the knife into her bedroom and hid it beneath her pillow. Then she took off her clothes and slid into bed. "Mmmm," she murmured as she allowed her hands to caress her body. Her fingers slowly traced a path from her neck to her thighs. Gently, her left hand dipped between her legs, and she began to rub herself.

She couldn't remember the last time she'd touched herself. Masturbation was not a usual part of her sexual repertoire, but tonight was different. Tonight she wanted to be perfectly in the mood.

Still gently stroking herself, Helen glanced at the clock. 6:15 pm. Gordon would be home any second now. He would come through the door expecting to find his dinner on the table, but it wouldn't be there. Helen pictured her husband's puzzled expression. She laughed, intensifying her rubbing. Gordon would call out her name, but she wouldn't answer. When he eventually got around to looking for her in the bedroom, this is what he would find. His loving, devoted wife playing with herself. What more of an invitation could a man need?

At first he might be surprised. He might even ask what was going on. But Helen wouldn't stop. She would stay silent, enjoying herself, but never taking her eyes off his. His eyes, of course, would be fixed on his wife's fingers. It wouldn't take him long to get the hint. Then he would take off his own clothes, all the while, unable to stop watching his wife masturbate. And, oh what a show she would put on.

Then Gordon would climb in bed, and just before she would allow him inside of her, Helen would cut the dick off of that cheating bastard.

Just like that Bobbit woman, she thought.

Helen arched her back and moaned. Partly from the pleasure she was giving herself, and partly from the excitement of the image of her soon to be dickless, philandering husband. *We'll see if he ever screws on me again,* Helen thought. *We'll see if he sticks his dick in someone else again.*

"So soon," she sighed as the first wave of orgasm washed over her body. Downstairs came the jiggling of keys at the front door.

June 11

Another ten minutes and Steve Wyckoff would officially be off duty. This was a minor inconvenience for McKeesport's senior detective, but it wouldn't do any good for someone to complain to City Hall about a police officer having a beer while still on the clock. Not that anyone in The Oaks would give a damn, but it was better to be careful, Steve decided. He sat in his air-conditioned car waiting for nine o'clock.

The summer hadn't even begun and things around the department were already getting out of hand. Besides four suicides in one week, Steve's office had been swamped with an abnormally high number of complaints that ranged from the potentially deadly (Charles Keaner shooting at his wife because she woke him up for dinner) to the absurd (the winner by far, Peter Lichfield's shit-covered bowling ball). There was always a rise in the crime rate during summer, but this first week of June was the worst Steve could remember. It seemed like a lot of people's fuses were getting awfully short all of the sudden. *Maybe it was the heat wave*, Steve hoped. *Heat can make people do some pretty stupid stuff.*

But heat usually didn't cause people to take their own lives. That was the center of Steve's concern. Gary had done some checking into the three suicides from what was now being referred to in the department as Slaughter Saturday, but found nothing out of the ordinary. "The only thing strange," Gary told him, "is that three reasonably adjusted individuals killed themselves."

Steve had agreed and told Gary not to press the issue anymore. With what had every indication of becoming a busy month for the police department, Steve decided it was best to bury the dead and let it go at that. "Chalk it up to sunspots," he told Gary.

Then Gladys Decorta killed herself, and the veteran police officer knew that it wasn't a sunspot that drove the popular high school teacher off the Josslin Bridge. But what was it that did?

That was the million-dollar question.

Steve glanced at his watch. Nine o'clock. He stepped out of his car and walked toward the metal front door beneath a blue neon sign that blinked: The Oaks: Dining and Drinks. Steve tried to remember the last time he had seen someone dining on anything except pretzels and the occasional hard-boiled egg at The Oaks. He pulled open the heavy door and stepped into the bar.

Taking a quick look around, he saw about a dozen people gathered throughout the smoky interior. Two girls were leaning over the jukebox while their boyfriends threw darts at an electronic dartboard. In a booth at the back end of the bar, three old men sat with a pitcher of Rolling Rock in front of them. One of the men saw Steve and raised his hand. "Hiya, chief."

"Hey, Tom."

The girls at the jukebox paid him no attention. *Good*, Steve thought. The regular crowd.

As he made his way to the bar, two large men at the pool table did notice Steve. The larger of the pair, Curtis Mayflower, a two-bit drug dealer Steve had arrested on two occasions, turned toward the cop and belched. "Well now, how's it hangin' chief?" The big man grabbed his crotch and laughed.

"You're a class act, Mayflower," Steve said, taking a seat at the U-shaped bar. He threw a wad of bills and a half-empty pack of Marlboros on the counter. Behind him he could hear Curtis Mayflower laughing and the sound of billiard balls colliding. Steve focused his attention on the bartender. "Hey gorgeous," he said.

Merilee Stepanich, owner and proprietor of The Oaks, turned from the cash register and held up a "I'll-be-with-you-in-a-second" finger. Steve watched her take several bills from the register and stuff them in the front pocket of her jeans. She then double checked a receipt slip, and with a quick flick of her wrist, slammed the register shut. She turned to the draft taps beside the register and called back over her shoulder. "Iron City?"

"Yup," Steve replied.

Merilee snatched two glasses from the rack under the long, mahogany bar, shoving the first under the tap marked I.C. When the brownish liquid reached the rim she slid it aside and inserted the second glass.

Steve watched as she poured the beers, much more interested in her curvaceous backside than the slowly filling Pilsner glasses. It was a firm and well-proportioned backside. Perhaps a little on the heavy side, but just the kind he loved.

Merilee turned toward Steve with a glass of beer in each hand. She was wearing a white blouse with the first two buttons left open revealing just a hint of cleavage contained between what was a substantial bosom. Her long brown hair hung loosely over her shoulders, a few out of place strands stuck to her forehead. She looked to be overworked and exhausted, and in Steve's estimation, the most gorgeous woman in McKeesport.

"Here you go," she said, placing one of the beers in front of Steve. The other glass she put in front of an older man perched on the corner stool. He was a thin, wiry man with scraggly hair and a three-day growth dotting his chin. "One for you, Morris." The older man's head snapped forward when he heard his name. He accepted the beer but said nothing.

"So," Merilee said, turning back to Steve. "How was your day?"

"Lousy. I'm just hoping that my night's a bit better."

Merilee's brown eyes widened. "Oh really? And what do you mean by that?" She bent over the side of the bar so that her head was to the side of Steve's ear. "I take it that you're planning to spend the night at my house," she said, lightly pressing her lips against his earlobe. Steve wanted to turn his head and kiss her but that would be breaking Merilee's number one rule. No public displays of affection, especially in the bar.

"Not fair," Steve said as Merilee straightened up. "How would you like it if I nuzzled you behind the bar?"

"Then, I would just have to call the cops."

Steve laughed. "In that case, I'll just sit here and drink my beer."

"Good choice."

A tall woman with red hair took a seat on the opposite end of the bar. Merilee turned to wait on her.

Steve lifted his glass and sipped at his beer. Out of the corner

56

of his eye he watched Morris Keyes, the thin man at the corner stool. Morris's frame looked even thinner than usual, making Steve wondered if the older man was sick. Steve wouldn't be surprised. To look at Morris's stick arms and hunched posture, it was a wonder that the man could even stand up. But Steve knew there was a lot more to Morris Keyes. He was a bona fide war hero, having received both a purple heart and a silver star in Viet Nam. Toward the end of his second tour, Morris had been wounded while evacuating some men onto a helicopter. The men made it to safety, but Morris had been captured by the Viet Cong. He had spent the next four years in a POW camp in Cambodia. Somehow, Steve had never learned the details; he had escaped. In 1973, Morris returned home to McKeesport, emaciated, broken and scared. Only thirty-six when he returned home from the war, Morris looked to be sixty.

Steve returned his gaze to the glass in his hand, but no sooner had he allowed himself to relax, an argument erupted from behind him. The two men who had been playing darts now wanted to play pool, but Curtis Mayflower didn't want to give up the table. "Come on," one of the dart players said. "You finished your game, now give us a turn."

Steve spun around on his stool in time to see Curtis shove the man away. "I'll give up the table when I fucking feel like it. And right now, I don't feel like it."

Steve rolled his eyes and sighed. Curtis was obviously getting drunk, and the last thing Steve wanted was to insert himself in the middle of a bar fight. But off duty or not, he was still a cop, so he lowered himself off the stool and faced the larger man. "Cool it, Mayflower. Give these guys their turn at the table."

Curtis turned toward Steve and glared. Behind him his companion, a punk Steve recognized but whose name he couldn't remember, started fidgeting. "Do as he says, Curtis," the punk chimed in. "I don't need this shit."

"Be quiet, Cooley," Curtis barked at his friend, though his eyes stayed fixed on Steve. Steve's mind clicked. Cooley Nettles. Steve had arrested him a few summers ago for stealing patio furniture.

"How's the furniture business, Cooley?" Steve asked casually, ignoring Curtis's glare.

"Oh," Cooley stammered. He forced a smile, a row of crooked, stained teeth emerged from behind his large lips. "I don't do that no more, sir."

Curtis wheeled about to face Cooley who was growing visibly nervous. Steve Wyckoff was a hard ass cop, Cooley knew that. But if you left him alone, he'd leave you alone. Curtis was the problem. The last thing Cooley wanted to do was piss off Curtis Mayflower. People who did that had a habit of getting their heads kicked in. "Don't you fucking *sir* him," Curtis growled.

"Curtis," Merilee yelled from behind the bar. "You just stop right now before you get yourself into trouble." Merilee looked toward Steve, but his attention was fixed on Curtis. Specifically, he was watching the hand holding the pool cue.

"Pussy," Curtis said to Cooley before turning his attention back to Steve. "What are you gonna do, Wyckoff? Arrest me for calling Cooley here a pussy. Huh? Sir."

Steve looked past Curtis to the two girls at the back of the bar. Their boyfriends had wisely abandoned the idea of playing pool and had joined them. Now the four stood quietly around the jukebox waiting to see what would happen next. The same went for the three old regulars in the side booth. For a moment there was complete silence in the bar, but Steve was tired, and he didn't have the energy for a showdown with Curtis Mayflower. "Go home, Curtis," Steve said, turning back to the bar. He slid his behind further onto the barstool and pushed his glass forward. "How about another?" Steve asked Merilee.

"Yeah, how about another for the pussy?" Curtis yelled over Steve's shoulder. The police officer was flabbergasted. This asshole just didn't know when to quit. But before Steve could say anything, a deep voice told Curtis to shut the fuck up.

Surprised, everyone sitting around the bar, including the recently arrived redhead, turned to stare at Morris Keyes.

"What did you say?" Curtis asked, surprised as anyone. It was the first time Curtis had ever heard Morris speak.

Looking down at his glass, Morris repeated, "Shut the fuck up, Mayflower."

Curtis slammed his pool cue onto the table and moved toward the bar. Positioning himself between Steve and Morris, Curtis stared down at the older man. "Shut the fuck up yourself, you senile bastard."

"Mayflower." Steve said the name slowly and deliberately. Things had definitely gotten out of hand. Steve shot a quick glance to Merilee and cocked his head toward the phone. Merilee nodded. "Just go back to your table," he said.

"Fuck you, Wyckoff. This is between me and the war hero."

Morris didn't move, he just stared at the backwash at the bottom of his glass.

"You're drunk, Curtis," Steve cautioned. "And you're digging yourself into some deep shit here. Now take my advice. Just walk away."

"Yeah, Curtis." It was Cooley who had safely positioned himself behind the pool table. "Come on. Let's just finish our beers and get out of here."

Curtis spun around to face Cooley, but as he did, his elbow slammed into Steve's glass sending it across the bar. Instinctively, Steve sprung from his stool and grabbed Curtis's right wrist. He bent it downward until the big man's fingers were nearly touching his forearm. Curtis let out a roar and tried to pull away, but the police officer applied more pressure and pushed the bent wrist even more. Mayflower's knees buckled beneath him as he slumped to the floor.

"Son-of-a-bitch," he cried. "You broke my fucking wrist."

"Not quite," Steve replied. "Now listen to me. You and Cooley are going to take a hike. You got it? You leave now, and I forget about your little tantrum. You stay, or even think about coming back here tonight, I'll snap your hand in two. You got that?"

Curtis looked around the bar. Everyone was staring at him. "Yeah," he mumbled. "I'm gone."

"Go home and sober up." Steve carefully released his grip. He wasn't taking any chances. Curtis outweighed him by about forty pounds, and if he wanted to make trouble, it wouldn't be easy to get Curtis down a second time. However, the embarrassment and pain in his wrist squelched any idea Curtis may have had of retaliation.

Curtis stood up and made his way back to the pool table. "You faggot," he muttered to Cooley who was moving toward the exit. As Curtis followed, a bit of his earlier bravado returned. "This is fucking police brutality. I'm going to sue you, Wyckoff. I'm gonna sue the fuck out of you." With that he spun around and kicked open the bar door and was gone.

While Curtis's tantrum provided quite a floorshow for the patrons, as soon as he was gone, things returned to normal. The dart game continued, as did the pockets of conversation. As Steve turned back to the bar, the redhead smiled at him. She was impressed.

Merilee, however, was not so happy.

"Oh that was just great," she said when Steve retook his seat. "That's all I need. Curtis Mayflower suing me." Merilee was furiously wiping the beer off the bar.

"You?" Steve began. "Why would he sue you? I'm the one he threatened."

Merilee tossed up her hands. "Yeah, but it's my place. I'm the proprietor. He'll probably say that I encourage police brutality or something. Damn it, Steve. I really don't need this."

"Relax," Steve said. "Mayflower's not going to do anything. God knows this isn't the first time he's made a dick out of himself. He'll go home and sober up, and that will be an end to it. Besides, what else could I do? I was defending myself, right? I mean, if I really wanted to brutalize him, I would have snapped his wrist off."

"That's right," the redhead interjected. "I saw the whole thing and . . ." She paused, tilting her head toward Steve. "I didn't get your name."

"Steve."

"Right." She smiled. "And Steve here was definitely defending himself. I certainly didn't see any police brutality." She turned her upper body toward Steve, allowing him a much better look at her extremely low cut blouse and full, tanned cleavage.

"Well thank you, miss."

"Nora," she said. "Nora Fuller."

"Thank you, Miss Fuller."

Merilee was not amused with the exchange. "Oh for the love of God." She set a bottle of Iron City in front of Steve. "Watch it buster," she whispered. "Now drink this and keep your eyes in your head. If you're going to be staring at someone's tits, you better be staring at mine. Got it."

Grinning, Steve took the bottle. "Yes Ma'am."

"Good." Merilee turned toward Nora Fuller and asked if she needed anything. The redhead lit a cigarette and said no.

Steve wisely took the opportunity to turn his body away from the visual temptation of Nora Fuller. "How are you doing, Mr. Keyes?" Steve asked. The thin man nodded awkwardly and returned to staring at his beer glass.

So much for small talk, Steve thought. But then again, he really didn't want to chat. Right now, all Steve wanted to do was sit with his beer, maybe steal a few peaks at Nora Fuller's knockers. Just a few hours of quiet, and then he and Merilee would go home together. Sometimes when he was anxious to get her in bed, Steve would stack the bar stools and sweep the floor while she tallied the day's receipts.

Looking at Merilee through his tired eyes, Steve hoped he could convince her to close a little early tonight.

***

The young one's pain was exquisite. It wrapped itself like a thread around his soul. So much pain. So much that he was willing, even eager, to offer up his mind. Anything. He said he would give anything to make the pain stop and to have just a few sweet drops of pleasure.

This young one was strong. Not like the others. Their pain was weak. They couldn't understand the sweet beauty of the gifts that were being offered.

He looked down on the boy, Nathan. He would be the vessel that would start the madness. The boy had tasted his revenge, had greedily sucked the life out of his father. And as he did, his last shreds of sanity also died. His dreams would now be torment, all beautiful pain.

But now was a time for caution. The death of the old one had given him only partial freedom. He was still weak. He needed time, and help, in order to become totally free.

He watched the boy.

Nathan.

"Nathan."

"Huh."

"Over here."

Nathan was lying on the floor of his bedroom, a pair of scissors gripped in his sweaty hands. Countless scraps of white paper lay discarded around him. Nathan rolled over onto his back and stared at the blown plaster above him. He imagined the small chunks of ceiling to be small, slightly deformed birds.

He was so happy. "Where are you?"

"Over here."

Nathan sat up and saw Coach sitting cross-legged on his bed. "Come here," Coach said, patting the space beside him. "Sit."

"Sure." Nathan got up and strolled over to the bed. He paid no attention to the thousands of baseball cards strewn across the floor. "What are we going to do today?"

"Talk," Coach replied.

Nathan was disappointed. "Oh. No ball games?"

Coach chuckled and placed a reassuring hand on the boy's left shoulder. "Well, I think we might be able to squeeze in a few innings at Fenway."

Nathan squealed with delight.

"But first, we need to talk." Coach sounded stern. "I need your help."

Nathan nodded. Of course. Anything Coach wanted, he would be happy to do.

"We have some very important work to do, Nathan. Do you understand?"

Nathan said he did.

"Good. But we will need help with the work. We will need others to assist us. And I," Coach said, resting his other hand on Nathan's right shoulder. "I need you to help me."

"Anything," Nathan replied. "What do you want me to do?"

"Are you ready to accept me, Nathan?"

"Of course," the boy said.

Coach smiled and pulled Nathan toward him. He hugged him, and at that moment, Nathan never loved anybody in his life like he loved Coach. Not his mother. Certainly not his father. The image of his father's body dangling from the water pipe in the basement came sharply into the boy's mind. "Anything," he repeated. And he meant it.

Nathan felt Coach's arms pulling him tighter into his chest. The hands that were on his shoulders slipped to the base of Nathan's neck. "Yes," Coach said, his fingers gently cradling the back of Nathan's head.

And then the fingers started to push, splitting open the back of the boy's skull. Nathan's eyes flew open and he tried to scream but all that emerged was a weak, gurgling cry. *This isn't right*, his mind protested. There's not supposed to be pain in a dream.

But as Coach's fingers pushed through the back of Nathan's head and began to probe into the soft gray matter of his brain, there was pain. An indescribable agony, Nathan realized with his last conscious thought, that had no place in the waking world. Nathan tried to free himself, but all he could do was tilt his head backward and stare at the flock of deformed birds above him. As Coach's fingers pushed forward, Nathan felt them wiggle behind his eyes.

Darkness swam about Nathan as he stared up at Coach's face. It was still gentle. He smiled softly at Nathan, and the boy couldn't help but smile back.

Then that part of Nathan that was his conscious-self slipped into a permanent dream. His body though, remained awake.

Chapter Five: June 12

Steve woke to the heavy sound of Merilee's breathing. It wasn't what he would classify as a snore; rather, a husky, but rhythmic sound that filtered up from the back of her throat. He classified it as a sigh. A throaty sigh.

There was no chance of him falling back asleep, but Steve closed his eyes anyway and concentrated on the sound of Merilee sighing in his ear. She was snuggled warmly beside him with her right arm draped across his chest. Steve sighed himself and listened to the morning. It was too quiet.

When he was a kid, Steve couldn't fall asleep without the background noise of the night shift at the mill. Even in the winter, Steve would leave his bedroom window cracked open a few inches in order to hear the clanging of steel at the blast furnace, or the periodic shrill of the whistle that signaled the end of one shift and the beginning of another. But one by one, those comforting night sounds had vanished, leaving only their memory to keep Steve company.

Now, listening to Merilee's low breathing, he finally found another comforting night sound. Even after two years, Steve had trouble believing the two of them were together. They met three years ago after Merilee had moved to McKeesport to manage The Oaks for her uncle, Ray Stepanich. Ray had lung cancer, and when he died six months after Merilee came to town, the bar became hers. Steve had always been a regular, but after Merilee took charge, he found himself spending more and more of his free time at the bar. He even made up excuses for stopping by while on duty. Ten years her senior, Steve didn't think there was much chance that Merilee would ever be romantically interested in him, but one dead Saturday evening when he was the only customer in the bar, Merilee asked Steve if he wanted to get a bite to eat. Steve said sure, so Merilee closed up early and the two had dinner at a local Dennys. Two weeks and three dates later, Steve spent the first of what would be many nights at Merilee's apartment. Since then, the two had been inseparable.

"Hey," Merilee purred. "What's up?"

His eyes still shut, Steve grinned as he felt the touch of her fingers tiptoeing down his mid-section toward his waist. "Not that." He laughed, grabbing Merilee's hand before it moved so far southward that he wouldn't want it to stop. "I'll be late for work." Steve rolled over and kissed her softly on the forehead before slipping out of bed.

Hugging her pillow, Merilee watched as Steve looked around the bedroom for his clothes. As usual, they were scattered across the floor. "Stop. Go take a shower," she ordered. "And brush your teeth. I love you honey, but you got some serious dog breath in the morning."

Steve stopped looking for his clothes. Raising his left arm high into the air, he took a loud, dramatic whiff of his armpit. He did it as a joke, but then a strong waft of grade-A body odor greeted his nose. "I think you've got a point," he said, and headed into the bathroom.

Once inside, he flipped on the shower and waited for the hot water to find its way out of the showerhead. On more than one occasion, Steve had just jumped into the shower only to be hit with a blast of near-freezing water. As he waited for the water temperature to rise, he caught a glimpse of himself in the mirror above the sink. What stared back at him was a pudgy, middle-aged man who had come to the conclusion a dozen or so years ago that he was about as attractive as Ernest Borgnine. At five ten, he was neither short nor tall; however, he was thick around the arms and chest, a trait he got from his mother. Unfortunately, that thickness had long since spread to his waist. Steve patted his round but firm stomach and chuckled. A few years back one of his fellow officers had joked that Steve looked like a thumb, only slightly taller than he was wide. At the time, Steve laughed, but now looking at his reflection, he had to confess that the description was not all that inaccurate.

Steve stepped into the shower, enjoying the feel of the lukewarm water rushing over his thumb-like frame. He let the water slap against his neck and shoulders for a few minutes before working up a healthy lather of Irish Spring and giving himself a good scrubbing. He had just finished washing his hair when he heard Merilee shuffling around in the bedroom.

"Hurry up in there," Merilee shouted from behind the bathroom door. "Coffee's ready."

Steve rinsed the sudsy lather from the thick mat of hair on his chest, shut off the water, and stepped out of the tub. He quickly dried off and wrapped the towel around his waist. "In a second," he called out. He brushed aside the steam buildup on the mirror and examined his face. He decided to forgo shaving; however, he didn't forget to brush his teeth. When he finished, he stepped out of the bathroom to a waiting Merilee.

"Here you go," she said, handing Steve a hot mug of coffee. She had retrieved his clothes and laid them neatly on the bed. "Are you going to want some breakfast?"

Steve shook his head. "Can't. I'll have just enough time to get back home and change."

"Okay." Merilee said. Steve took another sip of his coffee and handed the cup to her. He let the towel drop to the floor and reached for his underwear. He was in the process of pulling his drawers over his knees when Merilee spoke again. "Why don't you just move in here?"

The words blurted out of her mouth without her realizing it. Though the pair hadn't discussed living together, the subject had been on Merilee's mind for several weeks. For her part, she was certain that their relationship had reached this point, but seeing Steve in his underwear looking befuddled, Merilee realized that she could have picked a more appropriate time to pop the question. Embarrassed, her eyes fell to examining her coffee cup. Steve stopped dressing.

"Excuse me?"

Too late to go back now. "You heard me," she began. "You stay here almost every night anyhow; and face it, Steve, your apartment isn't exactly the Taj Mahal."

Steve resumed dressing, only a bit slower than normal.

"Look, we both know that we belong together. We say we love each other, and we spend all of our time together, so why not move in? We don't have to get married or anything, but living here will be cheaper, cleaner, and you'll eat better. And," Merilee added. "I'll even throw in free beer."

She was smiling, trying hard not to let on how nervous she was. Steve detected her anxiety anyway. "Don't have to get married and free beer? Now how could I pass up an offer like that?"

Merilee frowned. "Fine, fine. Just forget it." Steve had gotten his pants on and was now slipping his shirt over his shoulders. As he did, he kept his eyes trained on Merilee. She took a gulp of her coffee and shook her head. "Forget I said anything. I don't know what I was thinking."

But Steve had a pretty good idea of what she was thinking. He too had been thinking about the living arrangements and had arrived at roughly the same conclusion. "I've got to go," he said, buttoning the last two buttons of his shirt. Merilee nodded, a slight trace of embarrassed-red flushed her cheeks. Steve finished his coffee and handed the cup back to Merilee who took it without looking up. He bent forward and kissed her on the cheek. Merilee didn't move.

"I have to go," he repeated, adding, "but I want the right side of the closet."

Merilee wasn't sure she had heard him right. "Huh?"

"The closet. I want the right side. If I don't get the right side, it's no deal. Got it?"

"Sure." Merilee's voice cracked slightly. "Anything you want."

"Good. We'll talk about marriage after I get moved in. But the free beer, that's definitely a must."

Merilee nodded. There was nothing else she could do. She wanted to wrap her arms around Steve, to squeeze the breath out of him, but her hands still held the coffee cups. She gripped them like vices in order to keep her hands from shaking. Steve took a step forward and kissed her again on the cheek. "I do love you," he whispered into her ear.

Merilee watched as he made his way out of the bedroom and toward the stairs. She didn't start to cry until after she heard the outside door close.

June 12 continued

Curtis Mayflower was still pissed off. Over and over he pictured himself sticking his 13-wide cowboy boots straight up Steve Wyckoff's butt—ankle deep in ass. Curtis wanted Wyckoff bloody and begging for the beating to stop. Of course, Curtis would see no reason to oblige him. In his fantasy, he kept kicking until Wyckoff's face was a shapeless, bloody pulp. Only then did he stop. Then he would turn his attention to that Stepanich bitch. Oh she would get hers too. And that old man. Fucking mumbling bastard. He would get a serious hurting.

A real casualty of war beating.

Curtis rubbed the back of his neck with his right hand while his other hand gripped a half-empty bottle of Stoneys. On the floor beside the brown recliner where Curtis sank his butt at least six hours a day to watch television or sleep, four empty bottles were neatly lined up.

Curtis lifted his imposing frame out of the chair and, grabbing the empties off the floor, headed for the kitchen. Shirtless, he wore a pair of relaxed fit jeans and steel-tipped work boots. Though most of his muscular frame had been replaced by thick layers of beer fat, he was still one intimidating presence who didn't think twice about using his brawn to get what he wanted. Curtis Mayflower was one man who truly enjoyed being a big, mean son-of-a-bitch.

Curtis lived alone in a one-bedroom apartment above a candy

store that had long since gone out of business. His was the uncomplicated life of a small-time loser. When he wasn't committing larceny, he worked as a bouncer at a strip club. He also sold dope, marijuana mainly, to the locals. He had a TV, a stereo, and a footlocker full of porno and football magazines. What more did a swinging bachelor need?

Curtis tossed the empties into a blue recycling bin that overflowed with beer bottles and tuna fish cans. He opened the refrigerator and peeked in. Four more Stoneys, a jar of pickles, and a crusty container of Cool Whip. Curtis grabbed another beer. He was hungry but payday wasn't for two more days, and all he had in his wallet was three bucks. And he would need that if he wanted to eat lunch tomorrow. "Shit," he muttered, and slammed the refrigerator shut.

As he made his way back to the chair, Curtis paused to look at the only decoration in the entire apartment—a poster of Miami Dolphins quarterback Dan Marino. Ol' Dano stood in the middle of a pile of blurred lineman, his arm cocked back ready to toss another touchdown strike. Behind him, a linebacker was closing in for the sack. But, cool as ice, Dan didn't care. The linebacker would arrive too late. The pass would be off, and you could count up six more for the Dolphins.

Marino had been his hero ever since Curtis was in high school. In 1984, when Curtis became an All-State first round selection for McKeesport, he was hailed as the next great quarterback to come out of Western Pennsylvania, joining the ranks of Joe Namath, Joe Montana, and Marino himself. Curtis was big, fast, and had an arm like a cannon. When he received a full scholarship to New Hampshire University, Curtis thought he had a one-way ticket to the pros. Yet, despite his size and strength, Curtis was a bust, an undisciplined clown who didn't like to take a hit. After three semesters of academic probation and an arrest for breaking the jaw of a freshman who had bumped into him at a party, Curtis lost his scholarship and was sent packing. Only twenty, Curtis Mayflower, McKeesport's next big football hero, was washed up.

Curtis hoisted his bottle toward the poster. "You don't have to worry about food money, do you, Dan? You don't have to worry about a thing."

Curtis paused, half expecting the figure on the poster to answer. When it didn't, he took another swig, ignoring the drops of beer that dribbled onto his chin. Satisfied that he'd sufficiently humbled the poster, Curtis made his way to the recliner, but before he could sit down, there was a knock at the door. *Probably some kid looking to buy some weed*, Curtis thought. But he was out of it, which sucked because he could use the money. "Who is it?" he yelled. There was no response except for another loud knock. Annoyed and starting to get a headache from too much bad beer on an empty stomach, Curtis lumbered to the door. "All right, all right. I'm coming."

When he opened the door, Curtis wasn't surprised to find a skinny teenager standing in the hallway. "What ever you're looking for, I ain't got," he growled. "Come back next week, I might have something then."

The kid smiled, and Curtis thought he looked familiar. He also noticed something else. The smell of food. As if on cue, the kid lifted a shopping bag so it dangled beneath Curtis's nose. "Three quarter pounders with cheese," the kid said. "And fries."

Curtis snatched the bag out of the kid's hand and examined its contents. Sure enough, inside were three greasy hamburgers in leaking cardboard containers. "What do you want?" Curtis asked, not taking his eyes off the food.

"I'm here to talk business, Mr. Mayflower. May I come in?"

Before Curtis could tell him to take a hike (minus the food of course), the kid strolled into the apartment. He gave it a quick once over and casually slipped his skinny butt into Curtis's chair. "My name is Nathan Espy," he said. "But you already knew that."

Nathan Espy. The name did ring a bell. "You're Marcus Espy's kid, aren't you?"

Nathan nodded. "In the flesh."

"Yeah, whatever," Curtis muttered, ripping open the cardboard packing of the first sandwich. "How's your old man?" Curtis asked as he stuffed his mouth full of beef and cheese. "Haven't seen him in a while."

"Oh, he's fine," Nathan replied. "Never been better."

Curtis nodded. The first bites of the sandwich had gone far to settle his beer-filled stomach. As to the headache, that left him as soon as he started eating. "This is good," Curtis said, starting in on the second hamburger. This one he ate a bit slower. "Why are you here, kid? Did your dad send you?"

"My dad? Oh no. He doesn't know I'm here." Nathan grinned a wide, crooked-teeth smile that made him look like an emaciated version of the Joker. "I mean, if my old man knew I was here, we couldn't do business."

Curtis laughed out loud. "Christ kid, you brought me all this stuff just so you could buy some weed. That wasn't too smart. I told you I ain't got anything. Maybe next week, but right now I'm tapped out. So you," he said, pointing to the recliner, "can get the hell out of my chair."

"That's not the business I was talking about," Nathan replied, making no movement to get out of the recliner.

Curtis's first impulse was to yank the skinny kid out of his chair and toss him out the door. Hell, Curtis didn't even like Marcus Espy. "I told you to get out of my chair," Curtis said, taking a stride toward Nathan.

"No."

Curtis was stunned. All 261 pounds of him. And if Espy's refusal to get out of the chair wasn't surprising, Curtis certainly didn't expect Nathan's next comment.

"Would you mind getting me a beer, Curtis?"

Normally, Curtis wouldn't have hesitated to snap Nathan's pencil neck in half, but he stopped when he saw the boy's smile grow even wider. It spread out across the sides of his face, stretching the skin at the corners of Nathan's mouth to his ears. Somewhere behind all the layers of fat and beer muscles, behind the memories of the people just like Nathan Espy whom he had delighted in smacking around, a moment of perfect clarity knifed through Curtis's brain. When he saw Nathan's smile grow insanely wide, Curtis knew that he would never lay a hand on the boy. He would never touch him, because if he did, Curtis Mayflower was certain that Nathan's crazy grin would be the last thing he would ever see.

Curtis brought him the beer.

"Thank you." Nathan motioned for Curtis to take a seat on the coffee table in front of him. Curtis obliged, brushing off a stack of girly magazines before sitting down.

"So what kind of business?" he asked.

The grin on Nathan's face shrank to normal. "Oh the kind where you make a lot of money and get a bunch of perks."

"Such as?"

"The usual. Good food, some good dope, and . . ." Nathan paused long enough to take a sip of his Stoneys. "Pussy. Lots and lots of fine young pussy. Just like the old days, Curtis. Pussy lining up for you. Pussy like you could never dream of. Isn't that what you want most?"

Curtis laughed, his discomfort with Nathan momentarily forgotten. "What kind of business are you talking about? You want me to be some kind of pimp?"

This time they both laughed. "Pimping. Oh no, Curtis, nothing like that at all."

"Then what is it?"

Nathan made a teepee of his hands, resting his chin on his fingers. "All you have to do is run some errands, maybe deliver a few bags of dope. And, of course, hurt some people who Coach isn't fond of."

So that's what it was. Curtis was being recruited to be someone's strong arm. Of course, that was work Curtis felt himself particularly suited for. "Who's Coach?"

"Oh, he likes you, Curtis. He says you got what it takes to be in the big leagues. He'll tell you all about it himself tonight. I'm just here to deliver the message and to give you this." Nathan reached into the pocket of his Levis and pulled out a small, plastic bag. Inside it was what appeared to be some very fine weed. Nathan tossed the bag to Curtis. "For you."

Curtis opened the baggie and put it to his nose. He inhaled deeply. Ah, he was right; there's nothing like the sweet smell of good dope. "Hawaiian?"

"Peruvian," the boy corrected. "Finish your dinner and enjoy it. There's lots more of that."

Curtis was impressed. He pocketed the weed as Nathan lifted his beer to his mouth. "Here's to the casualties of war," he toasted.

June 13

Only 10:00 a.m. and already the temperature had reached eighty-two degrees. It was too hot for Steve to be wearing his only suit, a double-breasted navy-blue wool number that tugged, ever so slightly, against his stomach. Steve checked his watch to make sure that he wasn't late, and then looked up toward the Smith home partially hidden behind two huge oak trees that formed a natural archway to the front entrance. A narrow, stone path twisting between two rows of perfectly manicured hedges led from the sidewalk to the enormous front porch.

As Steve made his way to the first twist in the path, he wondered if he had made a mistake in asking to meet with Mrs. Smith. With the recent death of her husband, the last thing she needed was to be questioned about a remote connection between Dr. Smith and the suicides of Slaughter Saturday. Every ounce of common sense told Steve to turn around and drive away, to call Mrs. Smith and tell her he had made a mistake and that he was sorry for wasting her time. But Steve had asked Gary to check into the three suicides of Slaughter Saturday, and now, after the death of Gladys Decorta, Gary had found something.

"Steve," a voice called out. "Steve, is that you?"

Steve glanced up to see Linda Smith waiting for him on the porch. Dressed in a loose silk blouse and navy slacks, she was as elegant and beautiful as Steve remembered. "Hi," he said as he approached the porch.

"Steve, it's so good to see you." Linda opened the heavy, oaken door and motioned for Steve to follow her into the house. "Mother," she called out when the two were inside. "Steve Wyckoff is here." She paused and waited for a reply. When none came, she turned to Steve. "Why don't you head into the library, and I'll find Mother. Do you remember where it is?"

Steve remembered. "Down the hall, second door on the left."

"You got it." Linda turned to head down the hall then stopped abruptly. She looked back at Steve and said, "I'm glad you're here, Steve. So is Mother. We still owe you a lot."

Linda didn't wait for a reply. She turned again and headed down the hallway toward the kitchen. Steve remained a moment in the foyer listening to her footsteps echo off the hardwood floor. She didn't need to say that. No one owed him anything.

When he came to the library, Steve raked his knuckles lightly on the half-open door before walking in. It had been some time since his last visit to Dr. Smith's library, but as he stepped into the elegant room, he realized that nothing about it had changed. Thousands of leather-bound volumes lined over two thousand feet of bookshelves that covered three of the room's four walls. In the center of the library was a large couch, an antique coffee table, and three high backed chairs arranged in a semicircle. An eight-foot brick fireplace occupied the center of the room's shelf-less wall. To its left was a large mahogany entertainment center complete with stereo, video and a few electronic gadgets Steve didn't recognize. To the right of the fireplace was a full bar. And behind the bar stood Harris Smith.

"Hello, Detective Wyckoff," Harris said, holding up a glass filled with what Steve guessed to be Scotch. "Care for a drink?"

"No thanks, Harris. It's a bit early for me."

Harris snorted and tossed an ice cube into his own drink. "I don't really notice the time."

Steve was spared any further conversation with Harris by the timely entrance of his mother. Denise Smith strolled into the library with the practiced elegance of a social queen. In her early sixties, Mrs. Smith was still the kind of woman who turned heads when she walked down the street. Dressed in a tasteful, slightly short blue dress that offered Steve just a hint of her well-toned thighs, Mrs. Smith took Steve's outstretched hand and squeezed it. The touch was casual, oddly indifferent. "Detective Wyckoff, it's so good to see you."

"How are you, Mrs. Smith?"

"Fine. Just fine, Steve. And thank you for the bouquet and sympathy card. They were lovely."

Steve knew that of the hundreds of cards and flower

arrangements the Smith family had received, there was little chance that Mrs. Smith had even seen his. "I had a great respect for your husband, Mrs. Smith. I'm very sorry that he passed away."

"Yes, thank you, Steve." As she motioned for the police officer to take a seat in one of the high backed chairs, a stocky man in jeans and a white oxford shirt came into the room. From the corner of her eye, Mrs. Smith caught sight of the man, and for a brief moment, her smile wavered. "Oh. Detective Wyckoff, have you been introduced to my son-in-law? This is David Cavanaugh."

Steve moved toward the man. "Pleased to meet you," Steve said, taking David's outstretched hand. He had a good grip.

"Same here," David replied. "Linda has told me about you."

As her name was being mentioned, Linda walked into the library holding a silver tea service. She offered a cup to Steve and then one to her husband. David took his and slid toward the bar with Harris. Taking her cup of tea, Mrs. Smith again directed her guest to take a seat in the high back chair. When he did, she took a position directly across from him on the couch. Linda set the tea service on the coffee table, then moved next to her mother.

When everyone had their tea, except for Harris who still sipped on Scotch, Mrs. Smith turned to Steve. "Now Steve, what is it you wish to speak to me about? You said it had something to do with my husband."

Setting his teacup on the table in front of him, Steve turned to face Mrs. Smith. Feeling four pairs of eyes trained on him, he began. "The morning after your husband's death, three people in town committed suicide. Phillip Slaughter, Merril Toth, and a seventeen-year-old girl named Larissa Montgomery. Were you aware of that?"

Mrs. Smith nodded slightly. "I believe I read something in the paper about some suicides, but I don't believe I knew any of these people."

"Of course," Steve said, easing slightly back into his chair. "I'm telling you this because, as far as I know, there have never been two suicides in McKeesport on the same day, let alone three. And now with Gladys Decorta, four suicides in one week."

At the mention of Gladys Decorta, Linda sprung forward

letting go of her mother's hand. "Mrs. D. What happened to Mrs. D.?" Linda looked shocked, but Harris calmly sipped at his drink, his expression unchanged.

"She hung herself from the Josslin Bridge last Thursday," Steve explained, mentally noting Harris's demeanor. "You didn't know about that?"

"No," Linda gasped.

Mrs. Smith remained unmoved. "I apologize, Steve, for not keeping abreast of what is happening in our community. But I still don't understand what this has to do with my husband."

There was a distinct undercurrent to Mrs. Smith's voice that told the experienced police officer to proceed with caution. "Neither do I. And that's where I need your help. You see, the three people who killed themselves the day after your husband died had all been Dr. Smith's patients at one time."

Linda's jaw slipped open. "All daddy's patients?"

Mrs. Smith gently patted her daughter's knee. "Shh. Let Detective Wyckoff finish." She nodded at Steve pleasantly enough, but the gaze she fixed on him was hard and cold.

The moment was not lost on Steve. No longer on a first name basis, he was now Detective Wyckoff. "Yes, Ma'am," he began. "Phillip Slaughter received treatment on an out-patient basis from Dr. Smith several times between 1992 and 1994 for a cocaine dependency. Larissa Montgomery, the second suicide, saw the doctor several times when he was a counselor for the Youth Outreach Center. That was also in 1994. She was twelve at the time. And Merrill Toth was ordered to a nine-week stay at the Rehabilitation Center after his third conviction for public drunkenness. That was in the summer of 1994."

Steve stopped. For a few moments an uneasy silence hung in the air. Finally Linda asked, "And Mrs. Decorta? What about her? Was she one of my father's patients?"

"No she wasn't," Mrs. Smith began, surprising everyone in the room. "She was one of his nurses. Isn't that the point you were going to make next, detective?"

Steve didn't respond, he just looked at the brown liquid in the bottom of his teacup.

Mrs. Smith turned to her daughter. "Before she became a teacher, Gladys Decorta was a nurse when the clinic was still primarily a hospital for veterans. I believe she worked there until the early eighties. Isn't that right, detective?"

Steve didn't look up. "She was there until 1976."

David, who until this point had remained silent, moved to his wife's side. "Excuse me, Detective Wyckoff, but are you implying that Linda's father had something to do with the deaths of these people?"

Steve looked up quickly, though not at David. He directed his words at Mrs. Smith. "No. I'm not implying that in any way, shape, or form. Your father," he said, turning toward Linda, "had nothing to do with what happened to these people. But I do think that their connection to the Rehabilitation Clinic may provide some kind of clue as to why they killed themselves. Specifically, I need to know about a type of therapy Dr. Smith used called Addiction Pacification."

There was a brief pause where it seemed as if none of the Smith's was going to answer. "Excuse me?" Harris finally said.

Steve pulled a small, spiral notebook from his jacket pocket. "I have it right here," he said, flipping the notebook to the last page. "Mrs. Slaughter said that part of her husband's therapy was called Addiction Pacification," Steve read from the page. He closed the notebook and looked back at Harris. "I was wondering what that is."

The smirk that had been a fixture on Harris's face since Steve had walked into the library was now less pronounced. "Addiction Personification," he corrected. "The name of my father's treatment was Addiction Personification." Harris took the Scotch from behind the bar and freshened his drink. "Why do you ask?"

"Oh, I must have heard it wrong from Mrs. Slaughter." Steve took out the nub of a pencil and scribbled in the book, then slipped the notebook back into his pocket. "Well, since Merrill Toth's treatment was ordered as part of his probation, Dr. Smith had to file a report to the court as to his progress. That report mentioned Addiction Personification. So what is it?"

Harris emerged from behind the bar and made his way to the

center of the room. He casually waved his drink in front of him, but Steve sensed an undercurrent of nervousness. "My father recognized that a person who suffered from a dependency was addicted at both the conscious and subconscious level. However, he felt that traditional therapeutic approaches didn't pay enough attention to the subconscious elements of addiction. So he developed A.P. to help people build defenses against their addictive impulses at the subconscious level. That way they could fight their addiction even when asleep."

Steve shook his head. "You're beginning to lose me."

"It's like this. When a person is addicted to a certain substance—heroin, cocaine, alcohol, whatever, as long as that person is awake, he or she is aware of the addiction. As strung out as they may be, the addict can still consciously create some kind of defense to fight it. But when that person is asleep, the need for the substance is still present in the subconscious mind, but there exists no real mechanism for the person to fight it. For those eight or so hours the person is asleep, the need for the substance grows. So in the morning when he wakes up, the first thing that pops into his conscious mind is the need for the substance."

"Like a smoker who lights up before he's out of bed," Linda offered as an example.

Steve smiled, though the choice of illustration was a bit unsettling. How many times, he wondered, had he lit up before he was even out of bed?

"So how did A.P. work?" Steve asked, turning back to Harris.

Harris thought for a moment. "Well, it all starts with dream interpretation. You see, psychologists are fairly quick to interpret dreams; what they're not so quick to admit is that the only portion of a dream that can be interpreted is what a person remembers. But most of what goes on in the head when we dream is forgotten when we wake up. It's like looking at four or five pieces of a jigsaw puzzle and taking a guess as to the complete picture. There's just too much missing information. However, in the case of addicts, my father believed there was no reason to interpret their dreams. He believed that since a person's addiction superseded everything else in the conscious mind, there was no reason to believe it didn't supersede everything in the subconscious. In other words, an addict is an addict, awake or asleep, so all his dreams are about the addiction."

"No exceptions?" Steve asked.

Harris shook his head again. "My father didn't think there were. So instead of wasting time interpreting dreams, my father concentrated on using the dreams to help people fight their addictions. What he mainly tried to do was to make the patient remember more of what happened in his dreams, to fill in some of those puzzle pieces you might say."

"How do you do that?" Steve asked. "Get people to remember more of their dreams?"

"Have you ever heard of a lucid dream?" Harris asked. Steve said he didn't. "A lucid dream is one where the dreamer is aware that he is dreaming. In lucid dreams, the sights, sounds, and smells, are quite clear, so the dreamer can remember quite a bit when he wakes. It's not at all unusual. You've probably had a few lucid dreams yourself," Harris said, lifting his glass in Steve's direction.

Steve had no doubt about that. In fact there were a few dreams he could remember with a bit too much clarity. "True," he said. "But I don't think I had them on purpose."

"Probably not," Harris said. "But you could learn to have them. At least develop strategies for increasing the likelihood of having them."

"And this is what your father tried to do with his patients? Get them to have lucid dreams so they could remember them?"

Harris nodded. "That about sums it up."

"But where does the personification come in?" Steve asked. "How does that fit in with the lucid dreams?"

"Well, remembering what you dreamt about isn't all that much help for an addict unless it reinforces the desire to overcome the addiction. That's where my father's personification techniques came in. Simply, if you're hooked on something, you imagine the addiction to be a person or an animal. Something concrete and real. For example, if you're addicted to crack, you would pretend in your conscious mind that the craving for crack, the effects, everything associated with the drug is part of an animal. Let's say a bear."

"Now every time you feel the urge for crack, your conscious mind imagines a bear's claws ripping into your flesh. Whenever you see crack, pictures of crack, hell, whenever you step over a crack on the sidewalk, your mind pictures a big grizzly bear about to bite your head off. Now, at the end of the day, you're tired and you go to bed, but all day your conscious mind has been picturing this big bear. So you fall asleep . . ."

"And have a lucid dream of a bear," Steve said.

"Exactly. Well, with a little help from some directed suggestions and other therapies, but you got the idea. You dream about the bear, or lion, or whatever, and all the time your conscious mind says, 'I can kill this bear.' Eventually that's going to spill into your subconscious. When that happens, the bear will raise his ugly head in your dream, and low and behold, you're holding a gun."

"A gun?"

"Right. Part of the conscious suggestion you take into your dream is that you have a weapon to fight the bear. A dream gun you might say. So when he shows up, you shoot the bear until he goes away."

Steve was impressed with the apparent simplicity of the idea. "Did it work?"

"Oh yeah," Harris said quickly. "It worked pretty well. The only problem was that my father wasn't content with lions and tigers and bears."

Mrs. Smith lifted her hand and cut it. "Harris, I think we have wasted enough of Detective Wyckoff's time?" The sharpness of her tone took Steve by surprise, making him suppress the question he was about to ask her son.

But Harris wasn't through yet. "I might as well tell him the rest, mother. We all know that Steve's a smart guy, and I'll bet he's read a few of dad's articles. Being the curious detective, I'm sure now when Steve goes back through them, it won't be hard for him to put two and two together. So he might as well get the straight story from me."

Mrs. Smith glared at her son, angry that what he said made sense. "Very well."

Linda also looked hard at Harris, a furious reflection of her mother.

Harris ignored them and turned to Steve. "The more my father progressed with Addiction Personification, the more he got involved in the study of dreams. Not just the psychological and physiological aspects, but also the mythology of them. He became quite an expert on the subject. He was especially interested with myths about dream creatures who visit sleepers."

Steve looked surprised. "Dream creatures?"

"Sure," Harris said. "They're very common in the mythologies of many cultures. My father was especially interested in the myth creatures of Central Europe. For example, there was this one little guy called the Hugir who would appear in the shape of a beast, usually a wolf, and devour a person's dreams."

"Like a werewolf," Steve offered.

"Sort of. And then there's the Mara. This is where the word nightmare comes from. The Mara would bring horrible dreams to people and then get off by watching the sleeping person suffocate. There's a variation of the Mara called the Incubus; a male demon who would seduce women while they slept. Their legends are much like those of vampires. They supposedly drained the life out of people, or they brought madness."

"Jesus," Steve said under his breath.

Harris began again. "Anyway, the more my father studied these various myths and things, the more he encouraged his patients to personify their addictions as these creatures."

"Especially the Mara," Linda added quickly.

"Yes, the Mara. And that led to a few problems," Harris said. "It's one thing to make people imagine their addictions as animals, having them imagine their addictions to be the Mara or the Incubi is something completely different."

"Why?" Steve asked. "Wouldn't one thing be as good as another?"

"Technically yes," Harris replied. "But a few of my father's patients started to take their personifications a bit too seriously.

They developed what he called 'The devil made me do it' syndrome."

Linda took up the explanation before Steve could ask what Harris meant. "That is when the patient no longer accepts responsibility for his addiction and blames it on some outside force or person. A bear or a lion is a powerful image, but even in dreams, it's just an animal. The Mara, however, was supposed to be a thinking, evil creature. For a few of my father's more serious patients, it was too easy to give their control over to the suggestion of the Mara."

It became apparent to Steve what the problem was. "So if they couldn't control their addictions, if they took cocaine or crack or whatever, they could blame it on this Mara thing"

"Or the bear, or the Incubus, or whatever," Harris added. "I know it sounds far-fetched, but remember, my father was dealing with an emotionally unstable population. But like Linda said, this was only in very few cases. The vast majority of my father's patients responded extremely well to Addiction Personification."

"But the few who didn't?"

Mrs. Smith cut in, surprising the detective. "Those few became the focus of an investigation into the practices at my husband's clinic. That was 1995. As I am sure you are aware detective, that year my husband retired. End of story."

But there was one more thing Steve needed to know. "Of course, Mrs. Smith. I know this is difficult for you, and I do appreciate you and your family speaking with me. And I am only making these inquiries in order to help the families of the suicides. But I need to know one more thing. If Phillip Slaughter and Merrill Toth underwent Addiction Personification therapy, were they part of that group it didn't work on?"

"Oh, Steve," Mrs. Smith said. "I have no way of knowing that. What you are asking is very private and confidential information."

"I understand, but if I get permission from the families, could I have a look at your husband's files?"

Mrs. Smith's smile did not waver, but there was an undeniable finality to her voice: "No Steve, I can't allow that. My husband believed in the strictest of confidentiality when it came to his patients. And his patients trusted him implicitly to maintain that confidentiality. I cannot allow that trust to be broken for whatever reason." Mrs. Smith rose from the sofa, her stiff posture conveying the unmistakable message that the interview was over.

"Of course," Steve replied. Without further ceremony, he too stood up and thanked Mrs. Smith for her time, Linda for the tea, and Harris for the conversation.

"No problem," Harris said, pouring himself another Scotch.

"David," Mrs. Smith said, turning to her son-in-law. "Would you please show our guest out?"

"Sure." David ambled to the front of the library and stood in the doorway.

Steve thanked the Smith family again, then followed David back through the elegant hallway toward the front door. "So how long have you and Linda been married?" he asked when the two were out of earshot of the Smiths.

David grinned. "A little over a year now."

"Ahh. Still newlyweds."

When the pair reached the door, David opened it and motioned for Steve to step out. "You've known Linda and her family for quite a while," David said, following the police officer onto the front porch.

"Well, we don't really run in the same social circles, but the Smiths are a pretty prominent family in town. I think they know everyone."

David nodded. "Linda said you once saved her life."

For a moment Steve saw the image of Linda Smith crawling across the porch he now stood upon, a man by the name of Robert Monero pointing a shotgun at her back. "That was a long time ago," Steve said, forcing the memory out of his mind. "Ancient history."

"But I still want to thank you." David held out his hand.

It was a simple gesture, but one that touched the veteran cop. "No problem," Steve said.

The two men shook hands, Steve once again impressed with the strength of David's grip. "Take care," Steve said. He turned and walked down the stone pathway. When he got to the car, he quickly got in, turned the ignition, and flipped on the AC. Immediately a cold draft of air channeled through the vents on the front dash.

As he waited for the car to cool, Steve looked in the direction of the partially hidden porch, and thought about the night he killed Robert Monero. That was in 1979 when Steve was still a patrolman. He was in his cruiser, heading north on Bailey Avenue just a few blocks away when the call came over the radio that shots had been reported at the Smith mansion. Steve was the first on the scene. When he arrived, he heard shouting and then a shotgun blast followed by the sound of screams. Steve drew his weapon and raced from his vehicle to the Smith house. When he came to the porch, he saw twelve-year-old Linda Smith crawling on her hands and knees toward the front door. Robert Monero, who had his back turned toward Steve, was about six paces behind her, his shotgun trained on the girl's neck.

Steve yelled for Monero to drop his weapon. When he heard Steve's command, the man hesitated a moment, then wheeled about with the gun still raised. Steve had no choice but to shoot. He fired three shots, each one striking Monero squarely in the chest. As the first slug hit him, the shotgun flew out of Monero's hand and landed a few feet to Linda's right. Monero took a feeble step toward it, but the force of the next two bullets spun the man's body back and away from the shotgun. He took an awkward step toward Linda before collapsing on the porch.

Steve ran to Linda, keeping his gun trained on Monero who lay quivering in an expanding pool of his own blood. Steve scooped up the girl in his arms and carried her away from the dying man.

Less than a minute later, two more squad cars arrived. Two minutes after that, an ambulance, but by that time Robert Monero was already dead.

The shooting generated quite a bit of publicity in the local media and made Steve Wyckoff a minor celebrity in his hometown: The man who saved the daughter of McKeesport's most prominent philanthropist from a deranged killer. At least that's the slant The Daily News put on the story. For several weeks, the paper ran a number of pieces about the shooting, most accompanied by photographs of grateful members of the Smith family. In one picture, a nervous Linda Smith was standing between a stern looking Officer Wyckoff and a smiling Henry Smith. Clutched in Linda's hand was a check for twenty thousand dollars, a donation from the Smith family to the McKeesport Police Department. It was never made clear exactly what the donation was for, but eight days after the photograph was taken, Steve was promoted to detective.

As for Robert Monero, the paper reported an unspectacular life story. He had worked at the old Tube Works until the mid 1960's when he was drafted. He spent three undistinguished years in the army, and when he returned home, took up a job as a handyman. He never married or had any real friends to speak of. No motive for the attack had ever been found. In the end, he was made out to be just a small town loner who had lost his grip on reality.

Steve shuddered as he sat in the quickly cooling car. Even after two decades, he still couldn't shake the specter of Robert Monero. It was a constant presence hanging on the fringes of his memory. Whenever he shut his eyes, Steve could see Monero's broken body lying on the porch, the man's lips quivering, his eyes open but lifeless. He could smell Monero's blood and feel his own heart about to explode beneath his chest. But most of all, Steve could still hear Monero's dying words whispered to him in the few moments before the second squad car had arrived.

He told Steve that the devil made him do it.

***

As David headed back to the library, he could hear the sounds of an argument spilling out into the hallway.

"Why in God's name did you tell Steve all that?" Linda demanded.

"All of what? He wanted to know about father's work, and I told him. Christ, Linda, it's all public knowledge. Besides, you shouldn't underestimate Wyckoff. I bet I didn't tell him much that he didn't already know."

Linda's hands went to the side of her hips. "But why did you have to bring up the Mara and the sleep demons? Jesus, Harris, now Steve is going to think Father was nuts. That was dumb, Harris. For a second I thought you were going to bring up Dust."

Harris let out an exasperated moan. "Enough already. I'm not that stupid."

The pair paused, and David took that as an opportunity to enter the room. "Detective Wyckoff is gone," he announced.

Linda turned, surprised to see him. Harris remained facing the bar. "Oh," she said. "Good."

David headed toward one of the high back chairs. "What are you two talking about?" When neither Harris nor Linda was quick to respond, David continued. "I heard you say 'Dust,'" he said, addressing his wife. He placed a subtle emphasis on the word "you." "What is that?"

Linda exhaled slowly and shook her head. Harris had turned halfway toward David, his left elbow resting on the bar. In his right hand was a fresh glass of Dewers. "You might as well tell him, Linda," he said, raising his glass toward David. "After all, he is one of the family."

"David," Linda began, "Dust is just another part of the sleep myths my father researched. That's all."

"So why didn't you want it mentioned to Detective Wyckoff?" David glanced at Harris who seemed to be delighting in his sister's discomfort.

When Linda didn't respond, Harris did. "Because it hits a little too close to home."

David shook his head. "I don't understand."

"Dust is the name of a sleep demon in an old Indian myth."

"Native American," Linda corrected.

"Whatever." Harris rolled his eyes toward the ceiling and took a drink. "Anyway. This whole area once had a very large In-di-an population along the rivers. Well, during my father's research he stumbled across a little known dream myth that has its origins right here in the valley."

"Stop," Linda said. "If you're going to drudge up this nonsense, I'm going to check on mother." Linda moved to the door, expecting her husband to follow. "David," she said curtly.

When he didn't get up, she threw up her hands in disgust. "Fine. You stay here and listen to Harris's bullshit. I'm going to look after mother." She paused a moment, her eyes trained on her husband. When he didn't return her gaze, Linda stormed out of the room.

Harris began laughing and headed for the couch. He carried a second glass of Scotch, which David accepted without comment. "Brother, is your wife pissed at you," Harris said.

David took a sip. "So tell my about this Dust character."

"Right, him," Harris said, taking a seat. "Well, what my father was able to piece together was a Native American cross between a creation myth and Paradise Lost. According to the story, when the world was created, the Great Spirit divided everything into two realms, the world of men and the world of spirit. Men stayed in their world, the spirits stayed in theirs. However, one inhabitant of the spirit world, a trickster figure the Indians called Dust, wanted to live in both worlds. So he started popping into the world of men now and then, but when the Great Spirit found out what Dust was doing, he got pissed and banished him to the neither-places."

"Like Satan."

"Sort of. Only Dust didn't exactly go to hell. Instead, he was sent to the proverbial middle of nowhere. According to the legend, the Great Spirit took Dust up into the palm of his hand and blew on him, scattering him into a million pieces. Those pieces then rained down onto the Earth, becoming trapped where it's neither day nor night, east nor west."

David's puzzled expression prompted Harris to clarify the point. "You see, the Indians believed the neither-places to be a sort of transitional spot between things. Like the space at the top of a mountain where the mountain ends and the sky begins, or the moment when the sun is setting when its neither day nor night. These were the places in space and time where the remnants of Dust were supposed to have settled. The Indians who lived in this area believed that the most important of those neither-places was where the Youghioghany meets up with the Monongohelia."

"The rivers?" David asked surprised. "Right here in town?"

"That's how the story goes. Anyway, after wallowing in this particular neither-place for a few eons, Dust figured out a way to trick the Great Spirit and slip back into the world of men."

Anticipating what was next, David interjected, "Through dreams."

"Exactly. The Indians believed that their dreams were actually glimpses of the spirit world. So, when a person is dreaming, his mind moves away from the world of men and closer to the world of the spirit. However, the dreamer's body is still in the real world, so in effect, the dreamer has one foot in both worlds, but is not fully in either, making him neither here nor there. Which is exactly where Dust discovered he could get his revenge."

"Revenge?"

"Sure. Just like in Paradise Lost. Satan wants to get back at God, but he can't actually fight God, so he does the next best thing. He fucks with us. Same thing with Dust. He can't really get back at the Great Spirit, so he's going to take it out on men by giving them nightmares. But not your ordinary, run of the mill brand of nightmares. Oh no. Not for Dust. The ones he brought were your top-notch, scare-the-shit-out-of-you-for-the-rest-of-your-life kind of nightmares. The kind you could never get out of your mind. That's what my father called a dreamnikker." Harris chuckled to himself. "I always thought that was a stupid word."

"Is it a Native American word?"

Harris frowned at the question. "Good Lord no. It's a Henry Smith term; my father made it up." Harris shook his head slowly which made David feel like an idiot for asking the question. "He said it means 'dream stealer.' Supposedly, when Dust got into a person's dream, he took the form of whatever frightened the dreamer most and made it real. My father said that the ensuing nightmare would be so horrific that it would be impossible to forget. It seems that Dust's presence left some kind of psychic scar on the dreamer, leaving that person incapable of ever really having normal dreams again."

"Jesus," David said softly under his breath. "So what happened?"

"Well, it seemed that certain people were a little more susceptible to the influence of Dust than others. These were usually the infirmed, or the unbalanced. Anybody who lived with some kind of constant pain. They were easy pickings for the dream demon, so it was decided that for the good of the tribes, the sick and infirmed would be offered up to Dust."

"God," David said, surprised at the twist the story was taking. "They were sacrificed?"

Harris laughed. "No. Nothing that dramatic. Sacrificing wouldn't do any good. Dust needed people's dreams. Without them he was still a nonentity stuck in the neither-place. What the Indians did was construct a large hut near the river, a place they called the sleeping-room. And every night the sick were placed in it so Dust could have all the dreams he wanted."

"And the rest of the tribe?"

"Slept like babies. No problems. In the morning the people in the sleeping-room would be let out. Of course, they were usually a bit more infirmed or nuts, but it was better to sacrifice the dreams of the sick than risk the dreams of the healthy. This went on for years until a warrior named Mokera went into the sleeping-room to watch over his sick father. That night, no sounds came from the room. No screaming, no wailing. Nothing. In the morning, all the sleepers emerged. None the worse for wear."

"What happened?"

"No one knows. At least my father couldn't find anything in his research that explains what happened beyond the fact that Mokera said he defeated Dust in a battle of wills. However, from that night on, Mokera was the only person who slept in the sleeping-room."

"And Dust?"

"Not a peep. For the next twenty years, the tribes along the river lived in peace. No nightmares, no madness, nothing. It didn't take long until the people forgot about Dust. That is until Mokera died and Dust escaped. Only this time he wasn't going to be satisfied with the sick and infirmed. He let loose his dreamnikkers, and the morning after Mokera's death, about fifty men, women, and children in the village were dead. Hundreds of others went mad. Those who survived fled, leaving everything behind. By the time the white settlers came into the valley, the story of Dust and the dreamnikkers was forgotten."

David leaned back in his chair, surprised to discover that his glass of Scotch was empty. He didn't remember drinking any of it. "Why is this story any different from the others?" David asked. "Why not tell Officer Wyckoff about it?"

"Well there's a problem with that," Harris said. "You see, since this particular myth has its origins right here, my father thought it would be beneficial as a part of his Addiction Personification treatments. Dust was perfect for my father's patients to identify their addictions with. After all, he was evil, he lived in dreams, and it didn't hurt that he was somewhat of a local boy. Most importantly though, according to the myth, Dust could be defeated. All it took was a strong will. My father believed that if his patients could personify their addictions as Dust, and then imagine themselves to be like Mokera, they would have the perfect dream scenario for overcoming their addictions. It got to the point that almost all of his Addiction Personification treatment centered around the story of Dust."

"And the problem?"

Harris took a long gulp from his drink and glanced toward the library doors. "What my mother won't tell you, what she doesn't want Steve Wyckoff to know, is that Henry Smith became so caught up in his own theories and that goddamn Indian myth, that he got sloppy. He started making some stupid mistakes and that got a few people royally screwed." Harris shot David a troubled glance. "And that's how the story really ends."

June 14

"Well lookee here," the punk with the bleach-blond hair said when Curtis Mayflower stepped into the clearing the local high school kids called the Torrid Zone. The Torrid Zone wasn't much, about an eighth of an acre of flat, grassless land littered with beer cans, vodka bottles, and cinder blocks. But what made the Torrid Zone an ideal party place was the thick tree line that surrounded it. Just on the wooded outskirts of McKeesport's Renzihausen Park, the Zone was invisible from the park road. And if anyone of the law enforcement variety happened to stroll on in, they would first have to make their way through a twenty-foot thicket of trees. And even then, the woods around the clearing provided the partiers with a perfect escape route. For the cops, the Torrid Zone was a pain in the ass that was best ignored, but for the kids, it was nirvana.

"Hey shit head. What the hell is that in your ear?" Curtis asked bleach-blond.

"This," the skinny punk said, fingering a two-inch baby harp-seal earring. "This is a present your mama gave me after I fucked her."

Curtis gritted his teeth and forced a smile. Normally, a comment like that would have been rewarded with a slap to the back of the head, but not today. He was here on business. "Good one, Ace. How about a beer?" Curtis pointed to a well-worn blue Coleman sitting on a cinder block.

"Sure," Ace said. "Why not?" Ace glanced at a fat kid with greasy black hair who Curtis recognized as one of his regular nickel-bag clients. "Petey, give the man a Bud."

Not happy to be losing one of his beers, Petey reluctantly jammed his hand into the cooler and pulled out a can of Old Milwaukee. "It ain't cold," he grumbled, tossing the beer to Curtis.

"No problem." Curtis looked past Petey toward a girl in too-short shorts and a pink halter-top. She was perched on her tiptoes on one of the cinder blocks, clutching her beer with both hands. Curtis guessed that she was about fourteen. Definitely too young for this crowd. Curtis could tell from the dull expression on her face that she had already had a few too many Old Milwaukee pounders. "And who's this?" Curtis asked, taking a step toward her.

"She's nobody," a voice said from Curtis's left.

Curtis turned. Standing there was a large kid. Seventeen, eighteen, maybe, wearing jeans and a Motley Crue tee shirt that had its sleeves torn off. The kid was every bit Curtis's size, but where years of inactivity and hard living had softened Curtis's physique, this kid's muscles bulged sleek and hard beneath his skin.

"That's Fredo," Ace said before being asked. "He just moved

here from New York."

"Brooklyn," Fredo corrected. He said the word as if it would intimidate the big man who had just crashed his party. "So who are you?" he asked Curtis.

"Me, Mr. Fredo from Brooklyn?"

Curtis paused and took a long swig from the beer. As he did, he saw Fredo's biceps twitch. "I am the party man. The good time guy." Curtis held up his right hand for Ace to high-five him. "I'm Santa Claus."

Ace laughed and slapped Curtis's extended paw. "That's right. You are the party man."

Curtis took another sip, keeping his eyes trained on Fredo who was now rocking back and forth on his heels. Curtis could tell Fredo was fuming, especially when the young girl saddled up to Curtis's side. He looked down at her and smiled. "Yeah," Curtis said, turning his full attention to Ace. "I've got something for you." He reached into the back pocket of his jeans and pulled out a baggie bulging with pot. He tossed it to Ace. "I got a new supply. Thought you and your friends might like a little sample."

Ace stared at the bag that held two hundred dollars worth of marijuana. "Shit, Curtis. I can't afford this now."

Petey and the other greasers came up to Ace and stared hungrily at the dope.

"Who said anything about money?" Curtis grinned as all eyes turned to him. "Tell you what. Petey, you give me another of those piss-warm beers, and we'll call it even."

Petey looked at Ace, not sure what he should do. "You serious?" Ace asked.

Curtis burped out a "Yes."

Petey hesitated, but Ace was taking Curtis at his word. "Alright," he whooped, shoving Petey roughly toward the cooler. "Get the man a beer." Petey grabbed a can from the cooler, but instead of tossing it, he politely handed it to Curtis.

"Gracias," Curtis said. "My compliments folks. Enjoy. But," he added. "There is one condition. You have to share."

"Yeah, sure, Curtis. Anything you want." Ace stared at the bag as if it had magically appeared in his hand.

Miss No Name was also quite impressed with Curtis's generosity. It wasn't everyday she saw someone give away a bag of dope. She met Curtis's gaze and offered him an inviting, lip-glossed smile.

"Take care girly," Curtis said. "I'll see you later."

Curtis turned and headed back to the wooded pathway. Just before he came to the tree line, he looked back toward Fredo. "You too, Fredo. Enjoy yourself." Cocking a thumb at Miss No Name, he added. "Just make sure you get yours while you can."

Fredo huffed and crushed the aluminum beer can in his right hand. Curtis laughed out loud and slipped back into the woods.

***

It would not be long until he could let the madness escape to seek out the strong as well as the weak. But he grew impatient. For one who had languished in the eternal nothing even before man had built his first crude huts along the rivers, aware of only his being and the passing of time, this wait was excruciating.

When the old one died and the shackles were broken, he reached out, his hatred for the dreamers boiling. He would infect them as he had done before, filling their minds with bits of his own. But he was stopped, only a few, fragile vessels were open to him. Only a few wounded insects would let him enter.

But now the windows to the dreamers' minds would once again be opened. He anticipated their invitation, tasting their pain. It was sweet.

Chapter Six: June 15

Al Roker promised another scorcher for the North East, from the Great Lakes to the Jersey Shore. And, as usual, Al was right on the mark. It was only noon and the temperature was still climbing at ninety-one degrees. Even David, who had lived his entire life south of the Mason-Dixon line, had to admit that it was one of the hottest June's he'd ever experienced; it was most certainly the most uncomfortable. Unfortunately for David, much of that discomfort had nothing to do with the weather.

David had been purposefully avoiding the question of returning home. He had requested an emergency, two-week leave of absence from his job (which had been immediately granted), to which he'd added two of his four weeks of vacation time (also granted, but with less enthusiasm than the first request). During the few brief snatches of conversation he shared with his wife during their drive to McKeesport, Linda had told him that there might be some matters she would need to attend to after the funeral. Though she hadn't gone into any specifics, she said that she and David might need to stay in McKeesport for several weeks.

"That's fine," David told her.

But, with the exception of the funeral, nothing had really come up that required Linda's presence. The matter of the will had been quickly and efficiently settled (Mrs. Smith got everything). And despite Harris's pleading and an absurdly generous offer from

McKeesport's mayor, Mrs. Smith made it perfectly clear that she had no intention of selling the Rehabilitation Clinic and the surrounding property to the city. As for any kind of emotional support her daughter could offer, Mrs. Smith hadn't seemed to need or want any. Dr. Smith had been buried, and whatever passed for mourning in the Smith household was surely over. It was an awkward realization, but David and Linda were simply not needed.

Which left David with the problem of how to convince his wife it was time to go home.

Not surprising, when he went looking for her, he found Linda curled up on the couch in the library. Though the television was on, she didn't seem interested in the too-perfectly tanned and toned bodies of Sunset Beach; her attention was focused on some imaginary spot above the TV.

As David came nearer, Linda's attention didn't shift. He called out, but she didn't seem to hear him. "Linda," he repeated, this time more forcibly. A second later Linda's head snapped toward him.

"Oh," she said. "I didn't hear you come in." She clicked the remote, sending the television into blackness. "I just can't get into this." She looked up at her husband and smiled. "Sit here," she said, patting one of the cushions on the couch.

David sat down where his wife directed. "How are you feeling?"

She shrugged her shoulders and leaned back into the couch. "I don't know. I feel tired, like I've been out running all day. But I haven't been doing anything. I've just been lying around the house."

"Maybe that's it. Maybe you need to get some exercise. Get some sun."

Linda shook her head. "No. I don't think that's it. I'm sure some sun would help, but I just don't feel like I have the energy to get up and do anything. I just want to lie down and go to sleep." Saying this, Linda yawned and stretched out on her back, swinging her legs so they rested atop David's lap.

"Maybe you should see a doctor," David suggested.

With her eyes closed, Linda shook her head. "No. I just got a little touch of something. I'll be okay in a day or two."

"What I meant," David replied. "Is that maybe you should see a doctor back home."

Linda's eyes drifted opened. "I don't think that's necessary. I'm alright, just a little run down right now."

However, David wouldn't be dissuaded. "Fine. Forget about seeing the doctor. What about the home part?"

At the mention of home, Linda flung her legs off David's lap and sat back up. "Home? You mean back to Raleigh? Why? I'm free for the summer, and I know you can be out for a month. What's the hurry that we have to head back to Raleigh now?"

"There's no hurry," David said. "But we've been here two weeks, and there doesn't seem to be any real reason for us to stay any longer. Your mother and Harris seem to be fine. And besides, you haven't been yourself since we got here."

"Christ, David," Linda cut in. "My father just died. How the hell am I supposed to be?"

"That's not what I meant. I'm talking physically. You hardly eat anymore. You're not sleeping well at night. Look at yourself." David stopped and took his wife's hand. In a gentler tone he added, "I really think you should have someone take a look at you."

Linda's momentary anger abated. "I know you want to go home," she said, squeezing his hand. "I want to go back too. But we can't right now. Mother asked us to stay a while longer. Just for a few more days, maybe a week. It will mean so much to her to have us around."

"Maybe you," David replied. "But I don't think it matters to her if I'm here or not. In fact, I think she'd prefer it if I wasn't."

"That's not true," Linda said. "When she asked me if we would stay, I told her that I could, but you needed to get back home. I told her that a new exhibition was planned for July, and that you were needed at the museum. But she wouldn't hear of it. She insisted that you stay; she said she didn't want us to be separated." Linda sighed. "I know it's strange, but she made me promise that both of us would stay with her a little while longer."

David looked accusingly at his wife. "You promised her we'd

stay?"

Linda looked directly into his eyes and nodded. "What else could I do, David? She's my mother."

David didn't respond.

The decision had already been made.

June 16

It was all Ace's idea, to go out and, as he put it, "do a little damage."

The sun was close to setting on another balmy afternoon, and the six delinquents sitting around the Torrid Zone drinking beer were itching for something to do. Preferably something illegal.

"This is the way I see it," Ace began. Sprawled out in front of him on the hard ground was Fredo. Julie, the small redhead Curtis Mayflower dubbed little Miss No Name was stretched spread eagle on top of him. "We can sit around here playing with ourselves." Ace stopped and looked directly at Julie. "Or we can all play with you."

Julie glanced from Ace to the other three boys sitting on cinder bocks. Petey, Bip and Calvin had their eyes trained on her. She smiled and blew them a kiss, a subtle message that anything Ace might suggest would be just fine with her. As for Fredo, his hardness was quite apparent against her belly.

Julie giggled. It was not a nervous giggle. But, to her slight disappointment, Ace had other things on his mind. "Or we can go out on the town and cause a little mayhem."

Petey and Bip said nothing. For a brief moment, both had hopes that Ace might be serious about his suggestion about a gangbang. It wasn't beyond the realm of possibility. They had all done some crazy shit together, and Julie was always cool. She liked to flash her tits, and once, she went down on Ace in front of everybody just because Ace told her to. Though Petey and Bip's sexual experience with Julie was nil, it was no secret they would do anything short of chopping off their peckers to get into her pants.

"Mayhem." The calm voice belonged to Calvin. Unlike his

companions, Calvin didn't give a damn about screwing Julie, or, for that matter, screwing anyone. Especially not when there was the possibility for causing mayhem. He was a thin, gawky boy of sixteen who had spent half of his life being shunted between a mother who didn't want him and a series of group homes. He also had an IQ of 149 that had gone unrecognized all his life. "What kind of mayhem?" he asked.

"I'm glad you asked that." Ace jumped up from the cinder block and began pacing back and forth in front of the group. Both Calvin and Julie's full attention was on him. Petey and Bip sipped at their warm beers. They were both irritated that it didn't look like there was going to be a gangbang, but also anxious to just go out and do something. Fredo wasn't paying any attention to Ace. He would go along with whatever everyone else wanted to do. For now, he was having a good time seeing how far he could slide his fingers down the front of Julie's jeans.

"Well, just the other day," Ace began, "I said to myself, 'self, you haven't done anything fun in a while.' And you know what? I had to agree with myself. But then, all of a sudden, this idea comes popping into my head. Just this morning, bam, out of the fucking blue, it just comes popping into my head. And I am surprised. I mean I am exquisitely surprised at the quality of this idea."

Petey laughed and twisted his body in Ace's direction. "And what is this great idea?"

"That," Ace said, his voice rising dramatically, "we smoke this dooby!" In a wild flourish, Ace whipped an enormous joint from the breast pocket of the jean jacket he wore instead of a shirt. It was the last of the weed Curtis Mayflower had given to him, and just as Curtis asked, Ace was going to share it. He could be magnanimous now. Earlier in the day he had spoken to Curtis and asked if he was giving away any more samples of his excellent weed.

"Sure," Curtis told him. "Anything for you. But remember the rules. You got to share."

Ace said he would, but he did have to admit that he had no intentions of sharing the first gift bag Curtis had given him. After Curtis's visit to the Torrid Zone, Ace rolled a joint for the gang, but that was the extent he intended to pass the wealth. But after the second toke off the joint and the buzz started to hit him, Ace realized that this was not the kind of high that one should have alone. It was too good, too perfect of a high. It had to be shared. And from the satisfied, stoned faces of his companions, he could tell they felt the same way. They hadn't even smoked the joint down halfway when Ace pronounced that it was the best weed he had ever smoked. Even Fredo, who had taken an immediate disliking to Curtis Mayflower, agreed.

The absolute best.

Ace, who fancied himself a connoisseur of good weed, had trouble putting the exquisite, mind-numbing high of Curtis's dope into words. Not unlike the tons of grass Ace had smoked in his life, the first effects of the buzz brought with it a soothing calmness, a pleasant, mellow feeling that made his flesh tingle. As the effect intensified, Ace felt his mind growing hazy even as his senses were growing sharper. A damn fine buzz but nothing unusual for good weed.

Then came the jolt—a sudden awareness that rocked him out of his drug-induced stupor. It was an indescribable feeling of total control and power, a sensation of absolute clarity even while the hazy mellowness still clouded his mind. When it first hit him, Ace thought his head might explode. It was as if the back of his skull had been ripped away and all the sights and sounds he had never really paid attention to were forcing their way into his brain. A million different smells and noises collided into one massive chunk of sensory overload.

And for a second, it hurt like a son-of-a-bitch.

Then Ace opened his eyes and saw the world clearly for the first time. It was bright red.

Since that day, Ace kept up a steady stream of bong hits in an attempt to maintain the perfect balance of awareness and buzz the weed gave him. He liked the feel of the fire behind his half-closed eyes, the sounds of skin crawling across his body. It was his skin that had spoken to him. Whispered not only in his ear, but into his every pore and fiber. It was his skin that told him what to do.

Ace put the dooby to his mouth and lit it. A blue flame lapped against its tip, only to be replaced by the red glow of burning ash. Ace inhaled deeply, filling his lungs with the sweet smoke until he felt as if they would burst. He closed his eyes and held his breath. Already the tingling sensation of his flesh had begun. His whole body crawled with its own life, speaking to him in a language only he could understand.

When he opened his eyes to exhale, Julie and Calvin were at his side, eager to take their turns on the joint. Fredo was lifting his bulk off the ground, disappointed at Julie's departure but also eager to share the joint. Even Petey and Bip were showing some enthusiasm.

Ace passed the joint to Calvin and smiled. "And after this burns down," he said, repeating what his skin had been whispering to him all day, "we'll go and burn the city down."

Chapter Seven: June 18

David's choice was fairly simple—either take a long walk in the oppressive afternoon heat, or stay in the air-conditioned comfort of his mother-in-law's home. But that would mean having to endure another squabble between Mrs. Smith and Harris. Choosing the heat, David slipped out of the house unnoticed and started walking eastward toward the city.

It was the city's desire to purchase the land around the Rehabilitation Clinic and turn the area into an entertainment complex that fueled the current conflict in the Smith home. Harris wanted to sell the land, which his mother vehemently opposed. It was her intention to reopen the clinic. To David's surprise, Linda sided with her mother, even offering to take charge of the operation.

It was this bit of news that prompted David's walk. David wasn't sure if Linda had been serious about her offer, or if she was just saying it in the heat of the discussion to get a rise out of her brother. David certainly hoped it was the latter. For Linda to oversee the reopening of the clinic would mean that she would have to give up her teaching position at UNC and move back to McKeesport. Ostensibly, it would also mean that David would have to give up his own job if he wanted to be with his wife.

In this matter, David found himself siding with Harris. Reopening the clinic as some sort of tribute to Dr. Smith was both foolish and risky. As Harris pointed out, the city already owned the riverfront property directly in front of the clinic and almost a half of a mile to its right. "A rehab clinic that overlooks a hotel and two bars isn't going to do too much business," he said. David had to agree, despite his wife's objections. The best thing now was to sell the property at a substantial profit. But in the interest of retaining some semblance of marital harmony, David kept his opinion to himself and opted for the long walk.

David's walk took him past the downtown area toward the lower end of Fifth Avenue. He stopped when he came to the old Tube Works, a lifeless patch of concrete and twisted metal enclosed by a mile of chain-linked fence. To David, the remnants of the old steel mill looked like a strange, alien landscape, a graveyard of giant, rust colored smokestacks. A neatly stenciled sign hung from the metal gate of the six-acre lot: Mon-Valley Industrial Park: Future Home of Keening Cellular. Beneath the sign was a crudely drawn picture of a smiling cell phone.

David continued up Fifth Avenue and toward the new marina. After walking nearly a half-mile, he stopped again, this time to look at a flyer stapled to a utility pole. Atop it was a picture of a badly drawn speedboat. *Can't anyone in this town draw?* he thought. Beneath the speedboat in bold letters: GRAND OPENING, JULY 3; MCKEESPORT MARINA. FUN-FUN-FUN. David examined the list of fun things that were scheduled— MARCHING BANDS, FREE CONCERT by THE TEEZERS, FIREWORKS, PRIZES FOR THE KIDS, and AN APPEARANCE BY GOVERNOR HILL!!!!

Fireworks on July 3? Who the hell has fireworks on the third of July?

It was too hot for David to ponder such a deep question, so he turned away from the flyer and continued on his walk. When he came to the end of Fifth Avenue, David turned north onto Broadaire Street and headed toward the river. Directly ahead of him was the Smith building. A few hundred yards in front of it, the large docks of the new marina gently rocked with the river's current. During the funeral David hadn't realized just how close the new marina was to the Smith property, but now, approaching it from the opposite direction, David could fully appreciate Harris's point of view. The city's redevelopment plans would extend the new riverfront entertainment complex about a quarter mile on either side of the Smith property. Harris was absolutely right, now was the time to sell the land.

David turned off Broadaire and made his way up an uncut, grassy embankment that led to the new marina. Though not officially open, several small pleasure crafts and one cabin cruiser were already anchored in the dock. David trudged through the ankle-high grass to an observation platform that jutted about a dozen feet beyond the embankment. At the edge of the platform, David looked down at the brown water of the Youghioghany. A thin slick of oil rode the tiny waves, reflecting the sunlight into a quilt of red and dirty green. David worked a splinter of wood from the guardrail with his forefinger and flicked it into the oily water.

It didn't make sense, he thought. Linda and her mother's refusal to even consider selling the property. Even if it had been the family business for five generations, the clinic had long been closed, and there was no one left to take over the reins. What was the alternative? Leave it abandoned, to decay as it had been doing for the past four years? What else was there to . . .

"Hiya, Daviee-boy."

David spun around. He looked up and down Broadaire, but the street was empty.

"Yoo hoo. Davie, over here. Over by the trees."

David took a step toward a small patch of sickly looking Elm trees to the left of the observation tower. "Where are you?"

He was answered by a high-pitched giggle as a lanky teenager stepped from behind the trees. "What do you want?" David asked.

The boy grinned and casually made his way toward the observation platform. He was wearing jeans, army boots, and a ripped, black tee-shirt that hung loosely from his stick frame. At first, David thought he looked like some kind of sick skinhead, only this kid wasn't sporting a buzz cut. Resting on top of his head was a black ball cap with a skull and crossbones stitched across the front.

"I'm here," the kid said, "to bring you a message from Mr.

Biggler. He wanted me to tell you, 'Toot, Toot.'" The boy pumped his right fist into the air as he made the train whistle sound.

David felt the color drain from his face. "Who did you say?"

"Mr. Biggler," the kid said, doing a quick hop toward David. Though easily sixty pounds heavier than the kid in front of him, David took a few hurried steps backward. He was frightened, and the leering punk in front of him knew it. The boy stopped and reached into the ass pocket of his jeans. When his hand reappeared, it held a long, silver-handled switchblade. "Oh yeah. There was something else. Something about your wife."

David gasped. "My wife."

"Yeah, but I forgot what it was. But I know it had something to do with screaming." The kid snapped open the switchblade and pointed it in David's direction. He held his palms upward causing the sunlight to reflect off the blade back into David's eyes. "I have no idea what he's got against you, but like I said, I'm just the delivery boy."

The delivery boy stopped smiling and took another step forward. David judged the distance between himself and the kid to be about fifteen feet. Not enough space between the two for David to run. "Don't come any closer," he warned the kid.

"Sure," the boy said, not slowing down. "Anything you say."

The gap was now a dozen feet. It was obvious that the punk wasn't afraid of the much larger David Cavanaugh. For his part, David couldn't believe this was happening to him. Here, in broad daylight, he was being accosted by a kid with a knife . . .

A kid who knew about Mr. Biggler and Linda.

Which was impossible. There was no way the kid could know about the Toy Train. No way.

Yet he did, and he was less than eight feet away with a knife in his hand and a shit-eating grin on his face. *This son-of-a-bitch is enjoying himself*, David thought. *He's loving it.*

David let out a yell and lunged toward the boy, the sudden movement taking the punk by surprise. David slammed his right shoulder and forearm into the boy's chest, knocking the kid sideways against the guardrail. Carried by his momentum, David's feet got tangled with the punk's boots causing the bigger man to slip and fall face first against the wooden deck. But as soon as he hit the floor, David rolled to the right, barely avoiding the switchblade as it sliced toward the spot he had fallen. The knife missed its target and became embedded in a deck plank.

David heard a grunting sound as he staggered to his feet. He turned in time to see the punk yank the knife from the floor.

"Impressive," the kid said coldly. He held the knife out and made a half-hearted swipe in David's direction. "You're faster than you look."

Anticipating the punk's next move, David got into a crouching position. His fear had left him; now, he was pissed off and wanted to get his hands around the kid's skinny neck. "Come one," David panted. "Come on."

With the knife-hand fully extended toward David's chest, the boy took two steps to the right then dove. David sidestepped to the left and brought up his left hand, catching the punk's wrist before the knife was able to find its way into his chest. David twisted the punk's arm backward, then turned, slamming his right elbow into the kid's mid-section. The kid doubled over, but slipped free of David's grip. Instantly, the knife slashed past David's face, barely missing his throat but slicing his left bicep. David screamed and stumbled backward, his right hand clutching a fistful of the attacker's shirt. Falling against the back guardrail, David yanked as hard as he could, pulling the punk toward him. As he did, David ducked and caught his shoulder square into the kid's stomach. He jerked upward and threw the punk with his right shoulder, sending him over the guardrail above the embankment. The punk flew from the deck and landed awkwardly on a pile of rocks a dozen feet below.

David couldn't believe it when the kid jumped to his feet and started to brush himself off. Grinning, he glared at David, pointing the still-open switchblade toward the observation deck. "Toot, Toot," he shouted, then ran down the side of the river past the marina.

***

He had woven through hundreds of their dreams, tasting the fruits of their pain. Some dreams he devoured, feeding off their delicious energy. In some dreams he hid in the shadows, waiting for the right moment to step forward and reveal himself. As always, there were some dreamers who sought him out, offering their dreams to him in exchange for paltry tastes of ecstasy. To those, he most willingly obliged, giving them glimpses of their deepest wishes in exchange for their service. In the end, they too would feed him. They too would feel the last drops of their sanity wrung from the gray flesh that housed their dreams. When the last bit was sucked out of their brittle minds, he would be strong enough to escape the blackness of the abyss and bask in the pleasure of the waking world.

But until then . . .

June 19

Steve kicked his feet onto his desk and leaned back in his chair. Hands clenched at the base of his neck, he watched a thin trail of cigarette smoke snake its way to the cracked, stucco ceiling of his office. On his desk sat a pile of reports from the past two days.

He glanced at the stack of manila folders—each one a separate crime reported or complaint lodged in the past forty-eight hours, a total of thirty-seven. That had to be some kind of record. And that pile didn't even include the half-dozen suspicious fires that were reported over the weekend. "Christ almighty," he muttered to himself. "What the hell is going on?"

In the past two weeks his office had received over two hundred complaints. Steve wasn't sure of the exact number, but he knew it was bad. In fact it was the worst two-week span that he had ever seen in his career. Already, with a week and a half still left in the month, there had been a record number of assaults, DUI's, domestic disturbances, and thefts.

And there had been more suicides in McKeesport this month—seven—two more than the total for the past three years. The most recent had occurred Saturday when Marnie Baxter had walked into the Blue Note Tavern and fired three shots from a semi-automatic pistol into the jukebox before turning the gun on herself. Marnie had been spending quite a bit of time at the Blue Note recently, the owner told Gary Overton. "She kept to herself and seemed real nervous about something," were his words.

Marnie's file sat on a separate pile on Steve's desk atop a folder marked Gladys Decorta.

"It's got to be the heat," Steve muttered humorously. He flipped open the folder from the top of the pile, a domestic assault case, but before he could start to read, there was a knock at his door. He looked up from his desk as the door opened and a familiar face peeked in.

"Detective Wyckoff, am I disturbing you?"

Steve tossed the folder back onto the pile and motioned for David Cavanaugh to come in and take a seat. "No, not at all. Come in Mr. Cavanaugh. What can I do for you?"

"Please," David said, entering the office. "Call me David."

"Then you cut the detective stuff and call me Steve. Deal?"

"Deal," David said. He shook hands with the detective then lowered himself into the chair opposite Steve's desk.

Steve fished a cigarette from his pocket. "So what brings you to City Hall?"

"Police business actually."

"Oh," Steve said, surprised. He lit his cigarette. "What's the problem?"

"I was attacked yesterday by some kid at the marina. He gave me a good slice on the arm." David extended his right arm and rolled up his shirtsleeve. Steve leaned forward and examined the wound. A nickel-sized pink stain seeped through the white, gauze bandage.

"You okay?" Steve asked, still looking at David's arm.

"Yeah. I'm fine. Eight stitches." David rolled his sleeve back down. "I gave a statement to Detective Covey yesterday."

Steve nodded. Mike Covey was a good officer. "Do you know who attacked you?"

David shook his head. "No. I never saw the kid before."

Not unusual. "How old do you think?"

"Fifteen, maybe sixteen. Tall, skinny kid."

Steve laughed which puzzled David. "That's about half the junior class at McKeesport High," Steve said.

"That's just about what Detective Covey told me. If it helps, this kid was wearing a baseball cap with a skull and crossbones on it."

Steve nodded and pushed back his chair. "All this is in your statement?"

"Yes. I gave the officer as complete a description as I could. But I'll tell you, it was the weirdest thing. I never saw this kid before, yet he acted like he knew me. He called me by my name. He even mentioned Linda."

Steve folded his hands across his chin. "That's unusual, David, but it's not too far out. Especially if you consider all the publicity about Dr. Smith's death. I'm sure whoever it was just wanted to scare you."

The two men sat in silence for moment as David paused and looked toward the pile of folders on the desk. From the troubled expression on his face, Steve could tell there was more on David's mind.

"But there's something else, isn't there? Something about this kid?"

David looked up and nodded. "It's not just the kid. Though I'd feel a lot better if he was locked up. It's something Linda's brother said to me the other day. Something he didn't tell you about his father."

"Oh," Steve said, not surprised that Harris Smith hadn't been totally forthcoming. "What was that?"

David took a deep breath then proceeded to tell Steve the story of Dust. He related the legend in as much detail as he could remember, pointing out that Dr. Smith had spent years piecing the tale together from various fragments of myth. David told Steve about the sleeping-place, and Mokera, and how Dr. Smith had come to use the myth of Dust exclusively during his Addiction Personification therapy. David left nothing out, including the fact that some of Henry Smith's patients had suffered side effects from the treatment.

Steve listened intently. It was an interesting story, one that the police officer gladly filed into his inventory of historical anecdotes and tidbits, but, as he told David, he didn't think Harris's omission of it was a big deal. "He probably didn't want me to think his old man was a kook, or something."

David nodded and said that was probably the case. "But there's something else too. Something the kid said to me at the marina."

"Oh, what was that?"

David paused, suddenly uncomfortable sitting across from the detective. "When he attacked me, he said he had a message from Mr. Biggler."

"Who?"

David chuckled lightly, but Steve's expression remained fixed and serious. "This is where it gets a bit strange," David said. "When I was a kid, I used to have this recurring dream about a train full of toys. Mr. Biggler was the conductor."

Steve pursed his lips slightly and nodded. "A train full of toys."

"I told you it was odd. It's been years since I've dreamt of the Toy Train, but since I've come home with Linda, the dream keeps coming back. I can only remember little bits of it, but I'm standing at a railroad crossing and Mr. Biggler is on the train telling me to come aboard."

Steve bit his lower lip slightly and looked down at the desk. "And you say this kid who came after you knows about this train dream and Mr. Biggler." Still looking at his desk, Steve asked, "How do you think he could have found out about that?"

David shrugged his shoulders. "I don't know. That's why it's so strange. I haven't thought about the Toy Train in years. And I know I've never told Linda about it."

"What about Harris? Or Linda's mother? Could you have mentioned something to them? Or maybe someone at Dr. Smith's funeral? You must have spoken to quite a few people at that."

Once again, David shook his head. He had already replayed the events of the funeral over in his mind, trying to remember if there had been some conversation where he may have mentioned his recurring dream. But there hadn't been any. "No again. The subject has never come up."

Steve sighed and began rummaging through the papers on his desk. He found a page from a police report and looked it over. "Not to change the subject, but do you know a woman named Helen Bly?" he asked.

David thought about the name for a moment. "No, I don't think so."

"Well, she tried cutting her husband's penis off a few days ago. Almost succeeded too, but she got him in the upper thigh. Her husband was able to get away from her and call the police. When they arrived she told them that a man came to her in a dream and told her that her husband was having an affair. She said she met that man at a railroad crossing. Pretty weird huh?"

An awkward silence filled the room as neither man knew what to say. Finally, Steve glanced at his watch and pushed himself to his feet. "I don't know what else to tell you, David. But we'll find the kid who came after you, and that should clear everything up." Steve glanced at his watch again. "I don't want to be rude, but I got to get to a meeting with the mayor about the marina dedication."

David got to his feet and said he understood. "I'm sorry to take up your time, but I didn't really know who else to talk to."

Steve came out from behind his desk and ushered David toward the door. "Don't worry about it, that's what I'm here for. But call me if you think of anything else, or if you see this kid again." Steve pulled a business card from his shirt pocket and handed it to David. Several numbers were scratched on the card in blue ink. "If you need to get in touch with me, start calling those numbers. I'll be at one of them."

David slipped the card into his trouser pockets. "Thanks again, Steve," he said, closing the office door behind him.

Steve walked back to his desk to retrieve a report that he was to present to the mayor about the security for the marina dedication. He didn't want to let on to David that his dream about the railroad crossing bothered him. It was one hell of a coincidence, David's dream and what Helen Bly had told the police. But there was something else about David's story that was disturbing. It was part of the myth about Dust. About how he had been banished to a neither-place in the confluence where the Monongohelia met the Youghioghany.

The neither-place.

The spot where the two rivers converged.

Directly beneath the Josslin Bridge . . . where Gladys Decorta hung herself.

Steve balled his hands into fists and frowned.

Chapter Eight: June 22

There was no reason for anyone to notice the red Cavalier cruising eastward down Interstate 76. The car remained in the far, right lane of the highway, making no attempts to keep up with the stream of traffic whizzing past it. The Cavalier's speedometer remained at fifty-five mph, the driver satisfied with the steady progress.

Fredo, whose large frame was cramped in the backseat, was not so content with the vehicle's pace. He had been on the road for almost an hour, and his legs and ass were beginning to get numb. To make matters worse, that asshole Curtis Mayflower got to stretch out in the front seat. Fredo didn't give a shit if Curtis was passing out free weed, he simply didn't like the man. And one of these days, Fredo promised himself, he was going to show Mayflower just how much.

But that would have to wait. In the past week Fredo had smoked nearly an ounce and a half of Mayflower's dope. And as much as he didn't want to admit, it was the best stuff he'd ever had. "So it wouldn't do to piss him off now, not as long as he's giving it away." That's what Ace told him. "Just keep smiling and taking his shit while it's free. You can do what you want when he stops giving it away, but until then, don't fuck it up for the rest of us."

"Yeah, sure," Fredo reluctantly agreed. He promised not do anything to screw up the sweet deal the gang was getting. But it was this sweet deal that was beginning to make Fredo nervous. By his own estimation, Curtis Mayflower had given Ace about eight hundred dollars worth of pot. Fredo also heard Curtis boasting about supplying free stashes to other "needy folk," as he called them, around town. Curtis Mayflower was handing out a hell of a lot of grade-A dope, and Fredo was pretty certain that Curtis wasn't doing it out of the goodness of his heart. He had an angle, Fredo was sure of it. But until he found out what it was, Fredo would keep quiet and gladly accept Mayflower's charity.

But this afternoon things changed, and Fredo had a hunch he was about to find out just what Curtis Mayflower was up to. Ace had called Fredo at his home around noon and told him to be ready to be picked up at 6:00 pm. Curtis had an errand to run, and he needed a little muscle. "Fredo would do just fine," Curtis told Ace.

Fredo, however, didn't appreciate being summoned by Curtis Mayflower. "Tell him to kiss my ass," was what he said to Ace.

"Don't give me that crap. Curtis got something going down, and he says he needs a little muscular help. Understand?"

"Yeah," Fredo growled. Though helping Curtis Mayflower was not high in his "I wish I could" list, Fredo did like the sound of flexing a little muscle. It had been too long since he'd done some good head busting, and if the night's activities called for some fist action, Fredo was game. "Yeah, I understand. What is it he wants me to help him with?"

"I ain't sure. All he said was for you to be ready by six o'clock. Nathan Espy's gonna swing by your house and pick you up."

The name didn't ring a bell. "Who's Nathan Espy?"

One the other end of the line, Ace grew impatient. "What the fuck does it matter? Espy's a kid from school. He's been working with Curtis doing this and that. All you need to know is that he'll be there at six. Got it?"

"Sure. Whatever."

"Good." The line went dead.

Just as Ace had promised, at 6:00 pm a car horn honked three times in front of Fredo's house. As Fredo was leaving, his mother asked when he would be home. "Don't know," he answered, and then he was out the door and onto the sidewalk. In front of him, Curtis Mayflower's rust-colored Cavalier sat idling.

"Here," Curtis called from the passenger-side door. "Get in."

Fredo ignored Curtis and stood for a moment looking at the driver. He was a runt of a kid, about half Fredo's size wearing a black ball cap with the brim pulled down until it nearly covered his eyes. The driver was staring directly ahead, studying the bony fingers that clutched the steering wheel.

As Fredo got his first glimpse of Nathan Espy, Curtis stepped out of the car. "Come on, Fredo. Get in."

"Whatever." Fredo brushed past Curtis and slid into the Cavalier. He was surprised to see Julie in the back seat. "Hey," he said to her, but she didn't return the greeting.

As soon as Curtis was back in the car, the Cavalier sped off.

That had been an hour ago, and Fredo was starting to get pissed. When he asked where they were going, he was cut off by Curtis who told him to keep quiet. Subsequent inquiries were met with the same response.

Okay, Fredo thought. If no one was going to tell him where they were going, fine. He wasn't worried. He'd just sit back and go for the ride. But when it became clear twenty minutes into the trip that no one was saying anything at all, Fredo began to grow antsy. It was one thing to keep him in the dark about their destination, but it was strange as hell the way none of the other three were saying anything. Hell, the radio wasn't even on.

The whole damn trip was strange, but since Mayflower started supplying Ace and the gang with free dope, weird shit just seemed to happen. Like Ace and those fires the other night. At first it was fun, lighting a few bushes and tool sheds on fire. That was a kick. But when Calvin got the idea to set a dog on fire and toss it into someone's house, Fredo drew the line. He told Calvin he was a sick fuck, but Ace and the rest of the gang called Fredo a pussy.

"Call me what you want, but I'm not setting a fucking dog on fire," Fredo said before he headed back home while the rest of the gang went off in search of a dog.

"There." The silence of the trip was finally broken, and to Fredo's surprise, the voice that broke it belonged to the driver. Nathan was pointing to a long, two-story, brick building a few hundred yards up the road. "That's where we're going."

Fredo was disappointed. The building looked like a warehouse, not a place where Fredo might get an opportunity to do a little muscle flexing. Fredo pointed to the building. "What is it?" he asked.

"Construction company," Nathan replied, not taking his eyes off the road. When the car was within a hundred yards of the structure, he began to slow the Cavalier, pulling off to the side of the highway and into a large gravel parking lot. Steering past the front entrance, he drove the car to the back end of the building. Once the car was out of sight from the highway, Nathan killed the engine. Peering out the back window, Fredo could see a white, stenciled sign hanging above a set of metal double doors. CREW ENTRANCE, it read. Below that, CONWAY CONSTRUCTION.

As Fredo was checking out the sign, he felt a tug at his collar. Curtis had already exited the car. "Come on," he told Fredo. "We only got a few minutes."

Fredo got out of the car and followed Curtis to the double doors. He stole a quick glance back; neither Julie nor Espy had moved. Neither had even leaned over to close the door, leaving the car's dome light on like some kind of beacon. For a second, Fredo thought he should go back and shut the car door, but Curtis told him to move his ass.

Curtis produced a small brown key and set about opening one of the metal doors. "You got a key?" Fredo said surprised.

In reply, Curtis swung the door open and motioned for Fredo to go in. "Breaking and entering is always easier with a key," Curtis told him when the two were inside.

Once inside the building, Fredo had trouble adjusting to the thick darkness. He could distinguish Curtis's form directly in front of him, but beyond that, he was blind. "Lights," he whispered. "We need lights."

"Hold on." Curtis also whispered. Fredo could tell that he was reaching for something in his shirt. For a moment Fredo thought Curtis was going for a gun, but then there was a click and a powerful, thin beam of light pierced the darkness. "This way," Curtis said, pointing the beam down a narrow hallway. "Next to the last door on the left. That's storage." Curtis and the light started moving down the hall.

Fredo jogged behind, keeping his eyes fixed on the beam of light. "What are we doing here?" he whispered.

"I told you. Breaking and entering," came the quick reply.

When Curtis reached the door marked STORAGE, he pulled out another key and held it against the light. "Pay the right people the right kind of money, and theft is so much easier." He slipped the key into the lock and pushed open the door.

"Who are you paying off?"

"Not me, Espy. He's the one with all the cash."

"That skinny fuck in the car?"

Curtis held up a finger and turned toward Fredo. "Don't fuck around with Espy. You got me? He's the money man, so when he says shit, you shit. Now quit screwing around and come on."

When Curtis shone his light into the storage room, Fredo was surprised at its immensity. He half expected the room to be little more than a glorified closet, but what the beam of the mag-lite pierced through was nearly the size of a gymnasium, full of large wooden crates, machine parts, and tools of every imaginable variety. Curtis aimed the light against the back wall and proceeded to scan the room.

"What are we looking for?" Fredo asked as the light skipped from one item to the next.

Curtis didn't hesitate. "That."

Fredo looked to where the light had landed; a paint splattered orange tarp. "Beneath the tarp," Curtis said. "There are two crates. Go get them."

Fredo moved toward the tarp, careful to sidestep the tools and boxes strewn about the floor. When he reached the tarp, he snatched it up and tossed it to the side. Curtis wasn't lying. On the floor were two wooden crates, each about two feet long and a foot deep. Still standing just inside the doorway, Curtis trained the beam of light onto the crates. Fredo could see a series of long wood screws along the top and sides of the crate. "There's no markings on this," he called back to Curtis. "How do you know it's what you want?"

From behind him he heard Curtis grunting. "It's what we want.

Just get them and let's go."

Fredo reached down and hoisted the crates into his arms. Together they weighed about fifty pounds, heavy, but not awkward. Fredo would have no trouble carrying the load. "Come on," Curtis called out. "We only got a few more minutes."

Fredo quickened his pace but still managed to avoid tripping. When he made it to the hallway, Curtis came out of the room and relocked the door. He trained the flashlight down the hallway and onto the door that they had come in. "Let's go."

Once again Fredo followed the light, his large arms bulging from the weight of the boxes. Now that he was carrying them, the crates seemed to grow heavier with each step. Fredo was almost to the point where his arms were about to give out when the pair reached the exit. Curtis swung it open and stepped aside to let Fredo pass. Once outside, Fredo saw Nathan standing next to a large, white car, its trunk open. "In there," Nathan said, pointing to the trunk. "Carefully." Fredo didn't argue. His arms were beginning to quiver and his back felt as if it was about to snap. He shuffled to the car and lowered the cases into the waiting trunk.

"Good," Nathan said, slamming the trunk closed. By this time Curtis had locked the door of the building and was moving toward the group. Nathan lobbed him a set of keys and told him to take the white car. "You know where to go," he added.

"Right," Curtis said. He brushed past Fredo and slid into the diver's seat. He nodded once toward Espy and then took off out of the parking lot. The whole thing had taken less then five minutes.

Fredo watched as the taillights of the Lincoln turned westward onto I-76 and disappear down the highway. Now what? he thought.

But he didn't have long to wait. "Time to go," Nathan said.

"Yeah." Fredo turned to see that Nathan had taken off his ball cap. The kid was grinning, but it was as if his mouth was too big for his face. "Where did that white car come from?" Fredo asked nervously.

"A friend," Espy said, still grinning.

"Whatever." Fredo was getting pissed off. His arms hurt, his back hurt, and he didn't particularly like hanging out in the parking lot of a place that he just robbed. But he was still curious. "Hey. What was in those boxes we just lifted?"

"Stuff." Nathan said. "Stuff that bangs." The grin grew larger.

"Oh fuck this." Fredo spat out the words and started for the Cavalier. But as he did, Nathan shot his right arm out, catching the much larger boy in the chest. The speed and power behind the blow surprised Fredo, who crumpled to the ground in pain. His wind knocked out of him, Fredo tried to yell but all that escaped his lips was a feeble cough. Wasting no time, Nathan hopped over Fredo's prone body then flipped him over so that Fredo was laying flat on his back. Once done, Nathan grabbed Fredo's hands and thrust them to the side, forcing his arms outward. Gripping Fredo's wrists, Nathan did a quick hop and slammed his feet into Fredo's forearms. Fredo was still trying to catch his breath when Nathan Espy stood up, the heels of his boots grinding into the soft flesh of Fredo's trapped wrists.

"Don't move," Nathan ordered.

Fredo stopped moving. He looked up at Espy. Whether from the pain in his wrists or a trick of the light, Fredo thought he saw a gray trail of smoke snaking its way out of the back of Espy's head.

"You don't like me, do you, Fredo?"

Fredo tried to answer, but he still couldn't breath properly. And now that Nathan was slowly grinding down the bone in Fredo's left wrist with his boot, even if the former Brooklyn boy could make a sound, it would be a scream. "I just don't know what it is about you, but you don't want to be receptive. All your other little friends opened their dreams to me. But not you." The gray smoke coming out of Espy's head poured out faster as Nathan twisted his heel deeper into Fredo's wrist. "Maybe their pain was a bit more intense than yours." Another twist of the heel accompanied by the sound of cracking bone. "Maybe you don't have enough pain to really see me." Another twist, another crack. "Bet there's enough now."

The pain in Fredo's wrist shot up the length of his arm. It was excruciating, as if his arm was being crushed and burned at the same time. Fredo's head shot forward and his eyes rolled back into his head.

"Yes. You're feeling it now, aren't you." Nathan started to

twist his other heel.

Fredo's head snapped backward, sending his chin and neck skyward. A gurgling sound bubbled past his lips as the contents of his stomach began to force their way up his throat. Unable to swallow them back down, the acid and bile rushed up Fredo's esophagus, and just as it was about to spew from his mouth, Nathan lurched his body forward. Without releasing the pressure from Fredo's wrists, Nathan jammed his right palm under Fredo's jaw and pushed it upward, shattering both the jawbone and the bottom row of teeth. Shards of bone cut through Fredo's cheeks while broken fragments of teeth sliced through the gum line and into his nasal cavity.

"You should have opened yourself to me before," Nathan hissed.

Fredo didn't hear him. Blood poured into his broken mouth, mixing with the still-rising vomit. Unable to escape Fredo's clamped mouth, the vomit exploded into Fredo's nasal passage sending trickles of blood and puke seeping out his nose and eyes. A thin geyser of the bloody mix erupted from a hole in the boy's cheek where a piece of jawbone had broken through. The rest of his vomit though, had no means of escape, so it settled in his mouth and throat.

As his mouth became clogged with vomit, Fredo tried to wriggle himself free. Normally, he would have no trouble tossing Nathan Espy's skinny ass off, but the more he fought, the stronger Nathan's grip became. Only after he realized that he was no longer breathing did Fredo stop struggling and feel death washing over him. It started as a numbness in his feet that inched its way up his body. It tiptoed from his feet to his knees, and then up to his waist. Fredo felt the numbness, a sharp, cold, absence of feeling, creeping upward toward his chest. Like a heavy, wet blanket, it wrapped around Fredo's extremities, dulling the painful fire in his wrists and arms. It was a welcome coldness. After a minute it reached his neck, easing the agony of his broken face. Soon the cold would envelope his head and that would be the end of the pain.

As the numbness crept up his lip, Fredo's eyes flickered open.

Espy's face was no longer visible, obliterated by the swirling gray mist that poured out his head. Fredo looked into the mist and saw a shadow thing with dead eyes and a hungry mouth, a mouth that was an insatiable, devouring maw.

Convinced that he glimpsed the devil, Fredo died.

Chapter Nine: June 25

By 10:00 a.m., Steve once again found himself in all too familiar territory. The air-conditioning in his office still hadn't been fixed, and a new stack of police reports that needed his attention had found its way onto his desk. And like the reports from the last two weeks, this stack would go unattended for a day or two.

"Steve, you got a minute?"

Startled, Steve looked up from his desk to see Gary's large frame standing in the doorway. "There's someone here I think you should talk to."

"Sure," Steve said rising. He came around his desk and headed for the door. As he did, Steve got a good look at his partner. Deep black circles rung Gary's eyes, and his usual ruddy complexion seemed pasty. "Man, you don't look so hot," Steve said.

Gary coughed into his fist. "Damn summer cold," he said. "Can't seem to shake it."

"Oh." Steve accepted the explanation, but he was sure there was more bothering Gary than just a cold. The shoulders on the larger man seemed to droop under the weight of Gary's sport coat, and as the pair walked down the hall, Steve was certain that Gary had lost weight. *Probably too much work*, Steve thought. Lord knows that most of the cops in town had been forced to pull extra shifts since the start of the month.

Steve followed Gary down the hall and into the Detectives'

Room, commonly referred to as the "bullpen." The six detectives under Steve's command shared the bullpen using it mainly for interviews and paperwork. When the pair entered, the room was empty except for a large woman sitting to the side of Gary's desk.

"Mrs. Torach," Gary said, making his way toward the woman. "This is Detective Wyckoff." The woman nodded in Steve's direction. She was a massive creature. At least six-feet tall and nearly three hundred pounds. She wore a large, sleeveless cotton sundress that showed off the rippling folds of fat on her arms. With both hands she clutched at a small sequined purse, a disposable pack of tissue peaking out of its open lip.

Gary turned to Steve. "Mrs. Torach's seventeen-year-old son, Fredo, has been missing since Friday. She says that it's not unusual that he stay out all night, but he's never been gone for two days." The woman nodded sending slight ripples through her cheeks and chins. Gary rested against the side of his desk and leaned forward. "Now Mrs. Torach, I'd like for you to tell Detective Wyckoff what you told me about the last time you saw your son."

The woman sighed and clutched tighter at her purse. "It was Friday," she told Steve. "Fredo said he was going out with some friends."

Steve took the seat next to Mrs. Torach. "About what time was that?"

"Six. That's when they came and picked him up. I know because the news was just starting when he left."

"Did you know the people who picked your son up?"

Mrs. Torach shook her head. "No. I never saw them before."

"But you did see them Friday?"

"Oh yes. I was looking out the window. There was a big man standing by a red car. He was big, like my Fredo. He was on the passenger side, and Fredo got in the car behind him."

Gary cut in. "Mrs. Torach, tell Detective Wyckoff about the driver."

"Him. Oh yes. He was a little guy, but I couldn't get a good look at his face. He had a baseball cap pulled down real low over his eyes." Mrs. Torach let go of her purse and mimicked pulling an imaginary ball cap down her forehead. "Like this, real low. It had this picture of a skull on it. You know, like the one on a pirate ship."

Steve shot a quick glance toward Gary. David Cavanaugh's attacker had been wearing a skull and crossbones ball cap.

"Mrs. Torach, could you tell Detective Wyckoff about the phone conversation you told me about?"

"Of course. Earlier in the afternoon, my son got a phone call. I don't know who it was from, but Fredo sounded mad. His voice gets all huffy when he's mad, and that's how he sounded on the phone." Mrs. Torach pulled a tissue from her purse and loudly blew her nose. "I'm sorry," she said, choking back tears.

Steve put his hand on her meaty arm. "It's okay, Mrs. Torach. You're doing just fine." He gave her a few moments to compose herself before continuing. "When your son was on the phone, did you hear what he said?"

"No, not really. I was in the kitchen. But I did hear him say a name. Espy." She glanced quickly from Gary to Steve and then back to Gary. "Does that mean anything?"

"Espy," Steve replied. "Just Espy? Did your son mention a first name?"

The woman shook her head and sniffed. "I don't know. I think he might have, but I can't remember." She turned her head slowly toward Gary. "I'm sorry."

"That's alright." Gary glanced at Steve who was getting up from his chair. Steve cocked his head toward the door. Gary nodded. "Mrs. Torach, I'll be right back."

Steve turned toward Mrs. Torach and told her that as soon as Gary was finished taking her statement, they would begin a detailed search for her son. "We'll find him, Ma'am," Steve assured Fredo's mother. "Don't you worry."

Steve made his way into the hall where Gary stood waiting. "Black baseball cap with skull and crossbones. Same thing the kid who went after David Cavanaugh was wearing."

Gary nodded. "That's why I thought you'd want to talk to Mrs. Torach. The name Espy, does that mean anything to you?"

"Yeah. Marcus Espy. Big fat guy. He's been arrested a few times. Small stuff like public drunkenness and disorderly conduct.

Nothing major. I can't think of anybody else named Espy in town."

Gary considered that for a moment. "He could be the big man she saw."

Steve agreed. "And I'm almost positive Marcus Espy has a kid. How old again is the missing boy?"

"Seventeen."

"Okay. How long until you're finished?"

Gary glanced at his watch. "Fifteen, maybe twenty minutes. Her statement is pretty much complete. I just want to give her some details about what we can do for her."

"Good. When you get finished come to my office. I'm going to get a recent address on Marcus Espy."

"Twenty minutes," Gary said as he turned and headed back to a waiting Mrs. Torach.

When Steve was back in his office he dialed the extension for Sheila Markel, the police department's chief records-officer. "Sheila, this is Wyckoff, how are things in the hole?" The hole was the nickname for the square windowless office in the basement of City Hall that served as the records depository.

"Dark, but at least my air conditioning works." Since the beginning of the current heat wave, the lack of air-conditioning in Steve Wyckoff's office had become a departmental joke.

"You must be an important person," Steve quipped.

"Indeed. So what can I do for you?"

"Do you still have your collection of yearbooks down there?"

"Sure. What do you need?"

Steve considered his request for a moment." Just McKeesport High. Say, the last two years or so. Can you have someone bring them up?"

"No problem. I'll walk them up myself."

Steve thanked Sheila and hung up the phone. A few moments later there was a knock on Steve's door. Sheila came in carrying the two high school yearbooks. It was Sheila who suggested that the police department maintain a collection of yearbooks from the area's local high schools. She reasoned that in a pinch, the photographs might be useful for identification purposes, especially in cases involving missing kids. She was right. On several occasions when parents couldn't produce recent photographs of their children, the department had used photocopies of yearbook portraits in its investigation of missing kids and runaways.

Sheila stepped into the office and set the books on Steve's crowded desk. Looking about the room she chuckled. "And you call my domain a hole." Steve glanced over the covers of the two books. Both were blue, and each sported a picture of the school's mascot, a Tiger. "Are you going to need anything else?" Sheila asked.

"No, I think this will do. Thanks again."

"No problem," Sheila said, backing out of Steve's office. When the door closed behind her, Steve opened one of the yearbooks and flipped to the index. He scanned the names under the letter E, stopping when he came to Espy, Nathan. "Bingo," he said. Beside the name were three page numbers; 33, 129, 156. He opened to the first page, a collage of stills under the title "Tiger Life." Steve looked over the page, finding a small picture of two boys and an older man carrying a ladder. The caption read, "Jeff Tovarus and Nathan Espy give Mr. Conkle a hand."

Steve held the picture close to his face and examined it. Mr. Conkle stood grinning, overseeing his glum-faced charges. The two boys obviously weren't too thrilled about giving Mr. Conkle a hand, especially Nathan Espy whose expression seemed to be a cross between disgust and embarrassment.

Thumbing through the book, Steve came to page 129. Eight lines of thumbnail sized head shots stared out from the page. On the third row from the top, second picture to the left, was Nathan Espy. "There you are," Steve said, reaching for the phone.

***

When Gary finally finished with Mrs. Torach, thirty minutes had passed. Twice more, the woman had broken into tears. She was convinced that her son's disappearance was a result of her recent divorce and the subsequent move from Brooklyn to McKeesport. "He didn't want to go," Mrs. Torach said of her son. "He hated the idea of moving, just hated it."

After Mrs. Torach left, only after Gary promised that he would start looking for her son that afternoon, the detective started for Steve's office. As he neared it, he saw the chief of detectives in the hallway talking to a large, handsome man. Steve was ushering the man into his office when he saw Gary approach. He cocked his head and mouthed the word "Cavanaugh." Gary nodded and picked up his pace.

Once in the office, Steve introduced the two men and got down to business. He motioned for David to take a seat, and then, plopping into his own chair, thanked him for coming to the station on such short notice. "I know it's a difficult time for the family," Steve said, "but I think this is important."

"No problem." David was actually glad for the opportunity to get out of the house. Linda was looking worse but still refused to see a doctor, and Harris and Mrs. Smith had resumed their battle over what to do with the property adjoining the new marina. "It's only a few minutes drive."

"Good," Steve said.

Gary moved to the window and casually leaned against the sill. Out of the corner of his eye he could see the statue of Jack Kennedy that Steve was so enamored by. He was looking at the statue when Steve addressed David.

"I asked you down here because I think we might have a lead on the kid who attacked you." Steve handed the yearbook to David.

"High school yearbook?" David asked. "I don't get it."

Gary took the opportunity to explain their purpose. "Mr. Cavanaugh, a lot of times when we deal with cases involving juveniles, identifying them can be a problem. Often, the juveniles have no prior records, and we have no picture of them on file."

"But," Steve said, pointing to the yearbook in David's hand, "most of the teenagers who commit crimes in this city also live in this city. And if they live in the city, nine times out of ten, they go to McKeesport High School."

David tapped the heavy book with his fingers. "And so you use the yearbook as some sort of book of mug shots."

"That's about it," Gary replied. "Not your standard procedure, but effective."

"Okay," David said. "Now what?"

"Take a look on page 129," Steve instructed. David flipped open the book and started thumbing through the pages. "Third row, a kid named Walt Everett," Steve said when David reached the right page. "Is that the kid who attacked you?"

David examined Walt Everett's photo. It wasn't a very flattering picture. Walt Everett had a thin, cigar shaped head. His nose hung like a sharp beak between his small eyes and was bent to the left side. Walt was smiling, the corners of his mouth rising sharply into his acne-filled cheeks. From his picture, Walt Everett looked to David like a frail, awkward teenager who was going to have a hard time in life convincing people he wasn't a loser. He wasn't, however, the kid who had attacked him.

"Nope, not him."

"Are you sure?" Steve replied. "Take a look again."

David studied the picture a second time. No there was no way this was the kid who pulled a knife on him at the marina. He was a skinny teenager but . . . "Wait a second," David exclaimed.

Gary stepped forward, taking a position behind David's chair. "What is it, Mr. Cavanaugh?"

"This kid here," David said excitedly. "This is the kid." David spread the yearbook flat on Steve's desk.

"Are you sure?" Gary asked from over his shoulder.

"I'm sure," David replied, putting his finger to the side of the photograph cattycorner to Walt Everett's. "That's him." David leaned forward and read the caption. "Nathan Espy."

June 25 continued

Steve pulled McKeesport's only unmarked police cruiser to a stop in front of the Espy house. Beyond its weed-infested front yard, Steve could see that the shades were drawn over the windows making the house appear vacant. He took the last drag from his cigarette then snuffed it out in the vehicle's ashtray.

"This is supposed to be a nonsmoking vehicle," Gary said.

Steve caught the annoyance in Gary's tone. "You okay?" he

asked.

"Fine," Gary said through pursed lips. "I'm just not feeling well."

"Summer cold," Steve said. "Fucking things'll get you every time." The senior detective unsnapped his seat belt. "You ready?"

Gary did likewise. "Ready."

The two detectives got out of the car and headed for the door. "One more time," Gary said when they were halfway through the front yard. "Why are we here instead of a couple of uniforms?"

"Because this is part of an ongoing investigation. You know, detective work." Steve bounded up the front steps.

Gary remained at the bottom of the steps. "But the Cavanaugh assault is Covey's case. Why isn't he here?"

Steve moved to the door and rapped loudly. "It's Covey's day off." He knocked again, this time shouting "Police." Steve waited a few moments before pounding even louder. "Marcus, you in there?" Steve shouted. "Open up, Marcus, it's Steve Wyckoff. I need to talk to you about your boy."

"What now?" Gary asked when no reply came from the house. "We don't have a warrant."

Steve reached for the doorknob. It turned easily in his hand. "Door's open," he whispered.

"No probable cause."

"Find one later." Steve pushed open the door. Immediately the odor of stale air filtered out of the dark room. "Marcus," he called out, and then, "Nathan, you in here?" Getting no reply, he walked into the house. Reluctantly, Gary followed.

"You're going to get me fired someday," Gary whispered over Steve's shoulder.

Steve didn't reply as he stepped into a filth-strewn mess that was the Espy living room. Empty pizza boxes and junk food wrappers were spread about the floor along with dozens of spent beer bottles. Splattered on top of a console television was an impressive pile of vomit. Propped up in the middle of it, like a monument to the party life, was an empty bottle of Budweiser with an American flag poking out the neck. Several flies were buzzing around it.

Two paces behind his partner, Gary glanced about him, disgusted at the house's condition. Steve, however, had his eyes fixed on the coffee table in the middle of the room. Six large, grocery freezer bags containing equal amounts of a dried, green, leafy substance were neatly stacked in two piles. Next to the bags was a shallow basin, half filled with a pale green liquid. Instinctively, Steve undid the strap on his holster. "Look," he whispered.

Gary turned toward Steve and saw the cache on the coffee table. His voice, too, became barely audible. "That looks like a lot of dope, Steve."

Steve took a step toward the table but stopped when he felt the side of Gary's arm press against his chest. "Look at that," Gary said, pointing to Steve's right. Steve turned to face the Espy's overstuffed couch. In the middle of the left, back cushion was a wide and very distinct crimson discoloration. Before moving to examine it, Steve removed his weapon from its holster.

"What's that look like to you?" Gary asked. He too had drawn his weapon.

"Blood stain," Steve said, his mouth becoming suddenly dry. He surveyed the room again, not liking what he saw. Blood on the couch, dope on the table; it was certainly enough to kick his defenses into high gear.

Gary moved his face against the stain and examined it. "Definitely blood." Quickly, he stood up and turned to Steve. Both men assessed their situation and arrived at the same conclusion; they were knee deep in somebody's shit. "What now?" Gary exhaled.

Steve told himself to remain calm though he could feel his heart racing in his chest. "Touch nothing. Just one quick look around the house."

The house was a fairly simple design, one story with a kitchen, living room, dining room, and two bedrooms. Steve was sure he and Gary could be done with their look-around in two minutes. Then Steve would call for backup and the lab boys. He would also have to come up with a good excuse for entering the premises in the first place. But he could worry about that later. Right now he had a much larger and potentially deadly problem on his mind. Were they alone in the house?

With Steve leading, the pair crossed through the living room into the open dining room. It too was covered with the same kind of waste and filth. If anything, more flies seemed to have congregated here. Moving deliberately, the officers looked about the room. With the exception of several half-eaten pizzas that sported impressive coverings of mold, the officers discovered nothing criminal.

"Okay. Kitchen." Steve pointed to a white door at the far end of the dining room. Gary reached the door in three paces and put his shoulder against its side. He listened for a moment, then slowly pushed open the door with his foot and poked his head in. "Same thing in here," he announced after surveying the small room. "Crap everywhere."

Steve moved past Gary back into the living room. The stale air coupled with the heavy scent of mold and trash was beginning to choke off the older man's breathing. Another minute, he thought. Just another minute and he would be back outside having a smoke. "Alright. Bedrooms should be down the hallway."

Silently, the pair made their way to the first bedroom. The door was open and Steve walked in. While Gary stood in the hallway, Steve poked about the room, taking a quick look under the bed and in the closet. From the impressive collection of "Hustler" magazines and size forty-four boxer shorts draped across the unmade bed, Steve guessed the room belonged to Marcus. "Empty," Steve said as he stepped back into the hall. He pointed to the door directly across the hall. "Nathan's room."

This time Gary would investigate while Steve stood lookout in the hallway. Gary pursed his lips and looked at his partner. He stood to the side of the door and twisted the knob. It turned freely. As he did with the kitchen door, Gary gave the door a slight push with his foot and stepped into Nathan Espy's room.

"Good God," he said much too loudly in a voice that was a mixture of shock and disbelief. Steve moved up quickly and looked over his partner's shoulder.

Nathan Espy's room was covered with baseball cards.

Thousands of them had been glued to the walls and ceiling so that not one inch of plaster was showing. Topps, Fleer, and Upperdeck cards were all thrown together forming a wall-to-wall collage. Each card carefully staggered, side by side like flooring tiles so that the room was a seamless ocean of baseball players. Gary glanced down and caught his breath. Even the floor was covered with cards.

"There's got to be over ten thousand baseball cards here," Gary whispered.

Steve, too, was taken back by the sight of the baseball cards. Forgetting that he was supposed to be acting as a lookout in the hallway, Steve followed Gary into the room and peered at one of the cards. "Look at this," he said. "Look at the face."

Gary moved closer to the card Steve was pointing at. On the wall was a 1991 Topps Andy Van Slyke card showing the former Pirate outfielder chasing down a fly ball. Only the face on the card wasn't Van Slyke's, it was Nathan Espy's.

Both Steve and Gary looked about. On the walls, the ceilings and the floor, the condition of all the cards was the same. Where the player's face should have been was a thumbnail size picture of Nathan Espy. The same yearbook photograph David Cavanaugh had identified him with.

"This ain't normal," Steve said. "Look at this." He pointed to another card but stopped when he saw Gary move toward the end of Nathan's bed.

"There." Gary pointed to the floor near the right edge of the bed. "What's that?"

Steve crouched down beside the bed. Carefully he reached into his back pocket and removed his handkerchief. Draping it over his thumb and forefinger, Steve reached down and plucked a baseball from under the bed. He lifted it level with his eyes and then showed it to Gary. One side of the ball was smeared with blood.

Gary's eyes widened at the sight. "Oh, that's bad," he exhaled between clenched teeth.

The pounding in Steve's chest grew more rapid. Something very bad had happened in this house, and Steve didn't want to spend a second longer in it than he had to. "Yeah. Let's get out of here. The sooner this place is secured and the lab guys are here, the better."

Steve set the baseball back where he found it. Gary was already out of the room, retracing his steps to the living room. The two men were in the hall when Gary noticed a thin, gray door partially obscured by Marcus Espy's open bedroom door. "There," he said pointing. "Looks like a closet."

Great, Steve thought. A closet. Another closed door and a space just big enough to hold (*or hide*) a man (*or boy*). "I got it," Steve whispered nervously.

He gripped the door handle with his right hand and gently pulled it toward his body. There was no resistance as the door began to swing open. It hadn't opened more than a few inches when Steve heard a humming sound. He paused, and Gary stepped closer.

"You hear that?"

Gary nodded. The sound was faint, but distinct. "Sounds like an electric razor."

Steve inched the door back more and peered in. The humming grew louder. "Steps," he whispered. "There's a damn cellar down there." Steve looked back at Gary who stood poised, service revolver in hand, a strained expression on the younger man's face. Steve swallowed hard and fought back the urge to turn around and get the hell out of the house. *It's your job*, he told himself. It's your job to go into dark basements whenever you find baseballs covered in blood. Steve raised his revolver to chest level and took a step forward. "Okay. Here goes."

Steve started down into the basement, pausing at each step. To his right was the smooth, cold brick of the house's foundation. To his left was a shaky, chest-high wooden railing that didn't look as if it could support a man's weight. Steve put his right hand flat against the wall keeping his left hand, the one holding his weapon, trained toward the darkness in front of him. As he descended, the humming beneath him grew steadily louder. However, it wasn't until he made it to the fifth step that he caught a whiff of something emanating from the basement. It was a putrid stench, a vile orgy of shit, piss, and rotted cabbage. Steve's stomach did a quick flip. Behind him Gary exhaled loudly.

Halfway down the stairs, Steve could see all the way to the cellar floor, but the stairway and the wooden railing severely limited his left side view. It was a shame that the stairway didn't impede his other senses. Both the strange hum and the stench were growing stronger.

Steve made his way down two more steps and stopped. Only four more to go, then a sharp turn to the left and he would be in the open cellar. He took his right hand from the wall and transferred his revolver to it. Taking a deep breath he flung himself over the handrail and leapt to the cellar floor. As soon as his feet hit the ground he shot out his left hand and grabbed the side of the stairway wall. He pivoted to the left allowing him his first full view of the Espy basement.

He wished he hadn't.

Hanging from the ceiling was Marcus Espy. Only he wasn't alone. Tens of thousands of flies swarmed about his bloated, purple body forming a grotesque living shroud. The humming Steve heard from the steps now sounded like a chainsaw as the detective watched the black cloud of flies weave itself about Marcus's body. Everywhere there was a spot of congealed blood or pus, hundreds of flies bored into the hard tissue. They thrashed about the corpse, greedily sucking at the swollen pores of his flesh, the force of their feeding frenzy causing the body to sway back and forth as if it was being rocked by an unseen hand.

But that wasn't the worst thing Detective Wyckoff saw. Espy's fat body had ballooned to grotesque proportions, making his corpse look like some perverse, three-dimensional caricature. And in that first moment Steve saw him hanging from the water pipe, he knew why Marcus Espy had grown so fat. He was full of maggots. Millions of them wriggled beneath his skin, sending tiny ripples flowing across Espy's flabby torso. They were growing inside of Marcus, feeding off his organs. They crawled beneath his flesh until they popped out of the thick gashes in his legs where his skin had split open. Either that, or they made their way out his anus or urethra, falling to the basement floor to lay beside thousands of their wriggling brothers beneath Marcus Espy's still duct-taped feet.

Steve was able to suppress the urge to scream, but he couldn't control his gag reflex. The odor from the steps paled in comparison to the smell of rotting flesh that now assaulted his nostrils. "Oh shit," he choked, unable to hold back the vomit that was building in his throat. "Oh sweet Jesus."

When he saw his partner's reaction, Gary, too, jumped to the bottom of the steps. However, unlike Steve who had his head turned toward the basement wall and was puking his guts out, Gary could not take his eyes off of what hung in front of him. He stood mesmerized, his jaw hanging slack.

There was a putrid body covered with insects hanging from the ceiling, but it wasn't Marcus Espy that Gary was looking at.

It was Uncle Joe.

Uncle Joe. Family friend and baby sitter.

Good old Uncle Joe whom no one would ever believe was a pedophile and a rapist, and who, after raping a twelve-year-old Gary Overton for the first time, threatened to kill the boy's parents if Gary ever told anyone.

That Uncle Joe.

Gary took a step forward, unaffected by the stench that was making Steve sick. When he was within five feet of the corpse, Gray suddenly realized that it had been Uncle Joe that he had been dreaming about for the past two weeks. Dreaming about Uncle Joe forcing him on the ground. Uncle Joe ripping his jeans down to his ankles. That's why the cellar steps seemed familiar. It was in the Overton's cellar where Uncle Joe first raped Gary.

But now the son-of-a-bitch was hanging in front of him.

And then Uncle Joe opened his eyes.

"Haven't seen yah in a while boy," he said in a thick, raspy voice. "We gots lots of catchin' up to do. Yah know."

"No!!" Gary screamed, stumbling backwards. He slammed into Steve, shoving him face first against the basement wall.

Uncle Joe grinned, his bloated tongue lolling out the side of his mouth. "Come on, boy," it leered. "Give us a kiss." Gary screamed and opened fire, the bullets slamming into the bloated stomach of Marcus Espy.

A moment later it was raining maggots.

***

Fours hours later, after a shower, a change of clothes, and three shots of Wild Turkey, Steve Wyckoff found himself sitting across from Carolyn Markbury, McKeesport's mayor. At thirty-seven, Carolyn was not only the city's first female mayor, she was its youngest, and according to Steve, one of its best. "Right now, what's happening?" Carolyn asked, running her fingers through her short brown hair. It was an unconscious gesture, but one that drew Steve's attention to her face, especially her eyes. She had large, green eyes with thick, brown lashes. They could be kind eyes when she wanted. At the moment they were deadly serious.

"Lab guys are at Espy's house right now. They'll probably be there for three or four more hours. The body's been taken to the hospital, and an autopsy has been scheduled for this evening. The Daily News had a reporter over there, but none of the TV stations seem interested." Steve added, "No one in the media has had access to the basement."

Carolyn nodded. She was especially thankful that the three Pittsburgh television stations didn't think the story was worth reporting. With the grand opening of the new marina in just over a week, the last thing the city needed was the kind of public relations nightmare this situation had the potential to become. If all the details concerning the discovery of Marcus Espy got out, Carolyn could just imagine McKeesport being the lead story on Hard Copy. Without being asked, Steve continued his report. "We're admitting it's a murder, the media knows that much already. They also know that Marcus has a son, and that the boy is nowhere to be found. However, we're not officially naming Nathan Espy as a suspect yet. We've given a preliminary statement citing the cause of death as blunt trauma, but we haven't released any information about the condition of the body, or the baseballs. We're trying to make this look as routine as possible." Steve immediately regretted his choice of words. Since when did murder become routine in his hometown? "With any luck, any interest will die down in a day or two."

"With luck," Carolyn replied. She looked at Steve, thankful that he was the one who discovered the body. He had been around long enough to know that certain situations required a delicate touch from the police department. "Okay," Carolyn said, "now tell me what the hell happened."

Steve sighed and slouched deep into his chair. He took a deep breath and detailed the events of the afternoon. When he finished, the mayor grimaced. "How could a person do that?" she asked.

"I don't know." Steve's voice was low and rough. "Though we won't get any official word until after the autopsy, the lab guys are guessing that Espy's been dead for about two weeks or so." Steve paused and looked down at his hands. They had been shaking since he found the body. "They also said that it may have taken a few days for him to die."

"Christ," Carolyn sighed. "What about the drugs?"

"Pot," Steve answered matter-of-factly. "About two pounds. That's also at the lab."

"Was Espy selling it? Could this have been some kind of drug killing? Maybe a deal gone bad?"

Steve admitted that was a possibility, but he didn't think so. "To tell you the truth, I don't think Marcus Espy's murder had anything to do with the drugs we found."

The mayor was surprised by Steve's conclusion. "How do you figure? After all, you found a lot of dope in the house along with the corpse."

"Dealers don't kill each other with baseballs." The image of Marcus Espy's carcass hanging from the water pipe jumped into Steve's head. Even without a gut full of maggots, Marcus Espy was one big man. It would have taken a lot of time and effort to wrap him in duct tape and hoist him up to the ceiling. Definitely not the style of any drug dealer Steve had ever seen. "Besides, the dope was just sitting there. If it was drug related, why would the dope still be in the house? If I'm pissed off enough to kill some guy over a drug deal, I'm not going to ignore two pounds of marijuana sitting on the table. No, I think Espy's death and the drugs are two separate things."

Carolyn mulled over what Steve said for a moment before addressing the next of her concerns. "Now for the hard questions. What happened with Detective Overton? Sooner or later, and I'm guessing sooner, it's going to get out that Gary shot up the corpse. How is that going to be explained?"

"Nothing to explain," Steve replied. He was expecting the question and his answer had been carefully thought through. "We were in a very tense situation. We made one hell of a gruesome discovery, and Gary thought he saw something move. He reacted, but he was firing in self-defense."

Carolyn pursed her thin lips making her look as if she was pouting. "How can we say Gary was firing in self-defense? There wasn't anyone else there, Steve."

"Shit, Carolyn, I know that," Steve said. "But it was nothing like I've ever seen. Geez, you could see the skin bulging up from where the maggots were crawling around inside of him. It was a nightmare, and Gary got spooked and he fired." It was the simplest explanation Steve could think of. And it was the truth.

The mayor, however, wasn't completely satisfied with Steve's answer. "But you didn't fire." Carolyn's tone was blunt and factual.

"No," Steve said wearily. "I didn't fire. I was too busy puking."

Carolyn sighed and stared hard at Steve. From her stern expression, the Chief of Detectives knew the fate of his friend was being decided at that moment. After a few seconds, Carolyn asked if Gary Overton was easily spooked.

"No," Steve replied quickly. "No he's not."

"Alright," the mayor said. "As Chief of Detectives you'll have to order an investigation into the discharging of Detective Overton's weapon. You know that you can't lead the inquiry."

"Basic operating procedure. I know."

Carolyn nodded, and once again the hand slipped through the bangs of her hair. "And Detective Overton will be assigned desk duty for a few weeks until the investigation is over. Say four weeks?"

Steve allowed himself a slight smile. Gary's job was safe. "Four weeks sounds about right."

"Agreed." The mayor moved slightly forward in her chair. "Next question. Did the son do it?"

"I think so. Marcus Espy's been dead for about two weeks, but some of the food remains found in the house couldn't have been more than two or three days old."

"But how do you know that the boy's been there? Maybe the kid took off and whoever killed the father has been hiding out there."

"No. Nathan Espy's still around. David Cavanaugh positively identified Nathan as the kid who attacked him on the nineteenth. He's around all right. We just have to find him."

Carolyn exhaled slowly, she, too, was exhausted. "Okay. One more question. How worried should we be?"

Steve thought of the baseball cards that covered Nathan Espy's room. Thousands of cards, all bearing the smiling face of a skinny kid with bad acne. But only the faces on all those cards had been slightly altered. That's what he was about to point out to Gary when his partner discovered the first bloody baseball. All the faces had been touched up with two tiny dots of Wite-Out covering the eyes. Steve pictured thousands of pairs of Nathan Espy's blank, white eyes staring at him.

"We should be worried," he told the mayor.

Chapter Ten: June 25 continued

After his meeting with the mayor, Steve slipped out the building's rear delivery entrance. A good deal of the initial buzz over the discovery of Marcus Espy's body had died down, but there were still a few reporters from The Daily News and Pittsburgh Post Gazette hanging around. It had been a long, shitter of a day, and Steve wanted nothing more than to go home, pour three fingers of Old Crow into a can of Dr. Pepper and try to get some sleep. But before he could, he had one thing left to do.

Steve made it to his Taurus without being detected by the press corp. That was a lucky break, and if ever there was a day he could use a break, it was today. Once in the car, Steve removed a cellular phone from his glove compartment and dialed the number for The Oaks. On the second ring, a familiar voice answered.

"Hey," Steve said softly into the cell phone.

"Hey," Merilee answered. "Are you alright?"

"Yeah, I'm fine." Steve wasn't sure what to say next. He would have to tell her about finding Marcus Espy, but how much did Merilee need to know? Surely she could be spared the maggot-strewn details. "It's been a bad day," he said. "You'll read about in the paper tomorrow."

Steve heard the sharp intake of Merilee's breath. "What happened? Are you hurt?"

"No, I'm fine," Steve answered quickly. "Gary and I found a

body today. A guy was murdered over on Locust Street. It was pretty ugly, and we're trying to keep a close lid on it. I really can't tell you anymore right now. Okay?"

"Sure," Merilee said. From the sound of Steve's voice, she could tell that he was pretty shaken up. And if something could shake up Steve Wyckoff, Merilee knew it had to be bad. "I understand. Are you coming over?"

Steve thought about it for a moment. As much as he wanted to see her, he told Merilee that it would be for the best if he just went back to his apartment and got some sleep. "I've got a feeling things are going to be pretty crazy for a while."

"Okay." Merilee was disappointed but she knew not to press the issue. "I love you," she told him before hanging up.

Steve held the phone against the side of his head wishing that he was home right now. But there was still one more thing he had to do. He punched in another number and hit the send button.

***

"Thanks for coming," Steve said as David Cavanaugh slipped into the passenger's seat.

"No problem." Though he hadn't been expecting Steve's call, David wasn't completely surprised when it came. He thought that he might be getting an opportunity to ID his attacker in the flesh. But rather than a trip to the police station, Steve suggested meeting David on the corner of Fairview Street, two blocks from the Smith home. David thought it was an odd request, and when he saw the tired look in Steve's eyes, he knew that something was wrong.

When David was inside the Taurus, Steve slipped the car into park but didn't turn off the engine. "Tell me what you know about Nathan Espy," Steve said flatly.

The order took David by surprise. "I don't know anything about him except that he attacked me with a knife and he takes a lousy yearbook picture." David looked at Steve trying to gauge the officer's face for a clue to his blunt demeanor.

"Okay." Steve paused and turned fully to face his passenger. "Now I want you to think about your next answer very carefully.

Did you ever buy any drugs from Nathan Espy?"

David was stunned by the question. "Where the hell did you get an idea like that? Of course I didn't buy any drugs from him. Christ the kid tried to kill me." David balled up his hands into tight fists and pushed them into his thighs. "Where the hell do you get off asking me a question like that?"

Steve wasn't fazed by David's reaction. The police officer calmly closed his eyes and rested his head against the seat. "Okay. I believe you. I just had to ask."

"Why?" David shot back, angry at Steve's insinuation.

Steve proceeded to describe the events at the Espy house. He omitted nothing from the account, telling David of the large cache of marijuana he and Gary discovered, as well as the brutal way Marcus Espy had been murdered. He even told David about the missing Fredo Torach and his possible connection to Nathan Espy. "I don't think you're mixed up with the dope or Marcus Espy's death," he told David. "But it was because of your identification that we went over there in the first place. That's gonna come up in the investigation. I just want you to be prepared for that."

"Is that why you wanted to meet with me?" David asked. "To tell me my name might come up in the investigation?"

"No," Steve confessed. "That's not all of it." Steve reached into his pants pocket and pulled out one of the baseball cards from Nathan Espy's bedroom. "Here," he said, handing it to David.

David took the card and examined it, a 1996 Topps Mark McGwire. The smiling face of Nathan Espy grinned atop of Big Mac's body. "Jesus," David said when he saw the eyes.

"I took that out of Nathan's bedroom. Every inch of it was covered with those things."

David examined the card a few moments before returning it. Steve gave it a quick glance then shoved the card back into his pocket. "I don't know what Espy has against you, but I think you and Linda should head back to North Carolina as soon as possible."

David started to say something in reply, but Steve held up his hand. "Hear me out," he said. "Nathan Espy hung his father from a drain pipe and threw baseballs at him until he died. He broke just about every bone in his old man's body, but he kept pitching at him. There were baseballs all over the fucking cellar, dozens of them. Now I've been a cop for over twenty-five years, and this is the sickest thing I've ever seen. This kid is nuts, David, and I have no idea where he is."

"Do you think he's going to come after me?"

"I don't know," Steve said weakly. "But he did once, so I wouldn't chance it, would you?"

***

When he got back to the house, David found Linda alone in the library watching an episode of Jeopardy. She was stretched out on the couch, wrapped in a large, crocheted afghan. Her dinner, boiled chicken breast and a salad, sat untouched on the folding, wooden TV tray that David had set next to the couch. It was the third night in a row that Linda hadn't eaten.

Taking a seat on the edge of the couch, he wrapped Linda's hands in his. "Listen. I just talked with Steve Wyckoff, and he thinks that the kid who attacked me might come after me again." David squeezed his wife's hand, but Linda didn't respond. She kept staring at the television.

"Linda?"

No reply, only Alex Trebeck running down the categories in Double Jeopardy.

David slipped off the couch and knelt in front of his wife. He could hear her breathing, faint, but strong. "Linda," he said again, his voice slightly pleading. Still her eyes stared blankly ahead.

She was asleep.

David stood up and slowly backed away from the couch. He made his way to the television and turned it off just as a stockbroker from Michigan was telling Alex he'd take nine-letter-lingo for $400.00. When the television picture sank into blackness, David glanced over his shoulder, hoping that it would have jarred his wife out of her sleep. But there was no such luck. Her eyes, still open wide, were fixed on some spot deep in the black middle of the television screen.

David made his way out of the library and up to his and Linda's room. Once there, he slipped off his shoes and sat on the large, double bed. Resting his back against the headboard, he flipped on a small color television that sat on the nightstand. Some male model with spiked hair was doing his best to appear like a credible journalist reporting on the recent tragic breakup of some B-movie actress and her rock star husband. David watched, though he paid no attention to the show. It wasn't long until he too was asleep.

***

He was floating in a starless sky. Detached from the constrictions of gravity, David felt as if he was being swallowed in a cool, purple darkness.

"Davie, over here."

David turned to the sound of Mr. Biggler's voice, but he couldn't see anything in the impenetrable darkness that was his dream. He waved his arms, unseen, in front of his face. "Why is it dark?" he asked.

"That's the way you wanted it, Davie," Biggler replied, his voice coming at David from all directions. "Your dream, you're in charge."

David spread his arms out wider, making passes with them in front of his body. *Okay*, he thought. *My dream, I'm in charge. I want some light.* In his mind's eye, David pictured a single ray of sunlight penetrating the blackness around him.

Immediately, a white light seared through the darkness leaving David just as blinded as before. With the light came a rumbling sound that quickly became a thundering roar. David looked down and saw three thick wooden railroad ties beneath his feet. Instantly he knew where his dream had taken him; he was on the railroad tracks and the Toy Train was heading right for him.

David dove to his right, barely escaping the iron cowcatcher speeding by him. Landing on a patch of rock and gravel, David rolled painfully to the side, his momentum carrying him off the berm of the tracks and onto a wet, grassy patch. As he pushed himself to his feet, he saw that the blackness had turned to a pale, dirty yellow.

"Impressive, Davie," Biggler called out. "You wanted light and you got it."

David paid no attention to Biggler's praise. Instead he stared at the thing which stood leaning against the train car less than twenty feet away. Biggler looked comical decked out in his railroad conductor jump suit and ill-fitting cap that sat atop his misshapen head. A reptilian claw poked from beneath a pink ruffled cuff, fingering the white stick of a lollipop that stuck out the side of his fanged mouth. Biggler gnawed at the stick as if it was a bone. A cold sensation traveled up David's spine, settling in his brain. Things had changed since the last time he dreamt of the Toy Train; Biggler seemed more powerful, more in control.

But it's only a dream, that part of David's conscious mind that made sense of the insanity of dreams whispered. No matter how frightening, it's still all in your head.

Biggler's white eyes opened wider. "That's absolutely true, Davie-boy. Everything you see or feel is all in your in head. Even me." Biggler patted his round belly and chuckled. "As for this, you're the one who thought of this form. I'm only borrowing it when I'm here with you." Biggler looked downward, examining his body. With one long claw he brushed an imaginary speck of lint from his uniform. "Of course," he said, clicking his claws together. "I did add a little to the look. Your Mr. Biggler was a little too tame for my taste."

David stood confused. "What do you mean by borrowing it?"

The conductor sighed and pushed himself from his leaning position. Then slowly, he began to pace the length of the train car. "Look around you, Davie. All of this is yours. The train, the tracks, the odd yellow sky, even Mr. Biggler. They're all dredged up from the nooks and crannies of your subconscious. Oh, I'm sure that there is some deep psychological significance to your little train dream here, but quite frankly, it doesn't matter. This is just a playground I visit. When you wake up, I'll go somewhere else."

David took an angry step forward. "Bullshit. When I wake up, you'll be gone, and I'll have forgotten all about you."

Biggler chuckled and began shaking his head. "We both know that's not true, don't we, Davie? Deep down inside you, deep down in that part of your soul that dreams, you know that's just not true. You know that I can never disappear."

David's momentary rage was snuffed out like a flame. What Biggler was saying was the truth. He was there in David's dream, a foreigner who had no business on the Toy Train, who, nevertheless, couldn't be wished away in the morning. And now, Biggler didn't look so comical; the blank white eyes and leering grin had become a twisted mask of evil. "What are you?" David asked, his mounting fear nearly choking off his words.

"You know," Biggler replied. "You've always known."

"Dust."

For a moment the creature looked disappointed, then he nodded. "That's an old name, but it will do for now."

"I don't believe you," David stammered. "You're not real."

Dust offered no argument. "You're right. I'm not real. How can something that exists only in dreams be real? Yet I'm here, aren't I? That's the great enigma of my existence, I am who is and is not." Dust paused and turned toward the cattle car to his left. Its door slid open with a low rumbling sound. "I'm not real in the sense with which you are familiar, but I can assure you, he is real." Dust pointed to a solitary figure sitting Indian-style in the middle of the car.

David recognized him immediately. "Espy."

"Yes, young master Espy. He's mine now," Dust said. As he spoke, the door slid shut trapping the boy once again in darkness.

"What do you want from me?" David asked.

"I want you to avoid our young friend's fate, David. You see, I need your help. In the past, before the Old Warrior discovered the truth of my being, the dreamers came to me, hundreds of them. Their pain called to me. Their tormented minds invited me. And I fed on them, David. For generations I fed on their nightmares. First in the sleeping-place, and then in the home of the wounded."

David gasped as he realized what Dust was describing. "The veterans hospital. That's whose dreams you fed on, the men at Linda's family's hospital."

Dust nodded his enormous head. "Yes. The hospital. But the old one tricked me. He took from me what was mine and trapped me back in the neither-place. But now that the old one is dead and I am free, only a few dreamers remain. I need more, David. I'm still too weak to go in search of them, I need them brought to me. For that, I need you." Dust raised his clawed fist and pointed it at David. "Look at me."

The command came low and evil, but also compelling, like a strand of piano wire that bit into the flesh when it was tugged.

"Look in my eyes."

David tried to resist, but he found himself powerless to stop his gaze from focusing on Dust's dead, white eyes. Neither David nor Dust moved, but David felt himself being drawn by that same piercing thread into the void of the creature's eyes. As David neared them, Dust's eyes eclipsed both the Toy Train and the yellow dream sky. Like two pools of gray water, they swallowed David into their emptiness.

Then David was looking at Alex Trebeck.

Alex was smiling, informing a fat housewife from Topeka that, yes indeed, "what is the Glorious Revolution?" was the correct question for the first of today's daily double. The fat housewife, whose name was Gwen, gave herself a congratulatory round of applause as an extra fifteen hundred dollars was added to her score.

David's eyes were fixed on the television while Alex offered up another answer. As Alex spoke in his soothing but superior voice, a man stepped in front of the television. David watched as the man slowly moved backward, a caring but troubled look spread across his face. The man turned and clicked off the television. A momentary flash of recognition was followed by an incomprehensible wave of terror. David was watching himself from a few hours earlier. Watching himself through the eyes of his wife.

"No!" his mind screamed. "Not Linda." He felt himself being yanked from behind, and as quickly as he was sucked into Dust's eyes, he was hurled out. David felt his body sailing over the railroad tracks before slamming face first into the gravel footpath that ran parallel with the tracks. He lay there motionless, stunned, wondering if someone could pass out in a dream as the train's engine roared into life.

Ba-Boom

Ba-Boom

"I visit her dreams too, David. They're not as colorful as yours, but they are sufficient. I haven't revealed myself to her yet," Dust warned. "But if you refuse me, I will bring such dreams to her that she will never know rest again. I will turn her into a shell like that boy you saw."

"I have grown strong, David. With each day I grow stronger." Dust threw his head back, the veins and arteries in his neck forming a twisted map of red and blue flesh. They pulsated in time with the engine.

Ba-Boom

Then his body began to quiver, slowly at first, but then more violently until the ground beneath him started vibrating.

"See me," he yelled over the din of the shaking train.

David watched horrified as Dust lifted off the ground, his body swelling as it inched upward. The fabric of the conductor's uniform stretched across Dust's expanding torso until it shredded, sending dozens of dime-sized buttons hurtling like bullets through the air. As the remnants of his clothes fell to the ground, great chunks of flesh fell with them. The creature's chest, stomach, and thighs cracked like dried balsa wood, snapping away from his body with each thrust and gyration he made. His arms thrashed about the air before dissolving into thin wisps of smoke that curled like springs around the train car. Where there had been only two arms before, a half dozen now jutted from the creature's growing body.

All remnants of Mr. Biggler were gone from the creature hovering near the top of the train car. Dust had no definable shape that David could discern; what passed as arms and legs kept dissolving into the fluid motion of its body, only to reappear in another spot. It was like a cloud of swirling gray smoke. The only features that remained fixed were the pair of white eyes and the enormous, leering mouth that made up the bulbous protrusion that was the head.

When the transformation was complete, David saw that one trace of Mr. Biggler had remained. The white stick from the lollipop still jutted out of the creature's mouth. Only now, it was stretched to almost three feet in length. But rather than the smooth, paper surface of a lollipop stick, it had become dark and porous, bent at an awkward angle. At its tip, a small hand clutched frantically at the air.

"I can get to you," David heard Dust say, but the dream was beginning to melt away. A fragment of consciousness filtered into his mind telling him that he would soon be awake, away from the abomination his mind had created. Another second, he thought. Another second and nothing.

But even as he felt his body stirring in the safety of his own bed, his dream-self took a last look toward the ground. Around his feet hundreds of rats were in a frenzy, all snapping at his legs. One turned its head and glared at David. It had the face of Nathan Espy.

***

Alone in the dark library, David sipped from a glass of Scotch. Some of the details of his nightmare were already beginning to fade from memory. Unfortunately, most of the dream was still painfully vivid. Upstairs, Linda slept peacefully. How the two had switched places, he didn't know.

David knew there would be no sleep for the rest of the night. There was no denying that he had one hell of a nightmare, but, he kept telling himself, that's all it was. A nightmare. The attack by Espy, Linda's illness, and the strain of being away from the familiar surroundings of his home was starting to take its toll. No, there wasn't anything that unusual about David having nightmares considering all the stress he was under.

But this wasn't your normal kind of bad dream, a nagging voice inside his head reminded him. This was the worst fucking dream you ever had. The absolute worst.

With a shaking hand he poured the last drops of Scotch into his mouth.

Chapter Eleven: June 27

Ace never really had any reason to look at the sun before. He was a nighttime guy. But then Nathan Espy came to the Torrid Zone with Curtis Mayflower and told Ace of the beauty of the sun. As the two teens shared a joint, Nathan spoke of the power and majesty of the fire in the sky.

And now, watching it slip lower in the western sky, Ace couldn't take his eyes off the sun. He felt as if he could cry; never had he seen anything as beautiful as this sinking orange ball. How many sunsets had he missed? How many times could he have felt this numbing ecstasy if he would have only bothered to look? A single tear welled up in his eye and then slid down the smooth contours of his face. He made no attempt to wipe it away.

Forty yards beyond where Ace sat, the hill flattened out for about thirty feet and then sharply dropped off. A dozen wooden pegs had been pounded in the flat spot, three rows of six spaced evenly apart. Earlier, Bip told Ace that the city was planning on shooting off the fourth of July fireworks from Radaken's Hill, and the pegs were to be the foundation for some kind of platform.

From his vantage point at the top of Radaken's Hill, Ace could see the entire west side of McKeesport spread out before him: dozens of neighborhoods, each with its own churches and schools, its own grocery stores and a handful of corner bars. And houses, thousands of them full of families. There were so many people on the west side of town. Too many to count; all living and working and sleeping in that long, twisting valley on the bank of the river.

The base of the sun dipped below the horizon. As it did, a soft, orange glow reflected off the river. It lifted like a cloud, bathing the river in a warm, orange light. As the sun crept its way down the horizon, the orange glow washed over the sides of the river bank, up onto the newly paved streets of the Riverfront Park and out toward the west end of town.

Ace turned his head and looked about the freshly mowed expanse of Radaken's Hill. It had undergone quite a renovation in just a week. About half of the city's park employees swarmed onto the half-mile wide hill. First they picked up what amounted to two dump truck loads of trash and debris that had been collecting on the land since Phil Radaken sold his property to the city in the late 1970's. At the time there was a plan to terrace off the hill and turn it into a roadside picnic area, but when the economic problems of the early 1980's hit McKeesport, that, like all the plans for city improvement, was swept aside.

That is until now. With the new marina and entertainment complex set to open on the other side of the river, Radaken's Hill had been declared an eyesore. That's when the mayor sent in her summer help, and after a few days of picking up trash and attacking the side of the hill with weed whackers, Radaken's Hill had been transformed from a vermin-infested dump to an attractive manicured lot.

Ace hated it.

Like the Torrid Zone, Ace staked a claim to Radaken's Hill. It was one of the few places he felt comfortable, especially at night when he would sometimes lay down in the tall weeds and stare at the night sky. It was his place to be alone, to be hidden, but now the sons-of-bitches at City Hall took it away from him and turned it into a fucking lawn. Hell, they even started planting flowers along the side of the hill where it met the path by the riverbank.

But all that would change. Ace was certain of that.

The sun was now nearly halfway below the horizon. What was left of it in the evening sky blazed a dark, dull orange. The light pierced through the thin wisps of clouds that floated above the sun making them look as if they were on fire. And all across the west side of McKeesport, the orange glow that had started at the base of the river spilled out onto the streets. It flowed across the alleys, finding its way behind dumpsters and under rusting cars that had been abandoned to the side streets years ago.

Ace watched as the light crept along, washing over the houses and churches and people sitting on their porches. He watched as an old black man lifted a bottle of beer to his lips, and then stop as the orange glow reached his stoop. The old man stared as it moved up his steps and around his bare feet. Then he smiled and drank deeply from his beer.

Ace was also smiling. It was all so beautiful.

The sun.

The water.

The fire.

June 28

Curtis killed the engine of his Cavalier about a half block from The Oaks. Headlights off, he had a good view of the bar's neon sign jutting out over the sidewalk. Besides a rusted Ford Ranger, his was the only car on the street, which meant The Oaks was most likely empty. Except, of course, for Merilee Stepanich and that bastard, Morris Keyes. They were always there.

Curtis checked his watch. 11:45pm. He still had ten minutes to wait. On weeknights, Merilee always kicked out the last few stragglers around 11:50 so she could close at midnight. Espy told Curtis not to go into the bar until 11:55. And under no condition was Curtis to be seen by anyone. On that point, Espy was especially adamant.

Curtis leaned back into his driver's seat and smiled. This was one sweet deal he had gotten himself into. Since he started working for Coach and Espy, Curtis Mayflower's life had taken a definite turn for the better. He was raking in some serious cash, and had a stash of weed that kept him in a perpetual buzz. Of course, part of the deal was to pass out most of the dope to some of the locals, which didn't make any sense. But Curtis wasn't one to complain. He didn't know where Espy was getting the money, but as long as it kept rolling into Curtis's pocket, everything was cool.

And there were the chicks, just as Espy promised. That was the best part. Chicks that Curtis had been dreaming about since high school started showing up at his apartment in the middle of the night, all wanting the same thing, him. And Curtis was willing to oblige. Last night it was Carol Gorshen, just waiting for him to screw her. At least that's what she said. Curtis couldn't really remember much of the encounter. He just knew that he woke to her mounting him, and away they went. He fell back asleep after they finished, and when he awoke in the morning, she was gone.

Curtis glanced at his watch. Five more minutes. Impatiently, he began tapping the steering wheel. He wanted to act now, but Espy warned him that Coach wanted the big man to be patient.

Coach.

Now there was another funny thing.

He met Coach only once, the night Espy brought him the food and the pot. After Espy had gone, Curtis smoked a few bowls of the weed and got thoroughly hammered and passed out. He didn't know how long he was out, but when he came to, a thin, bald guy wearing a black suit and sunglasses was sitting in his recliner.

"Do I know you?" Curtis asked when he first woke up. He was still pretty high and not surprised to find that he had a visitor.

"We haven't been formally introduced, Mr. Mayflower." The man reached out and shook Curtis's limp hand. "I'm Coach."

Curtis slowly hoisted himself into a sitting position. "Oh yeah. You're the guy that kid wants me to talk to."

Coach lightly clapped his hands. They were thin with freshly manicured nails. "Yes. That's correct."

"Cool. I wasn't so sure that he wasn't full of shit or something."

"Of course," Coach replied. "But you did take young Nathan's food. And the marijuana."

Curtis eyed the man coolly. "Uh huh. What about it?"

"Nothing . . . nothing at all. I respect your caution. It's not everyday someone offers a man like you gifts, now is it, Curtis? It would only be natural for you to be suspicious. Greeks bearing gifts and such. But let me assure you. I, not young Mister Espy, am your benefactor."

"Espy, right Espy," Curtis said. "That was the kid's name."

"Yes. I came shortly after Nathan left. I knocked on the door but there was no answer. Seeing that it was open, I let myself in. You were a bit predisposed," Coach said, pointing to the bag of pot on the floor. "So I made myself comfortable."

"I see that." Curtis laughed, still groggy from all the dope he had smoked. "Okay. So you're here. What is it I can do for you? And more importantly, what are you going to do for me?"

Coach grinned. "I like that spirit. A real give-me-mine-and-fuck-the-rest attitude. First of all, there will be money. And much more of that fine dope. Plus," Coach added softly. "Her." Coach pointed toward the kitchen doorway. An attractive blond woman wearing a thin nightgown over an extremely curvaceous body leaned against the open door gently tracing her fingers up and down the sides of her torso. "Do we have a deal, Mr. Mayflower?"

On any other occasion, Curtis would have been a bit more curious as to how a woman that gorgeous just happened to find her way into his apartment. But with Coach sitting across from him tapping his perfectly manicured fingers against the arm of the chair, and the sweet scent of reefer still hanging in the air, Curtis didn't really give a shit how the woman got there. "That depends." Curtis was talking to Coach but he kept his eyes glued on the woman. She smiled at him and then playfully began to suck on her right forefinger. "What is it you want me to do?" Curtis asked.

"Nothing," Coach began. "Nothing that you haven't done before. A little robbery, an assault here and there. Mainly, I want you to purchase marijuana from some of your associates and then distribute it to certain individuals."

Curtis turned his gaze from the woman who was now orally satisfying herself with three fingers. "You want me to sell dope for you?"

"No, nothing like that. I want you to buy it, with my money of course, and then give it away."

Curtis took his eyes off the blond and stared at Coach. "I don't get it."

Coach reached into his pocket and tossed an envelope onto the coffee table. "There's five thousand dollars, Mr. Mayflower. For that kind of money you don't have to get it, do you?"

Curtis snatched up the money and began counting. His eyes grew wide at the sight of fifty, hundred dollar bills. "How do I know this isn't some kind of a setup?"

Coach began laughing and motioned for the girl to come over. "Please, Mr. Mayflower, don't flatter yourself. I don't think the police would go to all this trouble and effort to entrap someone like you. And anyway," Coach said, waving his left hand in Curtis's direction, "do you think a setup would contain this?" The blond woman strolled into the living room, her hands still caressing her sides. When she came to Curtis's chair, she undid the loose satin tie that held the nightgown together and let it fall to the floor. No sooner did the garment fall than Curtis rose from his seat and wrapped his large arms around her smooth back.

"I take it we have a deal then?" Coach asked a second time.

Curtis didn't reply; he was too busy kissing what he imagined to be an advance on his salary.

And Curtis had to admit, the pay was good and the work was pretty easy. Actually, it was all lightweight stuff, but a bit odd. Especially the first job. Curtis had been selling dope for a long time, and he knew that you didn't make any money giving the stuff away. But the day after Coach's visit, Nathan Espy showed up on his doorstep and told him that he was to purchase two thousand dollars of weed from one of his suppliers. He was then to give the weed to Espy who would return it to Curtis the next day.

"What do you want me to do with it then?"

"Give it away," Espy told him. "I'll tell you who and where."

Whatever, Curtis thought. He bought the pot as he was told and delivered it to Espy. And just as Coach said, the kid brought the weed back and told Curtis to deliver a bag of it to some of the losers who hung out at the Torrid Zone. When Curtis told him it wouldn't be a problem, Espy told the big man that Coach was pleased with his work and wanted to offer him a bonus.

"Oh yeah, what's that?" Curtis asked.

"Twins."

And sure enough, a pair of redheaded twins showed up in the middle of the night. Of course Curtis fucked them both, and in the morning when he awoke, the twins were gone, his red and sore cock the only proof that they had been there.

Curtis looked at his watch. Seven minutes till midnight. Instinct told him to get out of the car and get the deed over with. He was anxious to get his hands on Morris Keyes and that Stepanich bitch. But Espy warned him. No mistakes. Coach wanted it done in a certain way at a certain time. The plan was for him to go in at five minutes before midnight, no sooner. And only then was he to proceed to give both Morris and Merilee exactly one hundred kicks to the head. No more and certainly no less.

One more minute.

After Curtis delivered the first stash of pot to the punks at the Torrid Zone, the next few jobs were easy. A few tires got slashed, some kids got beat up, and one night, he broke into an old lady's house. He didn't steal anything, he was only to make noise. It was a fright job, Espy told him.

Curtis was content with doing what he was told. And after each job, Nathan Espy would show up with a few hundred bucks and a few other perks. After the break-in at the construction company, Nathan was waiting in Curtis's apartment with a bottle of Vodka. Curtis drank the booze and that night he was visited by a plump teenage chick. Like the others, he screwed this one for about an hour before passing out from too much booze and pot.

But then there was the thing with Fredo. There had been no sign of him since the robbery. It was no great loss, but Curtis thought it was odd that Fredo stopped hanging around the Torrid Zone. The last time he went to the hangout, Julie took Curtis off into the woods and screwed his lights out. She told Curtis that Fredo had split and that she needed a man.

And then there was tonight. Curtis was hanging out in his apartment hoping Julie would stop by when Espy called and said Coach wanted someone to get a "real casualty of war beating."

"One hundred kicks to the head," he told Curtis.

At first Curtis balked at the idea, but when he was told who would be the recipients of those kicks, he agreed.

"Good," Nathan said. "This is how Coach wants you to do it."

***

Merilee finished packing up a case of empty beer bottles and slipped it under the bar. It was supposed to go into the storeroom, but she was tired and had a headache. She could do it tomorrow. Actually, she decided, she would save everything for tomorrow. The restocking, the sweeping, even emptying out the garbage could wait for a day. *Screw it*, she thought, *I'm going to bed.*

Merilee glanced at the red and white Budweiser clock that hung above the dartboard. Eleven forty-five. As she wiped down the bar, her arms making wide circles on the smooth, wood surface, she gave up hope that Steve was going to stop by. Steve told her that with all that was happening with the Espy investigation and the search for Fredo Torach, he probably wouldn't be able to see her tonight. But still, Merilee was disappointed. When her wiping took her to the corner where Morris sat, she asked him if he wanted one more beer before she closed up for the night. Morris's head twitched slightly, but the man said nothing

Merilee took his glass and held it beneath the Iron City tap. Morris never was much of a talker, but he hadn't said a word for the last four days, and his silence was beginning to worry Merilee. "Straight from the Mon." she joked, placing the beer in front of him. Still no reply, just a quick, nervous twitch.

"You're welcome, Morris," she said kindly.

Merilee wiped off the rest of the bar before glancing at the clock again. 11:50 pm. "Time to knock off," she yawned. "Finish up, Morris, and I'll give you a lift home."

Morris eyed his half-empty glass as Merilee walked from behind the bar and headed to the front door. As she did, she cast a quick glance about the bar. It wasn't too messy, and nothing seemed to be seriously out of order. The chairs were in place, the pool cues were racked, and the tables were reasonably clean. Everything else could wait for the morning.

As she reached for the door, the Budweiser clocked read

11:51. Then the door swung open smacking Merilee squarely in the forehead. For a second, she saw a hail of flashing lights dancing in her field of vision. *You really do see stars*, she thought as she stumbled backward. Then the pain of the blow hit her full force. "Son-of-a-bitch!" she yelled, her hands groping toward the wound on her head. "Shit! That hurts."

"It'll get worse," a familiar voice growled.

Blurry from the pain, Merilee tried to focus on the figure coming through the door. She recognized it immediately and was even able to say "Curtis" before his powerful, right fist connected with her jaw. Merilee's head snapped back and she bit into her tongue as she fell over one of the small tables in the back of the bar.

"I'll be damned," Curtis said, glancing at the Budweiser clock. "My watch must be fast."

Merilee was sprawled out on the cold floor, the coppery taste of blood filling her mouth. Struggling, she managed to lift herself onto her hands and knees when Mayflower's steel tipped cowboy boot shot out and connected with her mid-section. The impact made a whumph sound as Merilee's breath exploded out of her mouth. She fell back onto the floor, gasping and clutching at her stomach.

"That's one," Mayflower whispered. "You got a whole lot more coming." He raised a thick finger toward Morris who had risen from his bar stool. He stood paralyzed, his eyes fixed on Merilee writhing on the floor.

Morris watched helplessly as Curtis kicked Merilee once more in the stomach before stepping over her prone body. Curtis's eyes were red and glassy, shrouded in a glaze of burning hatred. Morris recognized the look immediately.

Morris straightened up and faced Curtis. "I know who sent you," he said slowly.

Curtis laughed and slapped his hands together. "Do you now? Do you know why? Because to tell you the truth, I have no idea why Coach wants me to put a hurtin' on you. I don't know what you did to piss him off, but," Curtis said, his voice growing low and cold, "mine is but to do or die."

157

He started toward Morris but the old man didn't move. "His name isn't Coach. It's Dust. And he's a liar."

"That's fucking rich, you old shit." Curtis was about two arm lengths from Morris. "Dust, must, bust, I don't give a shit if he calls himself tinkerfuckingbell. He pays me and he pays me good. So fuck you." Curtis lunged at Morris. As he did, Morris swung his right arm around and hurled his beer glass at the former All-American. It shattered against the left side of Curtis's face, sending shards of glass into his cheek and chin. But the big man didn't notice them. They were tiny pinpricks when compared to the three-inch chunk of glass that was embedded in Curtis's eyeball.

"Oh motherfucker," Curtis screamed, his hands clutching at his wounded eye. As Curtis wailed, Morris shoved him aside and leapt toward Merilee who was pushing herself off the floor. But as he got past Curtis, the big man caught a handful of Morris's shirt and swung him backward.

"No," Curtis hissed, pinning Morris against the bar. Trapped, Morris looked up into Curtis's leering face. Blood and ocular fluid dripped from the jutting end of the glass; it rolled down Curtis's cheek, making a thin trail from his eye to his mouth. "Game fucking over," Curtis yelled, flipping Morris so that his stomach was pressed against the bar. "One hundred fucking kicks." He grabbed the back of Morris's head and slammed it into the mahogany bar top. "Ninety-nine more." Curtis lifted Morris head again, but before he could slam it back down, he was struck in the back of his own head with a force so hard that the glass shard in his eye popped out onto the bar.

Dazed, Curtis let go of Morris and spun around. Three feet in front of him, Merilee held the thick end of a pool cue, ready to swing it again.

"Get away from him," she ordered.

Curtis glared at her through his one good eye. "Fuck you, bi . . ."

Merilee swung the cue again, this time catching Curtis in the temple. She heard a snap and thought she had cracked his skull. Unfortunately, the snap was the sound of her pool cue breaking in half. Stunned from the blow, Curtis staggered backwards into

Morris who was still slumped over the bar. Merilee quickly brought her arm back ready to strike again, but as she did, Curtis's left foot swept out, catching Merilee's feet and knocking her to the ground.

"You bitch," he screamed, pouncing on top of Merilee. He grabbed her throat and pushed his thumbs into her neck. Merilee tried to fight him off but Mayflower's bulk and rage were too much for her. *This is it*, she thought. *This asshole is going to kill me.* She felt his grip tighten and closed her eyes . . .

Then Mayflower suddenly howled in pain and rolled off of her. Once the pressure from his fingers was gone, the air whooshed down Merilee's throat. She was gasping for air when a pair of strong hands gently lifted her to her feet. "You're okay now," Morris whispered.

Curtis's howling had turned to a wounded cry, and as Morris pulled Merilee toward the rear of the bar, she saw Curtis staggering toward the exit. A thick trail of blood followed. As Curtis threw open the bar door, Merilee could see the sharp point of the broken pool cue embedded in his left leg.

***

Curtis couldn't understand what went wrong. He had them both right where he wanted. "Fuck," he whimpered as he shuffled out of The Oaks. He was in too much pain to care about being seen. He had to get to his car and get out of there. He had to find Espy. He needed to know what to do.

Curtis forced his legs to move, but with each step a sheet of white-hot pain shot up his leg and into his back. He traveled only a few steps when he felt himself starting to black out. He lurched forward, collapsing against the window of the bakery next to The Oaks. He was about to pass out when he heard the engine of his car fire up. "Huh," he gasped as he saw it moving toward him. With the headlights still turned off, the car pulled up beside Curtis.

"Get in," Nathan Espy hissed from the driver's seat.

But Curtis wasn't looking at the driver. He was staring at the thing in the back seat, the thing that looked like a cloud. For a second the cloud floated harmlessly behind Espy's head, then it rolled over like a ball and revealed a giant mouth with razor sharp teeth. Thin, smoky tentacles wriggled free from the center of the cloud and reached out for Curtis. At the end of each tentacle was a razor sharp claw. "Get in," Curtis heard Espy say. "Man, did you screw up."

Then everything went black.

Chapter Twelve: June 29

Steve bolted through the Emergency Room entrance of McKeesport Hospital. It was empty except for a young man holding an ice pack against his swollen and purpled nose. Steve hurried to the admissions desk. "Excuse me," he said to the slightly plump middle-aged nurse sitting behind the counter. "I'm looking for a patient who was brought in here about an hour ago. Her name is Merilee Stepanich."

The nurse looked up at Steve and asked if he was family.

Steve snatched his wallet from his pants and showed her his detective shield. "Merilee Stepanich," he repeated.

"Oh," the nurse chirped. "Of course." She glanced down at a clipboard, scanning the names of the admits that had come in that evening. "Here it is. Stepanich, M. Admitted 12:34 a.m. She's in cubicle eleven. I'll get an orderly to take you to her."

"Thanks." Steve turned and started toward the door marked ER. "I know my way," he called over his shoulder.

He threw open the swinging door and had barely stepped into the ER when a young doctor in the middle of directing a tired orderly to collect a urine sample intercepted Steve. "You're not supposed to be in here," he said.

"I'm a police officer," Steve replied. "Where's cubicle eleven?"

The young doctor took a few seconds to eye up the detective before dismissing the orderly. "Right," he said, motioning for

Steve to follow him. "This way." He led Steve past a series of small cubicles, each one partitioned off by a nylon curtain. When they came to the end of the short hall, the doctor turned to his left and stopped. "Here," he said softly but firmly. "Miss Stepanich is resting now. She's suffered a pretty good beating, but she has no broken bones or any internal injuries. She's got some bad bruises, and she's going to be pretty sore for a few days, but she'll be fine." The doctor emphasized the word fine.

Steve nodded and the young doctor quietly slid the cloth partition to the side. "I'll be down the hall if you need anything," he said as he left.

Steve winced when he saw Merilee stretched out on the bed. She lay still under the starched white hospital sheets, her arms stiff at her sides. Propped up by two oversized pillows, Merilee's head and neck peeked out from beneath the tight hospital blankets. Taped to each forearm, a thin blue wire stretched across the length of the bed into the bank of electronic equipment that monitored her vital signs. The room was silent except for the beeping of the heart monitor and the slight whooshing sound that came from the oxygen tube suspended beneath Merilee's nose.

"Oh Merilee," Steve said weakly as he caught sight of the large, purple bruise that covered the left side of her face. It was in the shape of a crescent moon, extending from the upper part of her lip halfway up her forehead. Already, the eye had swelled shut. He moved beside her and gently stroked her hand with the tips of his fingers.

He had been in his office when the call came to the 911 dispatcher reporting a disturbance at The Oaks and advising that an ambulance was needed. The duty officer immediately sent a squad car to the bar and contacted Steve. When he heard what had happened, a primal rage grabbed hold of the detective. He peeled out of the parking lot, but instead of turning left onto Fifth Avenue and toward the hospital, he turned right and headed for Curtis Mayflower's apartment.

It took less than five minutes for Steve to traverse the few miles from the police station to Mayflower's apartment, but it was enough time for Steve's cop mind to rationalize his behavior. If he went straight to the hospital, he wouldn't be allowed to see Merilee anyway; he would only be in the way, and he knew that in his current state, his presence would be more of a hindrance than anything. No, it was better to do something constructive, like kick the living shit out of Curtis Mayflower and then haul his ass to jail. When he got to Mayflower's apartment building, Steve bolted from the car and ran up the back steps to the second floor. The door to Curtis's apartment was on the right. Without knocking, Steve lowered his shoulder and smashed through the wooden door, ripping the metal chain lock from the doorframe.

Steve tumbled into Mayflower's filthy kitchen, knocking over one of the two kitchen chairs that made up the room's only furniture. Steve's rage was uncontrollable now as he burst into the living room screaming the man's name. Finding no one there, he barreled his way down a small hallway and kicked open the bathroom door. Seeing that room was also empty, Steve went for the last room in the apartment.

Steve kicked in the door, sending it crashing into the plasterboard wall of Curtis's bedroom. Directly in front of him in the darkened room was a man laying on the bed. "Curtis," Steve barked, but the figure didn't move. Steve pulled his gun from its holster and aimed it at the bed. "You better fucking answer me, Curtis."

As Steve stepped into the room, an odd but familiar shit-and-piss scent greeted him. Not taking his eyes of the bed, Steve slid his hand across the bedroom wall near the door. Finding the light switch, he flicked it on.

He had expected to find Curtis passed out on the bed, but as the room became awash in the white light of the bare sixty-watt bulb that hung from the ceiling, Steve knew instantly that the mangled corpse on the bed was not Curtis Mayflower.

Less than ten minutes after Steve's discovery, two uniform officers arrived at Mayflower's apartment. As instructed, they did not turn on their lights or siren. It wasn't quite twelve-thirty, and with a little luck, the scene could be inspected and the body removed before daybreak. The pair of cops made their way into Curtis's apartment via the back steps just as Steve had done.

No sooner had Steve ushered the police officers into the apartment and showed them the body, than Assistant Police Chief Randy Bressler arrived. Without a word, Bressler did a quick once over of the crime scene then huddled for a moment with the two uniformed cops. His orders were succinct; he told them to wait on the back porch and make sure nobody else found their way into Mayflower's apartment. When they were alone, Bressler turned to Steve and said flatly, "You fucked up."

Steve was about to reply but Bressler cut him off. "Don't talk. Just listen. An APB has already been sent out on Mayflower. When you get grilled tomorrow, you tell the mayor everything that happened. How you had a positive identification of the man who attacked Merilee and Morris. And you make sure you tell her everything exactly the way it happened, except," Bressler said, pointing a thick finger at Steve. "The bit about the back door. It was open when you got here. Understand?"

Steve shook his head. "No one's going to buy that, Randy. The fucking door cracked when I came through it."

Bressler laughed dryly and pulled a brown lock chain from his pocket. "Don't flatter yourself," he said. "The thing was barely attached. When you busted in here the screws popped out. That's why it went flying. My granddaughter could have kicked this lock off."

Bressler pulled a Swiss army knife from his jacket pocket and opened up the flat head screwdriver attachment. "I already checked the front door and there's no signs of forced entry. And in about twenty seconds, this will be back on the door frame." He paused and looked hard at Steve. "So when you got here, you knocked, announced yourself, and then finding the door unlocked, entered the home of a dangerous man who had just assaulted two people. A man who is now wanted for assault and murder." Bressler arched his eyebrows. "Got it?"

Steve muttered a grateful thanks.

"Yeah," Bressler said. "You owe me one. Now go see Merilee."

Needing no further encouragement, Steve made his way out of the apartment, leaving the crime scene in the hands of the assistant chief of police.

Now as he looked down at Merilee, the rage that fueled him disappeared. In its place, a frustrating sense of helplessness gripped him like a sharp claw digging into his chest. Steve felt a real and physical ache jabbing at his breastbone, keeping time with his racing heart.

"Steve," a voice whispered from behind him.

Steve turned to see Morris Keyes standing in the opening to Merilee's cubicle. He, too, had a deep bruise on the side of his face only it didn't stop at his eye. Instead, it covered the area above Morris's right eye socket and then made a straight, ruler-sized line across the man's forehead.

"We've got to talk," Morris said.

Steve let go of Merilee's hand and took a step in Morris's direction. "What happened, Morris?" he asked. "Why the hell did Mayflower do this to her?"

Morris bristled at the mention of Curtis Mayflower. "It wasn't Merilee he wanted. It was me." Morris stepped into the small confines of Merilee's cubicle then carefully lowered his bruised frame onto the metal chair next to the bed. "Curtis was sent to kill me."

For a moment Steve felt his breath being sucked from his body as if he had been punched in the stomach. "What do you mean? Who would want to have you killed?"

Morris didn't answer immediately. Instead he buried his head into the palms of his hands and began to sway to and fro. "I thought this all ended," he said to Steve, only his words were directed to the floor, "twenty-five years ago. It was supposed to be over." The old man looked up at Steve. His swollen and puffy eyes filled with tears. "It's Dust. Dr. Smith said that he was dead; that he couldn't hurt anyone any more. He promised."

PART TWO

If but some vengeful god would call me
From the sky and laugh: "Thou suffering thing,
Know that thy sorrow is my ecstasy"
Thomas Hardy

Chapter Thirteen: June 29

Morris fingered the rim of his Styrofoam coffee cup, absently ripping off jagged fragments between his calloused fingers. He and Steve were sitting in a small booth of the hospital's mostly deserted cafeteria. Steve brought him there after Morris started babbling in the emergency room about Dr. Smith and the old veterans hospital. "Now try again," Steve said when Morris was calm enough to talk. Though the only other people in the cafeteria were two tired orderlies on their lunch break, Steve kept his voice low. "Who sent Curtis Mayflower, and what has this got to do with Henry Smith?"

Another flake of Styrofoam hit the tabletop. "It was him," Morris said softly. "Dust."

His patience beginning to wane, Steve stared hard at the older man. "Morris, I don't have time for this right now. You and Merilee got real lucky that Mayflower didn't kill the both of you.

So if you got something to tell me that will help me catch the son-of-a-bitch, tell me. If not, just drink your coffee, okay?"

"Damn it, Steve, will you listen to me. It was Dust. I know it sounds crazy, but you've got to believe me. I've seen it before. I think he got inside Curtis's head just like he did Bobby Monero."

The name hit Steve like a sledgehammer. "Bob Monero? Christ Morris, what the hell are you talking about?"

A sad, pained expression came over Morris's weathered face. "Back in the early seventies, Henry Smith concocted some kind of drug that was supposed to help folks remember their dreams better. He needed someone to test it out on, and Bobby and me were his guinea pigs."

Steve felt his guts twisting into long knots. "Guinea pigs?"

Morris nodded blankly. "Yeah. Henry helped me and Bobby quite a bit after we got back from Nam. We never had any money to pay him, so when he came to us and asked for a favor, we didn't think too much about it. He wanted the two of us to take this stuff he called the DK. He told us it would make our pituitary glands stronger, and it would help us remember our dreams more. Henry said the stuff was still in the experimental stage and that the tests were a secret, so we couldn't tell anyone. Like I said, Bobby and me didn't think anything of it. Henry Smith had always taken care of us before, and we owed him."

"So the two of you took this DK then?"

"Yup. But before we did, Henry tells us that along with remembering our dreams, he wants to help direct them a bit. Plant a subconscious suggestion, is what he called it. So he tells us this story about this dream creature named Dust."

"Yeah, I know about that legend," Steve interjected.

Morris eyed the detective oddly before continuing. "Then you know what a fucker he is. Anyway, Henry goes on about Dust for over an hour, so by the time I get to sleep, I've got this story running through my head. But only when I start dreaming, I'm not dreaming about any Indian tribe on the banks of the river. I'm dreaming I'm back in Nam, back in the jungle. And shit, it's like I'm really there. I mean, I could feel and smell everything around me like I had never left. And it was hot, Steve; hot like you couldn't imagine. I could even feel my sweat stinging me when it got into my eyes."

Morris let out a long, slow sigh. "Dreams aren't supposed to be like that, Steve. You're not supposed to feel anything in them like they're really happening to you. But I sure did," he said, roughly tapping his forehead. "It's still up here."

"So what happened?"

"I walked right through the jungle and smack-dab into a tiger. I knew I was dreaming, but it scared me, and I wasn't taking any chances, so I blew it away."

Morris paused and Steve noticed a definite tension cloud the man's face. "That's when it got really weird." Morris cast his eyes toward his hands. Slowly the older man began to tap out a one-two beat on the table with his thumb and forefinger. "I shot the tiger, and the thing's head exploded. It just blew up. Next thing I know I got all this tiger blood and brains all over me." The tapping grew quicker.

"After I blew the tiger's head off, Dust came wriggling out of the carcass. First these two arms come popping out of the tiger's neck, and then the whole thing starts shaking. By this time, I'm scared shitless, and I want to get the hell out of there. But I can't really go anywhere, can I? Cause it doesn't matter how real everything seems, it's still just a dream. So I tell myself to wake up, but I can't. I'm yelling and screaming and telling myself to wake the fuck up because I sure as shit don't want to be around when this thing gets out of the tiger."

Morris laughed nervously. "You know, it's kind of funny. Dr. Smith told me all about Dust being this big, evil monster. That he can take any shape he wants. But when he pulls himself out of the tiger, he's just a guy. He's not a monster or anything. He's just some skinny, bald guy all covered with tiger guts and shit. So when I see it's not a monster, I calm down. After all it's only a dream, right?"

Steve didn't know what to say. "What happened after Dust came out of the tiger?"

"He just stood there for a second. It was like he was surprised or something. And then he saw me. At least I think he saw me cause he didn't have any eyes."

"No eyes?"

Morris shook his head. "Nope. Just two holes in his head." He paused, taking a deep breath. "Then he smiled at me, and I thought I was dead. You see, Steve, he didn't have people teeth. He had these long fucking fangs. And they were all wiggling and moving around in his mouth. Christ, it looked like he had a mouthful of sharp fingers. When I saw that, I started screaming. That's when I woke up."

Steve expected for there to be more to the story, but Morris turned his attention back to rearranging the pile of Styrofoam flakes in front of him. "What about Bob Monero?" Steve asked.

"I didn't see Bobby that first night, but I think he had the same kind of dream I had."

"Why do you think that?"

Morris shrugged his shoulders, his attention still focused on the white flakes in front of him. "Just the way Henry was acting. Kind of nervous, and when I asked him about Bobby, he wouldn't give me a straight answer. He just said everything was fine."

"Anyway, the next night Henry wants to give me the DK again, but I don't want it. I told him that the dream I had the night before was too fucking lucid for me, and I didn't want any part of his sedative." Morris paused and bit the top of his lower lip.

"But you took it anyway," Steve said.

"Yeah, I did. Henry Smith had a way of talking you into things. He told me I had a bad reaction because I wasn't prepared for how real the dream would be, and that this time I would be just fine. It was all bullshit, but I bought it. He gave me the DK, and I was out like a light. The next thing I knew I was back in the jungle and Dust was waiting for me. Only this time, he ain't inside the tiger. This time he's sitting on a log wearing this black suit, just smiling and humming as pleasant as could be. When I came near him with my gun, that son-of-a-bitch even said hello."

"What did you do then?"

Morris huffed and lowered his eyes. For a moment it looked to Steve like the man was about to cry. "I fucked up," Morris said. "I don't know why, but I lowered my gun. Shit, I think I even said hello back to him." Morris lifted his head and looked up at Steve. "But as soon as I dropped my weapon, he dove on top of me. I tried to get a shot off, but he was too fast. The next thing I know, I'm on the ground and Dust is slapping me across the face. But he doesn't have hands no more, he's got claws, and he's ripping my face apart with them. I mean I can feel my skin getting ripped right off my face."

"You've got to remember, Steve, with this DK shit, it isn't like a normal dream. I can feel it happening to me like it's real. Do you know what that's like? Feeling your nose and eyes getting ripped off your face?"

Steve left the question unanswered. "How does Robert Monero fit into this?"

"Well, Dust's got a hold of me, and this time I know I'm a dead man when Bob Monero shows up. He comes busting into the clearing wearing his army fatigues and carrying an M16. When Dust sees him, he gets this funny look on his face and lets me go."

"What do you mean by a funny look?"

Morris shrugged his shoulders. "I don't know how to describe it really. Like he was confused or something. But I could tell that he was surprised to see Bobby. When he saw him, Dust got off me in a hurry and went for Monero. He got to him before Bobby could fire. I thought he was going to mess up Bobby like he did me, but Dust just whipped him around and put him in a half-nelson. Bobby was fighting like hell to get out of it, but he couldn't."

"While Bobby was struggling, Dust just started laughing. Then he takes one of his claws and starts pushing it into the back of Bobby's head. I'm still on the ground looking out of one eye, but I can see this plain as day. It was like Bobby's head was some kind of melon, and Dust was just pushing his hand right through. He got his entire claw into Bobby's head, all the way up to the wrist. I thought he was going to rip Bobby's head off, but then Dust just stops. Then he kind of leans his face forward and starts melting into Bobby."

"Melting?" Steve asked. "What do you mean?"

"I don't know how else to describe it," Morris replied. "It was like he was becoming smoke or something. Whatever was happening, Dust started pouring himself into Bobby's head, right through the holes he made with his claw. By the time I was able to get to my feet, about half of his body had become this smoke and was inside of Bobby. I don't know if Dust thought I was dead, or he just forgot about me, but he was still dumping himself into Bobby when I started shooting. I mean I just opened up on that mother."

Morris paused, his fingers nervously returning to the jagged rim of the cup. "That's the last part of the dream I remember. I woke up right after that and got the hell out of there. Didn't even bother getting dressed."

"Didn't Dr. Smith try to stop you?"

Morris shook his head. "Nope. He wasn't even around. Actually, no one was around, so I took off and went home. I thought Henry might come looking for me, but he didn't. But the next morning Bob Monero was at my door." Morris released the coffee cup and sighed. "And I'll tell you something. He was scared out of his mind. Now I'd known Bob Monero nearly all my life, and he was one tough man. But when I opened the door and saw him there, I couldn't believe it. He was crying, Steve. Just shaking all over and blubbering like some little kid."

"Did he say anything?" Steve asked. "Did he tell you what frightened him?"

"Yeah, he told me. Once I got him into the house he calmed down a bit. He told me that he dreamed of me the night before. Said I shot him in the jungle." A puzzled expression clouded Steve's face. Morris picked up on it immediately. "Yeah, I know what you're thinking. How can Bob have the same dream I did? And to this day I can't tell you how, but we did. Bob told me what happened in his dream, and every last detail was the same as mine. Only thing is, Bobby never really woke up."

"You lost me here, Morris. What do you mean he didn't wake up?"

"Just what I said. You see, when Dust got into him, he pushed into the part of Bob's mind that dreams. I stopped Dust before he could get totally inside Bob's head. But enough of him had gotten into Bob to send him over the edge. Bob said that Dust was talking to him, telling him to go to sleep. But if he did that, Dust would have control of his body. 'See with my eyes' is what Bob told me."

"I didn't know what to say to that, so I told him everything was going to be okay; that he just had a bad dream, and we weren't going anywhere near Henry Smith any more. That seemed to work a bit. After a few minutes he started to calm down, so I went to the kitchen to make him a cup of coffee. When I got back to the living room, he was asleep."

From the subtle change in Morris tone, Steve could tell the old man was struggling for the right words for what came next. "I didn't know what to think about what Bob was telling me. He was convinced that Dust was real and was in his head, and frankly, after seeing what I saw, I wasn't so sure Bob wasn't right. The only thing I knew for sure was that there was no way in hell I was ever going to take Henry Smith's DK shit again."

"When I went into the living room, I saw that Bob was out pretty heavy, so I just figured I'd let him be. But after a few minutes he starts fidgeting like he's having a bad dream or something. I go over to wake him, but before I can, he sits up and looks at me. Only it wasn't Bob Monero looking at me, it was Dust. I know because his eyes were all white. Solid white like a piece of paper. And he smiled at me just like he did in my dream, only he was smiling with Bob's face. It was like he was wearing Bob's face as a mask, but I knew who it was."

"Before I could say anything he jumps up and wraps Bob's hands around my neck. I tried to fight him off, but I couldn't. He just starts choking me, telling me that I know too much. That I should have opened my mind up to him. He kept saying that, and I was about to pass out when Bob's head snaps back and he drops me. I look up and Bob's standing over me, but this time it's the real Bob. He starts crying and says he's been to the neither-place. By the time I'm able to catch my breath, Bob took off out the door."

Morris stopped and pushed his chair back from the table. In front of him the pile of Styrofoam that an hour before had been a coffee cup sat like a mound of snow. "When I saw Curtis Mayflower at The Oaks he had the same look in his eyes that Bob had when he said he'd been to the neither-place. I know it sounds impossible, but you got to believe me, Steve. Dust is real, and he sent Curtis to the bar to kill me because I know what he is."

"And what is that, Morris?" Steve asked brusquely. "What exactly is Dust?"

"He's a dream demon, just like in Henry's myth. And he's trapped in the neither-place where the rivers meet. But he wants out, Steve. That's why he's back. Ever since Henry died, he's been trying to get himself free."

"This is nuts, Morris. I mean, do you expect me to believe that a pissed off demon from some Indian myth sent Curtis Mayflower to kill you? Come on." Steve pushed himself from the table and stood up. "Look I know you've been through a lot, and I am truly grateful you were there to save Merilee tonight, but I can't buy any of this, okay." Steve started from the table. "I'm going to check on Merilee."

As Steve walked away, Morris sat staring at the white flakes in front of him. He didn't adjust his gaze when he called after Steve.

"Steve, there's something else you should know."

Steve stopped and looked over his shoulder at Morris. "What's that?"

"The day that Bob Monero came to see me; the day that he said Dust was inside of him. That was the same day you killed him." Morris brushed the flakes onto the floor and stood up. "Henry Smith told me that Dust died along with Bob. But I don't think that's the case. I think he got into Mayflower, and I think he's gotten into some other folks in town too."

Chapter Fourteen: June 29 continued

Gary could hear two things very distinctly as he sat in Steve's office: the slow hum of the oscillating fan that did little to circulate the humid air, and his pulse pounding in his left temple. He paid the fan little attention as he massaged the side of his head and tried to come to grips with what had happened to him at the Espy house.

Sure he'd been scared when he went down the basement steps. It was dark and the place smelled like shit. And the flies—that had been the worst. God, Gary thought, there had to be a million of them. Anybody in their right mind would have been scared. Then there were the baseball cards. Thousands of them with Nathan Espy's face. All blinded. That alone was enough to freak a person out.

Gary began pacing about the small office. He desperately needed to talk to Steve and tell him what he saw in Espy's basement. He had to make Steve understand that there was something down there. Some unnatural thing, hiding, waiting for them to come down those steps. Gary stepped over to the window. Resting his large arms on the chest-high sill, he looked into the courtyard at the statue of Kennedy. "You've got to get a hold of yourself," Gary said out loud. "You've got to calm down." At least his job was secure. Steve had taken care to protect that. His partner had taken care of him just like he'd always done.

Just like ol' Uncle Joe took care of you.

Gary shuddered. Why after all these years had the memory of his abusive uncle come back to haunt him? Why now had the dreams of Uncle Joe's thick hands and sour breath returned? But Gary knew the answer to that one. Uncle Joe never really went away. Even after years of therapy and counseling, Uncle Joe's memory could never be completely erased. It was always there, just like Uncle Joe himself. Hiding, waiting for the right opportunity to play the "feel game." Gary understood the way things worked a long time ago. There was no way to get rid of Uncle Joe once he had you. After all, Uncle Joe was family.

Best not to think of it, Gary decided. Instead he focused on the statue of Kennedy, Steve's hero. For a few moments he was able to admire the detail and craftsmanship of the statue, then his mind slammed shut and his mouth flew open. What should have been a full-throated scream emerged as a weak gasp. Gary stood paralyzed, his breath trapped in his lungs, his fingers digging into the windowsill.

Kennedy's index finger, which normally pointed westward, was now aimed at the window and Gary. It wiggled from side to side as if scolding the detective.

Gary remained motionless as the twelve-foot bronze figure twisted its torso and took a jerking step forward. The sound of metal against metal was deafening, and for a second, the statue looked as if it would teeter off balance, but it quickly righted itself.

"Ah gots ta get mah land legs back," the statue said, the voice a malicious parody of a New Englander. "It's been too long since I got down. Yah know, Gary. Got down to business."

Got down to business. That was Uncle Joe's line.

Unable to move, Gary did the only thing he could—he screamed. And as he did, the Kennedy thing laughed. "Now, now. There'll be none of that on mah account."

Gary immediately stopped screaming and pissed himself.

Undeterred, the statue kept up its slow progress toward the window.

"You must excuse me," it said. The voice had lost its phony accent and was replaced by a much more familiar one. "Ol' Uncle Joe's moving kinda slow." A wide, bronze grin spread across its face. "At the junction." Kennedy/Uncle Joe laughed again, this time bringing both hands down onto his knees. "Whooh," it squealed, pumping its fist into the air. "Whooh, whooh."

Gary stepped away from the window. He didn't notice the puddle of urine at his feet, nor did he hear the two police officers banging at the locked office door. His attention was monopolized by the monstrosity grinning at him from outside the window, the moving hunk of metal that, Gary knew, wasn't really the former president. It was Uncle Joe in a Kennedy costume.

"Coming to get you Garyy-boy," Kennedy/Uncle Joe said. "And then I'm going to feel you up reeeaalll gooood!" The statue leered at Gary then leapt toward the window. For a moment, its massive bronze body was suspended in the air, then it crashed into the side of City Hall. The force of the impact shook the building, knocking Gary backwards over Steve's desk and onto the floor.

"No," he wailed as the statue's head and shoulders began to push through the window. Gary grabbed for the pistol he kept strapped to his left ankle. Whipping it out, he pointed it toward the window just as the statue thrust its metal arm into the office. The thick polished fingers snapped shut inches from Gary's face.

"Die you son-of-a-bitch!" Gary screamed. Sprawled flat on his back he fired six quick shots at the bronze figure. As he emptied his weapon, Officers Hank Lydel and Warren Turvel burst into the office, each had their weapons drawn.

"Gary!" Lydel shouted. "Gary!"

Gary stopped firing, leapt to his feet, and ran to the window. "Fucker," he yelled. "You fucker." With their guns still drawn, the two officers watched horrified as Gary began slamming his head into the windowsill. Though their eyes were trained on Gary, they both had perfect views of Kennedy Memorial Park and the statue of the thirty-fifth president pointing a single finger westward.

June 29 continued

Steve didn't get out of the hospital until nearly 6:00 a.m. After Merilee woke up, the doctor told him that she was fine, but he wanted her to stay for observation for at least another twelve hours. Though her x-rays revealed no broken bones or internal injuries, Merilee's heart rate was a little high. When told of the doctor's decision, Merilee was mad as hell, but Steve assured her that he would be back around dinnertime to take her home. The promise did little to placate her. "Just go find Curtis Mayflower," she told Steve. He kissed her softly on her bruised cheek before leaving.

"I'll get him."

Unlike his earlier trip to Mayflower's apartment, this time Steve drove slowly, hoping to get a handle on the conflicting emotions raging inside of him. What he'd told Morris was true; there was no way he could believe that a pissed off demigod from an ancient Indian myth was fucking with the heads of the people in McKeesport. There was just no way he could accept that. No way. And yet part of him couldn't shake the uncomfortable feeling that there was some bit of truth to what Morris had said. Too many strange things had been happening in McKeesport since Slaughter Saturday. Steve thought about that for a second then corrected himself. Slaughter Saturday wasn't the beginning; Henry Smith had died the night before. *Everything keeps coming back to Henry Smith*, Steve thought. Henry Smith and a man with no eyes.

Steve pulled up to the front of the former candy store where Mayflower lived, parking behind a large white van with bold letters stenciled across its side: MCKEESPORT POLICE: FORENSICS. That was a good sign. Steve was on pretty good terms with the lab boys, and if they came across anything interesting, Steve would be the first to know.

The steps to Mayflower's apartment were at the front right of the store, blocked off by an orange strip of CRIME SCENE- DO NOT CROSS ribbon. Steve stepped over the barrier and made his way up the steps. When he reached the top, he was greeted by a young man in a white lab coat. "Steve," he called out. "Just the man I've been looking for. Where have you been?"

"Been busy, Carl," Steve offered as an explanation. "What's going on?"

Carl glanced down at the clipboard. "Not much really. They took the body out about twenty minutes ago. That's when I got here. Rhonda is in the apartment now. She'll give you the low down."

Steve nodded, another good sign. Rhonda Hemmings was Allegheny County's best forensic pathologist and a good friend of Steve's.

Steve started toward the open apartment door, but Carl grabbed his arm. "Hold on a second, I've been trying to get a hold of you for two days now."

"Oh," Steve said, poking his head into the apartment. "Why?"

Carl said something about lab tests, but Steve wasn't paying attention; he was looking for Rhonda. It wasn't until Carl said, ". . . from the Espy house," that Steve turned to face him.

"What tests?" Steve asked quickly. "What are you talking about?"

"The dope that you found at Marcus Espy's house. It was soaking in that funky green liquid. You told me to check it out. Any of this ringing a bell?"

It was, now that Carl reminded him. "Shit," Steve said. "I'd forgotten all about that."

"Yeah, well you were busy being sick and all. I mean, man, that was one messed up scene. I'd never seen anything like it, you know, with all the maggots and stuff."

"Carl," Steve interjected. "What about the liquid?"

"Oh. Like I said, I've been trying to get a hold of you for two days now, but I guess we keep missing each other. Anyway, I ran a compositional break down analysis on the stuff, basic tests really. See what kinds of chemical compounds are in the substance, determine their ratios, that sort of thing."

"And."

"And I'll be damned if I know what that stuff is. I checked it against just about every database I could think of— pharmaceutical, corporate labs, chemical companies, everything. And nothing matched. Nada."

Steve shook his head. "I don't know what that means, Carl."

"It means," a woman's voice answered from behind Steve. "That whatever you found in Mr. Espy's house is not on the FDA's list of approved substances."

Steve turned to see Rhonda Hemmings. She was a good eight inches shorter than Steve and barely tipped the scales at a hundred pounds, but Steve knew the petite medical examiner to be one of the toughest women he'd ever met. Like Carl, she was wearing a white lab coat and carrying a clipboard.

"Hey Doc," Steve said.

"Hey yourself." Rhonda paused and nodded knowingly. "You look like hell." She gave Steve a firm squeeze on the elbow and asked how Merilee was.

"She's fine. Bruised and sore, but the doctors said that there weren't any broken bones. She's more pissed than anything."

"I can imagine," Rhonda said. She turned to Carl and handed him the clipboard. "Here's the preliminary stuff. Why don't you go get the paperwork started? I want to talk to Steve a minute."

Carl accepted the clipboard and headed down the steps. When Carl was gone, Rhonda let out a tired sigh and leaned against the doorjamb. She pulled a pack of Camels out of her lab coat and offered one to Steve. "You really do look like shit."

"Thanks." Steve took the cigarette, then flicked open his Zippo and lit both his and Rhonda's. "What's up?"

Rhonda shot a quick glance into the apartment. Satisfied that no one was around, she stuck her hand back into her lab coat and pulled out a small, plastic evidence bag. "This was on the body," she said. "Tucked in the shirt pocket. No one but me has seen it."

Even before the bag was in his hand Steve could tell what was in it.

A baseball card.

"Oh shit." Steve's hands were shaking as he lifted the bag to his face. A 1997 Topps Sammy Sosa. Of course Sammy's face had been replaced with that of Nathan Espy.

As Steve stared at the card, Rhonda told him what she knew. "The body was that missing kid, Fredo Torach. His wallet and driver's license were in his pants pocket. From what I can tell he's been dead for a week or so."

"Fredo," Steve half whispered, not taking his eyes off the baseball card.

Rhonda took another drag on her cigarette and absently flicked an ash on the floor. "You don't seem surprised."

Steve shook his head and explained how Mrs. Torach first made the connection between Nathan Espy and her son.

"That," Rhonda said pointing to the baseball card, "seems to be some kind of calling card, don't you think? A Nathan Espy Special."

Steve gave her a puzzled look as he handed the bag back to her. "Do you think it's a message?"

Rhonda crossed her thin arms across her chest and scowled. "I don't know, Steve, but I was in the Espy house. I saw that kid's room, and I saw what he did to his father." Rhonda stopped and looked hard at Steve. "I've been in this business a long time, and I'm telling you, that was the sickest thing I've ever seen."

Steve agreed. "Me too."

"So I think the card is a message," Rhonda replied. "And the message Espy is sending is simple: 'I'm having fun.'"

The two friends finished their cigarettes in silence.

***

Steve dropped Rhonda off at the police station a little after seven in the morning. He had every intention of heading to his office to get an update on the search for Curtis Mayflower, but Rhonda reminded him that Randy Bressler was in charge of the investigation, and considering the fact that Steve hadn't slept in over twenty-four hours, it might be a good idea for him to just head home. "Get some rest. Take a shower and clam down," she advised.

During the short drive to the station Rhonda gave Steve some more details concerning the liquid taken from the Espy house. It was nothing she had ever seen before, though its chemical composition was somewhat similar to LSD. "It looks a lot like some kind of acid, but there's definitely a strong organic element to it. I'll need to do a few more tests, but I'll find out what it is. Don't worry about that."

"What would do you think it does to the pot?"

This time Rhonda shrugged. "No way to tell, but my guess is

that it makes it a lot stronger. Something like lacing it with PCP."

After dropping off Rhonda, Steve decided to take a drive. He was exhausted and should have gone home, but he was still too on edge to think about resting. A disturbing picture was beginning to take shape for Steve. It was obvious that Curtis Mayflower and Nathan Espy were partners of a sort—both dealing pot out of Espy's house. Steve guessed that along with selling the dope, the two had probably smoked enough of it to fry their brains for good. Somehow, Nathan's father and Fredo Torach got in the way and were murdered—most likely a joint effort by Curtis and Nathan.

Steve made a left turn onto a narrow, brick street. Not paying attention to where he was going, he just let the car take him. The street, lined with two-story houses covered in decades-old aluminum siding, was not unlike most other street in McKeesport: small squares of neatly trimmed grass in the front, a bicycle, here and there, resting on its side in the driveway. Inside the houses, families were beginning their day—parents were getting ready to head off to work, kids getting dressed for daycare or church camp.

And outside those houses—well that was a different story, one of which the people of McKeesport weren't fully aware. Somewhere outside on the streets, two lunatics who got off on torturing people were loose. And Steve Wyckoff had no idea where they were.

Steve glanced at his watch. Almost 8:00 a.m. He was still too wired to sleep, but that didn't stop him from feeling like crap. He was hungry, he had a headache, and the smell of his own body drifted unpleasantly from the sweat-soaked clothes he had been wearing for almost two days.

He was also out of cigarettes,

Steve decided that the best thing for him was to make a quick trip back to his apartment to shower and shave. He could grab a bite to eat and a pack or two of smokes and be back at the station by nine.

Home.

Steve's fingers wrapped around the steering wheel like coiled springs as the car crawled past a weathered, brick house. "Son-of-a-bitch," he muttered, slamming on the breaks.

Steve loosened his grip on the wheel and pulled the car to the side of the road. Without realizing it, he patted the shoulder holster beneath his sports coat. The familiar bulk of his gun brushed comfortably against his chest. He then stepped out of the car and onto the sidewalk, muttering again, "son-of-a-bitch."

In front of him was the home of the late Marcus Espy.

Steve got out of his car and made his way through the weed-infested front yard to the porch where an orange CRIME SCENE-DO NOT ENTER tape hung limply at the top step. It had been ripped off and retied in a loose bowknot to the right corner of the handrail.

Steve stepped over the ribbon and onto the porch. He hadn't been back to the house since the discovery of Marcus Espy's body. Two uniformed police officers had been posted there in case Nathan Espy returned, but when Wednesday came around and there was still no sign of him, the officers had been reassigned. Steve knew that several squad cars had been assigned to do periodic drive-bys throughout the day, but at the moment, the house was empty and unguarded.

Steve was glad to find the front door locked. He examined the deadbolt, then reached into the breast pocket of his coat and removed a small silver key ring. Dangling from it were six thin strips of metal of varying sizes. Steve chose two, slipped them from the ring then slipped the rest back into his pocket. Satisfied that none of the neighbors was watching him, Steve slipped the picks into the deadbolt.

In less than ten seconds, Steve was inside the house, the deadbolt once again secure.

Not much was different from the previous Monday. Except for the bags of marijuana that had been removed, the living room was the same garbage-strewn mess. Steve made his way toward the hallway that would take him to Nathan's bedroom. As he passed the entrance to the cellar, he paused for a moment, laying the palm of his right hand against the door. Partly out of frustration, partly out of exhaustion, he closed his eyes and leaned his bulk against the door. In his mind's eye he could see Marcus Espy's bloated corpse hanging from the water pipe.

Then Marcus was standing in the middle of the cellar. His eyes staring straight ahead. He made his way to the steps, a line of maggots trailing behind him like the wake of a ship. He started up the stairs, one step then another. The eyes burning. Another step and he would be at the door. Another step and . . .

Steve's head jerked back as his eyes flew open. "Oh Jesus," he said, wiping the back of his hand across his forehead. Can't fall asleep now, he told himself.

Forcing the image of Marcus Espy out of his head, Steve pushed himself away from the door and headed to Nathan's bedroom. Like the living room, it too was in the same condition as on Monday. Only the bloodstained baseballs and a polyester uniform top from the Tasty Cone had been removed. Everything else was exactly as Nathan had left it.

Steve went to the bed and sat down. All around him thousands of blank eyes stared back from the walls and ceiling.

Steve looked about the room at the baseball cards. It must have taken the kid a week to cut and paste that many copies of his photograph onto the cards. It was a serious undertaking, and Nathan handled it fairly well.

But why ruin your entire collection of cards?

"Come on, Nathan. Give me something here."

But none of the thousands of Nathan Espy faces was giving an inch. They all stared back with the same blank eyes and crooked grin, mocking him, daring Steve to discover their secret.

But Steve wasn't going to give up. He trained his eyes on a group of cards directly in front of the bed. Besides their matching faces, they all were shots of batters in mid-swing. "In-action cards," they were called.

Sluggers, Steve realized as he examined the cards. Albert Belle, Barry Bonds, Mark McGwire, Roy Hobbes.

Steve laughed out loud. "I must be getting punchy," he said. Roy Hobbes was that guy Robert Redford played in that movie, The Natural. It was one of Steve's favorite movies, that and the other baseball movie. The one with Kevin Costner.

Field of Dreams.

Steve bolted off the bed. "That's it, isn't it you little shit." He moved to the wall, running his hand across the in-action shots. "You were putting yourself in them, weren't you, Nathan? Putting yourself in your dreams."

Steve inched closer to the wall. "That's it, you nut." Steve leaned forward, his nose nearly scraping a 96 Topps Barry Bonds/Nathan Espy. "You think you're really one of them, don't you?"

The face on the card said nothing.

Steve looked closer at the card. Bonds was in his patented post-home-run stance eyeing the ball as it flew somewhere beyond the left field wall. Behind him, a blurred sea of fans were on their feet, all staring off at that spot outside the card, following the path of the ball.

Steve gasped. Not everyone in the card was looking toward the fences. One man, his face no larger than the head of a pin, was staring straight ahead.

Straight at Steve.

Steve blinked hard and refocused his gaze, however, nothing changed. A thin, bald man in a black suit stood out in perfect clarity amid the thousands of blurred images captured on the card. His face peered out from just over Bonds's right shoulder. Even that minuscule, Steve could see his high forehead and angular jaw that jutted out from beneath his stern frown. And his eyes.

They were pinpricks of white, just like Espy's.

Steve stumbled backward, not able to take his eyes off of the man in the black suit. But the further Steve moved back, the more the man seemed to grow in stature behind Bonds's back. The face grew, magnifying until it blotted out the rest of the crowd.

When Steve felt the back of his legs brush against the side of Espy's bed, he stopped. At the same time the face in the card stopped growing.

But then the stern frown wavered and broke into a perfect imitation of Nathan Espy's crooked smile.

Steve screamed and felt himself falling . . .

. . . diving?

. . . into the water.

It was cold and black, but he wasn't afraid. His strong arms cut a path in front of him, propelling him forward even as the pressure in his chest urged him to break the surface and head up for air. Instead, he pushed on, farther into the blackness. When he could no longer ignore his body's need for oxygen, Steve pushed his arms down, sending his body upward. One more push and his head cut through the wet darkness to the bright sunlight of the surface.

Forty yards away on the river's shore, his friends, Larry Mizell and Ben Hazleton, were cheering. "A minute," Larry yelled. "You were under for over a minute!"

Steve let out a whoop and slapped at the dirty water in front of him. It was the longest he had ever been able to stay under water. And just about every warm day for the last two summers, ever since he turned thirteen, Steve Wyckoff had been coming down to the river near old man Radaken's boat dock to swim and see how long he could stay under water. And now he finally hit the minute mark. Not even Terry could do that.

But it didn't seem like a minute. It seemed more like a few seconds. He had just enough time to dive in and think about . . .

. . . baseball?

Yeah, that was it. He was thinking about baseball, and then he surfaced. It didn't seem like he was under water more than ten seconds. But Larry had the stopwatch, and Larry said it was a minute.

"Beat that," Steve yelled to his friends.

Larry and Ben remained at the river's edge, laughing and cheering. Steve knew they wouldn't try. Neither of them had the balls to swim this far out, and though Larry was pretty good at holding his breath, he never came close to a minute. The only kid Steve knew who could do that was Merrill Toth and he . . .

. . . was dead.

Steve shook his head, sending droplets of filthy river water flying. What was he thinking? Merrill Toth wasn't dead. Where did he get that idea? Steve had just seen him the other day working on his old man's Fairlane.

"Come on back," he heard Ben cry out. Only his voice sounded as if it was in some far away tunnel. "Come back."

Steve made a movement toward the riverbank.

"Whoah," he stammered.

He was now twice the distance from the shore he was a moment ago. This ain't right, his teenage mind told him. He couldn't have drifted this far out.

Steve stayed calm. He brought his arms forward and began doing an easy, deliberate breaststroke. Though he could feel the tug of the current running beneath his torso, he was in no trouble. Hell, it wasn't that far to shore. He started swimming faster, all the while keeping his eyes trained on Larry and Ben.

His two best friends. He was glad they were there. After all it wouldn't be much longer until Larry would head off to college and settle out in Wyoming with that girl he married. And Ben. Well Ben never really had his shit together. He was going to kill himself on Christmas day in 1979. No one ever knew why.

"Look at that," Larry called out, his hands cupped around his mouth like a megaphone. When Steve stopped his approach, Larry took his right hand from the side of his mouth and pointed to the sky.

No, not the sky, the bridge.

"There," he yelled. "Over there."

Steve's eyes followed the path of Larry's finger to the bridge. A woman was standing on the outside of the guardrail. A long thin . . .

. . . snake

. . . rope in her hand. She was waving at Steve.

"Hi Steve."

Steve waved back, not sure what else he could do. Beneath him the gentle tug of the current was starting to intensify.

"The devil made me do it," the woman shouted from the bridge. Only her voice was that of a man. A guy who used to be a friend of Terry's named Bobby Monero.

"The devil made me do it."

The woman jumped.

And Steve got sucked beneath the water.

Actually, he had just stopped treading water, too surprised at what was happening on the bridge. His head slipped beneath the surface of the river for a second, then he popped back out. By that time though, the woman's body had already hit the water. Her head though was hovering about sixty feet above the river.

"Wonderful view, Steve," she said. "You ought to take a look."

From the bank of the river, Steve heard his friends cheering just as they had done when he stayed under water for a minute. Steve began to shout for them, but when he saw the pair, he stopped.

They weren't his friends. They were two other kids. Kids he didn't hang out with.

"Come on in," Nathan Espy called. The other boy, the bigger one, Curtis Mayflower, said nothing. He just glared out across the water at Steve.

No, Steve's mind wailed. He can't go back to that side of the river. Those kids were trouble, they were . . .

. . . wanted for murder

Steve pivoted in the water and started toward the bank on the west side of the river, about a hundred yards away. He could do that. No problem. He switched from the breaststroke and started the sidestroke. Not much farther, he thought. A minute, that's all. A minute's swim. Hell, he could do it underwater.

The murky water of the Youghioghany began to grow choppy. It lapped up against Steve's face, slapping against his cheeks and eyes. Steve swam harder, trying to keep his head above water, but the water swelled beneath his chin, rising up to fill his nose. He started to gag when the water slapped at his body again, this time knocking him sideways. He couldn't go on; the choppy surf was too much.

Kicking with all his might, Steve pushed his torso above the reach of the river. For a moment the upper half of his body was fully extended in the warm, June air. Steve greedily swallowed as much air as his lungs could hold, then he plunged back beneath the river's surface. Back into the cold darkness.

Once underwater Steve pushed. One stroke, then two.

There was little current here to fight. In fact, it seemed to Steve that he was being gently pushed toward the shore. More at ease, he opened his eyes and peered into the murky blackness.

Only it wasn't all black. Below him a pale, yellow light glowed. Steve stopped swimming to look. Immediately he began to sink.

As he did, the light brightened until it looked like a white fire beneath the water's surface. Steve kicked wildly, trying to halt his descent. But for all his struggling, the most he could do was stop his body from sinking any further. He was stuck, ten feet below the surface of the river and God knows how far above the fire below him.

Steve looked directly into the light beneath him. Something was inside it, a dark shape emerging from its depths. Something was swimming upward.

Not something. Someone.

Steve tried to scream but when he opened his mouth, a rush of river swill flowed into it, choking him. He stopped kicking. There was no use struggling now. The river won this time. "Okay," he said beneath the water, the word echoing in his ears. Swimming out of the light came a man in a black suit. He was right below Steve now. Close enough that if Steve reached out he could touch him.

When the last of Steve's air gave out, the man lifted his head upward. It was Steve's brother Terry. Only this wasn't the Terry that Steve remembered. This wasn't the young, handsome Terry who used to play catch with his little brother in the backyard, or the Terry who taught Steve to play pinball down at Dutch's Bar.

Swimming toward Steve were the charred remains of what was left of Terry after the accident in the mill.

And he was grinning, a sly, crooked smile.

And he had no eyes.

Then he grabbed Steve's ankle . . .

. . . steering wheel?

Steve jerked forward, his chest smacking into the steering wheel of his Ford Taurus. *That hurt*, his mind registered. That hurt like hell.

Steve's eyes flew open. For a second the smell of oily water was fresh in his nostrils, but when he saw the dust-covered dashboard of his car, he was able to gain his bearings. "Jesus," he exhaled. It had been a dream. He had fallen asleep in his car and had dreamt the whole thing.

But that wasn't right. The last thing he remembered was looking at the baseball cards in Nathan Espy's room. And then he saw something in the Barry Bonds card. A face.

A face with no eyes.

What the hell was going on? He shouldn't be in the car; he should be in Espy's bedroom. How did he get back here? Steve turned to look out the window. In front of him was Marcus Espy's home, the CRIME SCENE tape still slung across the handrail of the porch steps.

But before Steve could make sense of what happened, his cell phone went off. Steve fumbled through his jacket, pulling the phone out on the fourth ring. "Wyckoff," he barked into the receiver. A voice stammered a message on the other end of the line. "Trouble at the station. Get here immediately."

The line went dead before Steve could respond. He tossed the phone onto the passenger seat then turned over the ignition and threw the car in gear. But before he sped off, he took one last look at the porch.

Someone had left the door open.

Chapter Fifteen: June 30

At first the pain was unbearable, but now in the cool darkness surrounding him, Curtis Mayflower was free of his previous agony. He didn't know where he was, but he was certain that he was outside; soft blades of grass pressed against his forearms and the back of his neck. And even though his eyes were opened, the darkness was all encompassing; there was nothing for him to see, no stars, no trees, nothing.

Curtis couldn't remember much of what happened after Espy picked him up in front of The Oaks. He was taken to a house on the north side of town. That Curtis knew for sure. And there was someone else there; he was certain that he heard several voices. And then came the pinprick and a warm sensation filling his veins.

And with it, the sweet darkness.

No pain, Curtis's mind hummed. I don't care where I am, just as long as there's no pain. Just as long as . . .

Just as long as that thing in the car didn't eat him.

Curtis shuddered. It had been one hell of a hallucination, that thing that looked like an octopus with a shark's mouth snapping at him from the back of his car. That was every bit as bad as the pain in his ripped up leg.

He had fucked up. Espy told him that. He fucked up, and Coach was pissed.

Coach.

He's called Dust. That's what Keyes said.

Curtis breathed in the night air, tasting a faint trace of dew. He would stay here, he decided. Stay here in the darkness and leave all the pain behind. To hell with Espy and Coach. He was finished with it. Finished with the lot of them.

And then the sun snapped on like a giant electric bulb obliterating the night with a million watts of piercing, white light. Curtis screamed and rolled over onto his stomach, his palms pressed tightly over his face. When the initial wave of pain subsided, Curtis cautiously lowered his right hand from his eye. When the light no longer stung, he removed his other hand and pushed himself to a kneeling position. "Holy shit," he said when he recognized where he was.

Right on top of the fifty-yard marker.

From a PA system a tinny voice blared out his name. "And starting as quarterback for the New Hampshire Bandits, McKeesport Pennsylvania's favorite son, Curtissss Mayflowerrr!!"

The last syllable of Curtis's name echoed against the stadium's forty thousand empty seats. Er-er-er-er. It reverberated between both ends of the stadium. But instead of dissipating, the echo grew louder and faster until it melted into one harsh metallic whine. Like the roar of a chainsaw, the noise sliced through the empty stadium, gaining momentum as it resonated through the upper deck until it blasted away the top three rows of seats.

Still on his knees, Curtis flung his head backward and shouted, "Stop it!"

The roar immediately ceased, replaced by the sound of a single pair of hands clapping. No longer in the middle of the field, Curtis found himself standing in front of the home-team bench, only a dozen feet from the first row of bleacher seats. Coach was sitting in the third row.

"Hello, Curtis." Coach continued to clap, but the sound that was coming from his hands no longer sounded like applause. Each time his palms smacked against each other, Curtis heard a child scream.

"Please," Curtis said, taking a wary step in Coach's direction. "Please don't do that."

"Certainly." Coach paused before slapping his hands together again. This time there was no sound as flesh hit flesh. "Is that better?"

"Yes," Curtis said weakly. "Thank you." Staring at the thin man in the third row, Morris Keyes's words came to the front of Curtis's mind. His name is Dust.

"That's right. Dust is one of the names I have been called. It is appropriate." Dust continued his silent clapping. Each time his hands came together, Curtis flinched. "Is the absence of sound not to your liking now, Curtis?" Dust threw his hands into the air and shook his head. "You are a particularly hard person to please. First you want this, and then you want that. Isn't that true, Curtis? You being a hard person to please."

"Where am I?" Curtis stammered. "What is all this?"

Dust sighed and rose to his feet. "Obviously, Curtis, you are here in this fine stadium. But . . . " Dust paused and stepped to the second row of bleachers. Curtis instinctively took a step backward, but as he did, he found his body sliding forward, halving the distance between himself and the man he knew as Coach.

"But we both know that you're really not here, don't we, Curtis? We both know that you are unconscious, sprawled out on the floor of an abandoned house. We both know that your eye has been plucked out, and that you were defeated by that decrepit old man and the woman. We both know that you should be dead right now. But you're not. Instead, you're here. Now how is that? How is it that you can be here and there at the same time?"

"Because you want me here." Curtis accepted that as the only explanation. Regardless of how realistic this dream was, he knew his body was laying on a cold basement floor in some condemned shack that Espy had dragged him to the previous night. And though he could feel no pain, deep within his consciousness he detected a dull, foreign pulse beating behind his eye. And Curtis knew that when he did wake up, he would do so screaming.

Satisfied with Curtis's answer, Dust lowered himself back onto the bleacher. "I am impressed," he said. "You do have some understanding."

Curtis nodded. "I'm dreaming this, ain't I? Just like I dreamt up all the chicks that came and screwed me. They were never there. They were all in my head."

"Does it matter?" Dust replied. "Didn't you get pleasure from their visits? Didn't they please you, leave you satisfied with the most beautiful of memories? So what if they came to you in your dreams?"

"Because that ain't real," Curtis shouted. "None of this is real. This is nothing but some kind of sick, drug hallucination. You," Curtis said, jabbing a finger at Dust, "you ain't real. And you ain't shit."

Dust swung his hands together creating a sound like a shotgun blast. At the same time, Curtis felt a sharp object slam into his chest sending him backwards over the bench. Twisting, he fell face first onto the hard ground, the impact knocking his breath out of him. Behind him Dust's voice thundered over the stadium's PA system.

"I could have brought you here every night. I could have filled this place with thousands of people whose sole purpose for being would have been to worship your pitiful existence. I would have made you a god in your own dreams. But you failed me. You could not destroy one pathetic, old man. One weak, insignificant man!"

Curtis lifted himself off the ground and wheeled about. "If you're so fucking hot, why can't you take care of him? Huh? If Morris Keyes is so insignificant, why can't you kill him?"

His fists clenched at his side, Curtis started back toward the bleachers. "That's because you can't, can you? That's why. You tried fucking with him before and that old bastard kicked your ass. That's it, isn't it? You tried to get into his head like you're doing with me, and he fucking kicked the shit out of you!" Curtis moved directly in front of Dust. "What did he do, huh? Did he grab your skinny neck and bitch-slap those white, bug eyes back into your head?"

Curtis grabbed the handrail of the first row of bleachers and hoisted himself up. There was only six feet separating him from Dust. "I'll wake up and that will be the end of this," Curtis growled. "But dream or no dream, right now I'm going to kick the living piss out of you."

He leapt over the first row of bleachers, but as he did, Dust vanished, leaving Curtis grasping at empty air.

"Fool."

Curtis spun around expecting to see Dust behind him, but when he looked up he saw the giant scoreboard at the north end of the field where an enormous image of Dust's face was being broadcast. His gaze was immediately drawn into the empty sockets that were Dust's eyes. Only now, a hazy speck of blackness floated deep inside of them. As Curtis stared, the speck grew and began to take on a shape.

"You will go nowhere when you wake," Curtis heard Dust say as the shape grew recognizable. It was a man.

No, two men. Two men standing at the foot of a flight of stairs.

"Your home," Dust announced over the PA system.

Two teenagers were standing at the back entrance of Curtis's apartment house. The figure on the left was Nathan Espy. The other was Fredo Torach. With one skinny arm planted in the middle of Fredo's back, Espy lifted him off the ground and started up the steps to Curtis's apartment. There was no hesitation in Nathan's steps, no awkward fumbling with his heavy load. When he reached the top, Espy put his hand against the door and pushed it open. Stepping inside, Espy's hand accidentally slipped from Fredo's back, and the bigger teen fell to the floor. When he landed, Fredo flopped onto his side, and Curtis got a good look at his face. It reminded Curtis of something he had seen in an old television commercial. He wasn't sure what the commercial was for, all he could remember was these oversized raisins dancing on some dinner table. Their faces were all purple and shriveled, but they were sporting sunglasses and having a good time, just happy as shit to be raisins. That's what Fredo's face reminded Curtis of, one of those happy, singing raisins.

Only Fredo wasn't wearing any sunglasses. Instead, his eyes dangled from their sockets, resting against the bloated, purple sides of his cheek. Only two thin strands of nerves kept them from detaching and rolling down the steps. Fredo's nose had been pushed back into his face until all that was left of it was a small, round hump. Directly below it, half of Fredo's upper-lip was peeled away from his mouth revealing the broken remnants of what used to be the top row of Fredo's teeth.

Below that there was nothing left of the young man's face.

With deliberate speed, Espy reached down and grabbed a handful of Fredo's shirt. He pulled, and the hefty teenager began to float upward. Espy lifted him waist high then led him deeper into Curtis's apartment.

From the scoreboard Dust blinked and the scene vanished, replaced by the white void of his enormous eyes. "That's what awaits you in the waking world."

Curtis screamed and the blazing stadium lights went dead. Only now, the contentment he originally felt in the darkness was replaced with an insane dread that left him quaking. "No," he whimpered. "I want to wake up. I want to wake up."

The stadium lights flickered on and Curtis once again found himself on the fifty-yard line. But now the stadium was full to capacity. In each of its seats sat Dust.

The voice of Dust thundered across the field. "It was applause you wanted. Accolades. Well here. Enjoy."

The stadium exploded in a cacophony of sound as forty thousand Dusts jumped to their feet and began clapping. They whooped and hooted in a pitched frenzy, their hands coming together so fast that Curtis couldn't see them. All he could make out was a blur in front of their chests that hung like quivering trails of smoke. And each time their hands touched, the sounds of screaming children filled the stadium.

Curtis stumbled backward, desperately trying to block out the sound. He jammed his fingers into his ears, shoving them so far that he could feel their tips scraping against his eardrums. But that did nothing to dim the noise. It came from all around him. An amalgamation of all the sounds of pain and terror that have ever escaped a human throat. It poked against him like a thousand iron fingers, each jab opening a tiny crack in his skull.

Curtis could feel his sanity leaking out the tiny fissure in his brain.

"This is your future. Each night when you sleep, when you

dream, I will bring you to this place. And each night it will be worse than the last."

Curtis nodded. It was all so obvious now.

He was in hell.

Chapter Sixteen: June 30

A few minutes after his meeting with the mayor, Steve strolled through the parking lot adjacent to City Hall and slipped unnoticed into his car. The mayor was royally pissed off, and considering the events of the last twenty-four hours, Steve couldn't blame her. Since yesterday, a cop had snapped and tried to shoot a statue, Linda Cavanaugh had been kidnapped, and Mrs. Smith was threatening to sue the city, the police department, and anyone else she could think of.

"Three days before we kick off the biggest economic revitalization project in the city's history, this happens," the mayor said, tossing the morning edition of The Daily News at Steve. The headline, in bold letters, announced: SHOOTING AT CITY HALL. Steve didn't read the accompanying article, his eyes were fixed on the photograph of Fredo Torach in the right hand corner of the page. It showed a smiling, handsome young man with wavy brown hair. In smaller bold type, the headline read: MISSING YOUTH SLAIN. Relegated to the lower left corner, but still front-page news, was a story about the disappearance of Linda Smith-Cavanaugh.

"Have you read this yet? Murder, kidnapping, and a cop going berserk on the front page. I got a call from the governor this morning, Steve. He said he has some reservations about appearing at the marina dedication. Can you believe that? I had to personally guarantee his safety before he'd agree to come." Carolyn flopped herself into her chair and slammed the palms of her hands against the desk in an uncharacteristic show of anger. It got Steve's attention. "And now Denise Smith is threatening to sic her pack of lawyers on the city. Goddamn it, Steve. What the hell is going on here?"

Steve wished he could offer up some kind of answer, some semi-rational explanation for why his hometown seemed to be going bug shit all of a sudden. But he'd been off the mark with his assessment of Gary, and in all likelihood, screwed up by refusing to connect Marcus Espy's death with the drugs he found, so it was a safe bet that his opinion didn't mean jack-shit to the mayor right now.

"First off," the mayor continued, her voice growing calm and business-like. "Gary Overton is history. As soon as he shows up, he's gone. There will be no mention of the shooting, but he'll take an extended leave of absence which will be followed by his resignation."

Steve nodded in agreement. What the mayor was proposing was in the best interest of both the city and Gary, but that fact didn't lessen the guilt Steve felt concerning his friend. Something had snapped in Gary, and deep down, Steve felt that he should shoulder some of the blame.

"Next. And this is a priority. I've ordered the chief to have every officer this city has at the marina dedication. The governor made me guarantee his safety and that is exactly what is going to happen." Carolyn pointed to the newspaper. "The only exceptions are to be you and whoever else you need to find Nathan Espy."

Carolyn removed her glasses and brought her hand to her face. With thumb and forefinger, she began to massage her tired eyes. Steve could see faint trace patterns of brown rings blushing through her flesh-toned make-up. When she looked back at Steve and spoke, her voice softened. "How's Merilee?" she asked.

"Fine. I brought her home from the hospital yesterday. She was cranky, but tired. Slept most of the night."

"I'm glad. And you're convinced that the guy who attacked

Merilee is mixed up with Nathan Espy, and that the two are responsible for killing that Torach boy?"

Steve didn't hesitate to answer. "Positive."

"Then find them," Carolyn said, her voice taking on its former sharp edge. "Do whatever it takes, but find them and stop them. Stop them permanently." Carolyn didn't give Steve a chance to reply. She snapped her glasses back on her head and told McKeesport's senior detective that the meeting was over.

Steve didn't argue.

***

Now, as he sat in the driver's seat of his Taurus smoking his tenth Marlboro, Steve had to admit that yesterday had been a hell of a day.

When Steve got the call that there was trouble at the police station, he paid little attention to the excited voice on the other end of the line. He was too busy wondering how he got from Nathan Espy's bedroom to the car. However, Steve did hear Gary's name mentioned before the cell phone lost the connection. That was enough to snap Steve back to his senses.

When he arrived at City Hall, he wasn't prepared for the circus that greeted him. Two squad cars were parked at the Josslin Bridge, stopping all traffic from entering or leaving the city. Six more were lined up in front of City Hall, their dome lights on and their blinkers flashing. A dozen uniform officers flanked the front entrance to City Hall while three groups of four officers were stationed at the remaining entrances to the building. Steve pulled up beside the row of squad cars, flicked on his blinkers and got out of his vehicle in a hurry.

He jogged across the grassy lawn in front of City Hall toward the phalanx of officers. Seeing Steve approach, one of the officers, Leslie Randell, a veteran of nine years, broke from the group and hurried toward him.

"Jesus Christ," Steve said as he neared Leslie. "What is going on?"

Leslie didn't answer until they were side by side. And then, her tone was hushed. "Somebody tried to assassinate the mayor," she whispered. "Just a few minutes ago. Tried to shoot her."

Steve couldn't believe what he was hearing. "Who the hell would want to kill the mayor?" Steve looked about at the row of police officers in front of him. They all wore the same grim expression. "Are you sure?"

Leslie shrugged. "That's what I heard. Bressler wants us to make sure no one goes in or out."

Steve frowned. "Thanks, Leslie. Where's Bressler now?"

"I'm not sure. Bullpen, I think. Either that or the mayor's office."

Steve headed toward the west side entrance, the one that led directly to the Police Department. When he got inside, he headed straight for the detective's room. The door was ajar, but when he poked his head inside, it was empty. "Bressler," he called out. "Where are you?"

A few seconds later Randy Bressler's voice echoed down the hall.

"Wyckoff, is that you?"

"Yeah."

"We're in your office."

Steve hurried to his office to find Assistant Chief Bressler with two uniformed officers, all looking out the window. "Where's the mayor?" Steve asked as he entered the room. "Is she alright?"

An uncomfortable look passed between the three police officers. The two uniforms, Hank Lydel and Warren Turvel lowered their eyes slightly as Randy Bressler proceeded to explain the situation.

"The mayor is fine," he said. "She's upstairs trying to keep a lid on this."

Steve moved closer to the three officers. Still, only Bressler would look him in the eye. "What's going on?"

"It's Gary," Bressler said. "Lydel and Turvel heard him shouting from your office about twenty minutes ago, then shots were fired. They came in and Gary was hanging out the window shooting at the statue."

Steve turned to the uniformed officers. "He was what?"

"We only saw him take one shot," Hank Lydel said. "And when we came in, he wasn't in the window yet. He was sprawled out on the floor here." Lydel made a sweeping motion in front of him. "But as soon as we got in the room, he jumped up and ran toward the window like he wanted to get out it. He was screaming and yelling, saying 'die you son-of-a-bitch.' Then he took off. Nearly knocked me on my ass as he went through the door."

Steve glanced over Lydel's shoulder toward the statue. "He told the statue to die?" Steve asked incredulously.

Both Turvel and Lydel nodded uncomfortably. "Called it a fucker too," Turvel added.

Bressler held up his hand. "I think Steve's got the idea, Warren." Officer Turvel didn't argue, he just let Bressler continue. "After that, Gary came running out into the hall waving his gun in the air. That's when all hell broke loose. No one was sure of what was going on, but all of a sudden, everybody got their guns drawn and were tearing around the building. No one knows where Gary got off to, but by the time Turvel here tracked me down and told me what happened, we had one full-scale cluster-fuck on our hands."

Steve took a step back from the other officers and leaned against his desk. It had been nearly thirty-six hours since he'd gotten any sleep, and it showed. Deep, dark rings circled his blood-shot eyes, and it was all he could do to keep them open.

Randy Bressler put his right hand on Steve's shoulder. "You look like hell buddy."

"I feel like shit," Steve replied.

Randy nodded sympathetically. "I know it's a lousy time, but I have to ask. Was Gary having some kind of problems the rest of us didn't know about? Drugs? A woman? Anything that might have made him lose it?"

"I don't know, Randy," Steve confessed. "I just don't know anymore."

Bressler started to ask Steve if he knew what Gary did when off duty when the sound of shouting came from the hall. "Oh, what is it now?" Bressler fumed, making his way to the door. Lydel and Turvel followed him out with Steve lagging a few steps behind.

201

When he got into the hall, Steve saw two police officers wrestling a large man to the floor. Steve's view was partially obscured by the men in front of him, but from the shouting and cursing, he could tell the cops weren't having much success in subduing the intruder. Lydel and Turvel bolted past Randy Bressler and were about to join in the melee when Steve got a clear look at the man who had forced his way into the building.

"Cavanaugh!" Steve shouted. "What are you doing?"

At the sound of Steve's voice, David stopped struggling. However, the two police officers trying to restrain him took the opportunity to overpower the larger man and force him to the floor. David thudded to the floor as one of the cops jammed his knee into the small of his back.

"Stop it," Steve shouted. He pushed past Lydel and Turvel and pulled the cop off David's back. "Get off of him." The police officer looked at Bressler who also told him to move.

"You two," Bressler barked. "Get back outside and make sure no one else comes in here." The assistant chief turned to Turvel. "Warren, will you and Hank please make sure that happens."

As the four uniformed officers made their way to the exit, Bressler reached down and helped Steve lift David off the floor. "You're Henry Smith's son-in-law, aren't you?" Bressler asked when David was on his feet.

David nodded, still panting from having his wind knocked out of him.

"You'd still better have a damn good explanation for forcing your way in here," Bressler said.

"I do," David managed to spit out between gasps. Reaching into his shirt pocket, he turned toward Steve. "It's Linda," he said. "She's missing." David pulled his hand away from his pocket. "I found this on her pillow."

Both Steve and Bressler felt the color drain from their faces as David showed them a baseball card with Nathan Espy's face on it.

It took David less than a minute to give Steve the specifics of Linda's disappearance. The night before, Linda said she was very tired and didn't want to be disturbed, so she asked David to sleep in one of the guest rooms. Linda had made the same request on two other occasions, so David wasn't surprised. The next morning when David went to the room to see if she wanted any breakfast, he became concerned when Linda didn't answer his calls. The door wasn't locked, so he went inside only to find the room empty.

"That's when I found the baseball card," he said.

As David recounted the events of the morning, Steve stared at the baseball card. Another Nathan Espy Special. This one, however, was particularly special.

It was a 1996 John Smoltz with the face of the Brave's pitcher replaced by that of Nathan. But unlike the others, the alterations to the card were not limited to the face. Espy had covered the pitcher's mound and infield with a collage of human faces. Each was meticulously pasted to the card, creating the effect that Espy was standing on a patchwork quilt of human flesh. The faces were turned toward the pitcher, each one projecting an image of unimaginable agony. Most of the pictures were of screaming children.

Behind the pitcher, what should have been the outfield of Atlanta's Fulton County Stadium had been replaced by a picture of a bombed-out city. A wall of fire engulfed the rubble and broken remains of several large buildings. The flames flared out from the background and licked at the perimeter of the pitcher's mound making the tortured faces at the pitcher's feet look as if they were being burned.

Steve placed the baseball card in the middle of his desk. "We have to go back to your mother-in-law's house," he told David. "There may be more evidence there." Steve looked toward Bressler who nodded in agreement.

"That would be for the best," Bressler said. "Get out of this zoo. Take two of the uniforms with you. Then call Rhonda at the lab and tell her to get her people to the Smith house." Turning toward David, Bressler offered a brief apology for the incident in the hallway. "But I assure you we will find your wife," he added, shooting Steve a quick, sideways glance. "Now go."

Steve opened the office door and ushered David out, but as Steve was exiting, Bressler held up a cautionary finger. "You stay focused on finding Mrs. Cavanaugh," he whispered. "I'll find

Gary."

"Right," Steve said quickly, though he knew it would be nearly impossible for him not to worry about his partner.

When David and Steve arrived at the Smith home, Mrs. Smith was standing on the porch. With her stern countenance, and arms held stiffly at her side, she looked like an MP on guard duty. As Steve and David hurried to the porch, Mrs. Smith didn't budge. "You're not needed here, Detective Wyckoff." Though she addressed Steve, her eyes were fixed on her son-in-law. They burned with an undisguised hatred. "This is a family matter."

David was about to speak, but Steve stopped him. Making his way to the bottom step, Steve addressed Mrs. Smith slowly and calmly, but he left no doubt that he was not going to be intimidated. "I understand how you feel, Mrs. Smith, but this is a police matter. From what David told me, your daughter's disappearance may have something to do with an individual who is already wanted in connection with two murders. If that's the case, Linda could be in great danger. So if you would please step aside, I need to go in the house."

Mrs. Smith folded her arms tightly against her chest, glaring at Steve with the same naked hatred she directed toward David. "No," she said defiantly. "You do not have a warrant to go into my house, and I refuse to give you permission."

Whether it was because he was exhausted or his degree of tolerance had simply been pushed past its limit, Steve was hit with a sudden urge to slug Henry Smith's widow across the chops. He bounded up the steps. "I'm tired of your shit, lady," he said, brushing past her. "I got a job to do."

David left a stunned Denise Smith alone on the porch and followed Steve into the house. "Linda's room," Steve said when the two were inside. Without hesitating, David started up the steps with Steve in tow. On the front porch, Mrs. Smith was yelling at the two uniformed officers who had just arrived.

"This is it," David said as the pair came to the bedroom's open doorway. Not entering, David pointed to the far end of the bed.

"That's where the baseball card was. Halfway tucked under the blanket just below the pillow."

Steve stepped into the room and asked David if he'd touched anything since removing the card.

"No, I don't think so."

"Good." Steve glanced about the large room. "Stay here," he ordered. "I don't want this area disturbed any more than it has been. That means not touching anything or even walking on the carpet. Okay?"

David nodded and reluctantly remained just outside the doorway. For his part, Steve gingerly stepped around the bed, bending over to examine a crease or a fold in the blankets, but all the while touching nothing. After his cursory examination he returned to David. "Are you sure you didn't touch anything except the baseball card?"

David was about to answer when Rhonda Hemmings called out from the stairway. "Steve, which one are you in?"

"In here. Second door on the left."

Still sporting her lab coat, Rhonda slipped past David and into the room carrying a black doctor's bag. "Espy again?" she asked. Steve nodded.

Just as Steve had done, Rhonda took a quick look about the room before fishing out a pair of latex gloves from the pocket of her lab coat. "What happened?"

Steve gave Rhonda a quick rundown of the situation, pausing to let David give his account of finding the baseball card. As the two brought Rhonda up to speed, Carl and another technician from the forensic lab waited at the top of the stairs. Once Rhonda gave them the go ahead, they would come in and do a complete sweep of the room.

When David finished, the pathologist frowned. "So Mrs. Smith was still here when you left." She looked to Steve, the frown growing deeper. "How do we know she didn't touch anything?" Rhonda cast a backward glance over her left shoulder. "I don't think we're going to get a lot of cooperation from her. She's down there raising Cain with your officers right now. When I came in she said she was going to sue me."

Rhonda snapped the palm of her glove against her skin, a sure sign she was ready to work. "You're keeping me too damn busy, Wyckoff." She turned from the two men and motioned for her team to follow her into the bedroom. Without looking back at Steve, she told him to make sure that she wasn't interrupted.

"Will do," Steve said, ushering David from the room. "Come on."

Steve and David had no sooner reached the top of the stairs than Mrs. Smith started shouting again. "Get these people out of my house this instant. You have no right to be here."

Flanked on either side of the woman was a uniformed police officer. They were there to make sure Mrs. Smith didn't interfere with Rhonda and her team, though they wisely refrained from physically restraining her.

"We have every right to be here," Steve said as he began to descend the stairs. "That man's wife may have been kidnapped. And that means a felony may have been committed in this house. And that means you're either going to cooperate, or I'm going to have these officers haul your ass to jail." Steve was on the third from the last step, about ten feet from Mrs. Smith. One of the officers raised a guarded arm in front of the woman, but Mrs. Smith didn't move.

"How dare you speak to me that way," she said, her eyes narrowing to slits. "If it wasn't for my husband you'd be nothing. He saw to it that you were promoted. He bought it for you."

So there it was, the dirty little secret about Steve Wyckoff that anyone who had put on the uniform of the McKeesport Police in the last twenty years knew. The secret that no one gave a shit about anymore was finally out in the open. Steve couldn't help but laugh.

"Ancient history," he shot back. "I don't owe you or your husband a goddamn thing." He stormed past Mrs. Smith and the two uniformed cops. As he did, detective Mike Covey came through the front door and into the grand foyer. Steve was relieved to see Covey; technically, Espy's attack on David Cavanaugh was still Covey's case, and the presence of another detective might help secure some degree of cooperation from Mrs. Smith.

"Bressler told me what's going on," Covey told Steve as the two huddled near the front entrance. While Covey updated Steve on the situation at City Hall, the senior detective kept one eye trained on Mrs. Smith. She hadn't moved from her spot at the base of the stairs.

"Anything on Gary?" Steve asked.

Covey shook his head. "No sign of him anywhere. It's like he vanished."

Steve cursed under his breath. There was too much happening at once. First Merilee and finding the body of Fredo Torach. Then Gary flipping out. And now Linda Cavanaugh and another Nathan Espy Special. Steve glanced toward the steps at David who still hadn't moved. A young, female police officer was standing next to him, her hand on his shoulder. David was crying.

Mike Covey took Steve by the elbow and pulled him toward the door. "Bressler wanted me to tell you to go home," Covey whispered. Steve began to protest, but Covey gripped tighter at his superior's elbow. "That's not a request. There is nothing else for you to do here." Covey shot a quick glance toward Mrs. Smith whose wrath was now directed at the officers next to her. "Besides, I don't think the lady of the house wants you around."

Steve snorted and rolled his eyes. "Tell me about it."

Perhaps if he wasn't so tired, Steve would have ignored the assistant chief's orders and remained at the Smith house. But exhaustion had set in hours ago. His entire body ached and he felt himself becoming increasingly disoriented. Plus there was Merilee. He was supposed to pick her up in a few hours. "You're right," he conceded. "I don't think I've ever been this shit-canned in my life. Just keep me informed if anything develops. Okay?"

"No problem, Steve."

"Good."

The front door opened and two more uniformed police officers entered, followed by an earnest looking woman in a lab coat. Before the door closed again, Steve slipped out of the house, unnoticed by anyone but Mike Covey.

***

Now, sitting in the parking lot, Steve lit a new cigarette off the burnt remnants of the last one. He knew that chain smoking was about the worst habit a middle-aged, out of shape guy like him could develop, but now really wasn't the time to think about that. Steve had other things on his mind.

Harris Smith for example.

The oldest Smith child was nowhere to be found when the police began their search for Linda. It wasn't until nearly 10:00 p.m. that Harris returned home with a vague excuse about being in Pittsburgh all day. Mike Covey grilled him for almost an hour about his sister's disappearance, and to no one's surprise, Harris claimed to know nothing. However, he did ask Covey to get a message to Steve. Harris wanted to meet the senior detective the next day at noon at his father's clinic.

Steve glanced at his watch. 12:15. *So, Harris wants to talk to me*, he thought. *That would be just fine.*

The car's engine roared into life.

***

"I'm glad you came," Harris said. He was standing in front of a large picture window in what used to be his father's first-floor office. With his back to Steve, Harris looked to be admiring the impressive view of the river. "I used to come down here all the time when I was a kid and watch the barges. Sometimes I'd sneak out and go down to the side of the river and try to hit them with rocks." Harris paused and chuckled softly to himself. "I never could though. Never had the arm strength."

Steve pursed his lips and frowned. He wasn't in the mood for small talk. "You told Mike Covey you wanted to talk to me about Linda," he said coldly. "So what is it?"

Harris nodded. "Of course. Before we get to Linda I have to tell you something about my father. He was a very brilliant man, Steve, you have to remember that. But he was also very impatient, always trying to find shortcuts that might produce better results in less time. He realized that the biggest setback to Addiction

208

Personification was the scant bit that his patients could remember of their dreams. Even with lucid dreams, the holes in their memory were just too big. So my father found a way to plug those holes with a drug, a type of sedative that kicked the pituitary gland into high gear, making it produce increased amounts of hormones the body uses to repair itself. As a side effect, the clarity of the lucid dreams grew immensely."

"Yeah," Steve said. "The DK. I know about that."

A surprised, almost bemused expression came over Harris's face. "Remind me never to underestimate you again, Steve. But yes, the drug was the DK. And you can probably guess that since I neglected to tell you about this aspect of my father's A.P. treatments, the use of the DK was not totally ethical." Harris paused and offered up a weak laugh. "But it did work. In some of my father's patients the DK worked so well that they couldn't forget their dreams anymore. That's when the problems started."

"What kind of problems?"

"In some of my father's patients, the DK affected their sleep cycles so they couldn't achieve REM sleep. Instead, they got stuck in what's called Stage-4 sleep." Harris stopped and turned his attention back to the window. He waited a few moments before continuing. "It's during Stage-4 sleep that people have what's called night terrors. Do you know what that is?"

Steve told Harris that the term was vaguely familiar.

"A night terror is a rather nasty type of nightmare; they're quite common in young children actually, but anyone can have them. Typically, a person having a night terror wakes up in an extreme state of panic, sweating, convulsing, usually screaming, but with no recollection of what the dream was about. It's as if the dreams are so horrible that the brain doesn't allow the person to remember them. All the dreamer knows is that he's terrified. For some of my father's patients, the DK caused them to have repeated night terrors. Only for them, the dreams weren't forgotten. They were completely lucid, and they wouldn't go away."

Steve stopped Harris there. "Listen, Harris, I talked to Morris Keyes and he told me all about the DK. He also told me all about the legend of Dust, and Morris is under the impression that this thing from one of your old man's stories is real and is messing with his head. Now, I don't have time for all this Freddy Kreuger crap, so I'd appreciate it if you would just cut to the chase and tell me what the hell all this has to do with your sister."

Harris slumped against the back wall and nodded. "The patients who were affected by the DK shared a disturbing commonality aside from their inability to achieve REM sleep. All of them claimed that Dust was in their dreams. Of course this was because my father insisted on incorporating that stupid myth into his A.P. treatments, but several people, Morris Keyes included, became convinced that Dust was real."

Steve glared at Harris, his eye brows furrowed into tight knots. "What about Bob Monero? Did he think Dust was real?"

"Unfortunately, he was more seriously affected than anyone else. He started having hallucinations—seeing things from his dream when he was awake. That's what was happening when he tried to kill Linda."

"Shit, Harris, why the hell didn't you tell me this before!" Steve shouted, his anger at the point of boiling over.

"Because it wouldn't have done any good," Harris shot back. "What happened to Morris Keyes and Bob Monero was a fluke. Most of the people my father gave the DK to had no side effects at all. The ones who did, didn't begin to have night terrors until much later, sometimes years after they were first treated." Harris reached into his pants pocket and removed a neatly folded sheet of legal-sized paper. "Here. This is a list of the patients my father treated with the DK."

Steve took the paper and scanned down the list of familiar names.

Baxter, Marnie.

Cotton, Susie

Decorta, Gladys

Paulette, Helen.

But Steve knew her by her married name, Helen Bly. He scanned further down the list, stopping at . . .

Slaughter, Phillip.

He stopped, stunned to see the next name on the list.

"Jesus Christ," he exhaled through clenched teeth. "Your father gave that shit to his own daughter?"

Harris nodded with his eyes closed. "That's why you've got to find her."

Chapter Seventeen: June 30 continued

Rhonda Hemmings was beginning to wonder if she would ever sleep again. Since the discovery of Fredo Torach's body, she'd been working around the clock. And there would be no concessions this time, she promised herself. No caving in to the mayor's hard luck stories about the town's poor financial status. She'd put in close to sixty hours this week already and by God, her paycheck was going to show it.

Rhonda sat alone in the small forensics lab, which the city was only able to half fund. Several glossy black and white photographs of Fredo Torach were strewn about the desk in front of her.

For Rhonda it was the missing jawbone that proved the most chilling aspect of the Torach murder. The police officers and members of her team who had seen the body had been equally sickened by its condition, all horrified at the sight of the boy's incomplete face. But it was only after the autopsy when Rhonda had an opportunity to fully examine the body that she understood the full extent of what had happened to Fredo Torach.

Fredo's jaw hadn't been removed surgically; it had not been hacked off with a saw. It hadn't even been crushed with a blunt object. Fredo's jaw had been ripped off by hand. Tugged at and pulled until it had popped free from the face.

And that would have taken a lot of tugging. Hours worth.

She had no doubt that Mayflower and Espy were responsible

for the murder, but now she was convinced that the pair may have had help. During the autopsy Rhonda found deep bruises on both of Fredo's shoulders and armpits. At first she thought they were a result of the same struggle that had left the boy's wrists broken, but upon closer examination, she discovered that they were too close in size and shape to be the result of a fight. They were too uniform. And she discovered, oddly familiar.

That's when she realized how Fredo's jaw had come off. Whoever had done this had crouched over Fredo's prone body with their feet firmly planted on the dead boy's shoulders. Tugging at the jaw with both hands, the killer had pushed off with his feet in an attempt to maximize his leverage.

It would have been a time-consuming process, Rhonda knew, but an efficient use of physics.

By examining the photos of the bruises under a magnifying lens, Rhonda was able to distinguish the outline of at least three different pairs of shoes. The outlines were faint, invisible to the naked eye, but they were there.

Three pairs of shoes had been planted on Fredo's chest. Of that, Rhonda was certain.

Espy.

Mayflower.

And who?

She took a last look at the purpled shoulders then tossed the photo back onto her desk. Rubbing at her red, tired eyes, she reached for the telephone. She'd have to tell Steve that the Torach murder was taking on yet another twist. It wasn't a message she was anxious to deliver.

Rhonda started to dial Steve's extension when she caught sight of the Nathan Espy Special that was left at the Smith house. It sat atop a thin, plastic casing on the corner of her desk. Lowering the phone back into its cradle, she reached across the desk and plucked the card up. She secured it between the thumb and forefinger of her right hand and brought it within inches of her face. The image of Espy standing on top of a mound of screaming faces was grotesque. But, she had to admit, oddly compelling. An image that was almost impossible not to stare at.

213

She scanned the tortured faces that had been affixed to the pitcher's mound. It reminded her of a word from her long past days as a practicing Catholic. Golgotha, she thought. The place of the skulls. That's where Christ was crucified.

Rhonda was about to return the card to the plastic evidence envelope when a sharp pain gripped her thumb and finger like a vise. She yelped as her fingers instinctively let go of the card, but the pain in her hand intensified, spreading from the tips of her fingers into the second and third knuckles. Clutching her wounded right hand with her left, she backed away from the desk.

She started toward the exit when the baseball card on her desk began to vibrate. Ignoring the sharp pain settling in her wrist, Rhonda headed back to the desk. The baseball card was shaking, fluttering from side to side so quickly that it became a blur. It reminded Rhonda of when, as a child, she had inserted baseball cards into the spokes of her bicycle. When the wheel spun, the baseball card snapped by so fast it was almost impossible to make out the picture on the card. Now on the top of her desk, the Nathan Espy Special was vibrating as if spun from some invisible bicycle wheel. All that was missing was the plup-plup-plup sound.

Without thinking, she reached out with her wounded right hand to grab the card, but when her fingers touched the snapping piece of cardboard, another, more powerful bolt of pain ripped them. This time the agony surged past Rhonda's wrist and elbow and up to her shoulder. She screamed as her right arm whipped backward sending Rhonda face first over her desk chair and onto the floor.

Rhonda caromed off the chair and landed sideways on the floor. The feeling in her right arm was gone, replaced by a quivering numbness spreading toward her chest. The pain was unlike anything she'd ever experienced, but Rhonda couldn't take her eyes off the baseball card. Geysers of white flame poured out of the card like a fourth of July sparkler, filling the air with the heavy scent of sulfur and carbon. Some of the sparks flew across the desk hitting Rhonda on the face and neck.

Pushing against the chair with her left hand, she managed to get to her feet and pull herself away from the desk. The thought of getting the fire extinguisher flashed into Rhonda's head when the baseball card stopped vibrating. For a moment it lay still on the desk, and then to Rhonda's terrified amazement, the pitcher stepped off the mound and began to push his way out.

Espy's baseball-card-sized hands emerged from either side of the card. They gripped its sides and began to push. Rhonda could see the strain on the face of the tiny pitcher as he struggled against an enormous weight, but he seemed to be succeeding as the sides of the card began to stretch. She heard a child-like giggle coming from the desk's surface just as a dime-sized version of Nathan Espy's head popped above the two dimensional surface of the baseball card.

Screaming, Rhonda ran out of the lab before Espy could free the rest of his tiny body.

July 1

Nathan wiped away a thick layer of dirt and grime from the attic window and peered out just as the first flickering stars became visible in the reddening sky. He looked out over the dilapidated rooftops and empty homes that spanned the northern edge of McKeesport. The street below him, a twisted path of broken bricks and gravel, was lifeless. Nathan began to hum, his fingers drumming across the filthy windowpane in time.

"Nathan," a voice whispered from behind him. "Everyone's down stairs."

Nathan didn't take his eyes from the window. He was staring at a lopsided garage across the street. In fluorescent green paint, someone had sprayed REST IN PISS. Nathan chuckled, the sound in his throat too deep and dark to be coming from a sixteen-year-old boy.

Nathan turned to face Ace.

"Who is everyone?"

Ace's face registered a moment of confusion. "You know, Petey and Bib."

Nathan nodded, pleased. "And Calvin. Our fire bug is here too."

Ace grinned and shook his head. "Oh yeah. He's been downstairs working on all those fuses and shit like you told him. Got them almost done." Ace paused and shifted uncomfortably on his feet. "Curtis is still here too. But he won't come out of his room."

Another satisfied nod, then Nathan turned back to the window. Outside, a man was making his way down the gravel road. Confused, he glanced from side to side, from house to house before stopping in front of the graffiti-covered garage door. "Don't worry about Curtis, he'll come out when he's told to." Nathan rapped slightly on the window. "There's someone outside," Nathan said. "Go down stairs and bring him in."

Ace turned to go but Nathan stopped him. "The girl," he said. "Has she done what I told her to do?"

Ace slapped his hands together. "Oh yeah. She got all dressed up and left about an hour ago."

"Good. Now go downstairs and get things ready. You and the others need to get high, but first, open the door for our guest."

"Right," Ace said before navigating the dark steps that led from the attic to the second floor of the house.

Nathan turned from the window and walked to the far side of the dark attic. Below him, stretched out on a wool army blanket, was Linda Cavanaugh. Nathan looked down at the sleeping woman. "Soon," he whispered to her in the darkness.

July 2

By the time the last of the Sunday editions of The Daily News had been delivered, the minor celebrity status of Curtis Mayflower and Nathan Espy had begun to diminish. Pictures of the two had appeared on the front page of the early Saturday edition of the paper, but by the next day, their photographs had been replaced by one of a smiling Governor Hill. The subsequent story promised that the governor would be making a major announcement at the marina dedication ceremony the next day. Already, there was talk that Pennsylvania's two-term governor was going to use the marina dedication to announce his candidacy for the presidency. It was still speculation and rumor, but it was enough to make the search for Mayflower and Espy page two news.

As for Carl Northrup of Northrup Fireworks and Pyrotechnics, he'd never heard of Nathan Espy and Curtis Mayflower, and even if he had, he wouldn't have cared. Carl sat in the air-conditioned comfort of his Chevy F-10, sipping at a hot cup of Tasty Cone coffee and thumbing through the sports page. The rest of The Daily News was tossed, unread, on the floor of the truck's cab. The Georgia native scowled as he scanned the pages looking for a NASCAR update. He found page after page devoted to football and baseball, and that was fine to the burly pyrotechnician. Even the basketball and golf news proved mildly interesting. But where was the NASCAR? Carl huffed and tossed the sports section with the rest of the paper. *Shit*, he thought. *What kind of a newspaper didn't cover NASCAR?*

"Fucking Yankees," he muttered before taking another mouthful of coffee. At least the coffee was good.

Having spent all of his life in the deep south, Carl's hide-like skin boasted a man who was used to hard work under a baking sun. He liked it hot—the hotter the better. And considering that fireworks was his line of business, a love of all things hot seemed only appropriate.

If only the two boys felt the same way.

Carl shook his head at the thought of his sons, Seth and Rubin. At twenty-two, Seth was the elder by two years, but the boy acted like he was sixteen. He was wild and irresponsible, not a bad kid, just the kind who never stopped to think. Seth had a careless streak in him—always did, always would. So far, Seth's screw-ups had been fairly minor, but Carl knew that kind of luck couldn't hold out forever. He regretted having to make the decision, but this was the last job he was going to let Seth work in the field. He hadn't told his son yet, but when they returned to Georgia, Seth was going to work full-time out of the office.

Carl sighed and swilled the last dregs of the coffee in his mouth. As he swallowed, he glanced in the rearview mirror and saw the front end of the boys' pickup truck pulling up behind him. He glanced at his watch. Almost 10:00 a.m.

About time, he thought, pushing open the truck's heavy door. "Let's get a move on," he called out to his sons. "We don't got all day."

"Coming," Seth answered, climbing out of the driver's side door. "We're coming."

Rubin climbed out of the truck and made his way toward his father. He was carrying a black toolbox and something wrapped in a canvas tarp. Seth carried nothing.

"You get the levels like I said?"

Seth cocked a thumb toward his brother who held up the canvas wrap. "Right here," Rubin said. "Got some extra electrical tape too."

"Good," Carl said. "Hand that toolbox to your brother and come on."

Seth took the toolbox without complaint as Carl led his sons down the newly cut path that led from the top of Radaken's Hill to the river. The trio marched down about fifty yards when they came to the first of the platforms for the fireworks display. There were three platforms in all, each forty feet long by twelve feet wide. They jutted from the side of the hill supported by post beams sunk three feet into the ground. The city was sparing no expense for its Independence Day celebration, which is why it gladly agreed to the twenty thousand dollar price tag for Carl's services. The city even agreed to construct the staging platforms required for the finale.

But none of the city's work would mean shit if the platforms weren't built to Carl's exact specifications.

Carl motioned to Rubin to put his bundle on the ground. "Take that level and check the support post first. If that's screwed up there won't be any sense in us checking anything else." Turning to Seth, he told him to get the measuring tapes out of the toolbox. "If this first platform is all level, me and you will space off the charge cradles."

Carl was about to ask Rubin if the post was straight when he heard his son curse. "Shit."

Carl and Seth hurried to where Rubin was kneeling. "What is it?" Carl asked.

"Look at this." Rubin pointed to the post where someone had taken a knife to it. Carved into the wood was ACE.

"Little bastards," Carl hissed. "Is the post straight, though?"

Rubin rechecked the air bubble in the level he held flat against the post. Dead center. "Yeah, the post is fine."

Carl moved in closer, peering over his son's shoulder. Beneath where someone had carved ACE, in smaller but equally deep lettering was written, n.e. was here

Carl stared at the letters, angry that someone had screwed around with his staging platforms. "Sons-of-bitches," he muttered once before going to work.

July 2 continued

When Rhonda said she wanted to meet somewhere in private, the first place that came to Steve's mind was The Oaks. The bar was closed on Sunday's anyway, and Rhonda was adamant that she didn't want to meet at either of their offices in City Hall. "Too many people," she said. "Too much craziness." Steve agreed and told Rhonda he'd get the keys from Merilee and meet her at the bar at noon.

Steve was waiting behind the bar when Rhonda came through the door a few minutes before twelve. "Hi, Rho. I just finished making coffee. Want some?"

Rhonda sidled up to the bar. "How about a beer instead? I'm not working today."

"Sure." As Steve reached for a beer, he noticed the thin, dark, crow's feet stretching from the sides of Rhonda's bloodshot eyes. He grabbed a bottle of Coors Light and placed it in front of her. "You look beat," he said. "You okay?"

He produced his pack of Marlboros and offered it to her. She took one, lit it, and after sucking in a sharp lungful of smoke, exhaled out of the side of her mouth. "Tired, that's all. I haven't slept in a few days."

Steve nodded and lit a cigarette of his own. He poured a cup of black coffee for himself then leaned against the bar in front of Rhonda. "I tried getting in touch with you yesterday. Carl said you called in sick."

Rhonda smiled and took another swig. "Not true. I was at County Hospital all day. I told Carl I was sick because I didn't want to be disturbed."

"Oh. What were you doing at County?"

"Tests." She slipped the thin strap of her purse off her shoulder. "County does our toxicology screens." Rhonda opened the purse and dumped the contents onto the bar, a half dozen Nathan Espy Special baseball cards and a plastic bag of marijuana. She looked over the baseball cards then pushed the one found at the Smith home toward Steve with the tip of her pinky. "The other day when I was going over the autopsy report on Fredo Torach something happened to me." Rhonda smiled nervously then proceeded to tell Steve what had happened at the lab.

"My God," Steve said when she finished.

"It scared the living hell out of me. I mean it was the kind of scared that makes you think you're going to have a heart attack. Do you know what I mean?"

Steve said he did and related what had happened to him when he was alone in Nathan Espy's room. He recounted the events in as much detail as he could remember, especially the figure he had seen in the baseball card and his dream of swimming in the river.

Rhonda listened attentively, not commenting until Steve finished. "I think I know what happened to us," she said.

"Really." Surprised, Steve leaned in closer to Rhonda.

"Yeah. Remember at Mayflower's apartment I told you that I wasn't sure what the pot you found at Espy's house was soaking in? Well, when I got the tox-screen back on Fredo Torach, some of the same elements were found in his blood system, but the toxicologist wasn't sure what they were. Anyway, it was right after I reviewed the autopsy report that I had my episode in the lab. I was pretty freaked out for quite a while, but when I calmed down, I had a hunch. I sent Carl to get that baseball card as well as some of the others from the Espy house. I also had him get me a sample of the pot." Rhonda spread her hands over the items on the bar. "What you see here."

"I took everything down to County and did some testing, and

guess what? The baseball cards are coated with the stuff that the marijuana is laced with. It's the same weird kind of acid. Which means that anyone who's handled these things without gloves would have come in direct contact with it."

"I'll be damned," Steve said under his breath. "Would just touching those baseball cards be enough to affect someone?"

Rhonda shook her head. "I don't think brief, casual contact would be a problem. But I think that if someone was to hold the card for a while, manipulate it a bit so that the acid had a chance to mingle with the sweat on the hands, there's a pretty good chance they'd be affected."

Steve felt a sudden emptiness in the pit of his stomach. "Gary and I both handled the cards on Espy's wall."

"And I've been handling the ones from Mayflower's apartment and the Smith house," Rhonda cut in. "Don't you see, Steve? When we were at Mayflower's apartment you told me you hadn't slept in over twenty-four hours. Then you went over to the Espy house and saw the face growing out of the baseball card on the wall. In my case, I was dead on my feet when I had my episode." Rhonda picked up her bottle and pointed the stem toward Steve. "In both instances, we were exhausted, barely standing. And that's when we had the hallucinations."

"Gary," Steve said. "He handled the baseball cards as much as I did. Could he have had some kind of weird episode too?"

Rhonda pursed her lips slightly and shrugged. "I don't know, but that would explain him freaking out. I know if I would have had a weapon the other day, I sure as hell would have taken a few shots at that baseball card."

Steve took a step back from the bar. "Tell me something, Rhonda. Could this stuff on the baseball cards be some kind of sedative?"

She gave Steve a puzzled look. "Why do you ask?"

He told her about his conversation with Morris and his involvement with Henry Smith and the DK. "A wild hunch," he said. "But what do you think?"

A grim expression clouded Rhonda's face as she reached into her jeans and removed a neatly folded square of paper. She put it on the bar and carefully smoothed it open. "This is the toxicology report on Fredo Torach," she said, pointing to a smudged line near the bottom of the page. "You said that Henry Smith told Morris that the DK was going to make his pituitary stronger, right?"

Steve nodded. "That's what Morris said."

"Well, Fredo's body contained extremely high levels of the kinds of growth hormones secreted by the pituitary gland during sleep. There was also an unusually high level of acetylcholine in his system."

"What's that?"

"It's a chemical in the brain that stimulates certain types of cells into action. In the case of acetylcholine, it allows cells called cholinergic cells to function in the brainstem."

Steve looked puzzled. "So?"

"Cholinergic cell activity is one of the things that triggers the dream process. It's complicated, but without the cholinergic cells, we couldn't formulate thoughts in our sleep or dream."

"And a lot of this acetyl-what-ever-you-call-it, was in Fredo's blood stream?"

Rhonda nodded. "Massive amounts."

Steve considered this for a moment. "Could too much of this acetylcholine end up affecting someone's sleep patterns? Maybe not allowing them to get to REM sleep?"

"I don't see why not," Rhonda replied. "There's no way of predicting exactly what would happen to someone's sleep cycle if their neural activity was increased. But inhibiting REM sleep sounds reasonable."

"What about hallucinations? What about what happened to us?"

"We were dreaming," Rhonda said emphatically. "There's no other explanation. Assuming that stuff on the baseball cards is Henry Smith's DK, we came in contact with just enough of it to have a limited affect on us. We started dozing and dreamt the whole thing. Hell, considering how much stress we were under and how we were exhausted, we could have seen anything."

Steve and Rhonda stared at each other from across the bar for a long twenty seconds. Neither spoke, neither moved. Steve finally broke the silence.

"So what do you think?"

Rhonda smacked her lips together and motioned for Steve to get her another beer. As he reached into the cooler, a thin frown came to Rhonda's face. She tapped out a cigarette from the pack Steve left on the bar. Keeping her eyes focused on the cigarette, she asked him if there was anything about the disappearance of Linda Cavanaugh that seemed unusual to him. "Don't you think it's odd," she said. "That there were no signs of forced entry in the house? No signs of struggle?"

Steve admitted to finding that curious.

Rhonda huffed. "Curious my ass. I went over that room with a fine-tooth comb, and I found nothing to indicate that she was abducted. Not one speck of physical evidence. And the only fingerprints we found matched those of Linda Cavanaugh and her husband."

"What do you make of that?" Steve asked.

"I think Linda Cavanaugh walked out of that house by herself and of her own free will. There's just no other explanation. If she had been abducted by Espy, there would have been some sign of a struggle. Something. But that room was completely clean."

"How did the baseball card get there then?"

Rhonda took a swig from her beer. "I don't know." She put her left hand up to her cheek and rested her elbow on the bar. "I just don't know, Steve. There's too much going on to think straight." A single tear slipped from Rhonda's right eye down her cheek. Embarrassed, she wiped it off with the back of her hand. "Damn it," she said. "I'm so tired right now."

Steve leaned forward and took her hand in his. "It's okay," he whispered. "I'll take things from here. You just go home and try to get some sleep, okay?"

Rhonda laughed and gave Steve's hand a pat. "Where have I heard that one before? But you're right." Rhonda was about to push the items on top of the bar back into her purse when Steve stopped her. An idea had popped into his head.

"Wait a second," he said. "Do me a favor."

***

Carl Northrup looked up from his crouched position on the third staging platform when he heard a car door slam. Beside him, Rubin was wiring the final spark switch to the last mortar. Three rows of fifteen mortars, each capable of holding shells of up to twenty-four inches in diameter, were evenly spread out on the platform. Once the spark switches were complete, the entire platform would be wired to a master control. The fireworks business had come a long way since Carl was his son's age. Back then, Carl would have to light the charge with a road flare and hope to God nothing went wrong. Today, all he had to do was wire the pots to the control board and plug in the computer. Push-button pyrotechnics Rubin had called it.

Carl nudged Rubin in the shoulder and cocked his head toward the crest of Radaken's Hill where an attractive young woman was standing beside a red car talking to Seth. "Who's that?" Carl asked his younger son.

Rubin glanced toward the girl and grunted. "Dunno. Seth told me that he might have plans tonight though."

Carl wiped his brow with the back of his thick hand. The woman was laughing, obviously impressed with something Carl's oldest son had said. The two spoke for another minute before the woman turned back to her car. She waved once to Seth from the driver's seat then sped away.

"Who was that?" Carl called to his son.

"Girl I met," he replied, smiling. "I got a date tonight."

Carl shook his head. "Date," he muttered, kneeling back down on the platform. He watched as Rubin finished wiring the spark switch. The boy did it quick and effectively. He had good hands. "Where the hell did your brother meet some girl? We've only been in town two days."

Rubin chuckled to himself as he rechecked the switch. "Aw, you know Seth. Always on the prowl."

Carl glanced up toward Seth who was collecting the tools. "That's the problem," Carl said, laughing. "Always thinking with his pecker."

"Yup," Rubin said still eyeing the wire. He gave it a gentle tug, and feeling no give, pronounced the job finished. "We're ready for tomorrow."

July 2 night

Seth leaned back in the seat and moaned. Eyes dreamily parted, he stared at the car's cream-colored roof while the little redhead writhed and bucked on his lap. She had her back to him so he could feel her tight ass wiggling against his stomach. Seth's strong hands were firmly planted on her sides, the tips of his fingers digging into the smooth flesh of her young breasts.

It was exactly the kind of date Seth loved. The girl picked him up at his hotel at nine and took him to a dive bar just outside of town. Midway through their third pitcher of beer, the girl asked if Seth wanted to smoke a joint. "Sure," he said. "Why not?" The two went back to the girl's car and took turns puffing on a dooby. When they finished, Seth was flying high on the best buzz of his life. He was also horny as hell, and when the girl didn't protest when he suggested they slip into the back seat, Seth knew he'd hit the jackpot. A few wet kisses later, the girl's panties were hanging from her ankles.

And now a familiar tingling sensation in his balls signaled the beginning of an unstoppable build up. Seth let out a deep moan and arched his hips forward sending his penis deeper into the girl. Immediately she slowed her pace.

"Don't stop now," Seth protested. "It's starting to get real good."

The girl flung her head back and laughed, sending strands of auburn hair brushing against Seth's face. Rather then resume the wild, hell-bent-for-leather hip grinding that was about to send him over the edge, the girl began to gingerly lift herself off Seth's swollen cock. "And your promise," she said in a husky voice. "You'll show me and my friends how to set off fireworks?"

Seth closed his eyes as the girl's hips lifted another delicious inch up his aching penis. "Sure," he muttered. "Anything you want."

The girl giggled and pulled herself free of Seth's throbbing member. Before Seth could protest further, she swung her tiny frame across his lap. She knelt on the floor of the car's backseat and gripped Seth's penis with both hands. Seth sighed as he heard the girl speak a variation of the words that all young men long to hear. "Just for that," Julie said, her mouth forming a tight O, "I'm going to shwonk your gator."

Another satisfied moan escaped Seth's lips as he was swallowed in ecstasy.

Chapter Eighteen: July 2 continued

Alone in Merilee's living room, Steve glanced at his watch—a few minutes before midnight. *Good*, he thought. Merilee had taken some of her pain medication and should sleep for a few more hours. Patting his breast pocket, Steve felt the thin, faint outline of the marijuana cigarette. Sighing, he tilted his head back and wished to God he'd never heard of Nathan Espy or Curtis Mayflower.

"Aw shit," Steve muttered in the darkness. How did things get so messed up? Just a month ago everything was fine. He and Merilee were cruising along, summer was just starting, and the only police matter that had really registered on the out-of-the-ordinary scale was the arrest of one of the middle-school's vice principles, Herb Carlysle, for masturbating in the men's room of a local Dennys. Then came Slaughter Saturday and all hell broke lose.

Steve shifted his weight in the chair to a more comfortable position as the sleeping pill he had taken earlier started to kick in. In his wildest dreams, the detective never imagined he would be sitting alone in a darkened room waiting for the right moment to get high. But if the marijuana he found at Nathan Espy's house had been laced with Henry Smith's DK as Steve suspected, then the chances were good that anyone who smoked it would have one of the lucid night terrors that Harris was talking about. And if that happened to Steve after smoking the pot he took from Rhonda, then Harris Smith was going to have a hell of a lot of explaining to do in the morning. Steve would be especially interested in Harris's explanation of how a teenager could have gotten his hands on Henry Smith's experimental drug.

Steve absently brushed his palm against his shirt pocket. *A few more minutes, then we'll see exactly what Espy's dope can really do.*

Correction, the cop-voice in his head chimed in. *We're going to see what that shit will do to you. And judging from how Nathan Espy and Curtis Mayflower turned out, it ain't going to be pleasant.*

I guess so, Steve answered himself. *Pretty stupid idea, huh?*

Not really. You've got to convince yourself that this stuff is the DK before you go after Harris. And this might be the only way to find out. So you just be careful old boy, okay?

Steve promised himself that he would as he took the joint from his pocket and fired it up.

As the red flame made contact, an image from his childhood popped into his head. He was nine and his mother had taken him to Ash Wednesday mass at St. Pius Church. He didn't want to go, but Steve didn't have a choice. When it came time to receive the ashes, he sullenly took his place in line, staring at the wide expanse of his mother's back as the line inched its way toward the altar rail. When it was his turn to receive ashes, his mother took a step to the side and pushed Steve within arm distance of Father Flaherty who didn't seem to notice the approaching boy. Father was looking down at his hands. Steve glanced down and watched as Father jammed his right thumb in a silver bowl of ashes made from the remnants of the palms from the previous Palm Sunday. The thumb emerged from the bowl black as night. Steve closed his eyes as the priest made the sign of the cross on his forehead.

Remember man that you were made of Dust.

And to Dust you shall return.

Dust.

Steve fell asleep.

***

The first thing he noticed was the lights. Harsh, white and blinding. He immediately brought his hands to his face to block the glare. The second thing he noticed was the pungent aroma of antiseptic soap—the smell of cleanliness—but behind it lurked the odor of rotting flesh and decay. It was the smell of warm blood and disease made palatable by a generous amount of Pine-Sol.

Cautiously, Steve lowered his hands from his face and opened his eyes. Though the glare forced him to squint, Steve's eyes adjusted enough for him to take stock of his surroundings. He was standing in the lobby of the emergency room at McKeesport Hospital, there was no mistaking that. Everything was exactly the same as he remembered from the night Merilee was brought in. The same three rows of plastic orange chairs were lined against the wall near the exit. A waiting area with no one waiting. The square receptionist's desk in the middle of the lobby also lacked an occupant.

"I'll be damned." Steve was impressed. He'd prepared himself for a lucid dream, but what he was experiencing was beyond lucidity; way beyond a simple heightening of his sensory perceptions. Every sight, every sound was as real as if he was actually at the hospital. Steve inhaled the cleaning-scent atmosphere, so clear that he could taste it in the back of his throat. For a moment he forgot his waking fear of what the dream might bring, then Steve turned back to face the receptionist's desk and that moment was over.

"May I help you?" a gentle but firm voice asked. "Visiting hours are over, you know."

Steve's eyes became two half dollar-sized ovals as the pleasant taste of pine cleaner turned into a bitter cocktail of blood and panic. His entire body began to shake, building up momentum for the scream of his life.

From behind the receptionist's desk, Gladys Decorta wiggled a long, teacher's finger at Steve. "Now, now, Mr. Wyckoff. There will be no hysterics. We just simply won't allow that."

Steve felt as if a wall of concrete had just fallen onto his head.

He couldn't scream. He couldn't move.

"Steven," Mrs. D. said. "Look me in the eyes when I'm speaking to you."

Steve did as he was told. Of course, to look Mrs. D. in the eyes, Steve had to shift his gaze from the headless figure of a nurse sitting behind the receptionist's desk, and direct his attention to the purple, bloated rock of flesh resting atop the desk addressing him.

The wet blob that was Gladys Decorta's head.

But now that head was swollen to nearly twice its normal size, causing its green and purple skin to stretch to the breaking point. Around the cheeks and forehead, patches of flesh had become translucent allowing Steve a glimpse of the thin network of veins and arteries that stretched just below Gladys's skin. Her lips and eyelids had been chewed away by small fish, leaving behind long tendrils of spider web flesh. At the top of her skull, her hair defied gravity, floating upward in a tangled mass. It moved slowly from the left to the right and then back again.

Which only seemed fitting, Steve realized. Because Gladys's head was still somewhere in the river.

Except, of course, in Steve's dream. Here, the head was perched in the middle of the emergency room receptionist desk on top of an issue of Vogue. The magazine acted like an oversized coaster to keep the blood and puss from Gladys's open neck from staining the desk. A thin, perfect arm of the cover model peaked out from beneath the bulbous mass. It was waving, a frantic cry for help from a suffocating supermodel.

A few moments passed before Steve could get his nerves under control. "Why did you do it, Gladys?" he asked when he finally stopped shaking. "Why did you hang yourself?"

A subtle change came over Gladys's misshapen face as a fusion of sadness and regret replaced the harshness of her previous expression. Even her corpse became less rigid. "You know the answer to that, Steve."

"I do?"

Gladys performed a decapitated nod. "It's your dream, Steve. You're responsible for what happens. For what you see. For who gets hurt."

Steve shook his head. "I don't understand."

"I didn't at first," Gladys replied. "But I figured it out eventually. We're responsible for what we let in our heads." Gladys rolled her eyes to the left. "It's their own fault what happened to them," she said.

Steve turned to where Gladys was looking. The "them" filled up the first two rows of orange chairs in the waiting area. All dead, all waiting, were the three suicides from Slaughter Saturday. Seated next to Merrill Toth was Marnie Baxter. Fredo Torach, his face uninjured, was next to her. When Fredo saw Steve, he casually uncurled the middle finger of his left hand. Behind him sat Marcus Espy.

Robert Monero was there too. "She's wrong, Steve," Monero said. "What happened wasn't our fault. It's yours. You shouldn't have stopped me. None of this would have happened if you would have let me kill that girl." Monero looked nervously toward the entrance. "It's all your fault, Steve."

"No," Steve said. "Your death isn't my fault. None of your deaths is my fault."

Marnie Baxter fixed her cold eyes on Steve. "He would have gone away if she died. But you had to go and save her. Now look at us." Marnie stood and started to scream. "You did this, Wyckoff! You're the reason we're all dead!"

Merrill Toth reached up and took Marnie by the elbow. "Sit down," he ordered.

Offering no resistance, Marnie collapsed into the chair. "He's coming," she whimpered.

"He knows," Merrill replied, turning to Steve. "He called him, didn't he?"

"What is it?" Steve asked Merrill. "What is it I'm supposed to know?" When Merrill didn't reply, Steve took a step closer. "Goddamn it, Toth, tell me," he shouted. He looked at Marnie, then Phillip Slaughter. Both were crying. Steve turned to Fredo who was punching his fist into the palm of his hand.

"Should've let her die," Fredo said. "Then there wouldn't have been a Slaughter Saturday. Then I'd still have my fucking jaw." Fredo pinched his chin with his right thumb and forefinger. "It still hurts, Wyckoff. Do you know that? We get all prettied up before we get buried, but the shit that killed us still hurts even after we're dead. That's what hell is." Fredo jerked his thumb over his left shoulder. "Just ask him."

"He's right, kid," a voice Steve hadn't heard in over thirty years said. "It still hurts like hell."

As soon as he heard his dead brother's voice, Steve squeezed his eyes shut. He knew if he opened them, he would see Terry standing just a few feet away. Standing so close that if he took three steps, Steve would be able to wrap his arms around him and hug him. And in a lucid dream like this, he would be able to feel his brother's embrace again. Touch him. Smell him. And Steve knew he would carry those sensations with him as a memory after he woke. A memory so clear and vivid he would swear it was real. But Steve also knew that unlike the others, Terry wouldn't look the way he did before he died. He wouldn't be the tall, handsome man with thick arms and a goofy smile. If Steve opened his eyes he would be looking at the burnt body of a man who died screaming in agony. It would be the Terry whose face was melted from his body; it would be the brother they had to bury in a closed casket.

Steve jammed his fists over his eyes. It's only a dream his mind repeated like a mantra. Only a dream. A really horrible lucid dream, but you will wake up. That's a promise. You will wake up. Only a dream.

The wailing of a siren exploded from somewhere outside of the waiting room. Steve slapped his palms over his ears and fell to his knees. Still, he kept his eyes shut tight.

Then silence.

Then a whisper.

"You can get up now, they're gone."

Steve shook his head, his hands still cupped over his ears. "No."

Again, the reassuring whisper.

"You have to open your eyes sometime. They're gone. It's just you and me now."

Steve lowered his hands to his side. Leaning forward he placed his palms flat on the floor. Tilting his head downward, he stared at the white tile beneath him. "Where are you?" he asked.

"Far away," came the reply. "Over by the door. I can't hurt you from here."

His eyes still trained to the floor, Steve twisted his head in order to see the waiting area. The rows of orange chairs were empty. Twisting his neck further, he peered back toward the receptionist's desk. That too was empty.

Steve paused for a second, then taking a deep breath, leapt to his feet, his right hand snatching his service revolver from its holster. He pivoted toward the entrance, his gun aimed chest high. It was a simple plan; just start shooting and to hell with the rest. *Only a dream*, Steve reminded himself. *Anything goes. Just shoot.*

"Hello."

Steve froze. In front of him, a thin, bald man wearing sunglasses and a doctor's smock was sitting Indian-style on a gurney. A pleasant, Nice-To-Meet-You smile on his face.

"I know you," Steve said, keeping the gun aimed at the man's chest. "You were the face I saw in Espy's baseball card."

"Well actually, Steven, I don't really know what you saw in that young man's bedroom. You were dozing off a bit. When that happens, when you're halfway between sleeping and waking, you can see just about anything." The man let his words sink in before continuing. "Like now. You know that you're dreaming, that much is apparent. But you are confused as to my presence. On one hand, you believe that everything you are seeing is a product of your subconscious. That I am nothing more than something created in some dark corner of your mind."

"Or there is the unpleasant alternative. Everything you are dreaming has been dredged up from inside your head, except me. And that's the possibility that has you terrified. Isn't that right, Steve? You're afraid that I'm the uninvited guest you've heard so much about who has found a way to sneak into your dream courtesy of Henry Smith."

"Are you?" The words fell weakly out of Steve's mouth. "Are you Dust?"

"And if I am?"

Steve didn't answer; instead, he fired. But in the time it took for Steve to squeeze the trigger, the dream demon vanished, leaving only a thin smoke outline of where his body had been. Steve's finger squeezed the trigger again sending a bullet through the smoke trail that a moment before had been the side of Dust's head. As the bullet ricocheted off the wall and slammed into the ceiling, the trail of smoke that outlined Dust's body began to swirl like a cyclone. Slowly at first, then picking up speed until it formed a long, funnel cloud as thick as Steve's arm. It stretched from the floor to the ceiling, rigid like a rope that had all the slack taken out of it.

It grew wider, doubling in width then doubling again. Steve watched, unable to take his eyes off the rope cloud as it expanded until it looked like a gray, swirling movie screen. Inside, the smoky outline of Dust stared at Steve. He looked like a gray shadow, its only distinguishing feature, two pale, white ovals for eyes.

"What are you?" Steve shouted.

"The Incubi. The Mara. The Prisoner. I am who is and is not."

The smoke outline around the white eyes wove back and forth, turning over on itself until a figure began to take shape. Steve gasped when he saw what was developing in front of him. A fanged abomination in a train conductor's uniform.

"Your friend David, this is what he sees when he dreams."

Behind the conductor was an old-fashioned engine car sitting at a railroad crossway. Thick, black smoke billowed out of the car as it rocked in place on silver tracks.

Steve immediately recognized David's Toy Train.

The black smoke poured out of the engine until it blotted the rest of the train from view. The same smoke whirled around the conductor until he too was swallowed in its blackness. Then the smoke separated like a curtain, revealing a frail, old woman in a green housecoat. She was hunched over, her spindly limbs swollen and misshapen. A look of agony was stitched across her face.

"This is what Gladys Decorta saw when she dreamed. Her mother, ravaged by age and arthritis. The mother that she smothered to death with a pillow."

The old woman jerked her head toward Steve and looked at

him with Dust's blank eyes. On the face of Gladys Decorta's mother, they looked like two empty moons jammed into the hollow recesses of her skull. She made a low, guttural moan then opened her mouth and the same black smoke that spewed from the Toy Train poured out of the opening.

"Gladys killed her own mother. She always told herself that it was a mercy killing. But that was in the days before it was acceptable to put a parent out of her misery. Back then you would have called it old-fashioned murder. And that is what Gladys couldn't live with, the fact that she was a murderer."

"That's not true!" Steve fired into the cloud where Gladys Decorta's mother had been a second before. The bullet split the new, smoky outline that was forming then disappeared into the cloud. Steve listened but there was no sound of the bullet making contact with anything. No broken glass, no high-pitched ricochet. Nothing.

"It is true, Steve Wyckoff. And you, more than anybody, know it. You know the history of this town, all its stories and secrets. You know the people; you have your suspicions. Don't deny your curiosity. I can show you what they dream of. All the people you've been serving and protecting. I can show you their dreams, Steve. I can show you how to live them."

Steve lowered his gun and took a step back.

"There is more to see."

The black smoke again dissipated, this time revealing a fat, naked man with a pockmarked face. Thick folds of flesh sagged from his chest and torso. He leered at Steve while his right hand stroked his erect penis.

"This is what your friend Gary dreamed about. His Uncle Joe. He was Gary's favorite. That is until he started raping his nephew in the basement."

The leering figure in the cloud began stroking with more urgency.

"When Gary followed you into the basement, this is what greeted him. Not Mr. Espy, but Uncle Joe hanging from the water pipe, just waiting to play the feel game. And do you know what? Part of your friend wanted to play. Part of him wanted to become thirteen again and feel his uncle's pole sliding into his nice tight ass. That's the part of Gary's dreams he never told his therapist. That's the part that only I know. The thing he couldn't live with."

Steve bowed his head and started to cry. He wept for Gladys Decorta and her mother. He wept for Gary. And he wept for himself because he knew what Dust was telling him was true. Every twisted thing was true.

"Enough," he said weakly. "Please, no more." When Steve looked up, the sight of Uncle Joe pounding his pud was gone, as was the gray cloud. In its place was the gurney. Dust, in his doctor's smock and sunglasses, was sitting on top of it.

"Why?" Steve asked. "Why Gary?"

"Your friend was no different than any of the others whose dreams are open to me. He had a secret he kept locked away up here," Dust said, tapping the side of his skull with his forefinger. "Secrets that he didn't want revealed, even to himself. So he buried them in the darkest part of his mind and convinced himself those secrets never existed. Only they came out at night. There was nothing he could do about that. And when they were free, oh the torment they caused him. You can't imagine the pain your friend lived with."

"It is the pain that calls me, Detective Wyckoff. Physical pain, mental pain. In dreams it is all the same. For me, pain is the invitation. The open door. All I need is a small crack to sneak in." Dust hopped off the gurney. "And then there are those like yourself who deliberately seek me out. Why is that, Steve Wyckoff? Why did you deliberately open your mind to me? Did you want to test me? To fight me? Or was it blind curiosity that brought me to you?" Dust pointed to the glass window behind him. "Look, Steve Wyckoff. Look at what is to come."

Behind the glass was a lineup of familiar faces.

"No," Steve gasped, his gun hand falling limp to his side.

"Very real," Dust answered. "Very dead."

On the other side of the glass, Gary twisted his head in the direction of Dust's voice. Thick rivers of dried blood made a path on each of his cheeks. Beside Gary, Morris Keyes stood motionless, his right hand pointing forward. His eyeless head turned upward and to the left. Next to Morris was David Cavanaugh.

"It's all your fault," Steve heard Gary say. "It's all your fault." The two other human statues turned toward Steve and started chanting, "It's all your fault. It's all your fault."

And that's when Steve knew he was going to lose his mind. They were right. It was all his fault. It didn't matter what they were blaming him for; it was his fault. That's what made Phillip Slaughter drink two quarts of Drano, and Merrill Toth drive off the overpass. They knew it was all their faults too.

Just like Steve had known for over thirty years that it was his fault that Terry was killed. Terry had traded his usual Thursday daylight shift for a Saturday night shift because he promised his kid brother he'd take him to see the Pirates play the Dodgers at Forbes Field. It was an early birthday present for Steve. A trip to the ballpark. But to make it happen, Terry had to switch shifts with one of his buddies.

"Can't just take a day off," he told Steve.

Everyone has something they can't live with.

You are so right Mr. Dust, Steve thought. Everyone's got something up their ass that itches.

Just can't take a day off.

Steve brought the gun up and put it to his temple. "It is my fault," he said aloud.

I know it is. Terry knows it too.

Steve nodded. That was the other cold truth that still plagued him. "If you kill yourself in your dream, do you die in real life?" Steve asked.

Yes Steve, that's the rule.

Steve nodded, the steel barrel of his gun planted firmly against his head. That seemed like a sensible rule. And after all, it was his fault.

Steve started to pull the trigger when his cop-voice got its two cents in. *What are the chances you're being a real dick-head right now?*

Steve whipped the gun away from his temple and got a shot off before Dust could react. The bullet caught Dust in the soft flesh between the shoulder blade and the side of his neck. A chunk of skin and muscle splattered against the window in a bloody mess.

Then Dust screamed.

It was unlike anything Steve had ever heard, a pandemonium of agony and darkness. The entire room vibrated from its force as if a thousand chainsaws had just been started. Behind Dust, the glass doors imploded sending countless shards of glass at Steve.

Steve shielded his eyes with his hands, but none of the glass touched him. All around him the room vibrated, but when he opened his eyes, Dust hadn't moved. "So you can be hurt," Steve said. He took aim at the creature's head and fired again.

This time the bullet sailed through a thin wisp of smoke and into the gray fog.

Steve fired three more times through the smoke. "Nothing's my fault, you bastard. Nothing. What happened to Terry was an accident!" Steve took a step forward and spat. The trail of smoke snaked to the left to avoid it.

"Come on you fucking coward. Why don't you fuck with me now that I know how to hurt you?"

The smoke swirled about, then flew out the open window. Once it was gone the vibrating stopped. Steve looked around the room. He was alone. There was no one behind the desk, no one in the chairs.

No longer afraid, Steve felt himself relaxing. It wouldn't be long until the dream was over. For some inexplicable reason, Steve knew he was on the verge of waking.

Then someone stepped back through the broken window.

Steve tried to focus on the figure, but his vision was growing blurry.

The figure moved within a few feet of Steve and stopped.

"Wake up now Steve."

Steve reached out to touch the figure but his arm fell short. "I know you," he said.

"Wake up Steve."

Yes. Steve nodded. It was time to . . .

"Wake up. Goddamn it, wake up!"

Merilee stood over Steve's body, her right palm open and ready to strike. Steve's eyes fluttered open saving him a right cross from his girlfriend. When she saw his eyes open, Merilee grabbed Steve by his shoulders and began shaking him.

"Snap out of it!" she shouted in his face. "Wake up."

Steve looked at Merilee but could barely make out her face. His conscious mind was quickly coming into focus, but part of him was still struggling to cast off the remnants of the dream. He was at Merilee's house, that he knew for sure. But all around him the strong scent of hospital antiseptic hung in the air. And just behind that he could smell . . .

. . . the burnt flesh of your brother

Roughly Steve pushed Merilee away from him. It was Dust's voice he heard, hollow and disconnected. He was still in his head, whispering to that part of Steve that was still dreaming. "No," Steve wailed, confused and frightened.

When Steve's head cleared enough that he realized where he was, he fell to his knees. "Oh what I saw," he managed to say.

Then Steve began to cry, and Merilee knew he had come back to her.

July 3

Steve pulled up in front of Marcus Espy's house a little after four in the morning. Someone had ripped the orange DO NOT CROSS tape off the porch and left it curled up in the overgrown front lawn. Steve got out of the car and headed for the porch. The front door was open, a pale, yellow glow illuminated the entranceway. Steve's mind quickly registered the source—a light was on in Nathan's bedroom.

As he entered the house, Steve felt as if he was stepping into the open jaws of a giant beast, a tiger like the one Morris Keyes had dreamt about. *Well*, he thought. *You crossed the line this time, and now you're going to get swallowed.*

Eaten alive.

Steve shuddered and quickly made his way to Nathan's bedroom. He entered to find Harris Smith with his back to the doorway staring at the wall of Nathan Espy Specials. Harris didn't move, eerily backlit by the forty-watt bulb that dangled from the ceiling. Steve took two steps into the room.

After Steve's nightmare, he immediately called Harris. Not certain if he was being coherent, the frightened cop told Harris about his dream. Harris was unfazed by the news, nor was he surprised when Steve demanded that they meet. However, it did take Steve by surprise when Harris suggested that they meet at the Espy house.

"I'm glad you called me," Harris said without turning around. "I was hoping it wouldn't come to this, but now you know the truth." Harris paused, stretching his arm out toward the wall of baseball cards. "Can you feel his evil just dripping from all these . . . things?"

Steve swallowed hard then took another step into the room. A few moments passed where neither man spoke. Harris stared at the baseball cards while Steve's mind replayed the memory of his dream. "What is he?" Steve asked, his whispered voice shaking.

Harris turned toward Steve. "I don't really know. No one does. Not me, not my father. Not even the Indians who mythologized him. All we know is that he feeds off dreams." Harris paused and cast his eyes briefly to the card-covered floor. "Dust forces his way into a person's subconscious mind and takes control of his dreams, turning them into night terrors. The more terrified the dreamer, the stronger Dust becomes."

"In an odd way, though, he's fairly harmless because the only time we know of his existence is when he causes night terrors. But like I said, we have a built in defense mechanism that stops us from remembering those dreams. People will wake up from a night terror scared to death, but with no memory of Dust. Unfortunately, my father found a way to bypass that defense mechanism with the DK and make the Stage-4 dreams so lucid that people wouldn't be able to forget them."

Harris sighed, his gaze still fixed on the floor. "When my father first came up with the DK, he truly believed it would revolutionize the way the medical establishment treated addicts. With the DK, people could literally dream themselves stronger and more in control of their lives. But my father had a history of acting impulsively. He tested the DK out on himself, and after taking it for several months, he convinced himself that it was a complete success, so he started giving it to the rest of his family."

"Good Lord," Steve whispered. "You all got it."

Harris nodded. "Yup. Me, Linda, my mother. And for a while, there weren't any problems. We'd take the DK, go to sleep, and in the morning tell my father what we dreamt about. Everything seemed fine, so he started giving the DK to some of his patients undergoing Addiction Personification. But then Linda started going through puberty. That's when we discovered Dust."

"Puberty? I don't understand," Steve said.

"During puberty the pituitary gland naturally becomes highly active, producing enormous amounts of growth and repair hormones. This heightened pituitary activity is especially prevalent during Stage-4 sleep. My father never considered the increased pituitary activity when he gave Linda the DK."

"So what has that to do with Dust?"

"Puberty has been linked for a long time with paranormal phenomenon because the increased pituitary activity creates enormous amounts of psychic energy. Most of the time, that energy is harmless, but in rare instances, the energy gets channeled and becomes manifested in physical phenomenon."

"And is that what Dust does?"

"In a way. He uses the energy to drive himself deeper into people's subconscious. In Linda's case, the combination of the DK and the onset of puberty produced incredible amounts of psychic energy. So much, in fact, that Dust was able to break down the barrier between her conscious and subconscious mind. Linda became obsessed with Dust. She started having hallucinations about him, saying she could see him every time she closed her eyes. My father thought she was going insane, then Dust found a way to use her psychic energy and push further into other people's dreams. That's when my father realized the truth about Dust."

"At first, only my father could pick up on it, but it didn't take long until my mother and I were also having night terrors about Dust. My father stopped giving Linda the DK, but by then it was too late. Dust had already used Linda to push into the dreams of Morris Keyes and Robert Monero." Harris paused, the pained look returning to his face. "You know what happened next."

"Monero went nuts and tried to kill Linda," Steve replied automatically.

"Yes. He knew Dust was using Linda as a power source. He thought if he killed her, Dust wouldn't be able to torment him."

"But why would Monero think that?"

Harris swallowed hard and bit his lower lip. "My father told me that Dust had been able to force himself into Robert Monero's subconscious and make Monero sleep when he wanted him to. Then Dust took control of his body, and Monero was helpless to do anything about it. He was stuck dreaming of the war while his body was out sleep walking." Harris glanced about the room at the baseball cards. "From the looks of all this, the same thing seems to have happened to this Espy boy."

"But if Dust was able to control Monero, why did Monero try to kill Linda? That doesn't make sense."

"Dust couldn't control him all the time. One of the things the myth says is that Dust is a coward. He's a tough bastard when there's no resistance, but remember, Monero was a soldier, a man who knew how to fight. Dust didn't like that. Monero was able to wake himself up. That's when he went after Linda."

Steve exhaled nervously and began patting the pockets of his jacket in search of a cigarette. It was definitely the wrong time to have run out of smokes. "Shit," he said when he realized the search was futile. He glared at Harris. "So what do we have to do to stop him?"

"We have to find Linda," Harris replied. "We have to find her and get her as far away from McKeesport as we can. The old Indian myth was right on one account. Dust's influence seems to be limited geographically. He's strongest near the rivers, but the further away from the confluence, the weaker he becomes. If we get Linda far enough away so that Dust can't draw any strength from her, that should be enough to break his grip on Espy and whoever else he's corrupted."

"Will that kill him?" Steve asked hopefully.

Harris shook his head from side to side. "No. In fact I don't think he can be killed. But," he quickly added. "Dust can be hurt, and he can be contained."

"Contained," Steve barked. "How the hell do you contain something like that?"

"By turning our dreams back on him," Harris shot back. "Listen, Steve, I know this is a lot for you to handle, and I don't expect you to believe half of what I'm telling you. But you've got to listen to me. I've been living with this for over twenty years, and I know what I'm talking about. Dust can be stopped, but it's not going to be easy. And it's certainly not going to happen unless we find Linda and get her the hell out of here."

"Okay, okay," Steve said. "Morris Keyes told me that he and Robert Monero fought Dust in one of Morris's Viet Nam dreams. Is that what we have to do?"

"No," Harris said to Steve's relief. "No confrontations like that. We might be able to hurt Dust, but we certainly wouldn't be able to contain him for long. Not with Linda nearby. No, what we need to do is force him into a dream he can't get out of."

Steve cast a puzzled look at Harris. "How?"

"There are rules that even dream demons have to abide by, and one of them is that he must come if he is summoned. In the Indian myth, Mokera summoned Dust into his dream and simply willed that he not leave it."

Steve expected more of an explanation but none came. "That's it?" he asked surprised. "Mokera just told Dust that he couldn't leave?"

Harris nodded. "Pretty much. Of course, Dust fought back by taking the form of everything Mokera feared, but the warrior wouldn't allow himself to be frightened. According to the legend, Mokera built a dream house of brick and stones and locked the demon inside. Afterwards, every night when he went to sleep, Mokera would summon Dust and force him back into the stone house. As long as he did that, Dust was contained."

Steve let out a long, low whistle. "I don't know, Harris. I mean, I'm still not sure that I believe all this, but if it was Dust I ran into in the dream I just had, I don't think he's going to sit still and allow himself to get locked up in some dream prison."

Harris agreed. "That's why we have to get Linda away from here. As long as he's using her as an energy source, he's too powerful to stop."

Steve wasn't convinced. "How do you know he can be stopped even if we do find Linda and get her away from McKeesport? How do you know he can be trapped even then?"

A tired, beaten expression spread across Harris's face as if he was a criminal about to hear his sentence. "Because that is what my father did for over two decades," Harris said, turning away from Steve. "I don't know if you remember, but shortly after the Monero incident, Linda was sent off to a private school in Connecticut. She was told it was to help her forget what happened to her, but the truth was there was no way to contain Dust as long as he was feeding off of Linda's energy. Once Linda was gone, Dust's powers were considerably weaker, and my father could hold him in a dream."

"Good God," Steve exclaimed. "He did this every night for the past twenty years?"

"Every night," Harris replied softly. "Then the night my father died, Dust escaped. I tried to stop him, but he was too strong, too enraged. He fled into the dreams of some of my father's patients who had been treated with the DK. I was able to summon him back again and trap him in a stone house like Mokera had done, but not before he had gotten into the heads of Phillip Slaughter and the Montgomery girl." Harris paused and looked toward Steve. "I tried to stop him, Steve, but I couldn't get to him in time."

Steve nodded. "But if you trapped him in the stone house, how did he get out again?"

"Linda," came the quick reply. "When she is asleep. Dust is still able to use her as an energy source. Once she came back to McKeesport, there was no controlling him. At first, I thought I could. I tried to wall him in, but he was too strong. After that I couldn't risk summoning him, not with him feeding off Linda like before. But I didn't think she would stay in town long, not with David and her job in Carolina. I planned on waiting until she went home before trying to recapture Dust. But then my mother convinced her to stay," Harris said contemptuously. "Her and that damn idea to reopen the clinic." Harris locked his fingers together, his palms pressing against the sides of his head. He looked up at the pale light bulb.

Steve took a step forward and placed a reassuring hand on Harris's shoulder. "What do we do now?" he whispered.

But before Harris could reply, the shrill ring of Steve's cell phone erupted from his jacket pocket, startling both men.

Chapter Nineteen: July 3 continued

Steve's right foot pinned the gas pedal to the floor as he sped through the dark streets of McKeesport's north side. Nervously sucking an unlit cigarette he found on the front seat of the car, Steve tried to make sense of the phone call he just received. Gary's message was brief and to the point. He wanted Steve to meet him as soon as he could at an abandoned house on Pirl Street. Gary said he found Nathan Espy.

"I can't go into any details," Gary said after giving Steve the address, his voice crackling on the other end of the line. "Just get here."

Now as Steve neared Pirl Street, a blend of trepidation and excitement began to burn in the middle of his gut. Telling himself to remain calm, Steve steered the car to the side of the curb and came to a stop just three blocks from where he was to meet Gary. He slipped the car into park and cut off the engine.

Steve forced three deep breaths into his lungs in an attempt to calm his racing heart. That didn't work so he lit the Marlboro. As he swallowed the first mouthful of smoke, he began to relax. No mistakes, he cautioned himself. No mistakes.

Bending his head slightly over the steering wheel, Steve looked down the pitch-black street. He was parked at the top of Helms Avenue, a twisting brick street littered with sharp potholes that rendered it nearly undriveable. This wasn't considered a major problem for the city since most of the houses that lined either side of the street were either condemned or abandoned. Steve patted the side of his chest feeling the comfortable weight of his service revolver snug in his shoulder holster. To get to the address Gary had given him, Steve would have to go two more blocks down Helms and then make a right. Driving the rest of the way was out of the question if he wanted to retain the element of surprise, so after grinding out his cigarette, Steve pushed open the driver's side door and stepped into the night.

With a quick and purposeful stride, Steve made his way toward Pirl Street. Even though he was in one of the worst sections of town, a neighborhood overrun with crack heads and drug dealers, Steve wasn't concerned with the locals. He had busted enough of them to know they weren't the type who actively sought out trouble with the police.

No, the neighborhood dope fiends weren't what concerned Steve. It was Curtis Mayflower.

Though Gary mentioned only Nathan Espy, it made sense that wherever Espy was, Mayflower couldn't be far behind. And wounded or not, Mayflower was still one dangerous bastard. Steve slowed for a moment and drew his weapon, holding it stiffly against his right side.

When he reached the intersection, Steve lowered himself into a crouching position and looked up and down Pirl Street. Like Helms, it was a thin, twisted road of broken brick and gravel flanked on either side by mostly uninhabited houses and weed-infested lots. As he examined his surroundings, Steve gently caressed the grip of his Smith and Wesson with his thumb. *Okay*, he thought. *Where are you, Gary?*

Steve shifted his weight and was contemplating his next move, when a figure emerged from between two houses about twenty feet from his position. For a second, Steve held his breath as every muscle in his body tensed. In that moment he got a good look at the figure, definitely a man, wearing jeans and a sweatshirt. Whoever it was, he was big. Not quite Gary's size and shape, but in this darkness, Steve couldn't be sure. Curtis Mayflower was also a big man.

Still crouched, Steve cradled his left hand under his right and aimed his weapon in the direction of the man's skull. Steve waited for a three-count, but when the figure didn't move, he slowly rose from his crouch. But no sooner did Steve lift his body out of its painful position, than the man darted across the street toward a dilapidated brownstone. Reaching the house, the man bounded up the steps and pushed open the front door. However, before disappearing into the darkness of the house, Steve was able to catch a glimpse of his face.

David Cavanaugh.

"Son-of-a-bitch," Steve hissed between clenched teeth. "What the fuck are you doing here?"

Carefully moving to where David first emerged, Steve kept his hands securely on his weapon and his eyes on the house. When he traversed the distance, he stopped and glanced about. Glass from a few broken beer bottles littered the sidewalk, and someone had crudely spray-painted REST IN PISS on the door of an abandoned garage. Not relaxing the grip on his weapon, he turned to face the brownstone. From where he stood, Steve could see the house numbers stenciled in white paint on the face of the top step.

It was the house Gary had told him Espy was hiding in.

912 Pirl Street.

This was a bad situation, and to Steve's chagrin, it was rapidly deteriorating. His first thought was to call for back up, but to do that he would have to use his cell phone and that was sitting on the passenger seat of his car. He cursed himself for not thinking to call for assistance as soon as Gary called, but between the surprise of hearing from Gary and his eagerness to get his hands on Espy, that fundamental rule of police work slipped his mind. "Stupid," Steve told himself. Even if he did go back to the car and phone the station, it would take at least ten minutes for backup to arrive.

And a lot could happen in ten minutes.

"Shit," Steve muttered before slipping across Pirl Street toward the abandoned house.

***

After entering the house, David paused long enough to let his eyes adjust to the darkness. It only took a few seconds for his night-vision to kick in, allowing him a glimpse of the living room's interior. Strewn about the dust-covered floor were pieces of broken and rotted furniture. An old console style television lay on its side, the picture tube smashed. In the corner of the room a sofa was propped up against the wall, the stuffing from its chewed up cushions hung out like the gutted innards of some animal.

The entire house reeked of mold and rotting wood, the wet acidic smell of decay and neglect. It was a heavy odor that nearly made David gag, but he forced himself not to give in to the stench. Linda's life was at stake.

Since her disappearance, David had maintained a steady routine of pacing back and forth across the library floor in the Smith house and staring at the telephone, waiting for some word about his wife. Until this evening, there had been none. Then came the call from Detective Overton. The police officer told him that Linda had been taken to an abandoned house, and that David should meet him there. No, there was no time for explanation, David was told. Just Linda had been found and a few sketchy directions. "Get there fast," the detective ordered.

David did just that, slamming down the receiver and tearing out of the house. Without permission, he took Mrs. Smith's car and raced toward Pirl Street. Just as the detective instructed, David parked the car a few blocks from the house and traveled the rest of the way on foot. Part of him recognized that what he was being instructed to do was odd, but an even stronger part of him didn't give a damn. All David could think about was finding Linda. To hell with everything else.

David took a few tentative steps into the house, trying to be as quiet as he could on the rotted floorboards. His eyes took another survey of the living room before resting on a wooden staircase to his right. He was about to head to the stairs when a powerful hand clamped itself over his mouth. Before he could react, David felt another hand jam something hard against his back. Instantly, he knew that there was a gun pinned between his shoulder blades. David's whole body went tense, but he didn't struggle.

"Don't move," a stern voice whispered in his ear. "Just relax and don't say a goddamn word. Do you understand me?"

David nodded and the hand across his mouth was taken away. However, the round barrel of the gun still poked into his spine.

"Steve," David whispered. "Is that you?"

"Shut up," Steve growled. The police officer took a step back and told David to turn around. "What the hell are you doing here?" Steve asked in an angry whisper when the two men were facing each other. Though he released David, Steve still had his weapon pointed in his direction.

David ignored the gun as he told Steve about the call from Gary Overton.

As David spoke, a sick feeling washed over the detective. "Oh shit," Steve said when David finished. "Gary called me too. Only he said that Nathan Espy was here."

A puzzled look came over David's face. "I don't understand. Why didn't he tell you about Linda?"

"Come one," Steve said, looking past David and scanning the darkness of the first floor. "We got to get out of here. It's a set up."

Steve went to grab David's arm but the younger man shook him off. In disbelief, he stepped away from Steve. "No," he said, his voice rising excitedly. "Linda is here, we got to find her."

David spun around and started for the steps. As he did, Steve reached out to try to get a grip on his arm, but just as his fingers brushed against David's sweatshirt, Steve heard a scraping sound coming from his left. David heard it too, turning, as Steve did, toward the source.

"Huh?" Steve managed to say as the sofa propped up in the corner came crashing toward him. Unable to get out of its way, Steve threw his arms out, but the weight of the sofa was too much to deflect. It slammed against his left shoulder knocking the cop backward, and bouncing his head off the wall. As the sofa thudded to the ground, Steve's feet got tangled with one of the loose cushions. He stumbled and slammed face first to the dirty floor.

A second later Steve was scrambling to his feet, blood from a gash in his lower lip pouring into his mouth. He looked up in time to see a feral young man leap onto David Cavanaugh. David screamed as the man knocked him flat on his back. Steve whipped his gun around and pointed it toward the wriggling figure that had David pinned to the floor.

"Freeze," Steve shouted, thumbing the hammer of his weapon. "Get the fuck off of him, or I'm going to blow your head off your shoulders."

For a moment the room was captured by a deadly silence as the trio froze. Then the man on top of David slowly turned his face to Steve and grinned. "Morning officer," Nathan Espy smirked.

At the sound of Espy's voice, Steve felt his breath hitch. There was no doubt that it was Nathan Espy straddled atop David Cavanaugh. It was a face that was permanently burned into Steve's mind. Yet what was grinning madly at Steve was not a sixteen-year-old boy. It was something all together different. Something that only looked human.

Nathan's face was a diaphanous, twisted mass of tissue-paper-thin skin stretched across a sharp, jagged skull. His lips were pulled back revealing a mouthful of yellow teeth poking through a set of blackened gums. Most of his hair had fallen out, and what remained, hung in thin greasy strands against his forehead. Small bloody sores oozing infection lined his pockmarked cheekbones just beneath the two sunken holes where Nathan's eyes should have been.

"Sweet Jesus," Steve choked out.

Nathan's grin grew wider as he blinked innocently. "Jesus. Moi? I don't think so." Nathan uttered a low, guttural laugh then twisted sideways against David. At the motion, Steve stepped forward and thrust his weapon out. "No, no, no," Nathan said, softly chuckling, as he leaned his head toward David's face.

Steve glanced down at David. The point of a thick butcher knife was pressed into the flesh below David's Adam's-apple. A thin trail of blood trickled from the wound.

"If either of you move," Nathan said. "I'm going to pin Mr. Cavanaugh's throat to the floor. Is that understood?" To emphasize his point, Nathan flicked the knife into David's flesh sending a spurt of blood several inches into the air. With surprising dexterity, Nathan then scissor-kicked his legs off David's lower body while pushing his torso upward with his left hand in a one armed push-up. His legs whipped behind him, and in an instant, he was crouched at David's side. Keeping his head tilted in Steve's direction, Nathan grabbed the back of David's head with his left hand and yanked the man to his feet. All the while the knife never wavered from his victim's throat.

"Step back, Officer Steve Wyckoff," Nathan ordered.

Reluctantly, Steve took three steps backward. However he didn't lower his weapon. "What do you want, Espy?"

Nathan laughed and slapped David's back with his free hand. "Don't be obtuse, Steve Wyckoff. We both know young Master Espy is not here. At least not all of him is here. But if it pleases you, you may call me by that name."

"Thank you," Steve said as calmly as he could. "But if only a part of Nathan is here, where's the rest of him?"

Nathan considered the question for a moment then turned his face within an inch of David's. "Actually, what's left of his mind is on Mr. Cavanaugh's Toy Train. I cannot tell you how grateful I am for that particular dream," Nathan said with a cold laugh. "I don't know why, but I truly find it quaint."

"I'm impressed," Steve began. "I thought you could only fuck with people when they're asleep. I didn't know you could possess them too."

Nathan waved his hand dismissively in the air, and for just a fraction of a second, Steve noticed that the hand that held the knife to David's throat seemed to relax. "I wouldn't actually call it possession," Nathan replied. "Borrowing is a better word. I'm merely borrowing young Nathan's body while he sleeps. To him this is all a dream."

Keep him talking, Steve thought. Keep him talking and pray to get a shot off. "Is that what you did with Phillip Slaughter and Gladys Decorta? Borrow their bodies?"

This time Nathan laughed heartily, the knife hand falling a good inch from David's throat. "Oh no, nothing like that at all. I merely made use of their proximity and visited them. They were extremely receptive to me, but unlike you, Detective Wyckoff, their minds were much too fragile to cope with my presence. I simply showed them one possible course of action to ease their pain; of course, it is not my fault if they can't tell the difference between the waking world and my world."

Nathan sighed and flicked the tip of the knife back into the flesh below David's jaw. "But this grows tiresome. After all, Davie-boy here came to see his wife." For a split-second, Nathan took the knife from David's throat and pointed it toward the stairs.

"Linda," David whispered.

"Yes," Nathan replied. "Our Linda."

Still clad in the silk pajamas she was wearing the night she disappeared, Linda Cavanaugh slowly descended the stairs. Her hair was in tangles and fine traces of dirt and grime filled the contours of her face, but as far as Steve could tell, she appeared to be uninjured.

She was also asleep.

"Linda!" David shouted. Nathan slapped his left hand back over David's mouth and tilted his head back, exposing even more of his blood stained throat.

"Shhh," he whispered into David's ear. "You might wake her."

David tried to free himself, but with every movement, no matter how slight, the sharp steel of the knife pricked through the tender flesh of his throat.

"Enough," Steve said. He cast a quick glance toward Linda then, with his gaze affixed on Nathan, addressed David. "Listen to me, David. He's keeping Linda asleep because he's nothing without her. Harris told me all about it. When Linda was a kid, Henry Smith accidentally turned her into some kind of energy source for this bastard. When Linda's not around, he can only screw around with people in their dreams." Steve shifted his gaze to Nathan. "But we forget them when we wake up, so what fun are they? Right. It's more fun to "borrow" a body and, to do that, you need Linda."

Steve turned his upper body and directed his Smith and Wesson away from Nathan, pointing its thick barrel at Linda Cavanaugh. Her eyes still closed, Linda stood transfixed on the bottom step. Steve heard a sharp intake of breath coming from Nathan.

"You wouldn't," he said murderously.

"I sure as fuck would," Steve shot back. "How many people are dead already because of you? Eight? Nine? More? I shoot Linda and we both know that you go out like a light. Back to your dream world . . ." Steve paused, a knowing grin playing at the corners of his mouth. "Where we can fuck with you. That's what you're afraid of, isn't it? That's how Henry Smith kept you in check all those years. He had all his patients personifying their dreams as you. And like Harris said, you have to come when you're called. And when they thought they were shooting their addictions with their dream guns, it was really your sorry ass they were blowing off. And that fucking hurt, didn't it?"

Steve cocked the hammer back on his weapon and took aim. So far his bluff was working. With a little more prodding, Nathan might push David aside and try to come after him. Then he could take care of Espy and get Linda out of the house and, preferably, a thousand miles away from McKeesport. "I kill her, then you go back to dream land. And then I'll come after you there and . . ."

Something solid struck Steve in the back of the head, knocking the cop to his knees. His gun hand fell limply to his side as the floor rushed toward him like a speeding car. Once again, Steve slammed face first into the floor, this time smashing his nose. As his consciousness melted away, Steve felt himself being rolled over onto his back. He tried to inhale, but his windpipe was too clogged with his own blood to allow any air down. He was surprised at how calm he felt at the moment of his own death. There was no pain, no fear. Only the warm, coppery taste of his own blood.

He blinked once and saw Gary standing over him, holding what looked like a brick. It didn't matter though. Nothing mattered any more. Steve wanted to tell his partner that everything was all right; that choking to death on your own blood wasn't such a bad way to die. But all he could do was close his eyes.

Then Steve felt himself die.

Chapter Twenty

The sun rose as it had done for eons, burning away the night and rousing the sleepers from their dreams. He felt them slipping from his grasp, shaking off the remnants of his presence as consciousness overtook their bodies. Some of the sleepers though, those whose pain was a sweet invitation to feast, still felt the numbing terror of his visit.

He submerged himself in their fears, feeling their anxiety become his strength. The old one, Henry Smith, had found a way to strip him off his powers, to turn him, the hunter, into the hunted. He had bore his own pain patiently, waiting for the time when he would be released from those who could hurt him.

Then the old one died and the girl was returned to him.

The girl. She was the one sleeper whose dreams bridged the dark chasm that separated the sleeping and waking worlds. She was his now, and he would see to it that she slept for eternity. And he would steal the power of her dreams and escape the neither-place.

But there were still those who knew he could be hurt. They were dangerous, but not without use. The girl's husband, the one who dreamt of trains could be converted like the boy into a sleepwalker. He would give anything to have his wife back.

The others though, they must be made to fear the coming of sleep before they died. They must know that their minds are being ripped apart, for the dread is always more delicious when it is accompanied by awareness.

Looking through the sleeping eyes of Nathan Espy, he watched the sun rising in the sky. His acolytes lay around him dreaming of fire and their own glorious deaths. "Arise," he said, his voice penetrating the recesses of their individual dreams. "It is time to begin."

July 3, 9:00 AM

Mayor Carolyn Markbury stirred three packs of sugar into her coffee while her eyes scanned the morning edition of The Daily News. The headline boasted: GOVERNOR HILL TO DEDICATE MARINA. Below it was a picture taken at the governor's yearly retreat of the governor shaking the mayor's hand. The governor was laughing at some private joke while Carolyn smiled politely. It was a good picture, and she was glad The Daily News picked it from their file footage.

Carolyn flipped open the newspaper and skimmed through the first few pages. They were filled with stories about the new marina and the expectation that the governor would be using the dedication ceremony to announce his candidacy for the presidency. Nowhere on the first six pages was there any mention of Nathan Espy or Curtis Mayflower. Pleased, Carolyn stopped stirring her coffee and took a sip.

But it was still a major pain in the ass knowing that those two were still at large. So far she had successfully used her influence to keep the lid on the matter, but she didn't know how much longer she would be able to contain the situation. The murderers had been too gruesome, too fantastic to escape widespread attention for long.

But all she needed was another twenty-four hours. Just enough time to convince the last handful of developers that the new Marina and Entertainment Complex was a prime investment. If she could get the final few investors in place, it would be the culmination of three years of wheeling and dealing to turn a useless stretch of riverfront property into one of Pennsylvania's premier entertainment showcases. The economic benefits to the town would be immense.

And, of course, when the money started rolling in, she'd be much too humble to take any of the credit. She'd blush as people praised her economic vision and concern for her hometown.

The Woman Who Saved McKeesport, they'd call her.

A catchy title.

It would work well during the next congressional election.

Congresswoman Markbury.

The Woman Who Saved McKeesport.

Yes, that sounded just right.

But there was still the nagging problem of Espy and Mayflower. After the dedication celebration and the final investors were all lined up, she'd get serious about apprehending them. The whole situation was a mess, and it was probably going to get messier, but Carolyn had no intention of letting it affect her political career. Sooner or later the shit was going to hit the fan about Espy and Mayflower, and someone was going to have to take the fall.

It's too bad, she thought, turning her attention to the comic page. She'd always liked Steve Wyckoff.

11:00 AM

A half-mile below the ridge of Radaken's Hill, Carl Northrup stopped his truck. He rolled the driver's side window down and stuck his arm out the side. The cop lounging against the side of the wooden barricade strolled over to Carl and took a small picture ID from his hand. The police officer casually looked over the ID, then handed it back to Carl.

"Okay, Mr. Northrup."

The young cop turned back to the barricade and pulled it to the side of the road, providing just enough room for Carl to get his truck through. As Carl went by, he stuck his head out the window and reminded the cop not to let anyone past the barricade who didn't have proper ID.

"Uh huh," the police officer said, dragging the barricade back across the street. "Whatever."

Once at the top of the hill, Carl parked his truck next to his sons'. Good. They were early for once.

Carl got out of his vehicle and called for his boys.

"Over here." Rubin was standing on the second staging platform rechecking for the third time the work he had done the day before.

"Everything okay for the charges?" Carl asked, making his way toward Rubin.

"Equipments ready," Rubin said. "But . . ."

Carl didn't let his son finish. "Shit," Carl said, whipping his baseball cap off his head and slapping it across the side of his thigh. He looked up and down the hill from the top where the trucks were parked to the bottom where it fell off sharply into the river. "Where is he?"

Rubin shrugged. "I don't know. He didn't come back from his date last night."

Carl slapped his ball cap back onto his head, then jammed his rough fists against his hips. Seth had pulled a lot of stupid stunts in his day, but to not show up when it was time to set the charges into the mortars was inexcusable. For a dozen different safety reasons, loading of the charges was a three-man job.

"This is the last time he ever pulls a stunt like this," Carl shouted.

Rubin remained silent. In the past, he often found himself covering for his brother's screw-ups, but this time was different. Not having the third man to help load the charges compromised their safety, and like his father, Rubin had no patience for anyone who took a half-assed approach to safety.

After a long couple of seconds, Carl wiped his mouth with the back of his hand. "Okay," he said calmly to Rubin. "I'm going to call the hospital and the police department, and see if your brother has been in some kind of accident or something. Then me and you are going to load those charges real carefully."

Carl didn't wait for a reply. He spun around and stomped his way up the hill. While he would never wish ill on his children, part of him was hoping that Seth had been in some kind of accident and was holed up in the hospital with a broken leg. Or maybe he got drunk and got in a fight and was sleeping it off in jail. It wouldn't be the first time that had happened. But if there was no good explanation for Seth's absence, Carl swore he was going to wring his eldest son's neck with his bare hands.

1:30 PM

Merilee looked at her watch for the third time in the past five minutes. There had been no word from Steve since he took off to meet Harris Smith nearly ten hours ago. Nervously, Merilee paced between her living room and kitchen, a total of nine strides in each direction.

"Damn it, Steve, where are you?" Merilee checked her watch again.

When Steve hadn't called her by 10:00 a.m., Merilee called Randy Bressler at the police station to see if Steve had reported to work. Randy told Merilee that there had been no sign of Steve. "He'd better get here," the assistant chief warned. "The mayor's looking for him."

After speaking with Randy, Merilee phoned Harris Smith who was also in the dark as to Steve's whereabouts. "He got a call on his cell phone," Harris told Merilee. "About four in the morning. He didn't say from whom, but he took off afterwards in a hurry."

The news only made Merilee more upset. Since six in the morning she'd been calling Steve's cell phone number but there was never any answer.

Frightened and unable to think of anyone else who might have a clue to Steve's whereabouts, Merilee snatched her phone from its cradle on the wall and began punching numbers. After the third ring, a tired voice said hello.

"Morris," Merilee said, "I need your help."

***

Propelled by some gentle, invisible hand, he drifted over the smooth, sloping hills. Beneath him, a vast ocean of green treetops swayed in the wind as he soared over the flattened peaks of ancient mountains and into the plush recess of a rich, fertile valley.

As he drifted above a twisting river that snaked through the valley, he felt his body slowing to match the speed of the water. He flowed with it, skimming atop its opal surface like a stone. He floated on, weaving through a dense forest of oak and pine until he came to a confluence where the water spilled into a wider, stronger river.

The two rivers slammed against each other with a great roar, forming a terrifying whirlpool, but he remained unafraid, safe above the churning water. He looked out past the confluence toward the riverbank where hundreds of tents were erected. Beyond them on a small hill overlooking the river, a cabin made of logs and mud sat apart from the rest of the community.

For a while, all was quiet then he heard a low, mournful wail. Soon the wailing was joined by hundreds of screams and angry shouts. One of the small tents in the middle of the village caught fire. Within moments, a dozen fires burned out of control, their flames rapidly spreading throughout the village.

Powerless to intercede, he looked on as men, women, and children swarmed from their homes and ran screaming toward the river. One woman, her torso engulfed in flame, grabbed a spindly, old man as he hobbled toward the water. Laughing, she wrapped her burning arms around him and wrestled him to the ground. The sound of her laughter lifted above the screams and cries of the others as her skin melted into the burning pores of the dying old man.

Unable to look at the carnage in front of him, the watcher turned his gaze toward the large hut overlooking the burning village. A man stood in the entranceway. His arms outstretched above his head, the man shouted toward the sky in a long, dead language.

alleta di rhasoon

alleta di rhasoon

The voice exploded over the screams of the villagers running toward the river. Some covered the sides of their heads with their hands in a desperate attempt to keep the sound from penetrating their ears. Others fell to the ground, their bodies writhing in pain as the chanting grew louder.

Horrified, a cold epiphany came across the watcher. He was witnessing the revenge of Dust, the sudden and terrible madness that was brought upon the people after the death of the warrior Mokera. This was where his dream brought him. To the past to get a glimpse of what lay ahead for the people of McKeesport.

When he realized what he was witnessing, Steve Wyckoff's eyes fluttered open. He was in terrible pain and barely able to breath, but at least he had come back from the dead.

July 3 continued

When Steve hit the floor, David was certain that the police officer's skull had been caved in from the brick that Gary Overton had pummeled into the back of his head. David tried to fight his way out of Espy's grip, but he was hoisted off the floor with all his weight pushing down on his twisted left arm. It was on the verge of snapping when Espy dropped him.

David collapsed in a pile next to Steve, the pain in his arm and shoulder excruciating. He tried to push himself up with his right arm but Gary Overton's foot slammed into David's wrist, sweeping his arm out from under him. David buckled and hit the floor chest first.

Immediately, David felt his wrists being yanked to the small of his back. There was a clicking sound, then came the sharp pinch of a pair of handcuffs being slapped onto his wrists. A second later, Espy's hands were under David's chin yanking the man's head upward. David heard the sharp sound of duct tape being ripped from its roll. Quickly, he gulped down a mouthful of air before the silver tape was plastered over his mouth. Once done, Espy released his grip.

"Bind his feet," Nathan instructed. "And toss him on the couch."

As Gary Overton carried out Nathan's orders, the boy whispered in David's ear. "Yes or no. Do you want your wife back?"

Eyes bulging from fright, David managed to nod yes.

Nathan patted the top of David's head. "That's what I thought. We'll talk soon."

Nathan stepped back and motioned for Gary to put the prisoner on the sofa. Taking hold of the cuffed wrists in one hand and the tied ankles in the other, Gary jerked David into the air and tossed him face first onto the couch.

"Don't turn around," Espy warned David. "If you do, I'll cut your wife's fingers off."

There was no doubt in David's mind that Espy was serious. He shuddered and buried his face deeper into the sofa's moldy fabric, his eyes stinging from tears and rage. Then he felt a pin prick in his leg and a sudden warmth ...

***

"Hiya, Daviee-boy."

David blinked in surprise at the sight of Mr. Biggler sitting on the edge of the railroad tracks.

"Short time no see," the conductor said pleasantly.

David pivoted his head from side to side. There was no doubt about it; he was at the familiar railroad crossing of the Toy Train, only now, a dramatic change had come over the dreamscape. The hazy, yellow sky of his previous dreams was now replaced by a canvas of brilliant blue. A cool breeze brushed past him bringing with it the faint sounds of swaying tree branches. The dull gray clouds that usually swallowed the steel tracks were also gone. Instead, David could see the tracks stretching in both directions for miles until they disappeared beyond the horizon.

David stopped surveying his surroundings and fixed his gaze on the conductor. "You're Dust," he said.

Mr. Biggler folded his hands into a teepee beneath his chin and nodded.

"But I didn't fall asleep," David replied.

Another knowing nod. "Not willingly, no. But you are asleep none-the-less. And I have it on good authority that you will be so for quite some time. For now, we have much to discuss, you and

I."

"Fuck you," David shot back. "What have you done to Linda?"

"Please, David," the conductor said patiently. "It's extremely rare that I treat your kind with such civility, so do not anger me. It would be nothing for me to turn this pleasant, little picture into your own private hell. It would serve you well to remember that."

"I'm not afraid of you."

Mr. Biggler dropped his hands from his chin and smiled. "I believe you, David. That's why we have a lot to talk about." Biggler paused, placing his palms across his knees. "But enough of this costume; I can see that it's become tedious for you." With that, Mr. Biggler pushed himself into a standing position. As he did, his conductor's uniform flaked away from his body like a layer of dried skin. It fell in chunks to the ground only to be blown away by a strong breeze. The same breeze whipped against Biggler's face, breaking off pieces of the conductor's jaw and cheeks with a sickening snap. When the breeze died down, all traces of Mr. Biggler were gone. In his place stood a tall, bald man wearing a black suit and sunglasses.

"I prefer this," Dust said. "Don't you?"

David ignored the question. "What do you want?"

Dust straightened up and spread his arms out to his sides. He raised his palms upward and began to sway. "I want to show you my home," he said. Dust looked upward at the sky that was beginning to grow dim, then he snapped his fingers and everything was swallowed in blackness.

Infinite nothingness.

And David was in the middle of it.

Chapter Twenty-one: 6:00 PM

The first thing Steve saw when he regained consciousness was a ray of sunlight peeking through a fist-sized hole in the cardboard that had been taped to the window. For Steve, the sight of the silver tape holding the cardboard in place brought an unpleasant association with Marcus Espy's corpse. But Steve quickly got that image out of his head. He was just happy that he wasn't a corpse himself.

And he had no intention of becoming one.

Steve was laying on his side with his hands cuffed behind his back while an electrical cord bound his ankles together. The right side of his face was smashed against the hard floor. Ignoring the throbbing pain in his cheek, Steve wiggled forward and pushed himself into a kneeling position.

Once on his knees, Steve was able to gain his bearings. He was in an upstairs bedroom. The door was to his right, closed and presumably locked. Steve glanced about, looking for a stick, a broken piece of furniture—anything that might be useful in helping him to escape. But the search was pointless; the room was empty except for the thick cloud of dust that hung in the air.

He glanced up at the beam of light coming through the window. It illuminated the left half of the room, sparkling off the floating particles and forming a hazy circle on the far bedroom wall. Steve leaned forward, concentrating on the floor just below the circle of light. There was something there, something barely visible in the corner of the room. Shifting his weight from knee to knee, Steve was able to push himself across the floor toward the object. It was the underside of a lid to a packing crate. Even in the bare light, Steve could see the warning stenciled to it:

DYNAMITE: USE EXTREME CAUTION

What the hell are you up to, Nathan?

Steve twisted his torso to the right and brought his cuffed hand toward the lid. It was a painful stretch, but Steve was able to grip the lid with the tips of his fingers and flip it over. On the topside was stenciled CONWAY CONSTRUCTION.

But before he could examine the lid further, Steve heard footsteps in the hallway. He twisted his body to the right, and moving as fast as he could, shuffled back to the center of the room. Kneeling, he watched the door fling opened.

"Hello, Mr. Wyckoff," Nathan Espy said politely. "You've been out for quite some time."

"Nathan," Steve said, surprised at the transformation that had come over the boy. Nathan's face no longer resembled the twisted mask from their earlier encounter. The much-too-wide grin was gone, and though still pale and pockmarked, Nathan's skin had lost its translucency. What stood in front of Steve was a gangly looking teenager. From all appearances, normal in every way.

Except for the eyes.

No longer turned completely up, Nathan's eyes still registered an insane intensity, wide and unblinking with nothing to hide the madness behind them. "You know, Coach said that people were going to be afraid of me once I teamed up with him. I kind of like that," Nathan said, giggling.

"Coach?" Steve asked.

Nathan waved his hand dismissively in the air. "Coach, Dust, whatever. He says he's got a lot of names. I call him Coach because that's what he told me to call him when he used to take me to play baseball. But we don't play baseball no more. We got more important things to do."

Steve detected a note of regret in Nathan's voice. "Listen, Nathan," Steve said quickly. "I know what's going on isn't your fault. I know how Coach has been making you do things. But you got to believe me, it doesn't have to be this way. I can get help for you, but you got to let me out of here. Please, Nathan. A lot of people have been hurt already."

A bored expression came over Nathan's face. "You don't get it, Wyckoff, do you?" Nathan moved forward and crouched in front of Steve so close that Steve could smell the fetid, pungent aroma of his body. Steve swallowed hard and held his breath. "I don't want your help, none of us do."

"Listen to me, Nathan. He's going to make you go insane."

"SO WHAT!! You're afraid of me. Everyone's afraid of me. AND I LIKE THAT!!" Nathan jumped up and moved behind Steve. "See, you got Coach all wrong. He ain't so bad. In fact, he can be a lot of fun."

Steve felt Nathan's thin fingers wrap around his neck.

"Like when we got my old man."

The fingers started squeezing.

"That was a fucking blast. I had the game of my life."

Steve tried to wiggle free, but the boy's grasp was too strong.

"In a way, I even think my dad was kind of proud of me. Oh, I know he couldn't tell me that because he was dead and all, but I think he was proud. Don't you think?"

Nathan leaned forward, tilting Steve's head upward as he did. For a second, the two made eye contact, and Steve realized that Espy was far past the point of ever reasoning again. Then with a dramatic flourish, Espy pulled his hands away from Steve's neck.

"Ta-da!"

Immediately, Steve began sucking in mouthfuls of the filthy air, burning his throat and lungs as he swallowed. Unable to keep his balance, Steve pitched forward into a ball on the floor, fighting for each painful breath.

"Coach says he wants you alive. He says you're gonna be useful when everything's done, but first you gotta get tenderized a bit." Another giggling fit struck the boy. "That sounds fun." The laughter lasted almost a minute then abruptly stopped. Nathan scowled at the man sprawled in front of him. "But right now we have to go. I'll come back for you in a few days. By then you'll be just right for Coach."

Nathan turned to go, but Steve stopped him. "Wait," Steve managed between gasps. "What did you do with Gary?"

"Oh, the big cop. I didn't do anything with him. Coach sent him to us. Turns out when he was a little kid, he had an uncle who liked to do him up the butt. That's really sick, you know that? I'm glad my old man wasn't into that kind of shit. Anyway, he's been having bad dreams all his life about that. That's the thing with us abused kids, Wyckoff. We all have bad dreams, and we'll do anything to get rid of them. His dreams made it easy for Coach to visit. And I guess Coach just took a liking to him, that's all."

"What about the dynamite, Nathan? What's that for?"

"Oh that." Nathan paused a moment to consider his answer. When it came, it was cold and emotionless. "We're going to set everyone in town on fire," he said, stepping through the door. "Then Coach will be free."

Steve heard the door close and the lock click in place. He lay still, trying to get his breathing under control as he replayed Nathan's parting words in his mind.

Set everyone on fire.

A few minutes later Steve groaned and began the painful process of getting back on his knees.

6:48 PM

Nathan paused at the top of the steps and looked down at the assembly below. At the base of the stairs, Ace, the perfect acolyte, stood at attention, his eyes wide and eager. Clinging to his left arm was Julie, still dressed in the red skirt and low cut blouse she wore for her date with Seth Northrup. Behind them, Petey and Bip rocked up on the balls of their feet, straining to see over Ace's head. Only Calvin, the firebug and electronics wizard, was missing out of the gang from the Torrid Zone. Nathan had dispatched him earlier.

To the right of Petey and Bip stood Mrs. Torach, smiling pleasantly while she clutched at the plastic strap of her purse. The smooth handle of a pistol peeked between the soiled folds of spent tissues Mrs. Torach had been stuffing in the bag since Fredo went missing. Only now, Fredo had come back to her, visiting her dreams and telling her that everything was going to be fine. He promised that they would be together again as long as she did exactly what Nathan Espy told her to do. And that promise was more than enough to get Mrs. Torach to stop crying.

The only person in the group not gazing lovingly upon Nathan was Curtis Mayflower. He sat alone on the couch at the far end of the room. Head hunched forward, he sat with his elbows on his knees, the palms of his hands pressed tightly against his ears. The wound in his leg seeped infection, and his eye burned from the tiny shards of glass that were still embedded in it, but neither pain compared to the agony that echoed within his skull as the screams of thousands of children reverberated between his ears. He kept his palms clamped against his head, but the screaming wouldn't stop.

As Nathan made his way to the bottom of the stairs, the group stepped reverently to the side so he could pass. He walked to the couch and stood next to Curtis. The big man didn't seem to notice Nathan's approach. He sat motionless, still trying to push his palms through the sides of his skull. Looking down at Curtis, Nathan addressed the group behind him.

"Is everything ready?"

Ace stepped forward and answered. "Yeah, Nathan. Everything's cool. The stuff is in place, and that Cavanaugh guy is doped up in the van like you said. He ain't gonna wake up in days."

Nathan showed no sign that he heard Ace. Instead, he reached out and brushed his fingertips across Curtis's greasy hair. Curtis flinched at the touch but did not alter his position. "And the fireworks guy?" Nathan asked. "Has he been taken care of?"

"Oh yeah," Ace said. Beside him, Julie began to giggle. "He's chilling in the trunk of the car."

"Good," Nathan purred, still stroking the top of Curtis's head.

"What about Wyckoff?" a woman's voice demanded. "Why is he still alive?"

Nathan shifted his gaze from Curtis and trained it on the figure standing in the open doorway that led to the kitchen. "I told you.

Coach doesn't want him dead. He thinks he can be of use after tonight's inferno."

"That's bullshit," the woman shot back. "Wyckoff is a threat, just like Cavanaugh. Both of them need to be killed."

Nathan chuckled softly to himself and returned his gaze toward Curtis. "I told you, Mrs. Smith. Coach has plans for those two, especially your son-in-law. So if I were you, I wouldn't try to fuck them up."

"Don't you threaten me you little freak!" Denise Smith screamed at Nathan. "Dust needs me a lot more than he needs any of you."

"Wrong." Nathan wheeled about toward Mrs. Smith, causing the woman to take a step backward. "You were necessary in the beginning when Coach needed money and the DK. But now your help is not required." Nathan spat out the last two words as a warning. "So you just keep your mouth shut and do what you're told, and you'll get your daughter back. And maybe, just maybe, if Coach is in a good mood, he'll let you keep her for a while."

For a moment, Mrs. Smith's eyes were fixed on Nathan's. Neither spoke, but the cold truth of Nathan's words began to sink in. "He promised me," she said, her voice trembling. "He promised me that he wouldn't hurt Linda or Harris if I helped you." She moved toward Nathan, pleading with the boy. "I don't care about who's been hurt already. I don't care what Dust wants to do to this town. All I want is my daughter back." Sobbing, Denise Smith fell to her knees.

Nathan flung Mrs. Smith to the side and turned back to his followers. "The time of revenge has come," he said. Around him came murmurs of agreement. "These people who have made him suffer will be washed away in a river of fire. And afterward, when they dream, they will be his food."

Nathan turned and knelt next to Curtis. He stuck his hand on Cutis's chest, patting the cylinders taped to the skin beneath his shirt. "And you, Curtis. Do what you have been commanded and the screaming will stop. Do you understand?"

Curtis lifted his head and said he understood.

"Good. Then it is time to go."

***

David was alone, surrounded by an endless, black void. He felt nothing; he heard nothing; he saw nothing. It was as if he was a part of the darkness, a black patch on the quilt work of infinity. Here there was no time, no space. Only nothingness and thought. That was the most terrifying part; he could still think. He was still conscious, still aware of who and what he was. And he could feel emotions. Fear, dread, loneliness.

He tried to speak, to shout out to someone in the darkness, but he couldn't tap into that part of his brain that controlled speech. He tried again, willing his voice to erupt from his mouth. But he had no voice. He had no mouth.

Deprived of form.

The thought was his, and yet it came from somewhere else. Somewhere beyond his consciousness.

I am here with you.

Yes, David answered. *But where is here?*

You call this the neither-place. The place that is nowhere. It is a prison of emptiness. I know its vastness, its infinite smallness. And like you, I am nothing here.

Why are you a prisoner?

I rebelled and was cast into this no place. Since the first dawn I was here. I was here when your kind swung from trees and walked on all fours. I was here when they stood upright and began to dream. It was their dreams that allowed me to see your world again. At first, those dreams were rare. Only glimpses, brief moments where I could see and touch. But always, I was forced to come back here. Then more and more of your kind came upon the land, and their dreams fed me. They let me see the sun and taste the air. But always . . . always, I return here.

As the words penetrated David's consciousness, they were accompanied by a feeling of unimaginable pain and despair as deep and black as the void that entombed him. But equally strong was the presence of a maddening chaos, an evil born of isolation and hatred.

And then the dreamer you call Linda came, your wife. She was just a child but her dreams were so powerful, more powerful than any I have ever felt. They were strong enough to release me.

I have tasted freedom, David. And I cannot give that up for another eternity here.

David concentrated, pushing the swirling confusion of Dust's emotions aside.

What do you want from me?

Much.

The blackness of the void wavered as David felt the weight of his body reunited with his mind.

Then he felt himself falling.

Chapter Twenty-two: 7:00 PM

Carolyn Markbury was all smiles as she allowed the governor to help her into the convertible that would carry the pair along the two-and-a-half-mile parade route. In an unexpected but welcome move, Governor Hill nixed the idea that he ride in a secured limousine, waving to the spectators from an open window. It was too nice a night to be stuck inside a car, he told Carolyn and his aids. He wanted to be where the people could see him. Would it be a problem? he asked Carolyn. If he rode with her?

No problem at all, she told the governor to the great displeasure of his security staff.

"Are all the major networks covering this?" the governor asked as soon as the two were seated. It was less a question and more a statement.

The mayor nodded smartly. "Local affiliates from here to Philadelphia, as well as FOX and CNN. They must think something big is going to happen tonight."

The governor laughed and began to wave to the enthusiastic crowd. "Then let's get this show on the road."

7:10 PM

From his bedroom window, Harris Smith watched his mother pull her white, Lincoln Continental into the driveway. When he saw her exiting the car, Harris stepped away from the window. He waited until he heard the front door open and his mother making her way to the staircase before going out into the hallway.

"Hello, mother," he said when she reached the top of the stairs.

Surprised at her son's voice, Mrs. Smith gasped, bringing her right palm to her chest. "Jesus, Harris. You scared me."

Harris grunted, keeping his eyes fixed on his mother's face. She looked disheveled; her hair hung in loose strands, and her usually flawless makeup was marred by dark brown smudges of dirt and grime. "You don't look so good," Harris said blankly. "Have a hard day?"

Mrs. Smith eyed her son suspiciously. "I don't know what you mean," she said as her hands flew about her face, pushing the loose hair back into place. She offered an affected laugh while she smoothed out her hair. "Oh, this. I just can't keep it under control."

"Uh huh." Harris took a step forward as his mother adjusted the last loose strand of hair. "Morris Keyes came to see me this afternoon," he said. "You remember him, don't you, mother?"

Mrs. Smith stopped fiddling with her hair. "Yes, I remember him," she said gruffly. "But unless he has some news about your sister, I am not interested in anything Mr. Keyes has to say. Now, if you'll excuse me."

Mrs. Smith made a motion to go around her son, but Harris blocked her path. "Morris came here to tell me that Steve Wyckoff is missing. He wanted to know if I had any idea where he might be."

"And why should that concern me?"

Harris reached out and grabbed his mother by the arm. "Because I met with Wyckoff this morning and told him everything about Linda and the DK. I also told him about Dust, but Steve seemed to know enough about him on his own."

"Really. And how would Steve Wyckoff come to know anything about Dust?"

"Because," Harris said, shaking her arm. "Dust pushed himself into one of his dreams. He got into Steve's head because Steve took some of the DK!" Harris shouted. "That's the other thing Morris came to see me about. The police found a bunch of

273

marijuana at Nathan Espy's house that Steve suspects has been laced with the DK."

Harris released his mother's arm and rested his shoulder against the wall. At that moment he saw Denise Smith for her true self. She was thin, pale, and frightened. And old.

"How did Nathan Espy get his hands on the DK?" Harris asked, his voice barely registering a whisper.

"I don't know what you're talking about." Mrs. Smith placed her palms on her hips and arched her back forward. She squared her jaw and narrowed her eyes in a calculated pose meant to intimidate her son. It was a pose her children knew well.

But it wouldn't work this time. "Please mother, we both know that you and I are the only people who have access to the DK. And we also know that I didn't give it to Espy." Harris's eyes drifted open. "So tell me right now what's going on."

"You're insane," Mrs. Smith snapped. "You're out of your mind." She sidestepped Harris and started down the hall, but Harris grabbed her by both elbows.

"You don't know what you've done, do you? You have no idea!"

Mrs. Smith struggled to free herself but couldn't break her son's grip. "Let me go this instant, Harris!"

Harris only gripped his mother tighter, pushing her roughly against the plaster wall. "Don't you get it? Everyone who has any contact with the DK becomes susceptible to Dust. When father died, there were only a few dozen of his patients left, not enough dreamers for Dust to grow too strong from before I could contain him again. But if Espy has been distributing pot laced with the DK, we have no way of knowing how many people have been affected. It could be hundreds. Thousands. Can you imagine that?" Harris asked, shaking his mother's arms. "Thousands of people whose dreams are open to Dust. How many of them do you think will end up insane like Robert Monero? Huh? How many of them will commit suicide?"

"I don't know!" Mrs. Smith shouted. "And I don't care! You were the one who let Dust escape. You were the one who was too weak to hold him. So if anybody dies, it's your fault. Do you understand me? It's your fault." Mrs. Smith slammed her palms into Harris's chest. The force of the blow took Harris by surprise, knocking him backward and causing him to lose his grip on his mother's arms.

"You're the weak one," she continued. "That's what he calls you, 'the weak one.' He knows that you can never hold him like your father did. You're nothing to him, Harris. Nothing."

"You're wrong," Harris stammered. "I can hold him."

Mrs. Smith laughed. "You can do nothing of the sort. If you could hold him, he wouldn't be free now, would he? He wouldn't be coming to me."

Mrs. Smith registered the stunned expression on her son's face and laughed again. "That's right. Dust has been in my dreams since your father died. He and I have an understanding. I give that freak Espy money and the DK, and Dust doesn't go after you and Linda."

"No," Harris said frightened. "Why didn't you tell me he was pushing his way into your dreams again? I could have helped you."

Mrs. Smith shook her head and rested her hand gently against her son's arm. "No, Harris. You couldn't have done anything to stop him. I did it for you and Linda. It was the only way to protect the two of you."

"Protect us?"

"Yes, protect us all," Mrs. Smith said, her tone softening. "All he wants is the Rehab Clinic to reopen. He needs a new sleeping-room." Mrs. Smith's fingers lightly brushed against the side of her son's head. "That's why Espy is giving away the marijuana with the DK in it; the clinic will need a new batch of patients. If we do that one thing for him, he'll be satisfied and let us go on with our lives."

"Good God, mother. You don't really believe that, do you?"

Mrs. Smith jerked her hand away from Harris's temple and glared at her son. "Do I have a choice? If I don't do what he wants, he'll destroy you and Linda."

Harris shook his head. "He'll come after me no matter what, but he won't hurt Linda. He needs her. That's why I have to find her and get her as far away as possible."

Mrs. Smith stiffened. "You can't do that. Not now."

For a moment, Harris was puzzled by his mother's response then a stark realization hit him like a brick. "You know where she is," he gasped. "You've known the whole time. That's why you didn't want Steve Wyckoff and the police involved." Harris pushed himself further away from his mother. "You let that creature take your own daughter."

"No, it's not like you think." Mrs. Smith went to grab her son's hand as he took another step backward. Harris jerked away from his mother's reach, but as he did, the heel of his left foot came down awkwardly over the top step. The stumble was negligible, but enough to make Harris lose his balance, twisting the bulk of his weight onto his left foot. It slipped off the step and landed sideways against the step below it. There was the sickening sound of snapping bone, then Harris screamed as his momentum sent him crashing down the staircase.

Mouth open, Mrs. Smith watched helplessly as her son's head and neck slammed against the hard marble steps. His fall carried him all the way to the next to last step where he landed in a twisted heap. Mrs. Smith hurried to Harris's side. He was out cold, his left leg slung over the side of the steps at an unnatural angle. Mrs. Smith gingerly ran her fingers along the top and sides of his head. There were no signs of fracture. She glanced down at her hands.

No blood either.

Mrs. Smith took Harris's left arm and checked for a pulse. It was quick, but strong. Satisfied that he was in no immediate danger, she bent forward and kissed him softly on the cheek. "Sleep baby," she whispered. "Everything is going to be just fine. I promise."

She got up from the steps and hurried out the front door, pausing only long enough to make sure that it was locked.

7:45 PM

Calvin had a prime, front row spot at the end of the parade route. Less than ten yards to his left was the dignitary's grandstand, all decked out in red, white, and blue bunting. A dark brown podium stood in the middle of the platform with a dozen folding chairs forming a semicircle behind it. The grandstand had been strategically arranged so that it overlooked the entranceway to McKeesport's new marina. It would be impossible for any of the network news cameras to get a shot of the governor without including the river and the new marina.

All around Calvin, thousands of McKeesporters buzzed with excitement as the sounds of the McKeesport High School Marching Tigers approached. Calvin closed his eyes and blocked out the noise. He pictured the grandstand, seeing it in his mind's eye as clearly as if he was gazing on it. The chairs, the podium, the patriotic bunting. It was all there in vivid color.

And it was all burning.

Calvin smiled to himself as the mental image intensified. The flames licked the sides of the podium, reaching upward. Calvin could see the governor, his skin peeling away from his body. Around him the charred bodies of the others writhed in agony. Calvin inhaled sharply. He could smell the sweet aroma of burning flesh, taste the blackened ash that hung in the air.

And the heat. It was everywhere. Surrounding him like an inferno. He quivered against its unbearably exquisite touch.

Calvin's eyes shot open. The Marching Tigers were coming up the street, led by a few scantily clad majorettes with batons and two fat kids holding a large red and blue sign:

MCKEESPORT WELCOMES GOVERNOR HILL

When the governor came in sight, Calvin joined the thousands who crammed the parade route in cheering on the man they hoped would be their next president. As the governor passed in front of him, Calvin whipped out his own miniature American flag and began waving it wildly above his head.

There were tears of joy in his eyes.

And the smell of burnt flesh in his nostrils.

7:50 PM

Steve was on his back, concentrating on the single ray of light that managed to stream through the covered window. For the past hour he watched it travel up the room's far wall, turning soft shades of orange and red as it did. Steve knew the sun would be setting soon, and he didn't relish the idea of being trapped in that room in total darkness. Focusing on the dying sunlight, he forced himself to remain calm.

After Espy left, Steve once again struggled to his feet and surveyed the room. Unfortunately, the examination only confirmed his initial suspicions; there was no way out. The locked door was too solid to break through, especially bound as he was, and the window was too high to smash. It was obvious that the only way Steve was going to get out of the room was for him to free himself first. Experience told him there was no sense trying to slip his chunky wrists out of the handcuffs, only the key would open those. But the cord that bound his ankles could be undone. When he was hopping around the room looking for a way out, Steve felt a slight give in the cord. The slack was hardly perceptible, but it was enough to give the police officer hope.

Steve plopped himself down on his back and rested his feet against the wall directly beneath the trail of sunlight. Slowly, he began rubbing his calves against each other. At first he could only move them an inch or two, but after a few minutes of rubbing, Steve felt the restraint slipping, allowing him to slide his calf an extra four inches. Fighting off the urge to force his way out of the restraint, Steve stayed focused and continued rubbing his legs together in the same, slow rhythm.

A half hour later, as the last rays of sunlight reflected off the thick dust, Steve managed to loosen the cord enough to slip his right foot through. He took a deep breath then gingerly began twisting his foot and ankle through the restraint. He was able to get his foot halfway out when the door flew open.

"Steve, you in here?"

Abandoning his attempt to free himself, Steve flopped onto his side and looked up. The darkness of the room was disorienting, but there was just enough light for Steve to recognize the figure standing in the doorway.

"Morris," Steve gasped.

Morris Keyes looked down and saw Steve sprawled on the floor. Immediately, he came over and helped him into a sitting position. "Jesus Christ, Steve. What happened?" Morris's hands flew to the cord around Steve's ankle.

"You were right," Steve said. "It's Dust. He's controlling Espy. Gary too. "

Morris grunted as he tugged the binds free from Steve's ankles. When Morris tossed them aside, Steve saw that the man was holding a pistol. "We got to get out of here," Morris said, helping Steve to his feet.

"The cuffs," Steve said when he was standing. "See if they left the key in my pocket. Left front."

Morris stuck his fingers in Steve's pocket and found the key to the handcuffs. "I'll be damned," Morris grinned. "The bastards ain't so smart after all."

"How did you find me?" Steve asked as Morris slipped behind him to unlock the cuffs.

"Merilee got worried and called me this afternoon. She said you went out to see Harris Smith late last night, so I went over and paid him a visit. He told me that the two of you met at the Espy house but then you got a call and took off." Morris snapped the cuffs from Steve's wrists and slipped them in his back pocket.

Steve began massaging his wrist with his thumb and forefinger. "But how did you know I would be in this house?"

Morris looked at Steve, an odd expression clouding his face. "You don't know where you are, do you?"

Steve shook his head. "Just some abandoned house."

"Oh shit, Steve. This is where Robert Monero used to live."

Morris was about to say something else when Gary Overton came charging through the open door. He slammed into Steve and Morris, knocking them both on their rears.

"No!" Gary screamed, looming over Steve's body. "If you leave he's going to send me back to Uncle Joe." Gary bent forward and snatched Steve off the floor as if he was a child. "You're one of the bad people. You like to play the feel game." Gary held Steve at arm's length, his feet dangling six inches off the ground. "He showed me what you do to the children, and I'm not going to let you do that anymore." Gary shook Steve's body and slammed him against the back wall. "You're just like Uncle Joe."

Stunned from the impact, Steve hung limply in Gary's grasp. He felt himself start to pass out when a movement at the opposite side of the room caught his attention. Morris Keyes was up and heading toward Gary. Summoning his last bit of strength, Steve shot his right arm forward, connecting it squarely with Gary's jaw. The blow snapped Gary's head back, causing the big man to lose his hold of Steve.

As Steve fell to his knees, Morris Keyes leapt at Gary. Gripping his pistol by the barrel, Morris whipped the butt of the gun against the back of Gary's head. Gary stumbled forward but didn't go down. Dazed, he turned toward Morris just as the older man swung again. This time, the gun slammed full force into Gary's right temple, snapping the young detective's head sideways. Then Gary collapsed onto the floor.

"Come on," Morris said, tugging Steve back to his feet. "We got to get out of here."

"But Gary," Steve said, looking down at his partner. "We can't leave him here."

Morris shoved Steve toward the door. "We can't help him. Not as long as Dust is inside his head." Morris pushed Steve roughly. "Now come on."

Still smarting from being smacked against the wall, Steve stumbled through the doorway into the hall. Morris followed close behind. "There," Morris said, pointing to his left. "The stairs."

Steve took a wobbly step toward the stairs when he heard shouting coming from behind him. Gary was standing in the hallway, his eyes murderously fixed on Steve. "Get back here."

Morris inserted himself between the two men and pushed Steve toward the steps. Steve stumbled forward, then lost his balance and found himself in midair, hurtling down the stairs. He landed on the fourth step and rolled end over end down the remaining eight. He hit the floor flat on his butt.

Dazed, but unhurt, Steve scrambled to his feet and looked up. Gary had gotten a hold of Morris's neck and was bending the old man backward over the top railing of the steps. Steve started toward the steps when he heard the sound of wood splitting. He looked up just as the railing snapped in half, sending Morris tumbling backward. With his hands still wrapped around Morris's neck, Gary followed him over the broken railing. The pair fell, one atop the other, toward the floor amidst the broken pieces of the stairwell.

A wooden rail post, no more than two feet long, hit the floor upright a millisecond before Morris came crashing down on it. Its jagged edge sliced through Morris back and out his chest cavity catching Gary in the base of the throat. Horrified, Steve watched as his two friends were impaled on the post. For half a second, the post stood upright, the two men flailing against each other. Then Morris and Gary fell to the side.

When their arms and legs stopped twitching, Steve took a wary step toward the pair. Two sets of dead eyes stared blankly back at him. Steve stopped as a pool of blood began to develop on the floor. It was an almost perfect black, this mixture of Morris and Gary's blood that bubbled from the holes in his friends' bodies and rolled across the dirty floor just inches from Steve's shoes. He began to take another uneasy step toward his dead friends then, stifling an urge to scream, Steve turned away and ran out of the house. He made it to the end of the unkempt yard and collapsed onto the ground.

"Steve," someone called out a moment later. "Oh my God, Steve. Is that you?"

Steve pushed himself onto his knees and looked up. Merilee was running toward him.

8:00 PM

Seth stopped the red Cavalier just before the barricade and rolled down his window. "I'm one of the pyrotechnicians," he said, thrusting out his identification card. The rookie police officer manning the barricade, Bill Steever, took the card and gave it a casual once over. He was hot and bored and more than a little pissed off that he drew this duty; making sure only official personnel went up Radaken's Hill. In the past seven hours, the official personnel amounted to one guy in a pickup truck. Unimpressed, Steever flipped the ID back to Seth before pushing the barricade to the side.

As the Cavalier made its way slowly up the hill, it never dawned on Officer Steever to ask the other four people in the car for their identification.

8:02 PM

Her arms wrapped about his waist, Merilee helped Steve walk the block and a half to his car. She was alarmed at his appearance; there was dried blood on the back of his collar, his upper lip was split open, and his nose purple and bent to the side. "What happened?" she asked as they neared the car.

"It was Gary. He tried to kill me. Morris stopped him, but they're both dead."

"Oh my God," Merilee gasped. She let go of Steve and spun back toward the house. "Gary and Morris are in there?"

Steve stopped and took her by the hand. "Listen, I'll explain everything later. But right now I need to get to a phone." When Merilee didn't respond, Steve gave her hand a sharp tug. "Come on! I got to get a hold of Randy Bressler. I think Nathan Espy is going to kill the governor."

Still staring at the house, Merilee allowed herself to be pulled to the car. "Why the governor?"

Steve didn't reply. He just kept pulling her to the car. When he reached it, he threw open the passenger side door and began rummaging about the seat for his cellular phone. When he found it, he punched in the numbers to Randy Bressler's direct line, but when he hit the "send" button, nothing happened.

The battery was dead.

"Shit!" he yelled, slamming the phone against the hood of the car. Small bits of plastic and electronics squirted out of his fist.

"Steve," Merilee said, her voice trembling. "What is going on? First you disappear, then Morris asks me to drive him to that house. Now you say he and Gary are dead, and you think Nathan Espy is going to kill the governor. What the fuck is happening?"

Steve wheeled about to face her. "You drove. Do you have my spare keys?"

Merilee nodded. "Yeah, they're on my ring."

"Come on." Steve maneuvered himself across the passenger seat and slid behind the steering wheel. "Come on," he repeated, this time motioning for Merilee to get in the car. As she did, she pulled her keys from her pocket and handed them to Steve.

"Where are we going?"

"The Smith house," Steve replied. Merilee shot him a puzzled look. "I know," Steve said, jamming the key into the ignition and firing up the engine. "I'll explain as we go."

8:04 PM

"That was very, very good," Ace cooed in Seth's right ear. "For a second there I thought I might have to waste ole deputy-dawg, but you were real cool." Ace chuckled and patted Seth on the shoulder.

Seth sat glued with his hands on the steering wheel. Out of the corner of his eye, he could see Julie in the passenger seat twirling her hair and looking bored. He didn't dare turn his head for a better look; if he did, the strand of piano wire wrapped around his neck would be tightened by the two punks sitting with Ace in the back seat. As it was, Petey and Bip allowed only enough slack for Seth to breath.

"Now we have to get your old man over here, do you understand?" Ace asked.

Seth felt the wire loosen a bit, allowing him to nod.

"Good. Now you call your father up here just like we planned. And if you and him don't fuck things up, you'll get to shoot off fireworks next year."

Seth swallowed hard and called for his father. "Dad," he yelled out the open window. "I'm up here."

A few seconds passed before Carl Northrup's lanky figure appeared at the top of the hill. When he saw Seth, a look of relief spread across his face, quickly replaced by a scowl. "Where the hell have you been?" Carl shouted as he scrambled toward the car.

When he came within a dozen feet of the car, Ace calmly emerged from the back seat. "Hiya, Mr. Northrup. Seth said we could watch you set off your fireworks."

"What?" Carl glared at the punk with the bleached hair before turning toward his son. "I don't know what the hell you think you're doing boy, but you get these kids out of here. Then you get your ass over to the truck."

"Aw, c'mon, Mr. Northrup. We won't get in your way." Ace grinned and took two steps toward the man. "Seth promised, you know." Another grin, another step.

Carl turned his back to Ace and grabbed the door handle. "God damn it, Seth," he yelled, yanking open the door. "What the hell is the matter with you?"

Carl stopped when he saw the thin ring of blood that circled his son's neck. "Dad," Seth choked out before Petey and Bip began tugging furiously on their ends of the wire. Seth's head shot back, his hands desperately trying to pull away the wire that was digging into his flesh. Carl reached out to grab his son, but as he did, Ace stepped forward and pressed himself against Carl's side. Carl barely registered the boy's presence or the hard pressure of the gun jammed against his ribs.

Ace fired two shots, blowing open Carl's torso and splattering blood and bits of intestine against Seth's face. In the back of the car, Petey and Bip planted their feet against the front seat in order to get better leverage. They pulled tighter with their arms, and pushed with their legs. As the pressure around his neck increased, Seth's arms and legs flailed wildly about, slapping against the dash of the car and his father's corpse. In his last moment of life, Seth thought he could hear the strains of a marching band. Then he saw his brother walking slowly to the car with an odd expression on his face. Then that odd expression turned to fear.

Then Seth died.

***

I'm still dreaming, David thought. *But where?*
Around him, a swirling gray mist wrapped around his body

284

and face. David tried to peer through the fog, but it was too dark and dense. However, he had no trouble hearing the sounds of moaning all around him. He was surrounded by it, the painful wailing of an unseen multitude.

"Where are you?" he called out.

"They cannot hear you." Dust's voice came from directly in front of David. "They are in the past. You are in the now."

David waved his hands furtively in front of him to clear the dense fog. "I don't understand."

A moment of silence followed. "Turn around."

When he did, the gray fog was gone. "It is the sleeping-place," Dust said. "Where the dreams of the sick were once offered to me. It is where I found life."

David stared amazed. He was in a large, thatched hut where dozens of men and women writhed about on the dirt-covered floor. Their faces were contorted in agonized masks of pain and terror, all with closed eyes. David looked away from the bodies and at the walls of the hut. They were transparent, no more solid than smoke. David peered beyond the walls and saw that the hut was in the middle of a much larger room. A hospital ward where hundreds of men, many of them missing arms and legs, lay on cots and dirty mattresses. They too were all asleep. "Who are they?"

"The infirmed; the wounded; the mad. They are the shells of the dreamers who were brought to this place." A firm hand clamped itself upon David's shoulder. "For centuries the dreamers were brought to me freely. First by the men who built their huts on the banks of the river, then by the men who built this hospital. For five generations, your wife's family has been filling the sleeping-place with the dreams of the wounded. Victims of war whose bodies were broken and mutilated in the most horrible ways. Imagine the dreams they gave me, David. Can you imagine the dreams of a man with no arms and legs? A man with no flesh?" The pressure on David's shoulder increased. "Oh, they were so exquisite."

David tried to turn around to face Dust, but the feeling of being weighed down was overwhelming. He couldn't move. "Why me?" he asked. "What do you want of me?"

"Since the Smith family built this hospital, I have been able to enter more deeply into the minds of the dreamers. At times, I could even move past their dreams and into their waking minds. For me, it is ecstasy to see through their eyes, to touch with their hands. It was the Smith family, David, who allowed me to do that."

"I don't believe you," David said weakly, unable to take his eyes off the diaphanous figures moaning in front of him. They writhed against each other, their arms and legs twisting through each other's incorporeal torsos. "I don't believe Linda's family would help you."

Dust found that amusing. "You'd be surprised how readily your wife's family has come to my assistance. But don't be confused. The family hasn't done anything to strengthen me. It is Linda. She is rare among your kind, David. She is the source of my strength now."

"You can't have her." David tried to free himself but the pressure on his shoulders was too great. "You stay out of her head, you bastard," he cried when he realized the futility of his struggle.

"You misunderstand me," Dust replied. "It is not her dreams I want. On the contrary, I have no intention of entering her dreams any more than is necessary. I know the kind of madness my visits bring. And though I'm sure her madness would be delicious, I cannot afford that. It is her presence I need, David. Her closeness to the neither-place."

"I am offering you a life with your beloved," Dust continued. "A chance to keep your sanity. All you need to do is make sure Linda doesn't leave this place again. If you do that, I will return her to you, and I shall never visit your dreams again. You will be together, free of me."

Dust stopped and David felt himself being turned to the right. The wall that was in front of him melted away, replaced by a large picture window offering a panoramic view of McKeesport's west side. David leaned forward and saw the new riverfront marina with hundreds of boats now moored to the new docks, all swaying with the rhythm of the river. He tilted his head downward and got a view of the street. Thousands of cheering people lined Broadaire Street, all waving flags and banners above their head. David shuddered when he saw they weren't alone.

Mixed in with the cheering crowd were hundreds of translucent figures like the ones trapped in the sleeping-place. Terrified, they were running through the bodies of the parade watchers, desperately trying to get to the river. Above the din of the parade, David could hear their screams as they hurled themselves into the brown water of the Youghioghany. As they did, orange flames shot from the water, licking the sides of the boats anchored in the new marina.

And no one noticed it.

Refuse me and this awaits you. An eternity of the past and the present, Dust said, his voice sounding directly in David's mind. *Together, in a dream.*

"What is happening?" David whispered.

My revenge.

And my rebirth.

Chapter Twenty-three: 8:08 PM

Mrs. Smith looked down at the sleeping body of her daughter, then glanced quickly at the monitor. Pulse, respiration, everything looked fine.

"How is she?" Nathan Espy asked.

"She's fine for now, but we can't keep her asleep much longer."

Nathan grunted and walked to the end of Linda's bed. "She won't need to sleep much longer." He stared at her for a moment then cocked his head to his left. "What about him?"

Mrs. Smith scowled before examining the numbers on the monitor that was hooked up to David's right arm. "He's fine too. He should be out for another twelve hours or so."

"Any chance of him waking up?"

Denise Smith shook her head. "None."

Nathan nodded, but he still reached into the back pocket of his grungy jeans and pulled out Gary Overton's handcuffs. He slipped one end over the bed frame and the other over David's left wrist. "Just to be sure," Nathan said, clicking the cuffs so tight onto David's wrist that they drew blood. "You keep an eye on them. I'm going to go watch the fireworks."

8:09 PM

"I can't believe it," Merilee blurted as she and Steve sped to the Smith house. "All this stuff about Dust is true?"

Steve nodded grimly but remained silent.

"Good God." Merilee brought her fist to her mouth and began to sob. "Why did Gary do it? Why would he want to hurt you and Morris?"

"It wasn't Gary. It was Dust." Steve sighed and pushed the image of his partner out of his mind. "Gary was abused as a kid, and Dust used that to get into his head. I think he forced Gary to dream about it, relive it, and that finally drove him over the edge. Back at the house, I don't think Gary had any idea who Morris or I was."

"What about Espy? And Mayflower? Did Dust do the same thing with them?"

Steve inhaled sharply. "I don't know about Mayflower, but it's different with Espy. Harris told me that in some cases, Dust can take over a person's body while they slept. He called that 'borrowing.' That's what he's doing with Espy."

Steve swung the wheel hard to the left. "There," he said as the Smith house came into view.

"Doesn't look like anyone's home," Merilee said.

Steve hit the brakes and skidded to a sideways stop in front of the driveway. In a single motion, he snatched the keys from the ignition and threw himself out of the door. "Let's go," he called over his shoulder, but Merilee was already out of the car. The two ran up the twisting walkway to the porch. "Harris," Steve shouted, banging his fist against the heavy door. "Mrs. Smith. Is anyone there?"

"Steve, look." Merilee stood to Steve's right, peering through the smoky glass on the side of the door. "On the steps. It looks like a body."

Steve peered inside. A crumpled figure lay twisted at the bottom of the stairs. Steve took a few steps back then hurled himself at the door. He hit it squarely with his shoulder, but it didn't budge. Steve flung himself at the door again, and this time he heard the wooden door cracking against its hinges. Taking a deep breath, Steve lifted his right foot and slammed it against the deadbolt. It broke away as the door swung open.

Steve bolted through the foyer with Merilee following a step behind. "Harris," Steve shouted when he reached the steps. "Can you hear me?"

Harris emitted a low moan and forced his eyes open. "Steve," he said when his vision cleared enough for him to recognize who was in front of him. Harris clutched Steve's hand. "Morris Keyes was here. He said you were missing."

"Yeah, I'll tell you about it later. What happened to you?"

"Dust has gotten to my mother." Harris squeezed Steve's hand for emphasis. "You can't trust her."

Steve nodded and said he understood. "Listen, Harris, I need to call the department. Espy has gotten his hands on some explosives, and I think he's going to do something to the governor."

Harris raised his left arm and pointed weakly toward the library. "In the library, on top of the bar, is a phone."

"I got it." Merilee started for the library, but Harris stopped her.

"Wait. In the bar, on the first shelf next to the ice tray, is a black satchel. Bring that too."

Merilee shot a puzzled look toward Steve before heading off to the library.

"I think I know what Dust wants," Steve said, propping Harris into a sitting position. "He's going to do it again. Take his revenge out on the whole town for being trapped."

Harris took a deep breath. "Yes, I think you're right. But it's more than just revenge. He'll draw strength from it. Become stronger, just as he did before." Harris grabbed Steve's wrist and squeezed it tight. "Steve, we have to stop him. With Linda here, he may become too strong to imprison again."

"But how?" Steve began, stopping when Merilee called out.

"I got it," Merilee said. She handed Steve the phone and Harris the black bag.

"Thank you," Harris said weakly.

Steve hurriedly dialed Randy Bressler's number. When the call connected he moved into the foyer and began talking furiously into the phone. While Steve was on the phone, Merilee leaned forward and examined Harris's wounds. "We got to get you to a doctor," she said. "I think your leg is broken."

Harris looked up at her and smiled. "It's broken alright. I think a few of my ribs are busted too, but no doctors right now. The pain is exactly what I need." Harris fumbled with the black bag and removed a small vial of clear liquid.

Steve hung up the phone and came back to the steps. "I talked to Bressler. He thinks I'm out of my mind, but he's going to alert the governor." Seeing Harris with the black bag, he crouched down beside him. "What are you doing?"

"You have to get to Linda," Harris said. He removed a syringe from the bag and inserted it into the vial. "No matter what happens, Linda is still his energy source." Drawing back on the plunger, Harris filled the syringe. "She'll be asleep, so you'll need to wake her." Harris slipped a small rubber cap over the needle and handed it to Steve. "This is Narcan. Eight c.c.'s of this will bring her out of any sleep."

Steve took the needle and carefully slipped it into his jacket pocket. "What about you?" he asked. "We can't leave you here alone."

Harris waved his hand in front of his face. "There's no time. Let the police handle Espy and whatever happens with the governor. You have to get to Linda. It's the only way to stop Dust."

"What about you?"

Harris slipped his hand back into the bag and took out another vial of liquid, only this one had a slight brownish tint. "The DK," he said. "Undiluted." He smiled and removed another syringe from the bag. "You find Linda, I'll keep Dust busy."

Steve squeezed Harris's shoulder then stood up. He didn't like the idea of leaving Harris alone, but there were no other alternatives. He turned to Merilee and made a motion toward the door. "We've got to go," he said.

Just as the two were at the door, Harris called out. "You know where she is, don't you?"

Steve looked back and nodded. "Yeah, the sleeping-place." Steve turned to Merilee and clarified. "She's at the Rehab Clinic."

8:10 PM

Randy Bressler pocketed his cell phone and looked about as the last row of marchers passed in front of him. He was standing next to a squad car parked at the east end of Broadaire Street. From his vantage point, Randy could see Governor Hill standing on the grandstand at the other end of the street. The mayor stood next to him, both laughing, both completely at ease. In between the two politicians and where Bressler stood, nearly ten thousand residents of McKeesport jammed the three-block area.

"What's the problem?"

Randy spun around to see Rhonda Hemmings. "Rho, am I glad you're here. I just got a call from Steve."

Rhonda's eyes perked up at the mention of Steve's name. "Wyckoff. Where the hell is he?"

Bressler shook his head and cast an uneasy glance toward the grandstand. "He didn't go into too much detail, but Steve said that Espy is nearby, and he thinks that he's going to do something to hurt the governor."

"The governor. What for?"

"I don't know. Steve just said that Espy has a shit-load of dynamite, and he might try to use it on Governor Hill."

Rhonda got on her tiptoes and strained to see the grandstand. The governor was just taking his seat as the mayor headed for the podium. "What are you going to do?"

Bressler glanced up and down Broadaire. Nearly three-dozen uniformed officers lined both sides of the crowded street. Another dozen were in plain clothes mingling with the crowd. "Shit," Bressler muttered. "There's too many people here." He opened the driver's side door of the squad car and slipped into the front seat. Grabbing the microphone of the car's radio, he quickly punched in the code that would broadcast him to all the mobile units. "Attention," he said calmly into the mike. "Attention all officers."

Bressler looked up in time to see nearly twenty officers simultaneously reach for the radio units attached to their service belts. He paused for a moment then spoke very softly and slowly.

"Listen up. This is Assistant Chief Bressler. I've just received word that there is a possibility that Nathan Espy and Curtis Mayflower may be planning some action against the governor. There is also the possibility that they are armed with some kind of explosive devices."

"This is only a possibility; this has not been confirmed. I repeat; this has not been confirmed. But I want everybody to keep a sharp eye out for Espy and Mayflower. If they are spotted, use extreme caution. The first priority will be to get the crowd and the governor away from their location."

Bressler switched the mike off, then punched in the code that would connect him directly to the governor's head of security, a bull of a man named Congreve who didn't seem too impressed with Bressler's news.

"No positive sightings or threats," Congreve replied. "Just a hunch from one of your detectives?"

"Basically," Bressler said. "But I wouldn't be too quick to dismiss it."

"Uh, yeah." Congreve said he would make the rest of the governor's security detail aware of the situation.

"Listen," Bressler began, but Congreve hung up on him. "That jackass," Bressler said to Rhonda who had slipped into the passenger seat of the squad car. "Idiot blew me off." Bressler stared at the radio in his hand before punching in another series of numbers. "Turvel, do you read me?"

"Uh, copy chief," Warren Turvel's nervous voice said over the radio. "Hey, is Espy really close by?"

"That's the word I got, but I don't know. Listen, I want you to do me a favor. You're partnered with Harrington above the marina, right?"

"Yeah, that's right."

"Can you see the Smith Clinic from your location?"

"Affirmative. I'm almost in its parking lot."

"Good. I want you and Harrington to take a quick walk around the grounds."

"Quick walk around the grounds," Turvel repeated. "Copy."

"Good. Radio me when you're done. Bressler out."

Bressler slipped the microphone back into its cradle and sighed. "Man, I hope Steve is wrong about this."

***

Officer Warren Turvel snapped his radio back onto his belt and frowned. Bressler wanted him and Harrington to do a once around the Rehab Clinic. But Neil Harrington went off to take a piss, and if Bressler found out that Neil left his post, the assistant chief would have Harrington's ass for breakfast. Plus, with the crowds at the porta-johns, it could easily be ten minutes before Neil was back. Turvel turned to his left and looked at the Smith building. Hell, it was only about a hundred yards away. He could take a quick stroll around it and report back to Bressler before Harrington got back.

Turvel hitched up his loose fitting service belt and hurried toward the Rehab Clinic.

***

Randy Bressler barely had time to pull his hand from the radio before the crackling of static indicated there was an incoming call. Bressler snatched the microphone from its cradle and held it to his mouth. "Bressler, what have you got?"

"Uh, Chief? This is Steever. I'm at the base of Radaken's Hill." Bressler could tell immediately from Steever's voice that the young officer was nervous. He glanced quickly at Rhonda who returned his gaze. She noticed it too. "Yeah, Steever," Bressler said calmly. "What is it?"

"Uh, a few minutes ago one of those fireworks guys came by. He had his identification, so I let him up the hill."

"So," Bressler replied.

"Well there were some kids with him. High school age, I think." A long pause followed before Steever added, "I didn't ask them for ID."

Bressler screwed his eyes shut and frowned.

"Uh, Chief. Do you want me to go up there and check them

out?"

"No," Bressler barked into the handset. "Stay where you are. Do you here me? Do not move until I get there. Do you understand?"

"Uh, yes sir. Don't move till you get here."

"I mean it, Steever." Bressler slammed the radio back into its cradle. He turned to Rhonda who was slipping the seatbelt over her chest. "It's probably nothing," Bressler said. "You don't need to go."

"True," Rhonda answered, clicking the buckle into place. "And then again it could have been Espy in that car." Rhonda opened her small pocket book and removed a key ring with three silver keys. Gripping one between her fingers, she bent forward and unlocked the steel plate that secured the unit's shotgun. "I am a cop too, you know. And besides," she said, lifting the weapon from its casing. "I'm a better shot than you."

Bressler turned the key and started the engine. "Everyone's a better shot than me."

***

Harris stood alone in the middle of an endless desert. Stretched out before him in every direction was a soft, golden blanket of sand. A pale, pink sun hovered just above the horizon. *There is nothing here*, Harris thought. *Nothing that can frighten me.*

He breathed in the cool air of his dream and felt a rush of adrenalin flow through his body. Of course he knew that his actual body was still lying in a crumpled heap on the stairs, his lower femur, most likely shattered. But here in his dream world, his body coursed with a furious electric energy. Harris had given himself twelve c.c.'s of the DK, three times the normal dose. How long his heart could handle the massive adrenaline rush was uncertain, but for now he was fine.

Closing his eyes, Harris concentrated, conjuring in his mind's eye the image of a crude, wooden shack. When he opened his eyes, a one-room, miner's shack was in front of him. It was dilapidated and looked as if a strong breeze could blow it down, but Harris knew the shack would not fall. He strolled toward the structure and examined the door. It was a heavy, oaken door nearly three inches thick. A thick, black chain hung from its side; attached to the end of the chain was a fist-sized padlock. Harris picked up the lock and felt the heavy, iron weight in his hand. His father always told him that he could direct his concentration more effectively if he had a tangible object to focus on. Like anything in the dream world, the padlock was nothing more than thought, its mass and weight illusionary. But like his father, Harris recognized the value of symbolism.

Especially in dreams.

Harris stepped back from the prison his mind constructed, and in a powerful voice that thundered across the vast desert of eternity, he uttered a single word.

A name.

A command.

Dust

***

David watched the governor stride across the grandstand, both hands aloft, waving to the enthusiastic crowd. The governor stopped to shake hands with the mayor, which elicited another roar from the crowd. As the pair shook hands, David saw a third figure crawling across the stage. Unseen by any of the smiling politicians, the figure dragged its way past the podium. The bright lights of the television cameras shone through his translucent body leaving behind the shadow of a shadow. The figure stopped and looked upward toward David. It was a man, his face and mouth contorted in pain. The man began to reach forward with his right arm, but then the governor released himself from the grip of the mayor and stepped through the crawling man on his way to the podium. As the governor's feet sliced through the transparent figure, the man again lowered his head and resumed dragging his body across the stage.

One of the survivors of the last purge, Dust whispered.

"The governor doesn't know he's there," David said, his gaze still fixed on the gruesome site of the governor's legs standing through the lower half of the tortured man on stage. As the governor raised his arms in a half-hearted attempt to quiet the crowd, the man crawled out from beneath the governor's feet and rolled off the stage.

They will all be broken for my rebirth. Now look.

David's head was forced painfully forward, giving him a glimpse of his own torso. Snaking around his waist and upper thighs were thin wisps of smoke. They wrapped around David's body like long fingers, squeezing into the folds of his flesh with an insatiable eagerness. Dust's voice continued echoing in his head. *What will you do to free Linda? Will you do anything? Will you submit?*

The pressure from the smoke intensified, nearly suffocating David. "Anything," he managed to say, though he wasn't sure if the words were spoken with his voice or his mind. "Anything you want, just let Linda go."

Good. I shall release her.

The pressure around David's stomach and chest became suffocating. The back of David's neck strained against an unstoppable pressure that forced David's head downward until his chin began to burrow into his chest. Though he could see nothing but the smoke that wrapped itself about him and the distant figure of the governor just beginning his speech, David knew that an immense clawed hand had clamped itself like a vise to the back of his head.

And we shall have her together.

David screamed through clenched teeth as he felt the sharp tips of Dust's hand begin to push their way into the back of his skull. The pain was unlike anything he could ever imagine, a wave of liquid fire melting into his skull. As Dust's fingers penetrated through the bone and into the gray matter of his brain, David felt the fire pouring into the holes in the back of his head. It filled him, mixing with his own blood and spreading throughout every fiber of his body. He was being filled with the spirit of Dust, and as the demon's consciousness flowed into him, David felt his own consciousness being sucked out of the holes Dust bored into his head. As Dust was entering him, he was entering Dust. But it wasn't a body he was being emptied into; it was the vast emptiness of the neither-place.

But before Dust could squeeze the last drops of will from David's mind, a voice called out, slicing through the blackness of the neither-place.

Dust.

Chapter Twenty-four: 8:12 PM

Rubin was face down on his belly, his arms outstretched like an inverted crucifix. Petey sat on the backs of Rubin's thighs, twisting the man's legs into a figure-four-leg-lock while Ace's knees were planted on Rubin's shoulders. In his left hand, Ace fingered the pistol that minutes before had killed Rubin's father; in his right hand, he gripped a red, masonry brick. Ace jammed the brick against the side of Rubin's face. "Now let me see if I got this straight," Ace said, giving the brick a twist. "I type in 1-GO on the computer then hit enter, and the grand finale goes off, right?"

Rubin made a muffled cry, which Ace took as a yes.

"And if I want to set off the fire works one at a time, I just flick those little black switches in the back of those metal tubes, right?" Ace removed the brick from Rubin's face.

"Yeah," Rubin stammered. "But you can't . . . ."

Ace swung the edge of the brick down on top of Rubin's head sending thick shards of the pyrotechnician's skull slicing into his brain, killing him instantly.

Without a word, Ace lifted himself off Rubin and motioned for Petey to do the same. "Go help Bip with those tubes. Make sure they're all pointing at the marina."

Petey jumped up and scampered over the crest of Radaken's Hill.

Ace turned toward the white pickup truck with the Northrup

Pyrotechnics sign on its side. Sitting in the driver's seat was Julie. Beside her was a laptop computer with a single cable protruding from its back. The cable made a direct path to the three staging platforms. "Come out of there," he commanded. "And bring the computer."

Julie popped her bubble gum and slid out of the truck. "Here," she said, handing Ace the laptop.

As Ace took the computer, he held out his left hand. "Take this," he said, waving the gun toward Julie. "Enjoy yourself."

A big grin spread across Julie's face as she accepted the weapon. "Oh baby," she purred.

He pivoted sharply on his heels and went to join Petey and Bip at the staging platforms. Julie lagged behind a few moments staring at the gun.

Petey and Bip were just finishing resetting the angles on the firing mortars when Ace reached the first platform. "All done," Bip said.

Ace smiled and smacked Bip in the shoulder with the palm of his hand. "Excellent." Ace jumped on top of the first platform and inspected the firing mortars. His eyes fell to the first mortar in the second row, a thick shell containing a twenty-four-inch charge. He bent forward and followed the angle of the shell with his eyes. "Very excellent," he said. He set the laptop on the platform beside him and looked up at his friends. Petey, Bip, and Julie all looked down at him with wild, eager eyes. "Let the games begin."

Ace flicked the black switch on the mortar. For a moment nothing happened, then the shell ignited, shooting off the firework with its unmistakable "whoosh." As it sped across the river toward the marina, no one on Radaken's Hill heard the sound of the approaching police car.

*** *** ***

As Steve skidded to a stop, the back end of his car fishtailed to the right sending a spray of gravel against a blue minivan. The tiny rocks bounced off the vehicle, leaving a shotgun pattern of a half dozen thumbnail-sized chips in the driver's side door. Oblivious to the damage he had done to the minivan, Steve snatched the keys from the ignition and hurried out of the car. He was parked on a narrow, gravel, walking path that ran along the north end of the Smith Rehabilitation Clinic parking lot. Less than a dozen yards away, the edge of the parking lot narrowed into a concrete walkway leading to the building's service entrance.

Steve looked about the parking lot. It was overflowing with cars, some, like his, parked on the gravel walkway. From his vantage point, Steve could also see the grandstand. The mayor was standing at the podium, the governor a few feet to her left. Both politicians were waving to the thousands of McKeesporters who had come to see the new marina dedicated. As he scanned the crowd, an unsettling realization came to him. The only time Steve had seen so many people gathered in downtown McKeesport was when John F. Kennedy visited.

"What now?" Merilee asked, following Steve out of the car.

Steve scrambled to the rear of the vehicle and opened the trunk. "We've got to find Linda." When the lid popped open, Steve glanced about the trunk. His eyes lighted on a red duffel bag inconspicuously placed beneath a discolored tire-iron. Steve tossed the tire-iron to the side and scooped up the bag.

Merilee watched as Steve removed a revolver from the bag. As he loaded the chamber, Steve kept glancing at the entrance to the Clinic. "I'm going to get Linda."

"I'm coming with you," Merilee said without hesitation.

Steve looked up and shook his head. "I don't have time to argue, Merilee. You're staying out here."

"No." Merilee slipped her hand into her purse and pulled out the small chrome-plated pistol Steve had given to her the previous Christmas. "Mayflower tried to kill me, remember? I'm going with you."

Steve saw the fierce, determined look in Merilee's eyes and knew there was no way he could make her stay behind. "Okay. But you stay right by my side. And if we run into Espy or Mayflower . . ." Steve paused, motioning toward Merilee's gun with his own weapon. "You aim for their heads and shoot. No hesitation, understand?"

Merilee pursed her lips tightly and nodded. Steve returned the gesture. "We'll go in through the service entrance. There's a back stairway there that should take us to the fourth floor."

"How do you know she's on the fourth floor?"

Steve started for the concrete driveway with Merilee close behind. "That's where Henry Smith gave Morris the DK."

When the pair reached the service entrance door, a roar erupted from the crowd as the governor was introduced. Steve ignored the noise and inspected the door. A simple dead bolt separated him from the inside of the clinic. "Stand back." Steve lifted his right foot and slammed it to the right of the doorknob. The door swung open with a loud bang. Steve waited a moment, his fingers squeezing the handle of his gun. When no one appeared in the small hallway, he motioned for Merilee to come to his side, then the two went in.

"Over there," Steve whispered, gesturing to a metal door about twenty feet from where they stood. "The stairs."

The two began to make their way toward the door. When they halved the distance, they were surprised by the sound of an unmistakable dull boom coming from the direction of the river.

"Fireworks," Merilee said, casting a quick glance over her shoulder. Seeing no one behind her, she turned back toward Steve. "But they're early."

Steve didn't take his eyes off the metal door, but he was troubled by the fireworks. They weren't supposed to go off until after the governor officially opened the marina, and that wasn't supposed to happen for another forty-five minutes.

"Here," Steve said when he reached the door to the stairwell. Merilee slipped beside him and brought her pistol chest high as Steve gripped the doorknob. He took a deep breath then flung the door open. He stepped into the stairwell, making a sweeping arc with his gun hand. Satisfied no one else was in the stairwell, Steve turned toward Merilee and said, "Clear."

Merilee moved forward as Steve started up the stairs. Behind her, the heavy metal door swung shut with a click.

Then came the sound of an explosion, and with that, the screaming.

***

"All right!!!" Governor Hill shouted into the microphone when he took the podium. "I cannot think of anywhere I would rather celebrate Independence Day than in the beautiful city of McKeesport!"

At the mention of its hometown, the crowd erupted in a thunderous round of cheers and whoops. Governor Hill paused and smiled broadly. Three decades in the political spotlight had taught him how to work a crowd. He waved smartly to the people, casually turning to the right so he was fully facing the CNN cameraman. The gesture was met with another round of cheers.

"I've spent a lot of time in McKeesport over the years, and like you, I've seen this town go through some pretty tough times. But I'm here to tell you, that those tough times are over. Today, with the dedication of your new marina and entertainment complex, I can guarantee you that McKeesport is back on track!"

Another raucous outburst of cheering ensued, causing the governor's smile to deepen. Everything was perfect. The governor's speech was intended as a fluff piece, nothing but pure political sugar. But the people were gobbling it up, whipping themselves into a patriotic frenzy. This has got to be great footage, the governor thought in the few moments it took for the applause to die down. He glanced over at the CNN cameraman who was busy panning the crowd. *Perfect.*

Everything was just perfect.

The cameraman spun back toward the podium as the governor inched closer to the microphone. "But I understand that there have been some rumors going around that I was considering a run for the presidency. Well, before we continue with the evening's festivities, I want to take a few minutes to put those rumors to rest."

The governor paused, and in that moment, a collective hush fell over the crowd as ten thousand people inhaled at once. There wasn't a single person jammed onto Broadaire Street who didn't think that Governor Hill was about to announce that he was, indeed, a candidate for president; and yet, the realization that they were on the brink of hearing him officially declare his candidacy left the audience breathless. Everyone knew that history was about to be made.

The pause, just a five second gap between sentences was a well-rehearsed and calculated ploy on the part of the governor. But just as those seconds ended, a high-pitched whine filled the air, breaking the governor's grip on the audience. As he opened his mouth to continue, the eyes of the crowd veered away from him toward something coming out of the eastern sky. A few mouths opened in silent gasps, and one young boy pointed upward, but no one spoke.

Governor Hill had just enough time to realize that his grand announcement had been upstaged when the firework Ace shot off exploded above his head, sending waves of red, white, and blue sparks across the stage. Luckily, the concussion from the blast knocked most of the platform party off their chairs, so the nickel-sized bits of flame passed harmlessly over their heads. However, the governor was sent forward into the podium by the initial blast. As the first sparks bit into the back of his neck, Governor Hill instinctively ducked, covering his head with the palms of his hands. Momentarily blinded, he stumbled to his left, nearly falling off the platform as the colored sparks rained around him.

The crowd, who a few moments ago had been cheering wildly, was stunned. Many of the people in the first few rows dove to the ground as the remnants of the firework flew past the grandstand and onto Broadaire, but most of the throng remained motionless, their bodies frozen in disbelief. Only two people made any movement toward the grandstand when the firework hit: Bill Congreve, who was scrambling up the right side of the platform, and a skinny teenage boy in a heavy varsity jacket who had been waiting for this moment for the past five hours.

By the time the firework burnt itself out, Calvin had been able to slip unnoticed to the side rail on the left end of the platform. Just as Bill Congreve reached the governor, and the mayor and the other city dignitaries were slowly lifting themselves off the floor, Calvin hopped over the railing and bounded straight for the podium.

Bill Congreve saw him first. A funny looking kid in an out of season jacket. The security chief instinctively whipped his arm around the governor's torso, and placed himself between Governor Hill and the approaching boy. The boy stopped, and for a moment, he and Bill Congreve's eyes met. *They're empty*, Congreve thought. *Completely blank.* Congreve thrust his hand beneath his suit coat and yanked out his weapon. At the sight of the gun, an eruption of screams burst from the crowd, but Calvin paid no notice to them or the gun. He reached to his left and grabbed Mayor Markbury by the back of her head. In one deft motion, he yanked the mayor off her feet and tossed her in the governor's direction. Before Congreve could shout out a warning, Calvin ripped open the front of his varsity jacket.

"Oh shit," Congreve said when he saw the sticks of dynamite strapped to the kid's chest. Without a word, Calvin slid his hand into the pocket of his jacket and pulled out a detonator. When he saw the device, Bill Congreve knew that everyone on the grandstand, including himself, was about to die. Without realizing it, Congreve slammed his left hand into the governor's shoulder knocking him off his precarious spot at the edge of the grandstand and into the air. The weight of the governor's body had barely escaped Congreve's hand when Calvin squeezed the detonator, killing McKeesport's mayor, the town's city council, and special agent Bill Congreve, who never liked McKeesport anyway.

***

The clear pink sky of Harris Smith's dreamscape peeled back like a torn curtain with the approach of Dust. Bracing himself against the shack, Harris stared into the blackness forming above him as it swallowed half the sky. Deep within its inky darkness, Harris saw a massive wall of gray smoke spiraling like a whirlwind toward him. As it twisted along its path, trailers of smoke violently spun off the funnel revealing a figure trapped within the spiraling cloud. As the funnel came closer and more of the smoke trailers broke free, the man's shape became more pronounced, even recognizable.

"David!" Harris shouted when he saw whom Dust had trapped.

At the sound of Harris's voice, the remaining strands that bound David snapped away from his body. For a moment, Harris saw his brother-in-law suspended above him, caught in between the blackness of the neither-place and the pale sky of his own dreamscape; then, like a gunshot, David was slung backwards through the emptiness of the neither-place, his body shrinking until it disappeared into the nothingness. Harris shouted for David but his words were met with silence. There was nothing left of David Cavanaugh, only the infinite void of the neither-place.

And Dust.

Once David disappeared, the gray whirlwind roared toward Harris, pulling in its wake the folds of sky that had been split open. Harris stepped away from the dream shack, and feeling the full force of the approaching tornado blasting against his face, thrust his arms out and closed his eyes. In his mind's eye he saw an unbroken pink sky surrounding him. He concentrated on the image, willing it into being. When he opened his eyes the whirling gray cloud had stopped its approach, hovering precariously above the desert floor. Behind it the torn sky sealed itself like an enormous zipper closing.

"There is nothing here that can harm me," Harris said, his eyes fixed on the gray twister. "There is nothing here I fear."

The cloud stopped spinning.

Then it dropped like a curtain to the ground.

And Dr. Henry Ellis Smith stepped out of its folds.

Chapter Twenty-five

David felt the universe hurling past him at an incalculable speed. Light, darkness, sound, and motion all melted into a single, furious blur. It rolled like a tidal wave, carrying him out of Dust's grasp and into the neither-place. At the far end of the cacophony, only a pinprick of light at the limits of his vision, he saw Harris. He was standing beside a ramshackle hut in the middle of a great desert. David saw his brother-in-law for only an instant, but it was time enough for David to hear Harris's voice whispering directly in his mind.

Wake up.

Then Dust tumbled through the light, and David was catapulted back through the neither-place.

When he was finally free of Dust's grasp, David's first thought was of his wife. He had to find Linda, to wake her and get her as far away from McKeesport as possible. But how? He was asleep; everything around him, the whole spinning universe washing over him was all inside his head.

How do I get out?

But the answer to that was obvious. He couldn't get out because he couldn't wake up.

Yet that wasn't right.

When Dust pushed his way into his mind, David felt as if he was being crushed in Dust's grasp. And as Dust forced himself deeper into his subconscious, David was pulled into the mind of Dust. Until the moment Harris's summons broke Dust's grip, the demon's thoughts were open. Every thought, every memory, every secret lay exposed and unguarded.

And from that glimpse, David came to understand the extent of Dust's control. Every person, every soul whose dreams he invaded had a small piece of their personality stored away in the demon's consciousness. These were the shells Dust collected, the translucent shadows of who the dreamers used to be. But the shells became empty only after the death of the dreamer; while the dreamer lived, the bits and pieces of stolen consciousness were still alive. Still capable of thought.

That's why Dust had to keep them imprisoned.

David's eyes flew open. Even in the swirling chaos, his mind's eye was able to generate the image of a finely detailed memory.

The Toy Train, his mind shouted. *Linda's on the Toy Train*!

If he could get to the Toy Train and find Linda, then maybe he could wake her up. As the thought burned itself into his brain, the swirling maelstrom of light and sound began to lose its intensity. The blurring wind that raked his body slowed to a soft, reassuring hum. Around him a wall of gray unfolded out of the darkness, and behind that wall, an enormous iron monstrosity waited to greet him.

Ba Boom

Ba Boom

When the last of the whirling chaos finally melted into nothingness, David stepped through the gray veil, out of the neither-place and once again into his own dream. Near him, a train whistle split the night.

***

"Oh shit," Officer Steever hissed in the back seat of Randy Bressler's squad car as the rookie cop caught sight of Seth Northrup's body dangling out the driver's side of a red Cavalier. "That's one of them fireworks guys."

Bressler's right hand reflexively shot into the air telling Steever to be quiet. The young cop did, looking nervously out the window while the assistant chief brought the car to a stop about a dozen yards behind the Cavalier. Bressler looked at Rhonda and swallowed hard. "That guy looks dead," he said flatly.

Rhonda brought the shotgun to her chest and undid her seat belt. She too had a good view of Seth's body and there was no doubt in the pathologist's mind that she was looking at a corpse. "That's the car the kids were in?" she asked Steever as she scanned the hill for any signs of life.

"Uh yeah," Steever replied. "Four kids, I think."

Bressler grunted and removed his service revolver from its holster. "Steever, you and me are going to walk over toward that white truck over there. Rhonda, you stay . . ." The sound of an explosion cut off the rest of Bressler's sentence.

"What the fuck?" Bressler threw open the driver's side door and hurled himself from the vehicle. Thrusting his weapon in front of him, he scrambled to the crest of Radaken's Hill. Taken aback by the blast, Officer Steever sat stunned, unable to move until he felt a sharp poke in the side of his chest. Rhonda was jabbing at him with the barrel of the shotgun.

"Move it!" she shouted.

"Right." Steever whipped his own revolver from his holster and bolted out of the car with Rhonda just a few paces behind. The pair had nearly caught up to Bressler when the burly cop stopped. "Freeze," he shouted.

Before Rhonda could see whom Bressler was addressing, the sound of a small caliber weapon exploded. Bressler screamed as his left leg came whipping around, the kneecap blown off. Bressler pivoted toward Rhonda on his right leg, and for a second, it looked as if she could grab his jacket and pull him toward her. But just as she reached out to snag him, Bressler lost his balance and tumbled backward down the hill.

As Randy Bressler disappeared from her sight, Rhonda heard two more shots. Instinctively she hit the ground but not before seeing Officer Steever turn toward her, his eyes wide and confused. He tried to speak, but a geyser of blood shot out from the hole in his throat where his Adam's apple used to be. His eyes met Rhonda's; they were full of tears.

Steever took another shaky step forward before he too tumbled down the side of Radaken's Hill.

Fueled by a surge of adrenalin, Rhonda Hemmings leapt to her feet and bolted over the crest of the hill. The first thing she saw was Randy Bressler laying about twenty feet away. His fall had taken him down the slope of the hill toward the first staging platform. A few feet to his right, a teenager with bleached blonde hair was laughing and waving a laptop computer over his head. Another boy, a fat one with greasy black hair stood on the edge of the first fireworks platform. He too was pointing at Bressler and laughing.

Rhonda realized that they didn't see her.

"Freeze!" she shouted leveling the shotgun at the boy with the computer. "You move an inch, and I'll blow your head off."

The boy looked up toward Rhonda and shook his head. "Blow me," he shouted, earning an appreciative giggle from the fat boy. Rhonda was about to repeat her order when she detected a movement to her right. She spun around in time to see a young girl pointing a pistol at her head. Rhonda didn't hesitate; too many years on the firing range had sharpened her reflexes to a deadly degree. Rhonda squeezed the trigger before the girl could get a shot off.

The blast from the shotgun struck the girl squarely in the chest, lifting her off the ground and tossing her back a dozen feet. Red bits of flesh and clothing sprayed from her body as she flew through the air. She was dead before she hit the ground.

"Fuck!" the fat kid on the platform yelled. "She shot Julie." The blonde remained silent, fixing Rhonda with an icy stare. A long few seconds passed, then Rhonda saw the blonde cock his head to the right and say, "Bip, kill that bitch."

Rhonda wheeled to her left. Less than ten yards away stood another greasy-haired punk. This one was holding Steever's service revolver. "Die," the punk said as he pulled the trigger.

Rhonda heard the gun fire, then felt a sharp burn rip across her right thigh as the bullet sliced through the top two layers of skin. Her knees buckled and she started to fall to the right, but as she did, she saw that the punk had underestimated the kick from Steever's gun. After he fired, the gun nearly smacked him in the head. He hadn't considered that his shot wasn't on the mark, so he was in no hurry to re-aim the pistol. Rhonda saw this all in an instant, and as she fell, she managed to quick pump the shotgun and fire.

Bip's face was taken off.

"NO!!!" The bleached blonde punk roared. "You're going to burn," he said, thrusting the laptop in Rhonda's direction. "Burn!"

Rhonda hit the ground and rolled. When she stopped, she was flat on her back, her fingers coiled around the shotgun. Out of the corner of her eyes she could see the punk tapping out something on the keyboard.

"There," he yelled, tossing the computer to the ground. Almost instantly, the sound of fireworks igniting filled the air. Rhonda watched horrified as the grand finale of McKeesport's Fourth of July fireworks extravaganza erupted. Dozens of deep popping sounds were followed by the whoosh of the fireworks in flight as they sped across the Youghioghany toward the crowd gathered at the marina dedication. One of the rockets exploded from its mortar and caught the fat punk still standing on the edge of the first platform square in the chest. The boy yelped as the rocket knocked him backward and off the platform. The yelp turned to a scream when the boy slammed to the ground with the twelve-inch rocket snagged in his clothes. A second later the firework exploded showering the staging platforms in a sea of white sparkles and blood.

Rhonda tucked her head beneath her hands as the tiny bits of flame spiraled down around her. When the flaming bits stopped singeing her neck, she glanced up toward the staging platform where the rockets from the grand finale continued to shoot off. She looked to the left, then to the right but saw no sign of the boy with the blond hair.

Pushing herself up with the shotgun, Rhonda got to her feet.

"Not so fast."

The voice came from behind her.

Rhonda felt something solid slamming against the back of her head, knocking her forward. She no sooner hit the ground than the shotgun was ripped out of her hand.

"Oooh wee." The blond punk giggled. "You shouldn't have messed with Espy's business, girly girl. I mean, I don't really give a shit that you killed my friends, but you nearly stopped me from doing my job." The punk pumped the shotgun and put the barrel to the side of Rhonda's temple. "And I'd be fucked if I didn't get my job done, you know. When the man says burn the city down, you burn it down."

Rhonda gasped as the punk lifted the barrel toward the top of her head, but before he could pull the trigger, a bullet struck him dead between the eyes. The blonde's head jerked back, and his knees buckled. For a half a second he stood silhouetted against the evening sky before crumpling into a heap of filthy clothes and limbs at Rhonda's feet, his dead eyes staring upward.

Rhonda rolled on to her side and started to cry. Randy Bressler, his gun still smoking, began to drag himself toward her.

***

"It's not going to work," Harris said to the approaching figure of Henry Ellis Smith. "You're not my father."

The figure stopped, tilted his head in one of Dr. Smith's trademark mannerisms and addressed Harris in the calm, detached tone of his father. "Please Harris, you have to understand. I'm not even sure if I can explain it, but the truth is that not all of me died last month. A part of my consciousness still lives inside of Dust." Dr. Smith smiled pleasantly and patted his chest with his palms. "It's still me, but I'm a dream now, son."

"I don't believe you."

Henry Smith nodded. "I know it's tough to accept, but it's the truth. All those years of taking the DK and willing Dust into my dreams connected a part of my mind to his. Even death couldn't sever that connection. I'm in him, Harris, don't you see? That's why your mother helped Dust. He let me visit her dreams." Henry's gaze fixed on the cabin behind his son. "If you try to imprison him in that," Henry said. "He'll never let me out again."

Harris stared hard at his father. "There's an invisible wall between us," Harris said. "I will it to be there."

A puzzled expression came over Dr. Smith. "I don't understand, son. What do you mean?"

"I took three times the normal dose of DK," Harris replied. "You know exactly what I mean."

The puzzled expression quickly turned to amusement as Henry reached forward and struck the invisible wall with his fist. "Good," he cooed, his tone losing the familiar traces of Henry Smith's voice. He pounded the wall again. "Very, very, very good."

"Lose the disguise," Harris ordered.

Immediately the vestiges of Henry Smith melted from Dust's body and blew away like ash. What remained was the black-suited, nondescript bald man with dead white eyes that fixed themselves mercilessly on Harris. "You've come prepared. Stronger than the last time." Dust smiled and raked the invisible barrier with the tips of his clawed hands. "I thought seeing the old one might catch you off guard." The clawed fingers continued strumming against the barrier. "But you're much too smart for that. Aren't you, Harris?"

"I'm not going to let you leave this dream." Harris turned to the side and pointed to the shack. "You're going in there. That is my will."

Dust shot his head back and roared with laughter. "It's not that easy, weak one. You have to do more than just tell me to crawl off into your prison. You have to put me there." Dust pushed himself from the barrier and spun around. As he did, the smooth, round features of his face and head hardened, becoming a sharp and angular mask. His chin jutted forward and his ears grew pointed as his pale, white skin took on a greenish tint. When he faced Harris again, the last step of his transformation was complete. Two narrow fangs jutted like twin spikes out the front of his mouth.

Dust had become the Nosferatu from the old silent movie, the vampire that had given Harris nightmares as a child. At the sight of the vampire, Harris shuddered as the memory of hundreds of night terrors spilled into his mind's eye.

Dust sensed the fear. "Ah, I see you haven't forgotten our old game," he said, his voice hissing snakelike. Dust pulled his arm back, then shot out a clawed fist against the barrier that separated the two men. At first nothing happened, then a long, thick fissure appeared, knifing its way from the cloudless sky downward. When it reached the ground, a pattern of spider web cracks split across the sky. "Your father never lost his grip." Dust shot his arm out again and smashed through the barrier. "He was old, but he wasn't weak."

As the invisible barrier crashed around him, Harris felt his power over the dream slip away. He had lost control again. Staring at Dust in the guise of the Nosferatu, his fear boiled over into an uncontrollable rage. He remembered all the helpless nights he dreaded going to sleep for fear of the Nosferatu. How many nights, he wondered, were the nightmares of his own making? How many of those vampires were really Dust?

And now, here he was again, face to face with the creature who had haunted his subconscious all his life. A dream creature in a physical form. A dream creature who could be hurt.

"I'm not weak!" Harris screamed, hurling himself toward Dust.

Chapter Twenty-six

Curtis Mayflower's eyes snapped open at the sound of the explosion. Concealed in the darkness, Curtis felt safe from the sound of screaming children that Dust had left in his mind. For these few minutes he lay in this tomb-like blackness breathing in its stale stagnant air, his mind was his own again.

He had no way to understand what had happened to him, how his sanity had been shredded by that thing that called itself Coach. All he knew was that he had been played for a patsy by some twisted creature of the night. *Morris Keyes was right*, Curtis thought. *That son-of-a-bitch Dust lies.*

And he likes to hurt people. That was fucking-A for sure. Curtis found that out the hard way.

And now the only way to stop the hurting was to do one last thing for Dust. Espy called it the "big bang." "And the screaming will go away," Espy promised after strapping twenty sticks of dynamite to Curtis's torso. "Just squeeze the trigger at the right time, and you'll never hear the screams again. Won't that be nice?"

With tears of gratitude streaming down his cheeks, Curtis took the detonator. It was so simple, Espy told him. Just wait in the trunk of Mrs. Smith's car until he heard the explosion. Then come on out. When the people running away from the first explosion came near him, push the button.

"It will be a helluvalot of fun, Curtis," Espy told the former

315

quarterback as he helped him into the trunk of the car. "You get to do some serious ass kicking." Then Espy smiled and closed the trunk and that was the last thing Curtis saw.

But now the sound of the explosion prompted Curtis to action. He pushed open the trunk lid and gingerly rolled his body out, making sure the dynamite didn't scrape against the car. He had to set the bomb off at the right time; Espy was adamant about that. It was the only way to ensure that the screaming would stop.

After he got out of the trunk, Curtis looked in the direction of the new marina. Most of the grandstand had been blown away, and what was left was engulfed in flame. Even from a hundred yards away, Curtis could see several bodies writhing within the inferno. One figure, Curtis guessed it was a man from his size, was still on its feet. With his entire upper body awash in flame, the man stumbled toward the end of what was left of the grandstand and fell off. He hit the ground, rolled over once, and then lay still. Almost instantly the flames from his body ignited the dry grass around him.

Curtis gripped the trigger with his right hand and waited for the crowd to head in his direction. At first, the throng didn't move. Stunned by the explosion, most of the people watched helplessly as their mayor and city council were incinerated. There was quite a bit of screaming, but for the most part, the people stood with wide eyes and slack jaws, unable to believe what was happening in front of them. It wasn't until the deep booming sound of fireworks filled the air that the crowd realized that it was in jeopardy. Almost to a person, every neck in the crowd twisted in the direction of Radaken's Hill where the fireworks were being set off.

Then the first firework exploded at the south end of Broadaire Street, landing in the middle of a group of senior citizens who had been bussed in from Pittsburgh to see the parade. A tail of green flame over thirty-feet-long whipped around the end of the rocket as it spun like a top in the middle of the street. It skipped across the paved road burning the people on both sides of the street in a shower of green and silver sparks. No sooner had the first firework singed a path across Broadaire Street than the rest of the grand finale began raining onto the crowd.

The crowd's stunned reaction to the explosion of the grandstand quickly dissolved into a frenzy of screaming and shoving as dozens of eighteen-inch rockets exploded up and down the length of Broadaire. Most of the people on the east side of the street turned and ran down the embankment toward the river, but several of the fireworks had exploded on top of the pleasure crafts moored on the new dock setting them on fire. Within a minute, a wall of flame was rapidly spreading over the dock as the first wave of people pressed forward to the river. Many in the crowd tried to turn around and flee the direction of the fire, but the initial push toward the river was too great as the inertia of hundreds of feet trampled the few who had fallen or stopped. Pushed on by those behind them, the first rows of people avoided the growing inferno by diving into the murky brown water of the Youghioghany.

On the west side of Broadaire, the crowd dispersed in the opposite direction, stampeding away from the river toward the parking lot of the Smith Rehabilitation Clinic. A solid wall of screaming people pushed forward as dozens of fireworks exploded in their midst. One eighteen-inch Roman candle landed near the center of the onrush erupting in a geyser of white flame. Lisa Perral, a part-time librarian heard the high-pitched whine of its approach but was unable to get out of the rocket's way. It burst less than a foot in front of her, the flame so hot that it instantly melted away the top three layers of skin on her face.

Curtis watched impassively as the fireworks streaked across the sky. He paid no attention to the flames that engulfed the marina nor to the screams of those being incinerated in the inferno. Nothing else mattered than the wall of people moving toward the end of the parking lot. A few more seconds and they would be swarming onto its blacktop surface trying desperately to find shelter among the minivans and SUV's. Once they made it to his position, once they swarmed around him, it would be time to squeeze the trigger like Espy said.

Time for the screaming in his head to stop.

But as the crowd came closer, another sound found its way into Curtis's brain. Faint at first, it grew louder, mingling with the screaming children Dust had pushed into his head. Soon, it overpowered the screams, silencing them.

It was cheering.

Thousands of people chanting his name, cheering their heads off because he'd thrown another touchdown pass. It was a sound culled from the only corners of his memory that Dust couldn't poison, a sound Curtis remembered as pure and perfect. It was the sound he had been coveting for the last fifteen years, the sound that echoed through all his dreams. And it was the sound Dust had stolen, the sound he had replaced with the screams of a football stadium full of damned souls.

But for all his power, Dust couldn't destroy that memory. There had been a time when those cheers had been real, when they weren't just broken fragments of Curtis's dreams. Not even Dust could destroy so perfect a memory.

Curtis let the detonator slip from his hand as the crowd swarmed around him. If they knew that he had just saved their lives, they would cheer for him right now.

Curtis smiled at the thought. In his head he began the old familiar chant.

Curtis . . . Curtis . . . Curtis

Ignoring the burning pain in his leg, he pushed through the wave of parade-goers trying to escape the carnage at the marina. He hadn't gone six steps when he bumped into Cooley Nettles. Cooley's eyes bugged out when he saw his old drinking buddy. "Saved your life, Cooley," Curtis said, tapping the bulging vest of dynamite strapped to his chest. Cooley didn't reply. He just let out a tiny gasp and pushed himself back into the safety of the crowd. Curtis watched him disappear into a sea of arms and legs.

Then turning his gaze toward the Smith Rehabilitation Clinic, Curtis made his painful way toward its front door.

***

"What the hell is going on?" Merilee shouted.

Steve glanced down the steps and shook his head. "I don't know. Sounds like they're shooting off the fireworks." For a moment he hesitated, not sure if he should continue up the stairs or bolt out the back door of the clinic and see what was happening outside. Merilee solved the problem when she started up the stairs.

"Come on," she urged. "You've got to find Harris's sister."

When the pair reached the turn before the second floor landing, Steve shot his left arm out, a sign for Merilee to stop. Merilee pushed her body against the smooth stairwell and gripped tighter at her pistol. "What is it?"

Steve didn't respond. Instead he lowered himself into a crouching position and aimed his gun at something at the other end of the stairwell. "The door," he said. "It looks like there's something propping it open." Steve paused and licked his dry lips, the sharp taste of blood stabbing his tongue. "I'm gonna take a look. You stay here."

Merilee didn't flinch as Steve straightened himself and headed up the steps. Her heart was racing and she was suddenly struck with a powerful urge to pee. *Get a grip girl*, she told herself. *Can't lose it now.* She tightened the muscles that controlled her bladder, which did little to ease her discomfort. She contemplated following Steve when she heard him mutter a low, "Damn it."

Instantly, the urge to pee vanished as Merilee pushed herself from her position against the wall. "What is it?" she asked, rounding the corner. Steve was standing in front of the door that led to the second floor of the clinic. Jutting out of the bottom of the doorway were two twisted legs.

"Warren Turvel," Steve said, not turning around. "He's been shot in chest."

Merilee moved closer, but Steve's position in front of the door prevented her from getting a clear look at the body. "Is he dead?"

Steve nodded. "Uh huh. Whoever did this, shot him at close range with a big fucking gun. Most of his neck is gone." Steve stood still for a moment then spun around to face Merilee. "Let's go. We'll tend to Warren later." Steve stepped away from the body and allowed the door to gently close itself against the dead cop's legs.

Merilee and Steve made their way past the third floor without incident. But with each step, Merilee grew increasingly nervous, her gun hand trembling almost to the point that she thought she might drop the weapon. She hovered two steps behind Steve, keeping her eyes trained on his back and hoping that Espy and Mayflower were long gone.

When the pair reached the door that led to the fourth floor, Steve turned and offered Merilee a sad smile. "You don't have to come with me," he said. "I'll be fine by myself."

Merilee knew that Steve was lying, and she wasn't going to let him get away with it. "I've been a cop's girlfriend too long," she whispered, "to not know when I'm being bull-shitted. I'm coming with you."

Steve brushed his rough fingers gently against the smooth, bruised skin of Merilee's cheek. She closed her eyes, and he allowed his hand to linger by the corner of her mouth.

God, he loved her.

Merilee's eyes fluttered open. "Let's go," she said.

Steve nodded and turned toward the door. He gripped the handle with his left hand and gently inched it forward. When he got the door opened a foot, he stuck his head through the space and scanned the long, narrow hallway. On both sides were three doors, all shut except for the last door on the left side. Bright fluorescent light spilled out from it into the hall. Steve held his breath and listened. Except for the sounds of chaos that still filtered in from outside, he heard nothing.

Keeping his eyes locked on the far end of the hallway, he pushed the door open another foot and slid his bulky frame through. Merilee followed close behind, peering out from behind Steve's back. Slowly, they made their way down the hall, Steve pausing to test each of the doors. They were all locked.

Steve made his way to the edge of the open door and looked into the large room formerly known as the amputee ward. Despite the bright fluorescent lights, the ward was empty except for an overturned filing cabinet pushed near the black metal frame of a hospital bed. He rounded the doorway and took a half step into the room.

"Linda!" he shouted as he saw the two hospital beds that had been placed side by side at the far end of the ward. Occupying them were David and Linda Cavanaugh.

At the sight of the couple, Steve bolted from the doorway toward the beds. "She's here," he shouted over his shoulder. "They're both here." Steve made it to the side of Linda's bed before turning to see if Merilee had followed him. When he caught sight of her, the excitement of finding the Cavanaughs vanished. As she was coming through the doorway, Merilee saw Linda and David Cavanaugh and stopped. It was only for a second, but that was the moment Steve turned around.

That's when he saw Espy.

Steve tried to warn her, but Espy was too fast. Before Merilee had a chance to react, Espy grabbed her right wrist and twisted it behind her back. Merilee felt her wrist snap when Espy ripped the gun from her grasp. "No," Steve yelled, as Espy twisted Merilee's body forward and jammed the barrel of her gun against her temple.

For several agonizing seconds, no one moved, no one spoke.

"Let her go, Nathan," Steve finally said, forcing himself not to look at the terrified expression on Merilee's face. He had to stay calm; that was the only chance Merilee had. "I can still get help for you, Nathan, but you have to let her go."

Nathan forced Merilee into the center of the room. "Too late for that," he said. "Don't you hear that outside, Wyckoff? It's already begun. Coach is burning the shit out of this town, and when he's finished, he's going to be a badder motherfucker than ever before. And you," Espy said, laughing, "are going to be one sorry cop when he gets through with you. I mean, he's fucked me over good, and he likes me. I can't imagine what he's going to do to you."

"God damn it, you freak. Kill him!"

Surprised by the voice, both Steve and Espy turned toward the doorway as Mrs. Smith barged in. "Kill him. I told you he was dangerous."

Espy turned his attention back to Steve and began laughing which only enraged Mrs. Smith more. "He has to die!" she screamed.

"People are going to die," Espy calmly replied. "That's a given." With his gaze still fixed on Steve, Espy dropped the gun from Merilee's temple and aimed it at Mrs. Smith who was oblivious to the motion. She was staring at Steve, about to say something when the bullet from Merilee's gun entered her right eye socket and came out her left temple. Before her corpse hit the floor, Espy had retrained the gun back onto Merilee.

"Not so pretty now, is she? I told her to watch her step, but the stupid bitch would not shut up. I mean, I told her that Coach didn't need her any more, but would she listen? Would she keep her mouth shut? Oh no."

Espy pushed the gun tighter against Merilee's skull. "But that's neither her nor there, now is it? We got ourselves another problem, don't we, Wyckoff?"

"What's that?"

Espy's left hand traveled slowly up Merilee's torso, over her breasts and to her throat. "I don't know if I should shoot her or strangle her."

Steve stood helpless as Espy began to squeeze.

***

David stepped through the gray veil that separated the neither-place from the familiar landscape of his own dream. In front of him was the Toy Train, but any similarities between this train and the dream train of his childhood had long vanished. What waited before him was a twisted steel abomination, an enormous snaking line of black box cars as far as the eye could see. Sitting on rusted wheels atop a broken network of browning tracks, the boxcars bulged at the sides as if whatever was trapped within them was struggling for release.

But David knew what the boxcars held. He had felt them when he'd become one with the darkness of the neither-place. They were the nightmares, thousands of bits of memory and consciousness collected over the centuries. All of them stolen and perverted by Dust. They raged against the walls that confined them, causing the string of cars to rock back and forth on the tracks. They wanted out.

David forced himself to remain calm as he walked slowly along the sides of the tracks toward the engine car. Oddly enough, it was Dust's warning that allowed him to keep his composure. *You're responsible for what happens in your dreams.* David wouldn't forget that. No matter what might happen, he was in control.

David stopped at the front of the train and examined the engine car. The thin, cigar shaped smoke stack of his boyhood dreams had become a towering cylinder of red-hot steel belching out a plume of ash and black fire. The graceful contours of the car's smooth cowcatcher had been ripped apart, replaced by rows of serrated steel pipe twisted in the shape of an enormous, bloody mouth. Lacking only eyes, the engine car looked like some giant prehistoric shark set against a black ocean. This is what Dust does to dreams, David thought. Turns them into shit.

David shook Dust from his thoughts and looked past the engine to the passenger car, the car that held the toys. A dim yellow light peaked out from the crack at the bottom of its closed, sliding door. Unlike the cattle cars, the sides of the passenger car were not strained to the breaking point. David eyed the innocuous looking car for a moment before bounding across the gravel path that separated him from the tracks. As his foot cleared the steps and he landed on the car's platform, a piercing whine sliced through the black sky as hundreds of rust-coated wheels rolled awkwardly into life. For a moment David lost his balance as the train lurched forward, but he was able to grab the handle of the sliding door to keep from falling. He righted himself, then throwing open the heavy door, David leapt into the belly of the beast.

***

"Drop the gun," Espy ordered. "Or I'll rip her throat open."

Steve trained the weapon on the sliver of Espy's face that peeked from behind Merilee's head. Just his left eye and a corner of his forehead, enough of a target that Steve might hit eight out of ten tries at the shooting range.

Nothing he would try with Merilee's life at stake.

But still, if he dropped his gun there would be no . . .

"Drop the fucking gun, Wyckoff!" The sliver of Espy's face disappeared behind Merilee as Espy's fingers choked off her airway. "She ain't breathing now."

Steve dropped the gun and held his hands out. "There," he said. "Let her go."

Espy laughed, and the grip on Merilee's throat relaxed significantly. A half moon of Espy's face peeked around Merilee's shoulder. "Put your foot on the gun and kick it backward."

Without looking, Steve did as he was told. He flicked at the gun with his right foot, sending it skirting across the linoleum floor. Steve heard it bang against something metallic and come to a stop.

Pleased, Espy took his hand away from Merilee's throat and slipped it to the back of her neck, grabbing a fist full of her hair in the process. Yanking on the hair, he snapped her head backward, the pistol still snug against her right temple. "I don't know what it is about you, but Coach wants you alive. He says you're gonna be real helpful in the days to come. New world order and all that shit." Espy paused and stroked Merilee's cheek with the gun. "She, however, don't mean nothing to Coach."

"You hurt her and you'll have to shoot me too, Nathan, because I'll be coming to kill you. And I don't think that's what Coach wants."

Before Espy could respond, another voice came from the open doorway. "His name is Dust."

Both Steve and Espy wheeled about toward sound of Curtis Mayflower's voice. When he saw the dynamite strapped to Mayflower's chest, Steve felt his knees buckle. All he could think to do was get to Merilee and wrap his arms around her before Curtis blew them all sky high.

"Mayflower!" Espy shoved Merilee forward, hard enough that she stumbled into Steve's arms, and headed for Mayflower. "What!" he screamed. "Are you doing here? You were supposed to blow up the people in the parking lot!"

Curtis shot a hasty glance toward Steve then cast his eyes to the floor. "I . . . I tried," he stuttered. "I pushed the button like you said, but the thing wouldn't go off." Curtis held out his hand with the detonator as proof.

His arms wrapped about Merilee's trembling body, Steve leaned forward and whispered in her ear, "Don't move. Don't say a word."

Espy slid next to Curtis's side and backhanded the big man across the face. "Not go off? It wouldn't go off? So what! You should have made it go off. Put a road flare against your chest. You got a lighter, you could've just set yourself on fire!" Espy slapped Curtis a second time. "You were supposed to blow yourself up!"

As Espy was pummeling Curtis, Steve unwrapped his arms from Merilee and took a careful step backward. But no sooner had he moved then Espy spun back around and leveled the gun at Merilee's chest.

He said nothing but the stiff tilt in the way he held his head and the quick motion of his hand told Steve that Espy was going to shoot. Merilee gasped and tried to duck as Steve managed to get his right hand on her shoulder in an attempt to push her out of the way. But neither movement would be enough; Espy had her dead center.

But before Espy got the shot off, Curtis wrapped his massive arms around Espy's thin frame and flung him into the air. He pressed the teenager above his head, then, with his left hand wrapped around Espy's gun hand, Curtis body slammed Espy to the floor. There was a sickening sound of bone crushing as Espy's wrist snapped in half, but somehow, he managed to hold on to Merilee's gun. Curtis dove to the ground jamming his right forearm into Espy's throat and pinning the smaller man's gun hand to the floor.

"You lie! You and Dust are both fucking liars!" Curtis screamed in Espy's face, pushing his arm deeper into the thin folds of the boy's neck. Curtis turned his head to Steve who was helping Merilee off the floor. "Get out," Curtis said hoarsely. "Both of you."

"What about them?" Steve pointed to the Cavanaughs.

"Just go," Curtis pleaded. Tears began streaming down his face. "Hurry. The screaming has started again."

Steve bolted to the table where David Cavanaugh lay and tried to pick him up. "He's cuffed to the bed!"

"Go!" Curtis shouted again. He still had Espy pinned to the floor, but he was losing his grip. It was only with every ounce of what was left of his sanity that he was able to fight off the urge to jam his fists into his ears. His body began to shake and his hold on Espy's throat weakened.

Espy began laughing.

Steve didn't hesitate. There was no way he could free David's wrist, so he ran to Linda's bed and scooped her up in his arms. "Come on," he said to Merilee and ran to the door. Seeing Steve's gun on the floor, Merilee picked it up and headed after him.

Tossing Linda over his shoulder in a fireman's carry, Steve made a wide berth around Curtis and Espy. "You can't escape him," Espy yelled when Steve made it into the hallway. "You got to sleep sometime."

Steve didn't slow down. He ran straight for the back stairwell, but when he was within a dozen feet of it, the door suddenly swung open.

Mrs. Torach, all three hundred pounds of her, was blocking his exit. On top of her sweaty, round head, Warren Turvel's uniform cap sat at a jaunty angle. "I'm going to see my Fredo," she said pleasantly before pulling a handgun out of her oversized handbag and training it on Steve.

Steve skidded to a stop as the sound of gunfire reverberated down the hallway.

Mrs. Torach's head snapped back sending Warren Turvel's hat flying into the stairwell as four crimson pools of blood swelled up on her yellow sundress. Mrs. Torach's great flabby arm dropped to its side as Merilee fired two more shots into her abdomen, but the enormous woman wouldn't go down.

Instead, she started to re-aim the gun.

Merilee let out a howl and hurled herself into the woman sending the two of them into the open stairwell. Driving her shoulder into Mrs. Torach's midsection, Merilee doubled her over, knocking the gun out of her hand. Pinned against the wall, the big woman stood dazed for a moment, then offering Merilee a motherly smile, collapsed dead in an enormous, fleshy pile.

"Move," Steve shouted. With Linda still slung over his shoulder, he was already stepping over Mrs. Torach's corpse. Behind him the sound of Espy's laughter grew loud in the hall. "You don't have the balls," Espy was shouting. "You don't have the balls to die."

Merilee took a last look at the woman she had just killed, then started down the stairs.

Chapter Twenty-seven

Harris was knocked to the desert floor as the Nosferatu's taloned fingers sliced through his chest. When the vampire saw the three crimson streaks down Harris's chest, he stopped his attack, bent over his victim and licked the drippings of blood off his claws. "Delicious," it said. "Even in dreams, there is nothing like the taste of blood."

Gripping his wounded chest, Harris struggled to his feet. The Nosferatu stared at him with its unblinking white eyes and grinned.

"Stop it," Harris said, his voice caught somewhere between a plea and a command. "We both know what you are." Harris staggered backwards until he came upon the shack.

"What I am is irrelevant," the vampire said coldly. "Didn't your father teach you that? What is important is how you see me. How you make me. Don't you understand, weak one? I pluck my form from your mind. A snake, a tiger. Whoever you want me to be." Chuckling, the Nosferatu spread his arms out. "I become."

The Nosferatu snapped his claws open and began to advance on Harris. "I feel you losing control of your dream, Harris. Don't you? It won't be long before I'll be able to push myself right out of here." The vampire came closer, still clacking his claws together. "But not before I gorge myself on every ounce of sanity you have left. This will be my gift for you, weak one. Your own dream; I return it. And every time you dream, you will come back to this place of your creation, and I will be waiting to eat your soul."

Harris screamed and threw out his arms in a futile attempt to repel the attack, but Dust batted away Harris's arms to the side and fell slobbering upon the man. But as Harris was knocked back against the shack, as he was fighting for his sanity in the pale sand of his dreamscape, he chanced to catch a glimpse of the sky.

It was splitting open.

***

The walls of the Toy Train dripped blood. From behind the thousands of amputated arms and legs that had been tacked to the walls, flowed tiny rivulets of rust-colored liquid. The liquid seeped over the once yellow walls and spilled onto the floor, swallowing the toys in thick, sticky pools. In those spots where the blood hadn't reached, layers of dust and cobwebs blanketed what was left of the piles of broken and charred toys strewn about the train car. The Toy Train of David's youth now resembled the scene of a mass execution. David shook his head sadly and breathed in the fetid stench of warm blood and death. He was surprised that it didn't make him gag.

He started making his way to the back of the car, kicking aside shit covered piles of toys when something Harris had told Steve Wyckoff about Addiction Personification surfaced in his mind. Linda's father would condition his patients to dream of weapons to use against their addictions. Harris called them dream guns.

"My God," David said. "The Phaser rifle."

As a child, David wanted a Star Trek Phaser rifle more than anything in the world. It was nothing but a gold-painted, toy rifle with the Star Fleet insignia on the side that shot little plastic rings. It was a cheap, ten-dollar toy gun, but for reasons David never understood, he never got one. He waited and hoped as Christmases and birthdays rolled by until he had outgrown toy guns, and the Star Trek rifle was forgotten.

Trembling, David turned and started back to the front of the toy car.

Because the Phaser rifle had never been totally forgotten. It had only been moved from the front of his mind to one of the back rooms of his subconscious and tucked safely away on the Toy Train. It had always stayed with him, that one perfect toy.

David came to the front of the train and scanned the wall. In the spot where the Phaser rifle should have been was a crusty mass of congealed blood protruding from the wall. David took a deep breath and plunged his hands into the mass. No sooner had David's hands broken through the hard surface, his fingers wrapped themselves around the smooth, plastic barrel of the Phaser rifle. "Dream gun," he shouted, yanking it free.

But David had no time to savor the moment. The train jolted forward sending David sprawling to the side, the Phaser rifle clutched tightly against his chest. Above him, hundreds of shit covered baseballs began falling from the silver threads that held them to the ceiling. They slammed into David's arms and chest with painful velocity. Not loosening his grip on the rifle, David flipped over onto his back and pushed himself to his knees.

That's when he saw the black hobbyhorse.

Except it bore only a slight resemblance to an actual horse. Its head had ballooned to grotesque proportions becoming a misshapen lump of flesh sporting a pair of white, bulbous eyes. Its smooth and muscular flanks had been twisted into an unrecognizable mass of misplaced limbs and bone, all covered in scales. What was once a horse's mouth split open revealing an enormous cavity lined with uneven rows of razor sharp teeth.

David scrambled to his feet as he recognized that the thing in front of him was an obscene amalgamation of a thoroughbred and a great white shark.

Without thinking, David leveled the Phaser rifle toward the creature and squeezed the trigger. A single plastic ring about the size of a thumbnail shot out of the gun and floated toward the charging beast. When the creature saw the ring, it reared up on its hind legs and tried to skirt out of its way. The pellet struck the horse-thing just above the right, front hoof shattering it as if it had been struck by a shotgun blast. The horse screamed through its shark mouth and kicked wildly with its good front leg.

David wasted no time clicking off six more rounds.

The pellets struck the horse in its torso and back legs, shattering the creature into six unequal parts. The largest part, the head and half of the left shoulder, landed near David's feet. The creature's jaws worked furiously, snapping at the air in an attempt to get at its prey. David lowered the rifle toward the horse's white eye and shot again. As soon as the pellet made contact, the head exploded leaving nothing behind but a black stain on the floor and the smell of burnt wood.

David stepped back from the splintery remains of the horse and started for the lone black door at the back of the toy car. The door that led to the first of the cattle cars that were hitched to the Toy Train.

***

Harris saw the darkness of the neither-place spilling into the fabric of his dream just as Dust's hand clamped over his face. Whether he sensed the approaching darkness or recognized a new terror in Harris's eyes, Dust stopped pushing his claw into Harris's skull and glanced over his shoulder at the sky. Harris felt the demon trembling as a loud cry echoed across the sky.

Dduuusssstttt

A surprised look came across the Nosferatu's face. "I am being called." Dust released Harris and tossed him to the ground. "There will be time for you later, weak one. But now, I must go to where I am summoned."

Again, the voice reverberated across the sky.

Dduuusssssttttt

Harris pushed himself off the desert floor as the sand at Dust's feet began swirling about him, wrapping his legs and torso in a funnel cloud. Inside the whirling sand, the features of the Nosferatu began to melt into a formless cloud of smoke. Only the deep, white eyes remained intact, staring from out of the cyclone at Harris. When the last trace of the Nosferatu was gone, the swirling cloud turned toward the blackness of the neither-place and began to lift off the ground.

"NO!"

Harris dove headlong into the cloud. Fighting off the sand that bit into his flesh, he flung his arms around the cyclone, but his hands found nothing to grab. His momentum carried him blindly into the vortex of the cloud where he felt a fierce tug at his midsection bending him backward and pulling his arms and legs in opposite directions. For a moment, Harris thought his limbs were about to be ripped off his body, then the pressure subsided, and Harris was spit out of the cyclone. He let loose a muffled cry before crashing face first against a cold, hard surface. No sooner had the force of the impact registered in his brain, than the floor beneath him began to melt away. It dissipated like smoke, losing its solidity and, for a brief second, Harris thought he might tumble through the floor. Then his vision cleared and he realized that the wooden floorboards of the train car weren't melting away.

He was.

Then he heard a single word spoken from somewhere above him.

"Dust."

David was standing in the middle of an empty boxcar, his Star Trek Phaser rifle pointed at a hulking mass in front of him. Dust had once again taken the shape of Mr. Biggler, only now the conductor was four times his previous size.

"You're on the train, Davie," Dust said. "Congratulations."

"What have you done to Linda?"

Dust chuckled and waved a bloated arm across his body. "I'm sure if you look close enough, you may find her somewhere in these shadows." Dust snapped his head to the right and glared at Harris. "Like this weak one."

David allowed himself a quick glance toward the corner of the boxcar. Barely visible in the corner was a shadowy form of a man. "Harris?"

The specter nodded.

"What have you done to him?" David asked, inching his Phaser rifle toward Dust.

"Nothing. The fool followed when you summoned me, but he is nothing here. He can do nothing." To prove his point, Dust swung his arm around, passing his fist harmlessly through the wispy outline of Harris's figure. "He has no substance in your dream." Dust laughed and took a step toward David. "I, on the other hand, am a different matter."

"I know that," David shot back. "I summoned you, remember."

"Which was a mistake. You are strong, much stronger than that pitiful thing in the corner, but I will underestimate you no longer, David Cavanaugh. I hoped, through you, to keep Linda near me, but your will is too strong. I guess you should be congratulated. Few of your kind have been able to resist me as you have done. But your resistance grows tedious."

Dust lunged forward before his sentence was complete, but David was ready. He swung the Phaser rifle upward and fired off four plastic pellets. They whizzed out of the gun's gold barrel, slicing through the coveralls of Dust's conductor's uniform and into the creature's chest. Unlike those that destroyed the hobbyhorse, these pellets didn't explode on contact; instead, they bored into Dust's flesh like tiny saw blades, not stopping until they emerged out the opposite side of the creature. Dust howled in agony as a flurry of pellets ripped through his shoulders and neck.

David kept up a stream of fire, aiming the blast of the Phaser rifle directly at Dust's face and chest, turning the demon's massive clown face into a bloody pulp. For a moment, the weapon held Dust in his tracks, but the fury and momentum of the dream demon couldn't be stopped. With a scream that shook the cattle car, Dust slammed his massive fist into David's right shoulder, knocking David to the ground and sending his dream gun skidding across the floor.

With surprising quickness, Dust snatched up the Phaser rifle and snapped it in two. He tossed the pieces to the side and turned to face the rising David. "No more," he bellowed. "I gave you a chance to keep your wife and your sanity. Now you lose both." Before David could get out of his way, Dust wrapped his hands around his throat and hoisted him into the air. "When you wake, I will have you killed," Dust growled. "But until then, I am going to savor ripping your flesh off strand by strand."

Kicking furiously into Dust's midsection, David tried to free himself, but the creature's hands were too large and powerful. Trying to get to the demon's eyes, David swung his fists against the side of Dust's face, but the blows proved glancing and ineffective. His struggle was useless, the dream demon was too strong. Unable to continue, David's arms fell limply to his side as the pressure around his throat increased. "Linda," David choked out just before Dust crushed his windpipe. "Linda."

Chapter Twenty-eight

Steve and Merilee were just rounding the stairwell to the second floor when they heard the fireworks exploding outside. "What the hell was that?" Merilee shouted.

Steve didn't reply. He just tightened his grip on Linda Cavanaugh and continued down the stairs. When he made it to the first floor he paused to let Merilee slip ahead of him and open the fire exit. "Let's get out of here," he said breathlessly.

Merilee pushed the heavy metal door open and looked about. It was a scene of total chaos; thousands of people were swarming through the parking lot, most of them screaming. Bypassing the narrow lanes between the parked cars, the crowd ran through and over the vehicles, tipping dozens of cars and minivans onto their sides. Several people, who managed to make it safely to their vehicles when the barrage of fireworks began, were now trapped inside, unable to escape the onslaught of the massive crowd. With Linda still slung over his shoulder, Steve lumbered out the door and pushed his way through the mob and up the cement apron to the gravel path of the parking lot. Reaching his car, Steve gently lowered Linda to the ground then plopped himself down next to her.

"Come on," Merilee shouted. "We have to get out of here."

Steve shook his head and began fumbling in his jacket pocket. "We got to wake her up first," he shouted over the din of the horde. From his pocket, Steve took out the syringe Harris had given him. He removed the rubber tip from the end of the needle then shot a nervous glance toward the exit where he and Merilee had just come out. Satisfied that Espy hadn't followed them out of the building, he plunged the syringe into Linda's arm and shot her full of the Narcan.

"Is it working?" Merilee asked, kneeling next to Steve on the pavement.

"I don't know," Steve replied, slipping the syringe back into his pocket. Taking his eyes off Linda, the detective looked out across the parking lot toward the river. He couldn't believe what he saw. The river was completely ablaze in an orange wall of fire that spread the entire length of the new marina. Where the fire had spread onto the oil slicks and leaking gasoline that was spilling into the river, plumes of thick, black smoke snaked their way skyward. Most of the pleasure craft that had been moored to the new dock were either on fire or drifting down the choppy river. As Steve stared at the inferno engulfing the riverside, a well-dressed man with a deep gash across his forehead stumbled blindly past him. It was a few moments before Steve recognized that the man was the governor, but before he could go after him, Merilee grabbed Steve's forearm.

"Look," she said, pointing to Linda. "She's waking up."

***

David's head snapped backward as the pressure that had been crushing his windpipe suddenly relaxed. Instinctively, David brought his knees upward and kicked his feet forward into Dust's chest. The blow took Dust by surprise, sending him stumbling backwards across the train car. David sailed in the opposite direction, slamming his back against the sidewall of the car. Still gasping for breath and stunned from his impact with the wall, David collapsed to the floor.

"NO!" he heard Dust wail as he hit the ground. "THIS CANNOT BE!"

Gulping down a mouthful of air, David scrambled to his feet

and spun around to face the demon. But where a moment before Dust had taken the form of Mr. Biggler, there now stood a tall, bald man. Shaking with rage, Dust examined himself, surprised at the alteration. No longer in the form of Mr. Biggler, Dust craned his neck toward the ceiling and screamed. Not sure of what was happening, David took a wary step backward. In the corner of the car, the shadow figure of Harris was frantically waving his arms. Catching the movement out of the corner of his eye, David shot Harris a puzzled look.

Linda is awake, Harris's voice whispered directly into David's mind. *That's why he's losing control. He's weaker now.*

With his hands balled in fists and his eyes clamped shut, Dust remained fixed in the middle of the train car, his entire body quivering. Not taking his eyes off Dust, David gulped in more air. Already the pain in his throat was beginning to subside.

Take control, David, Harris whispered frantically. *Don't let him escape. Whatever you do, don't let him leave the train. But be careful, you* . . .

Without hesitating, David threw himself forward, slamming his shoulder into Dust's chest. Wrapping his powerful arms around Dust's torso, David lifted him into the air and body slammed him to the floor. "My dream; I'm in charge!" David yelled as he planted his knees atop Dust's chest and proceeded to pummel the demon with a furious barrage of punches. "No more fucking tricks," David shouted as his fist crushed the bridge of Dust's nose. "I will not let you leave this train!"

David slapped his palms together and lifted his clenched fists above his head. He was about to bring them crashing onto Dust's skull when a sharp, burning pain sliced across his abdomen. "It's not that easy," Dust hissed through clenched teeth.

For a second, the fiery pain that ripped through his torso made it impossible for David to move. Then his hands flew to his chest as a torrent of hot blood erupted out of the gash that ran from David's waist to just below his right nipple. David slapped his hands across the wound but that did little to stop the blood from pouring out between his outstretched fingers. It flowed unchecked, staining Dust's amused face in gluey dots of dark burgundy.

Effortlessly, Dust tossed David off his chest, laughing as the man writhed in agony on the floor.

"You're no warrior," Dust said, rising to his feet. As he did, the smooth, round features of his bald head began to sharpen and become more angular. The nose that, moments before, David had crushed, was now straight and narrow. The blank white eyes too grew narrower, almost serpent-like. Dust thrust his right arm out so David could see that instead of a hand, a single, bloodstained talon protruded from the end of his wrist.

The Nosferatu, Harris's voice whispered in David's head. *Oh God, David, he's become the vampire!*

Standing fully erect, Dust loomed over David's bleeding, prone body. "Did you really think you could hold me in your pitiful Toy Train? This is no jail, no prison." Dust glared at David for a moment before slashing his taloned arm downward. It caught David in the neck, ripping open his throat and slicing through his collarbone before entering the deep valley that had already been cut into his chest. Three of David's fingers were separated at the second knuckle with the pass of Dust's talon and flew into the air. "Before you can trap me, David, you have to make sure that I do not take a form that can hurt you. Even that fool Harris knows that."

Dust knelt down beside David and gently cradled the man's head in his left hand. The lone taloned finger, he twisted deep into David's bowels. "But you understand now, don't you. You understand why some of the dreamers gladly take their lives. They cannot bear the agony that I bring to them. The agony you are feeling now," Dust said, pushing his claw through David's bowel and into his liver. The pain sent David's eyes turning upward in their sockets; unable to endure the agony of his own evisceration, David's mind struggled desperately to discover some way to escape the pain.

With the point of his talon still embedded in David's liver, Dust whispered. "What happens when pain is too great in the waking world, David? You lose consciousness, and your mind retreats into the safety of sleep. But where do you escape to when the pain is too great in the dream world and you can't wake up?

What do you do then?" Dust laughed and gave his arm another agonizing twist. "You do nothing, Davie-boy, because there is nothing to do. There is no place for your mind to go, no refuge in sleep. In your own head, you must endure the pain or go mad. That is the rule."

Dust pulled his hand out of David's torso, bringing with it twisting strands of entrails. Laughing, Dust greedily licked the loose threads of David's organs off his blood-soaked hand. "So how long do you think you can endure this, Davie-boy? How long before your sanity crumbles around my fingers?" Dust brought his face next to David's. "Tell me, David. How long can you survive knowing that we will play out this little scene every night for the rest of your life? Remember, David, you are the one who is keeping me in your head; you said I couldn't leave the Toy Train."

David peered into the blank ovals of Dust's unblinking eyes. They looked like two, pale moons, two twin lakes of white fire eagerly waiting to suck up David's sanity. *Give him what he wants*, David's mind screamed. It was the only way to stop the pain now, the only way to escape the night terror that was now the Toy Train. But as his mind began to retreat into the safety of madness, David heard a voice that was part scream, part command, filtering its way through the walls of the Toy Train. It was a voice from the waking world, a voice that came from just a few feet from where David's sleeping body lay handcuffed to a metal bed frame. And Dust heard the voice too; and for the briefest of moments, there was fear reflected in the twin fires of his dead, white eyes.

"*Mayflower*," Nathan Espy screamed. "*Don't you fucking do it.*"

Then the world turned orange.

And then black.

Chapter Twenty-nine: August 5

For the first time since Slaughter Saturday, the afternoon temperature was below eighty degrees. It was a most welcome respite for Steve who stood on the walkway of the Josslin Bridge staring across the river at the burnt remains of the marina. An unlit cigarette dangled off his lower lip. Absently, he clicked open his Zippo but made no motion to light the cigarette.

The final body count for the July 3rd inferno, as the local papers were calling it, stood at thirty-two. Included in that number was Mayor Caroline Markbury, the entire city council, and Peter Litchfield who was crushed beneath the feet of one of the high school marching bands that had participated in the parade. Also listed among the dead was Miss Nora Fuller who was killed when a sixteen-inch roman candle found the delicious curve between her two perfect breasts and exploded.

As for Governor Hill, he never did announce his candidacy for the presidency, but the graphic footage of his narrow escape from the explosion that killed everyone on the grandstand had become a near-nightly feature on the national news. And in the latest CNN poll, the unofficial candidate for president was leading all challengers by over twenty points.

Steve sighed, lit his cigarette, and let his gaze drift across the expanse of the riverfront. The marina fire raged for nearly six hours, requiring the efforts of seven fire companies from four neighboring towns to bring the blaze under control. By the time the sun rose on July 4th, an area roughly the size of four city blocks had been reduced to cinders. Damage estimates ranged anywhere from three to eleven million dollars.

So much for economic revitalization.

As Steve stared out over the river, a black minivan pulled to a stop behind him. He heard its approach but didn't bother to turn around. Even when he heard the side door slide open and someone exiting, his eyes remained fixed on the burnt carcass of McKeesport's west side. It was only when Harris Smith was standing next to him that Steve acknowledged his presence.

"How's the leg?" Steve asked, still looking at the riverfront.

Harris glanced down at the plaster cast that ran from the middle of his left thigh to the base of his foot. "Not too bad. The doctor thinks the pins can come out sometime in October."

Steve nodded. "That's good."

For a few minutes, the two men stood in silence, each one staring at a spot across the river. Steve's gaze was fixed on the four charred support poles that stuck thirty feet out of the water like long, thin fingers. They were all that was left of the new marina.

Harris's eyes were trained on the remains of the Smith building. When Curtis Mayflower ignited the dynamite strapped to his chest, the resulting explosion blew away most of the building's top floor. The force of the blast also caused the remaining three floors beneath the amputee ward to pancake one on top the other, ultimately settling in the building's basement. It took excavators over a week to search through the rubble and debris in order to find enough body parts to account for all the people who were in the building at the time of the explosion. But even after four weeks of meticulous search, there were still limbs left unaccounted.

"As soon as I get permission," Harris said, breaking the silence. "I'm going to have the building razed. Just bulldozed over."

"Yeah, that's probably for the best."

Harris turned to face Steve. "Look, Steve, I didn't get a chance to say this before, but I want to thank you for not implicating my mother with Nathan Espy and Mayflower."

Steve shook his head and told Harris to stop. "It doesn't matter, Harris. A lot of people are dead, and if everyone thinks your mother was just another one of Espy's victims, so be it." Steve took a last, quick drag on his cigarette then flicked it into the air. It tumbled for a second before being swallowed by the brown water of the Youghioghany. "You and I are the only ones in this town who know what the hell really happened last month, and I think it should stay that way. The FBI and the state police both want the book closed on this mess as soon as possible, so they're perfectly willing to lay the blame entirely on Espy, Mayflower, and those fuck heads up on Radaken's Hill. So it really wouldn't help matters any to talk about your mother and the DK. Got it?"

Harris nodded. "I understand. The less said the better."

"Good." Steve fished another cigarette from his pocket and lit it before turning to face Harris. "Now tell me again that Dust is dead."

"He's dead; he has to be." Harris shuddered as he remembered the last moments of his brother-in-law's dream where, unable to help David, he was forced to watch as Dust disemboweled him. He had tried to warn David, to tell him to erect a mental barrier between himself and Dust. That was the only way to stay clear of the deadly reach of the dream demon. But before he could deliver the warning, David attacked.

"There's no other explanation," Harris continued. "He was physically in David's dream when David was killed. I saw it happen, Steve. One moment Dust was ripping open David's stomach, then the next, everything was a ball of fire. I'm telling you, there was no time for Dust to get out of David's dream before he died."

Steve pursed his lips and nodded. He wanted to believe Harris; he needed to. "And what happens when the dreamer dies?" Steve asked.

"The dream, and everything in it, dies with him."

Accepting the simple logic of Harris's explanation, Steve nodded and leaned his tired body against the guardrail. "So what happens now?"

"I'm not sure," Harris said. "Linda is still pretty broken up over

David and Mother. But thankfully, she doesn't remember anything that happened after her disappearance. Right now she's staying with some friends in Pittsburgh, but after I get the clinic dozed over, I'm going to take her on an extended vacation. Maybe Europe." Harris paused and glanced back toward the charred remains of the Smith Rehabilitation Clinic. "Maybe we'll never come back."

Steve couldn't help but chuckle. "Yeah, I know what you mean. Merilee and I are flying out to Vegas tomorrow. She wants to get married in one of those little chapels on the strip. Who knows, we might just stay out there for a while. Maybe I'll get a job dealing Black Jack."

Steve pushed himself away from the guardrail and glanced down at the murky water beneath the bridge. And as it had done for untold years, it flowed on, silently passing over the spot where Gladys Decorta's still-missing head had fallen into its depths and was swallowed by the darkness of the neither-place. *The river doesn't care*, Steve thought. *It didn't care who lived on its banks or who swam and pissed in it. It just flowed. Persistent. Patient.*

"Merilee said she wants us to get as far away from this place as possible," Steve said, flicking another half-smoked Marlboro into the river's brown water. "And I don't really blame her for feeling that way, do you?"

The End

A Spectral Visions Imprint
Now Available

Riverwatch

By
Joseph M. Nassise

From a new voice in horror comes a novel rich in characterization and stunning in its imagery. In his debut novel, author Joseph M. Nassise weaves strange and shocking events into the ordinary lives of his characters so smoothly that the reader accepts them without pause, setting the stage for a climactic ending with the rushing power of a summer storm.

When his construction team finds the tunnel hidden beneath the cellar floor in the old Blake family mansion in Harrington Falls, Jake Caruso is excited by the possibility of what he might find hidden there. Exploring its depths, he discovers an even greater mystery: a sealed stone chamber at the end of that tunnel.

When the seal on that long forgotten chamber is broken, a reign of terror and death comes unbidden to the residents of the small mountain community. Something is stalking its citizens; something that comes in the dark of night on silent wings and strikes without warning, leaving a trail of blood in its wake. Something that should never have been released from the prison the Guardian had fashioned for it years before.

Now Jake, with the help of his friends Sam Travers and Katelynn Riley, will be forced to confront this ancient evil in an effort to stop the creature's rampage. The Nightshade, however, has other plans.

Ask for it at your local bookseller!

ISBN 1931402191

www.barclaybooks.com

A Spectral Visions Imprint
Now Available

Spirit Of Independence

By
Keith Rommel

Travis Winter, the Spirit of Independence, was viciously murdered in World War II. Soon after his untimely death, he discovers he is a chosen celestial knight; a new breed of Angel destined to fight the age-old war between Heaven and Hell. Yet, confusion reigns for Travis when he is pulled into Hell and is confronted by the Devil himself—the saddened creature who begs only to be heard.

Freed by a band of Angels sent to rescue him, Travis rejects the Devil's plea and begins a fifty year long odyssey to uncover the true reasons why Heaven and Hell war.

Now, in this, the present day, Travis comes to you, the reader, to share recent and extraordinary revelations that will no doubt change the way you view the Kingdom of Heaven and Hell. And what is revealed will change your own afterlife in ways you could never imagine ...

Ask for it at your local bookseller!

ISBN 1931402078

www.barclaybooks.com

A Spectral Visions Imprint
Now Available

The Apostate

By
Paul Lonardo

An ancient evil is spreading through Caldera, a burgeoning desert metropolis that has been heralded as the gateway of the new millennium. As the malevolent shadow spreads across the land, three seemingly ordinary people, Julian, Saney, and Chris, discover that they are the only ones who can defeat the true source of the region's evil, which may or may not be the Devil himself. When a man claiming to work for a mysterious global organization informs the trio that Satan has, in fact, chosen Caldera as the site of the final battle between good and evil, only one questions remains…

Is it too late for humanity?

Ask for it at your local bookseller!

ISBN 193140132

www.barclaybooks.com

A Spectral Visions Imprint
Now Available

Phantom Feast

By
Diana Barron

A haunted antique circus wagon.

A murderous dwarf.

A disappearing town under siege.

The citizens of sleepy little Hester, New York are plunged into unimaginable terror when their town is transformed into snowy old-growth forests, lush, steamy jungles, and grassy, golden savannas by a powerful, supernatural force determined to live...again

Danger and death stalk two handsome young cops, a retired couple and their dog, the town 'bad girl', her younger sister's boyfriend, and three members of the local motorcycle gang. They find themselves battling the elements, restless spirits, and each other on a perilous journey into the unknown, where nothing is familiar, and people are not what they at first appear to be.

Who, or what, are the real monsters?

Ask for it at your local bookseller!

ISBN 193140213

www.barclaybooks.com

A Spectral Visions Imprint

Now Available

Psyclone
by
Roger Sharp

Driven by the need to recreate the twin brother who had been abducted more than twenty years ago and using himself as a model, renowned geneticist David Brooks develops the ability to clone an adult human being. His partner, Dr. Williams, is closing in on a break-through that will let them implant a false set of memories, thoughts, and emotions into the newly formed clone's mind to give it a sense of the past. Before Williams succeeds, however, an ancient demon possesses the clone's empty shell and takes the doctors hostage. Is what the demon reveals about the fate of his brother true? Can they escape and stop the demon clone's rampage before too much damage is done?

Ask for it at your local bookseller!

ISBN 193140019

www.barclaybooks.com